The Song of the
Eternal Aeons

Other Works
by Johann M. Moser

Verse

Most Ancient of All Splendors

Late Autumn at Dumbarton Oaks
And Other Poems

Farewell . . . and If Forever
And Other Poems

Prose

The Ivory Fount
A Novel

Love of the Blossoming Hills
New England Stories and Sketches

Tutelary Presences
And Other Stories

Translations

O Holy Night
An Anthology of Classic Nativity Verse

Devoutly I Adore Thee
Prayers and Hymns of St. Thomas Aquinas
(with Robert Anderson)

The Song of the Eternal Aeons

A Phantasmagoria

*From the Lineage of Knarry Wood-Gnome
of the Western Ponderosa Clan of Oval-Earth
as Aided by the Stylus of the Ancestral Tree*

Faithfully retrieved and redacted by
Johann M. Moser

The Diamond Ledge Press
Sandwich, New Hampshire

For more information, please contact us at:
https://diamondledgepress.com/

978-1-964001-18-0 (hardback)
978-1-964001-19-7 (paperback)

Library of Congress Control Number: 2025930186

Dedicated to the memory of

Olaf Tollefsen
(1944–1989)
of St. Anselm College
Manchester, New Hampshire:

Friend, colleague, philosopher,
without whose initiative, guidance,
and participation in the very early phases
of this work *The Song of the Eternal Aeons*
would never have been sung.

The sleep of reason gives birth to many monsters.
Spanish proverb

Those who are awake live in one universe;
those who are asleep live in many.
Herakleitos

Who does not know the good itself, or any particular good
through the exercise of reason, by dreaming and dozing
through this life, he will descend into the depths
of the underworld and fall asleep forever.
Plato

For in that sleep of death, what dreams may come!
William Shakespeare

Contents

The Third Codex
The Great Upwelling

Exordium

AGAIN, AND YET AGAIN, having come to the twilight of my animate days, I set to parchment those transient and ever-fading memories bequeathed to me by my father and to him by my grandfather Knarry. For Knarry was there at the time of the Great Upwelling, and he trod in the footsteps of those who liberated us and who, having crossed the Golden Mountains, raised the Legion of the Wind and sang for us the Song of the Eternal Aeons.

Even now I tremble to think of that heroic quest, both of its unspeakable terror and its unfathomable beauty. And Knarry knew it all — knew its speech and its measure, its ever-recurrent hardships and its discoveries beyond all the discoveries made in the history of the Oval-Earth peoples.

Then Knarry lived out his allotted days and went to his metamorphosis on the Northern Taiga, his boughs spreading and rising into the finest of all the conifers of the forest. Two hundred years later, my father, too, hearkening to the summons of the deep-rooted soil and the eternal skies, went to his metamorphosis as well, but not without imparting to me the laborious duty of preserving for posterity those unsurpassable events that even now grow dim with age and forgetfulness.

My lamp burns low. The confines of my earth-house grow heavy around me. My eyes grow weak; my skin flakes and hardens into barky scales; and my spirit longs for the final trek to the Northern Taiga. Yet I will fulfill my father's charge and lay to rest this great travail upon me. The annals of the past have once again grown hushed, and even my father's words resonate as hollow and distant echoes in my ears. Soon my own ears, too, shall be as silent as the stars above the woodlands.

I have one consolation — the wooden Stylus shaped from the Splinter of the Purloined Staff. Indeed, it is the only remnant of that powerful artifact, which was hewn out of the great Ancestral Tree on the Northern Taiga and which caused such irremediable harm in that age of distress.

The Stylus embodies still a segment of its original power. Even as I write upon the parchment, it quivers and flexes in my hand and speeds beyond the thinking of my mind, grafting its own words on the aged vellum and lunging by itself into the black maw of my ink-well to slake its insatiable thirst.

The Stylus will remember, even when I do not; its voice will speak when my voice falters; and the imperishable earth-power, drawn from the soil through aeons of time upon the Northern Taiga, will leave nothing unspoken that must be spoken. In the great density and darkness of my advanced age, as I thicken and blossom into an unending fountain of life, I shall trust to the alacrity and lightness of my Stylus, which is so eager to serve me.

I pray my beneficent lector of ages to come to shake the dust of millennia from this venerable manuscript. Such times as are recorded here had never been before, nor shall they come again as long as we remember the words of the Eternal Song.

If these words should be forgotten, and the great desolation once more befall this most bounteous earth, may this manuscript itself reenact that most heroic of all quests for any generation that may be in need of it.

Burn high again, my lamp, for just this final task; be patient, my greedy and unbridled Stylus, for this chronicle is but your very first, which will be for me my very last.

The Passing of the Grand Master

Chapter I

The Bitter Seasons

I n the time of Knarry, the four hundred and fourteenth descendant in the
lineage of Brindle-Cone from the western clan of the ponderosa wood-
gnomes, there came upon the inhabitants of Oval-Earth a succession
of strange and bitter seasons: short summers of burning heat; autumns and
springs of acrid dust and barren skies; and long winters marked by brittle
cold and howling winds.

During these long winters, from the Northern Taiga to the Southern Hill
Country, from the great Rock-Falls in the west to the eastern Moor-Plains,
the lands encompassed by the oval band of the Golden Mountains lay buried
for months in impenetrable snows. At the center of Oval-Earth, the shimmering, milk-white waters of the oval-shaped Midland Sea froze over for
the first time in recorded history. The fishermen who lived in little villages
by its shores, for want of anything better to do, came up with the ingenious
idea of fashioning iron hoops and attaching them with leather straps to their
boots. Then, having muffled themselves up in their thick burlap capes, they
skimmed across the glossy white surface of the frozen sea.

Even as they raced one another, scudding and falling and raucous with
laughter, they stayed close to the shores, following their traditional practice,
when, in more clement weather, and sailing their fishing craft into the open
waters, they avoided the mysterious round Isle at the center of the Sea where
towering boughs of bright-blue spruce trees enshrouded the domicile of the
dreaded Brotherhood of the Drowsers. It was rumored that, under the jet-
black marble tower at the center of the Isle, the domicile of the Brotherhood
descended through countless chambers and gnarled tunnels into the depths
of the earth. Generations of fishermen enjoyed passing on an old folktale

that alleged that the fretful dreams of the Drowsers sometimes became real and drew men and skiffs down to a watery demise. The fishermen heeded the warning of the old folktale and did their newly discovered ice-skimming on the outer rim of the Sea.

As the seasons grew worse, the crops failed. Barley perished in the fields, apples and pears and paliotynes plopped unharvested from the rotten boughs of orchards into the mire below, and entire villages sank into sloughs of mud and ice. Houses tipped sideways, bridges fell into streams and were washed away, barns split open while their now sparse remnants of livestock huddled into corners and crannies for warmth. Since all commerce ground to a halt during the winter, the commoners' spare and monotonous diet became even more spare and monotonous. The farmers longed for a "proper year" for growing turnips, cabbages, and the other staples of the Oval-Earth diet. Yet such a prospect seemed ever more unlikely. Instead, at the onset of winter, they watched with horror the giant funnels of snow that spiraled in the frozen winds over the peaks of the Golden Mountains and the avalanches that roared downwards into the valleys from the glaciers above. And they watched as the twin lavender moons of Oval-Earth languished behind the ponderous cloud formations that collected like huge, clotted willow mats in the arching heavens.

The people shrugged their shoulders. It was their way. They shrugged their shoulders in weariness and dismay. The Imperial Government could offer little help. From the Capital, the Ministry of Historical Records issued sporadic reports assuring the citizenry that the climate of Oval-Earth habitually underwent long, cyclical changes; that they were nearing the end of such a cycle; and that in a few more years the seasons would begin to improve. The citizenry was not deceived. The lengthy imperial reports—verbose, convoluted, contradictory, and pompous—were regarded as pronouncements of little worth.

Further, everyone, whether in the Capital or in the outlying regional districts, knew that things could be a great deal worse. Nothing that climatic change could bring, nothing that could ensue from all the gathered anguish of the bitter seasons, indeed, nothing at all could ever overshadow the grim memory of the ancient War of Desolation, which had lived on through the ages in the hearts of the people. This memory was accompanied by the fearful prophecy that one day the War would start up again and that once more Oval-Earth might be beleaguered by the implacable forces of the Kingdom of Darkness that lay in wait, mustering its lethal forces somewhere beyond the Golden Mountains.

The Government continued to issue its reports, even though the Inter-Regional Couriers Network, once proudly staffed by a regiment of the Emperor's Riders, had long ceased to gallop on their elegant white moose along the Radial High-Roads bearing imperial tidings to the far-flung villages and farmsteads of Oval-Earth. The imperial throne had been left unclaimed for centuries, and a recent Viceroy, one of a long succession of Viceroys acting as "interim" heads of state, had declared the Riders a drain on the impoverished treasury of Oval-Earth. Indeed, they seemed but an easily expendable reminder of a bygone era, now that the Radial High-Road System had fallen into disrepair. Consequently, the decaying barracks of the regiment were closed down, The Imperial Moose Stables—once the celebrated studfarm and training grounds for the moose herd that the regiment had used as mounts—were converted into storehouses for government documents.

The dissolute power and influence of the Imperial Government did not go unheeded by some of the less-savory elements in the rural population; Oval-Earth saw a slow increase in the number of thugs who specialized in robbing the more isolated farmsteads. The locals grumbled about the problem, muttered threats about gathering armed vigilante bands to patrol the countryside, and said that it was a shame that the Viceroy could not staff a proper constabulary. But the dismal truth was that even banditry was a dispirited profession that prospered little better than any other.

"It's gotten easier to steal," murmured a certain drunken, lifelong thief to himself. He was seated in a dark corner of a broken-down shack that passed for a tavern in a small village at the edge of the Moor-Plains. It was early evening. A single lantern swung dimly over the bar. "But there's nothing out there to steal!" he added disgustedly.

The thief hung his densely bearded face over a large crock of turnip beer. Wrapped in his heavy woolen robe in the cold room, he was the last customer of the day.

"Turnips!" he muttered sleepily. "Turnips! Turnips! Turnips! That's all they got here. Turnips! What else could they use to make this foul stuff! It even tastes like bad turnips!" Clasping the earthen crock in his hands, the thief slowly lowered his head down onto the table between his outstretched arms, continuing to mumble there as sleep overcame him: "No, nothing left to steal, nothing at all, no honor for thieves in this world!"

The innkeeper, still behind the bar, stared at the old thief slumped on the table, mortally afraid to awaken the angry old man. He might be passed out drunk, but he still could act with astonishing speed. That knife under his robe would be deadly.

In the dim light, the thief looked peculiarly enlarged and distorted, as if possessed by some strange demonic force. Perhaps this strange appearance was caused by the half-light of the lantern and its shadows, perhaps by the heavy, uneasy breathing of the thief himself; yet his neck was twisted around unnaturally and his face, suddenly staring with reddish eyes at the innkeeper, was twisted into a diabolical grimace.

Long after midnight, the thief awoke, his beard and robe stained purple with turnip beer, the lantern out, and the innkeeper gone to bed hours before. It was time to retreat to his hovel, where he could crawl out of the rain and the sleet and sleep most of the coming day.

He stood unsteadily up, reached for his crossbow, and walked slowly over the creaky floorboards to the door of the tavern. He swung it open, looked out for a moment at the bleak village, and then descended the rickety stairs into the street without closing the door behind him.

It was dark, except for the feeble glimmer of the bailiff's torch. No one of sensible mind was using wood for torches this year, what with the threat of another winter like the last one coming on. The wind had picked up; it was colder and damper than ever; a thin sleet had begun to fall. It clung like a cold hand to the old man. "It will snow," he mumbled to himself, "if it gets much colder." He remembered the thick, crippling snows of the previous year, wrapped his woolen robe more tightly around himself, shivered, and glanced briefly down the long muddy rut that had once been the main street.

The world was wearing away to nothing.

What did it matter? What did anything matter?

The old thief shuffled down the street past the office of the bailiff, who, wrapped in warm robes and despite the chill, was sitting on the porch of the jailhouse, his feet propped up jauntily on a railing. The bailiff did not like to admit to himself that he had once dreaded this man. Now he could sit at his leisure and spit at him as he went by. The thief, in turn, shook his fist and ambled on. The bailiff laughed.

The thief headed out along a country lane towards a grove of thin, barren trees. Here he had constructed a hidden lean-to, using boards stolen from a nearby barn. Once inside, he scraped together some leaves and lay down on top of them, gathering his filthy robe up around his head to stay warm.

He tried to sleep, but sleep came only in fitful patches. A curious dream kept troubling him.

A creature—or was it a creature?—was staring at him with dull, narrowed eyes, eyes that seemed yellow and pale but without pupils in them; eyes that, in all their inexpressible torpor, were voraciously hungry. The thief awoke with a start, sweat beading his lips and his brows. He was trembling. "Too much turnip beer," he thought. He tried to sleep again, but again the dream reappeared with the same mute and terrible figure fixing its glare upon him.

The thief awoke once more. He shook in terror. He felt as if he were standing at the edge of some fathomless void, a hollowness so deep that, once a person began to fall into it, there would never be an end to that falling. He tossed the robe from his face and scrambled to his feet, as his head collided with one of the boards of the lean-to. He felt dizzy, unbalanced, sore from the collision with the roof, confused as if an inrush of sour beer had unhinged his brain and poisoned his limbs. He knew, somehow, that it was too late to escape whatever it was that was now threatening him in so overpowering a manner.

The entire grove was filled with a presence that was strangely an absence—a lack, a vacuum, a voracious appetite that wanted him, that desired to draw him within itself, that wished to engulf him into its own unutterable misery and horror. The thief didn't know what to do. He couldn't figure out if the threat was somehow external to himself, or inside himself, or both somehow.

He struggled and groaned in his broken, gruff voice. He kicked and thrashed his arms, and, not knowing why he did it, he threw himself on the ground in an effort to crawl under a bush, as if the bush, or anything he could crawl under, would save him. But yellow eyes — yellow eyes everywhere and nowhere, multiple and single — flashed out of the emptiness that surrounded him.

Slowly and hideously, he felt himself being dragged from underneath the bush and into the desperate hollowness of the apparition. He lost his grip on the stem of the bush, and his face was scraped along in the wet dust and gravel as his hands frantically grabbed for anything that would retard his movement. But the ingestion was steady and gruesome, and soon the thief found himself falling down a dark, bottomless well, whirling and spinning around inside an infinite chasm of nothingness.

Moments later, the old thief — or something that looked like the old thief — was lumbering out of the grove and trotting back down the country lane towards the village through the rain. His feet drummed mechanically on the surface of the road like heavy metallic hoofs. He was drooling in his beard and puffing heavily as he strode. With grim determination, he rounded the corner at the leather shop and chugged blindly towards the bailiff's office.

The bailiff was still sitting on the porch, his legs flung over the railing. He saw the thief coming and guffawed loudly. He spat upwards in a wide, arching angle, hoping to hit the thief square in the forehead. He missed. Then he rose in alarm, or tried to, for his feet caught on the railing, causing his chair to tip over and sending him sprawling on one side of the porch as the chair bounced and clattered on the other side.

The thief was aimed directly at him.

But it was not the thief — it was something that looked like the thief, something larger than the thief and filled with a savage energy the bailiff had never seen before. It puffed and inhaled with tremendous force, like the huge bellows once used in the old ironworks of the mining districts.

The terrified bailiff picked himself up and bolted through the office door. He tripped over the furniture in the office as he tumbled across it and threw himself headfirst into the iron-ribbed jail cell at the back of the room. The thief slammed into the office door and stopped, being now too swollen to pass through it.

Even as the bailiff swung the iron-barred entrance to the jail cell shut, thinking that he would be safe there, the rotted timbers of the building began to disintegrate, and the decrepit furniture, already strewn through the room by the bailiff's desperate retreat, was pulled by a powerful suction towards the thief. It slid in wild disorder across the floor and crammed up against the doorframe momentarily, until it shattered, spraying fragments of wood and upholstery in every direction.

The doorframe collapsed and much of the front wall with it. Seconds later, the iron bars of the jail cell were ripped out of the floor joists like toothpicks.

Instantly, the bailiff found himself being dragged across the floor, screaming and grasping for anything he could get hold of, while a typhoon of papers and pieces of wood whirled about him. He was finally sucked into the body of the thief, who stood panting heavily at the door.

The building fell into a dusty heap on top of the thief, followed by a strange calm as the dust settled.

Several villagers, led by the tavern publican, ran up to find out what had happened. They stood in the cold rain and gaped stupidly at the tangled mound of what had been the bailiff's office. But the calm did not last very long.

The rubble began to tremble slightly, then to heave violently backward and forward, until a huge form, as big as the entire jailhouse had been, exploded out of the rubble. It was neither the thief nor the bailiff but some dreadful combination of the two. It stood on massive legs and shook old plaster and boards from its head. It strained its colossal hulk around at the waist. Its head bent around in spasmodic little jerks, tilting gruesomely up and down as it moved. Its eyes glittered yellow and vague in the gray rain that fell about it. Its loathsome pit of a mouth was twisted into a leering smile.

It was looking for another victim. The villagers who had collected by the former jailhouse fled away as fast as they could; but for some of them, including the tavern publican, it was too late. They, too, were drawn into the entrails of the monstrosity; they, too, became the monstrosity.

And it became bigger.

Bigger and bigger.

The monstrosity laughed and shrieked in its delirious joy, and it wept as it laughed, spewing out from its empty eyes a bloody and acrimonious rain of tears, and its terrified victims, still alive in its swirling vacuity, twisted and turned, screaming and crying in the precipitous void.

Chapter II

The College of Wisdom

In the second great winter after the onset of the bitter seasons, Garug-Caroch, Master Sage and occupant of the prestigious Grand Master's Chair at the College of Wisdom, renounced the somnolent life of the College's venerable old cloisters and quadrangles and withdrew into the seclusion of his private quarters. In the long nights of the winter, he would spend hours at a time sitting by the fire in his shadowy chambers and sipping from a steamy tankard of fragrant grog.

He was a tall, stooped, aged man with a long, frazzled white beard and huge, cavernous eyes that gazed mournfully from underneath the great arch of his forehead. His nose was as arched and as craggy as his forehead, and thick white brows, like the heavy banks of wattle-weed that grows along the rim of moorland streams, hung low over his eyes.

Despite the warmth of the fiery hearth in front of him, he was wrapped in the cumbersome woolen robe traditional for his office; it was dark blue and bordered along its edges by golden tassels, now seriously frayed and often missing in places. His scarlet ceremonial hood, marked here and there by jagged moth holes and by the patches sometimes clumsily applied to them, lay loosely over his head and around his neck; it served to protect him, however inadequately, from the chill drafts that eddied around him from the deeper recesses of his chambers and that curled, like long, icy tongues of serpents, into the blazing fire of the hearth.

As he sat in his high-backed, throne-like, intricately carved Grand Master's chair, Garug-Caroch meditated on what he now had come to understand as the decay of the College over the previous millennium. Every nook and vault of the ancient institution, with its numerous carvings and inscriptions, attested to a former life of the College that had been vital and purposive.

It was said in the few surviving fragments of older college history that his own professorial chair had once been occupied by scholars of brilliant intellect who attracted the brightest students from every corner of Oval-Earth. Now, from among the many students who still flocked annually to the College, only a few students sought him out as mentor and guide, and even those few eventually drifted away from the College, often to find themselves inexplicably drawn to the tiny felucca at the rim of the Midland Sea. There they were ferried, by an odd little ferryman appointed especially for the task, over those shimmering, milk-white waters of the oval-shaped Midland Sea to the Isle of the Drowsers, where, it was said, they would join a mysterious Brotherhood and sleep out the remainder of their lives twitching and moaning in the midst of feverish dreams.

Garug-Caroch gazed into the blazing fire for hours at a time, occasionally stirring his grog or rising to toss another log into the flames, the sparks billowing and flashing into the cold, musty air of the chamber. Suspended from a rod over the fire, a copper kettle bubbled with the hot grog that warmed his aged bones and weary heart. Indeed, even his own life had become indolent and sluggish. Except for several hours a day when he bent over his well-worn game board, fulfilling what he still regarded as his obligatory daily exercises at rolling gemstones through the complex mazes of the Game of Spheres, he did little but sit by the fire and gaze, somewhat vacantly, at the flickering play of flame and shadow.

Infrequently, relinquishing for a while the lonely sanctuary of his chambers, he would pace anxiously through the drafty cloisters of the dilapidated College buildings. He would study the old inscriptions and carvings with searching, restless eyes. Whatever meaning they once conveyed had long since been forgotten, though Garug-Caroch could make out that some of them were memorials to great debates and significant discoveries that had occurred within the College precincts.

He often wondered what it was that those Masters and students of old had debated about with such vigor in the lecture halls of the College, and what there was to discover, and what it was about those discoveries that the ancient collegians would consider fitting to celebrate in those elaborate carvings upon the walls.

It was peculiar too, he mused, how the recorded history of the College, as it presently stood, began at the invention of the Game of Spheres, some thousand years earlier, as if there has been little previous to that time worthy of memory.

The information about the invention and its impact on the College life was vague. Soon after the invention of the Game, made by a brilliant and supremely self-obsessed professor of philosophy, Rorpigan the Shrewd, it had come to dominate the life of the College. All those who had opposed this domination, and the gradual displacement of the older studies it produced, were eventually driven from their posts at the College and replaced by a new generation whose attention was devoted solely to the pursuit of the Game. The Master Sages, as a group, held out the longest in their opposition to the Game of Spheres but finally succumbed to its seductive influence.

What had those Master Sages of so long ago discerned about the Game of Spheres that had been the cause of their initial resistance? Collegial history did not preserve even a fragment of their arguments against the Game and against what it was doing to the intellectual life of the College.

Thereafter, all academic distinction was based on proficiency in playing the Game. Election to the rank of Master Sage, and to membership in the honorable Board of Sages, was granted purely by skill in the Game. Accordingly, the main lecture hall of the College was converted into the Hall of Games; at its center was a large game board surrounded on all four sides by rising banks of steps that served as benches for the rapt audiences that witnessed the games.

The ancillary lecture hall, located at the opposite side of the College buildings, was transformed into the Ale Hall, a place for students and faculty to discuss the Game at length over heavy earthen crocks of college-brewed ale. Such discussions were often unruly and quarrelsome, and many a time the college gendarmes had to clear the Hall of its frenzied and inebriated crowd.

When, as a young man, Garug-Caroch had entered the College for the first time, the Game of Spheres was the sole activity for the faculty and students to pursue. He had been surprised by this, naively expecting that the

College might have, conceivably, something else to do, and he had wondered, in the vague way that the young so often wonder, what the "wisdom" might be, or might have been, in a place still referred to, rather archaically, as the College of Wisdom.

His surprise was not at all unusual for a new student arriving at the College from some province or another, for, in outlying areas of Oval-Earth, the condition of the College was largely unknown to the populace. Further, in his first months at the College, Garug-Caroch had been haunted by the crumbling remnants of the past that marked every corner and niche in the College and that now, in his old age, had come back to haunt him more than ever.

Of course, at the time of his matriculation in the College, he accepted, as everyone did, that the physical dilapidation of the buildings here (as elsewhere in Oval-Earth) had been caused by the War of Desolation, even though no one seemed to know exactly when this war had occurred, or to have any specific account of its events, or to understand why later generations had not bothered to rebuild much of anything after the war was over.

Eventually Garug-Caroch — again, like everybody else — adjusted to what was expected of him as a student, except that he had prospered at it in an exceptional way. Indeed, he had triumphed in the Game, rolling the glittering gemstones over the intricately carved wooden board while he guided their motions by applying and resolving immensely complex mathematical formulas at almost instantaneous speed.

His triumphs had led to his investiture, at an unusually young age, as a Junior Master, later as a Senior Master, then as a Master Sage (one of the fifteen in the College), and finally as the Grand Master — the Master Sage who presided over the Board of Sages. Indeed, he had achieved some of the highest scores recorded in recent times. Years of practice trained his concentration and taught him how to channel the flashing gemstones as they whirred through spiraling rings and ovals into mathematical patterns of increasing complexity towards the center of the board.

At the annual tournament in the Hall of Games, the skill of Garug-Caroch dominated the Game for decades and dazzled all potential contenders for the Chair of Grand Master. In fact, Garug-Caroch was the only player resident at the College in his lifetime to have rolled, on more than one occasion, the *Darii*—the seventh circle.

As the greatest known living practitioner of the Game, he couldn't help but revere the words chiseled into the archway over the entrance portal of the Hall of Games:

> *The Mind is the Cosmos.*
> *The Game is the Mind.*
> *Power over the Game is power over the Cosmos.*

How could one believe otherwise? Nothing he knew of could engage the power of the intellect in such a dazzling display of sheer mental energy and skill. Nothing he knew of had such immediately remarkable effects, for the gemstones lit up with a ferocious, almost blinding inner light as the intensity of the Game increased and as they spun at dizzying speeds through the intricate channels.

Yet it all seemed so curiously empty too, and the inscription above the portal tantalized his curiosity in another way; for its large uneven lettering had been crudely stamped over an older inscription, whose ancient words were no longer legible but whose elegant demarcations still faintly shimmered when a rare shaft of sunlight bent downwards from a high window and lit up the old panel where the inscription was carved so long ago.

For all this, though, Garug-Caroch had grown weary of the Game, and even more weary of the tedious and tendentious discussion of the Game that went on incessantly in collegiate circles. He no longer wished to defend his Grand Master title in the annual tournament. Though he continued the routine of playing for several hours a day at the board, he did so without pleasure. He had begun to lose his faith in the Game.

Over and over, the doubt arose in his mind: one thousand years of the frantic rolling of gemstones and of compiling endless lists of players and scores. What had been achieved through the Game? Where had Rorpigan's ingenious invention led, and what had it achieved?

These, and other speculations, troubled the long winter nights of Garug-Caroch. Occasionally he would rise from his great looped and carven chair in front of the fire and pace restlessly from one end of the darkened chamber to the other, perhaps scraping away some frost on his narrow window to look out into the frozen, snow-filled quadrangle below or to listen to the hoarse drinking songs that floated through the winter air from the Ale Hall in the adjoining quadrangle. He would then turn back to the hearth and ladle out for himself another tankard of hot grog from the simmering kettle and sit down to gaze once more into the embers.

He was glad that he had his own private preserve of the sweet Hill wine and the sachet of fragrant spices which his friends, Tundra-Bear and Fox-Foot, gave him as a going-away present each summer when he vacationed among the Hill people. Their gifts were deeply appreciated. At least he did not have to resort to imbibing the wretched turnip brew served up in the Ale Hall.

He could not help smiling whenever he thought of the Hill people—of their innocence and of their remarkable beauty. The Hill people alone of all the peoples in Oval-Earth seemed to have eluded the demoralization and hopelessness that affected the other populations. Even the wood-gnomes, those most sturdy and tenacious of creatures, had not been left unaffected by the universal decay that touched all aspects of life in Oval-Earth.

As he tenderly blended his wine and spices and stirred them in the copper kettle over the flames of the fire, he was beset by question after question.

What had happened to the College?

What was happening to Oval-Earth in its devastating turn of weather?

Was some catastrophe at hand, perhaps—as everyone seemed to believe—a second War of Desolation was poised to wreak its havoc over the mountain-rimmed solitude of Oval-Earth?

Was some desperate and malicious force now in control of the weather in an effort to soften up the people of Oval-Earth before it struck, as if the people were capable of offering any resistance anyway?

What about the Kingdom of Darkness, reported to exist beyond the Golden Mountains and inhabited by an implacable enemy with its apparently nameless and faceless hordes?

Most of all, why had he, Garug-Caroch, come to ask the questions he was asking?

What had jolted him out of his own bedimmed awareness and led him to his multitudinous and obscure questions?

Garug-Caroch knew that there could be only one explanation, and he recalled it time and again. As he sat in his great armchair and stared into the fire, he attempted to reconstruct in his memory, moment by moment and thought by thought, the astonishing event that had happened to him in the spring of the previous year in front of the great ivy-covered Gate-Tower of the College. It was this event that had changed his life.

Shortly before the ominous shift of seasons had begun, he had taken a walk in the pleasant meadows that surrounded the College. The day was clear and sunny, and a rare breeze blowing out of the east temporarily wafted away the dank mist that perpetually enshrouded the vast Moor-Plains which lay at the eastern edge of the College pastures.

The extraordinary clearness of the day allowed him to discern far across the flooded fens and byways of the Moor-Plains the tiny but exotic cupolas that arose from the city of the Gethsarbim in the distance. These strange, diminutive people with their sparkling coin-like eyes were known for their wealth of proverbs and proverbial lore; in previous times, they were sought out by the other peoples of Oval-Earth for consultation in practical matters of all kinds.

As Garug-Caroch treasured this rare experience of being able to gaze out upon their distant and solitary city, he happened to recall an old story according to which the College of Wisdom had originally been founded on this borderland by the great Emperor Ospeth. Ospeth had desired that the future generations of collegians take advantage of the practical counsel of the Gethsarbim, so that the flights of the speculative intellect would not ignore the needs of every-day common sense.

Of course, no one at the College now took the Ospeth legends seriously. About the time the Game was beginning to dominate the scholarly studies of the College's faculty—a group of exegetes, pressed into service by the Game's advocates and using some of the most purportedly advanced methods of textual criticism, had shown that the Ospeth stories were mere re-workings of older legends that predated the rise of any true civilization in Oval-Earth.

The stories, accordingly, were dismissed by the exegetes as childish nonsense, though, soon thereafter, the exegetes themselves were dismissed as childish fools, for the College no longer had need of exegetes or anyone else not devoted fully to the Game.

As for the Gethsarbim, they were consulted less and less often in recent centuries. Indeed, the few visitors who now ventured into the Moor-Plains hunting for the famed waterfowl or for the sumptuous crayfish and fresh-water oysters of the vast swamplands returned with accounts of an elfish people gone mad and prattling endless nonsense. The Gethsarbim now led an isolated existence in their watery domain and under the incessant fogs that shrouded them in obscurity. They were a ruined people living in the remains of a ruined city.

Allusions to the War of Desolation were invoked as ever to explain this unhappy turn of events.

The good Emperor Ospeth, as befitted the legendary founder of a civilization, also played an important role in other stories regarding the early history of the College, for it was he, so one particular legend claimed, who was responsible for the erection of the lofty ivy-covered Gate-Tower that arched over what had once been the entrance to the College.

Its staunch and formidable battlements, facing the eastern Moor-Plains, were built by Ospeth, so the story said, as a reminder to future scholars that even the deepest intellectual learning required the moral virtues of vigilance and fortitude in order to withstand the temptations of scholarly pride. This reminder was treated in the more satirical versions of the story as a quaint and outmoded platitude of a happily bygone epoch and was the brunt of many a coarse joke in the Ale Hall.

The Gate-Tower, now almost a ruin, had been the original formal entrance to the College. Passing through its once regal portals, one would have walked along a broad, tree-lined pathway made of finely fitted paving stones to the granite steps that led up to the immense oaken doors of the Library.

The Library stood at the center of the College grounds and had been surrounded by the pleasant lawns and gardens, the fountains and cloisters of the old college quadrangles. But that was many centuries ago; it was later abandoned by the collegians.

Now, since the decay of the Gate-Tower had made it dangerous to walk through the gates, the entrance to the College had been shifted from the Gate-Tower, which stood at the center of the eastern wall, to a nearby service portal adjacent to it. The service portal passed through the same eastern wall;

its original purpose was to provide purveyors and deliverymen access to the larders of the College refectory.

At about the same time, since the Library was also in a state of decay, a hastily built and rather clumsy stone barrier was erected around the Library to keep people away from the danger of falling roof-slates and other debris that occasionally tumbled from the ancient edifice. This protective barrier, however, was connected by a walled passageway through to the old Gate-Tower, so that if anyone was foolish enough to want to enter the Library, it was possible to pass through the Gate-Tower, to traverse the passageway and arrive at the doors of the Library.

Such a venture would be foolish indeed, for the Gate-Tower's huge, vaulted portcullis and the passageway beyond it were clogged with centuries of accumulated thorn-brush, weeds, and fallen masonry. For all practical purposes, in effect, entrance to the Library was blocked.

It didn't matter. No one had any use for the Library anymore; in fact, no one could even imagine what was in it and what it had ever been used for in the past.

On that fine, exhilarating day in spring, reveries about the Gethsarbim and about the good Emperor Ospeth induced Garug-Caroch to wander past the old Gate-Tower and to examine it, as he had never done before. The outlines of the crusty stone building could be scarcely made out beneath the heavy growth of ivy and other vegetation. The crest of its walls on the northern and eastern flanks had collapsed—a casualty, it was alleged, of the War of Desolation.

As he studied the imposing ruin of the Gate-Tower, admiring the skill that had constructed it, his attention was drawn mysteriously to a badly corroded stone carving that stood out like a kind of heraldic escutcheon over the main arch of the entry. Some birds had nested there, and their nests had partially obscured some of the stonework.

Garug-Caroch found it curious that he had never noticed this carving before; on the other hand, as he reminded himself, he had never looked very carefully at the Gate-Tower before. Indeed, he wasn't sure he had ever looked very carefully at anything before, except at the Game of Spheres, which had the peculiar effect of distracting one's attention from everything else. But Garug-Caroch studied the carving from below as best he could.

At one point, he fumbled through his blue robe with the frayed golden tassels and drew out a pair of spectacles. These spectacles looked like two flattened diamonds wrapped up in an ungainly mass of copper wire. They were bent and tilted in awkward ways and were held together precariously by bits of golden tassel clearly snipped from the robe for this purpose. But Garug-Caroch managed somehow to get them to teeter on the arch of his nose and squinted through them.

What he saw looked like a festoon of flowers carved in weather-beaten granite.

But no, not at all! Garug-Caroch observed that the objects were not flowers; they were stars. "Yes," he had mused, "a festoon of stars." He was silent for a moment, studying further the old carving.

It was difficult to make out the exact configuration of the badly eroded surface, especially since — and it was certainly very astonishing indeed — the carving, as if it were aware of the scrutiny to which it was being subjected, seemed to have become curiously active, almost as if it had some interior life of its own that beckoned to him and began to quiver vividly before his eyes.

He pulled off his glasses and wiped them with the dangling blue sleeve of his robe. He wondered if he was having a delusion of some kind or if something was disturbing the optic refraction of his spectacles. He perched the spectacles on the high, craggy ridge of his nose, bent backward, and looked again.

"Flowers, not stars!" he spoke aloud. "No, stars!"

But how could one have a festoon of stars? They must be flowers with star-like petals. And it was not a festoon either; the shape was rising in the center, an arc, a garland more strictly speaking, a garland of flowers. "Yes, a garland of flowers!"

Meanwhile the stone carving became ever more agitated, and the stellated forms began to flicker and shine.

"No," he spoke out loud again, "not flowers. Stars certainly! What are they? What am I seeing?"

His head seemed to spin, his spectacles flew off his nose, and his mouth stammered as strange and powerful words welled up and formed inside him. A mysterious energy seemed to shudder through his entire being.

"*A Garland of Stars!*" he exclaimed, practically shouting these words.

As he pronounced the words, the entire Gate-Tower shook violently. Clumps of masonry and vegetation broke loose from the decaying parapets. The nesting birds fled in wild, twittering circuits of flight. An old battlement, balanced precariously on a few jutting stones, came thundering down the side of one of the walls, and a thick cloud of dust puffed up from the ground as pieces of the fallen battlement collided with the debris below.

The words themselves rang with a power and life of their own.

They had the strange effect of engendering another image of the Gate-Tower, wholly different from the wreck that tottered under their impact, as if the ages of ruin that encrusted it were dissolving, falling away, and revealing beneath them another Gate-Tower, a Gate-Tower that had a permanent reality of its own, somehow immune to decay, and that arose before Garug-Caroch's imagination as fresh and magnificent as the day it was built.

At that moment, as Garug-Caroch gaped at the Gate-Tower, the world somehow shifted around him, and he glimpsed for a moment something beyond both remembering and forgetting, something so luminous, so replete with beauty and grace, that he noticed, for the first time in his life, an elaborate tapestry hung before his eyes, a strong-textured, dense, and cohesive web of tightly bound threads that made up the universe and all that was in it.

Before, he had seen only what was little else but a faded grid of worn-out, spindly strands of fabric. Now he sensed that he himself had become like that fabric — thin, straggly, insubstantial, threadbare, a decaying phantasm where something solid and real should have been.

Just as suddenly, the vision was gone.

Confused and dizzy, Garug-Caroch sank to the ground. He lay there for a while — he didn't know how long — half aware of what was happening and half asleep. A patch of damp moss beneath him gradually soaked his robe and chilled his skin.

He groped around in a tuft of grass to find his spectacles. When he found them, he stood up and peered again at the Gate-Tower. The glasses now distorted the Gate-Tower beyond recognition; he realized he didn't need them anymore and tossed them aside.

Meanwhile, the Gate-Tower stood high above him, looking as it always had: old, crumbling, the coarse gray of the stones' eroded contours splattered with lichen and hidden behind the spring growth of vines that clung to every part of the ancient structure. Its passageway was still choked with weeds, and the view through to the Library was just as dismal as ever. Even the birds nestled sleepily again in their perches scattered over the carving. The dust from the fallen battlement settled down slowly over the mound that it had made.

Garug-Caroch stumbled across the field in front of the eastern wall of the College. He tripped over stones and branches as he went, catching at his robe and trying to steady his tread. Attaining finally the College enclosure, he pushed his way through the heavy door of the service portal into the kitchen larder. A cook, pulling a roast pumpkin out of a big, greasy oven, stopped to watch the breathless old man as he made his way into the refectory and then out into the quadrangle.

As Garug-Caroch crossed over the quadrangle to his quarters, he noticed another spectator—one not nearly as beneficent looking as the College cook. A grotesque face stared intently at him from an upper window over the quadrangle cloister. Its glaring reddish eyes, embedded in a soft, pallid face, followed his movements across the quadrangle.

Garug-Caroch was not sure that he recognized the face; but he was troubled by the malevolence of its glare. He also noticed that the joyous spring day was quickly becoming overcast. A thick fog had blown in out of the eastern Moor-Plains and smothered the College in a sodden blanket of yellow-gray, malodorous mist.

That very day, the bitter seasons began.

Suddenly, the weather in Oval-Earth became vicious and painful. It was not long before Garug-Caroch concluded that his experience at the Gate-Tower was somehow connected with the alteration of the climate, as if some dark power had recognized that Garug-Caroch's vision was a threat to its domination and was now acting to defend itself from that threat.

During the cold year that followed, Garug-Caroch struggled through the semesters at the College, fulfilling his duties in the most perfunctory way and performing in the Hall of Games without enthusiasm or interest.

At the beginning of the second great winter, having thought often of his experience at the Gate-Tower and having told it to no one, Garug-Caroch submitted his resignation of the Grand Master's Chair, effective at the end of the following summer, and made his final withdrawal into the seclusion of his quarters at the College.

He was only vaguely aware that the faculty and students, thoroughly accustomed to the soporific pace and wholly predictable course of life at the College, were taken aback by the resignation of its most esteemed member. For the first time in the history of the College, a Master Sage and occupant of the Grand Master's Chair was, apparently, abandoning his privileges and turning away from the College life.

Rumors, naturally, spread rapidly through the College. Some believed that Garug-Caroch, who was accustomed to spend his holidays in the Southern Hill-Country, had met one of the shy and rarely seen Hill maidens, reputed to be of unmatchable beauty, and decided to run off to spend the rest of his days with her in the luxuriant high valleys of her homeland. That was, naturally, a wildly improbable story. Those who knew anything about the folkways of the Hill people knew this explanation was especially groundless, since the Hill people were engaged to be married while still children and married only their own kind.

Others speculated that Garug-Caroch had decided, like many before him who had been endowed with especially gifted minds, to seek out the tiny felucca and be ferried across the milk-white waters of the Midland Sea to the Isle of the Drowsers, there to join its sleepy Brotherhood and never to emerge again. But the rumor was dismissed by the more knowledgeable, for only the young went to join the Brotherhood. Garug-Caroch was much too old for that.

The more practical sorts at the College took a different view of the situation. "He's old, and he's cracked," declared Arfla, a rather flabby Junior Master noted for his prowess in the refectory as well as in meddling in others' affairs. A twist of nastiness quivered in his thin smile. "He really can't handle the responsibilities of Grand Master, so we are well rid of him," he expounded, "and I scarcely need to point out that the Grand Master's Chair will be vacant, do I?"

He didn't need to point this out to the students and to the other Junior Masters who gathered around him during the ale-hour, swooshing the foaming brew around in their crocks. The furious competition for the Grand Master's Chair would supply months of diversion, to say nothing of the boisterous riots it could be expected to induce in the Ale Hall.

But they were resentful and mute. They despised Arfla's petty ambitions; yet they could acknowledge that he might be right.

Perhaps Garug-Caroch was simply "old" and "cracked," as Arfla said he was. What other explanation of Garug-Caroch's unprecedented resignation could there be?

But Arfla's influence was limited to his small band of sycophants and cronies; most of the students and Junior Masters avoided his company, and the Senior Masters and the Master Sages held themselves aloof from any association with him. They regarded him as a fraud who should never have been given the appointment of Junior Master in the first place.

Yet the Master Sages were curiously afraid of him. He seemed to possess unusual powers and had advanced rather a bit too swiftly through the many difficult stages of proficiency in the Game of Spheres, even while being unable to demonstrate much in the way of advanced mathematical skill.

And his physical appearance was frightening too — it was bloated, pale, distorted; he had reddish, disarming eyes that often glared intently at anyone he didn't like.

Meanwhile, winter deepened.

Blizzard after blizzard buried Oval-Earth in towering snow drifts. The Radial High-Road System, or what was left of it, closed down, and the College of Wisdom, marking the terminus of the Eastern Arm of the System, became isolated. Besides the endless barrels of turnip ale, only the large, though ill-nourishing, supply of pumpkins, garlic, and rancid vats of moose butter kept the faculty and students from the worst extremities of hunger.

Arfla, more out of self-interest than communal concern, had seen to that; through a combination of extortion, fraud, and downright raiding of local farmers' limited supplies by bands of miscreant students under his leadership, Arfla had stocked the larders well for the rigors of winter. As much as many collegians hated Arfla, they felt gratitude for his provisions.

Garug-Caroch kept to himself, as he had since he had submitted his resignation, and continued his long, brooding meditations before the blazing hearth of his chamber. Again and again, he thought of the Gate-Tower, of the carved garland of star-like images that arched over the portal and that had sparkled like tiny pinnacles of light before his eyes, of the words he had uttered that had so shaken the Gate-Tower, and the earth around him, and his own bedimmed awareness of things.

He knew that the carving had been made to commemorate something, something that had special words associated with it — words that he had accidentally spoken and that had unlocked, for a moment, a deep and ancient and wonderful mystery.

Late one dark and particularly cold evening, he alternately dozed and fretted in his chair, his conscious but uncontrolled dreams blending into an oppressive anxiety. Suddenly he was startled into awareness when he heard a wood-hard set of knuckles cracking heavily against his door.

He rose quickly from the warmth of his chair before the fire and almost tripped over his heavy blue robe as he groped through the dark antechamber leading to the door. This he unbolted and flung open. It groaned loudly as it swung on its massive rusty hinges and admitted a heavy blast of cold air into the room. Garug-Caroch blinked for a moment as his eyes adjusted to the darkness.

The torchlight at the end of the hallway illuminated from behind a shadowy figure standing at his door that looked like a snow-covered pine tree from a mountain forest.

"Knarry!" he exclaimed. He could just barely make out the massive, gnarled figure of the wood-gnome standing before him in the hallway and filling up practically the entire doorway.

"Well, let me in," Knarry growled impetuously. "I need to do some serious melting."

Garug-Caroch stepped to the side as the burly wood-gnome stamped past him into the room, bringing the sense of a wintry woodland with him into the musty antechamber and shedding snow around him in small avalanches that toppled off his huge frame in heavy clumps. The chamber door groaned shut on its hinges once again, and Garug-Caroch slid the iron bolt back into place.

Knarry advanced straight to the hearth, picked up a bulky log, tossed it into the flames, and stepped backward to avoid the shower of sparks that flew wildly in every direction. Garug-Caroch knew that Knarry must be cold, for wood-gnomes were normally shy of wood fires.

Meanwhile, Knarry stood in the warmth emanating from the hearth. He was dripping like a mountain slope in a winter thaw and allowed the crust of snow gradually to melt off him in flowing rivulets, revealing, as it did, the shaggy woolen mantle drooped over his enormous shoulders; the leathern jerkin underneath it was bound at the waist by a wide buckthorn belt with a brassy buckle and was secured by a row of round moose-antler buttons and thongs. Leather straps attached a pendulous carry-sack firmly to his side. His gigantic bark boots were rimmed at the top by scarlet woolen stockings.

His square jagged head, a block almost, was capped with thickly snarled hair; his broad face was stretched by high cheekbones and a tawny, wood-grained skin. Globular amber eyes rolled deep inside knotty enclosures beneath lowering banks of tangled brows. His nose and ears were protuberant and knobby; and his mouth was a cavernous orifice when he spoke, gaping like a densely encrusted knothole opening into the hollows of an ancient tree.

"On my way to the Woodlands of Morbihan I was, when the storm began," Knarry grumbled solemnly, as he shrugged off a few icicles still clinging to his sleeves. "I don't think I have ever seen the snow fall so fast. And the wind! That wind could cut even the hardiest gnome to ribbons, or rather to shavings, if you get my meaning. I take it you know the roads are closed. I had to trek overland. No easy task, that!"

Approaching closer now to the fire, he rubbed his brown, corded hands together; the snow in his coarse hair and tangled eyebrows was only just beginning to melt.

Garug-Caroch dragged a heavy chair from a distant corner of the chamber over to the fireplace, even though he knew that wood-gnomes usually prefer to stand rather than sit. Pouring out some Hill wine from a ewer into a copper kettle and adding some spices, he prepared a fresh batch of grog. Then he sat in his chair, pulled the scarlet hood up over the back of his head again, and listened. His white beard quivered just slightly as he watched Knarry's form continue to emerge slowly from the final vestiges of its snowy mantle.

"There's something wrong out there, something—yes, unnatural!" Knarry announced abruptly. "A wood-gnome should know when a storm like this is coming. But I had no premonition of it at all. I could barely find my way—even when I arrived on the College grounds, I couldn't recognize the buildings because the snow is piled so high around them. I don't like this at all."

"But why were you out there?" Garug-Caroch asked, his head having finally cleared from the troubled reveries that had clouded it.

"Plague," Knarry answered grimly. "Plague raging in the valley hamlets up beyond the Woodlands of Morbihan. I came this way because I thought I might be able to use the Eastern Arm of the Radial High-Road. Foolish thought, that! Anyway, I must get there ... too much for the local gnomes to handle, I've heard. I'm afraid some lives will be lost because I'm delayed."

"Human lives," Garug-Caroch mumbled. He wondered if humanity could survive without the gnomes to heal their diseases. At last, he spoke: "Well, Knarry, warm up by the fire while I pour you something hot to drink. You're right, you know, about something being wrong. Something is very wrong. But I just don't know at all what it is."

Moments later, sage and gnome were deep in conversation. Knarry decided to use the chair and sat down heavily in it. The spicy aroma from the tankards of hot grog rose around them as they talked. Outside, the wind howled. Grains of hail and snow pelted the window that faced down over the quadrangle. The fire in the hearth burned ever lower as the logs sank into glowing embers.

"I'm stumped," said Knarry, "if you will forgive the expression. I can't say anything about the business at the Gate-Tower." He shook his large, shaggy head. "There's nothing in gnome-lore about the Gate-Tower, or about these words you spoke, or any of the rest of it. And then the weather changing! You seem to think that the weather changed somehow *because* of what happened at the Gate-Tower! That's an odd conclusion—I don't know what to make of it."

Knarry stopped, peering down into his tankard, as if he expected to find some answer there. He was deeply troubled; he would have liked to ascribe Garug-Caroch's experience to some moment of madness, a fleeting but irrational episode that had no significance. Yet he knew, as all the wood-gnomes did, that something very strange was going on in Oval-Earth.

"What bothers me," Garug-Caroch said, "is that I spend a lot of time trying to remember precisely what occurred. I go over it again and again, yet I cannot recapture all of it. It's as if there were things involved that were beyond the ability of my mind to grasp." Both Knarry and Garug-Caroch stared into the dying flames in the hearth for a while, and then Knarry finally murmured something to himself.

"What's that?" Garug-Caroch asked. He bent forward as if he thought his hearing was somehow failing him.

Knarry repeated what he had said, slowly and hesitantly.

"The what?" Garug-Caroch asked again, putting one long, bony finger behind his ear and tipping the cusp of his ear forward.

"The Library!"

"The Library?"

"Yes, the *Library*! We need the Library!" Knarry repeated emphatically.

Garug-Caroch gasped at him. "Knarry! You know very well that no one has used the Library in recorded memory! It was walled up centuries ago! You are mad! Anyway, it's dangerous. Do you want to get your skull split by a falling stone? And you never know when the whole place will give way and disintegrate into a shapeless mound of rubble. Worms, mold, and moss-mice are its only inhabitants. What would we have to do with them?"

Knarry chortled. "Actually, the Library does have an inhabitant — other than the worms, mold, and moss-mice you speak of. There has been a wood-gnome in residence there as a custodian for hundreds of years. There is a medical library on the main floor that's filled with information some of the gnomes need to practice their healing arts effectively."

Garug-Caroch was incredulous. "A gnome in there … on College property … without the knowledge of the Master Sages? And why do the wood-gnomes need a medical library? I thought you healed by earth-power. I didn't know there was a medical library there."

Knarry chortled again. "It's all perfectly legal. By the time of Stavan-Kresh's tenure of the Grand Master's Chair about eight hundred years ago, the College had pretty much abandoned the Library. Under these circumstances, the gnomes made a covenant with Stavan-Kresh allowing them access to the Library in return for custodial services. Soon after that, all records concerning the Game of Spheres having been removed to the Hall of Games, the masters simply forgot about us and the Library altogether.

"As for the medical library, we are not magicians; we do heal through earth-power, but we occasionally need gnome-lore, the recorded experiences of gnomes through the ages, to help us in the proper application of earth-power. Hence, the Library is useful for our work.

"That is why the passageway from the Gate-Tower to the Library was built — so that we could have access to its collection without having to pass through the confines of the regular college cloisters. We wouldn't want to interrupt the students at their studies by subjecting them to the sight of an occasional gnome disturbing their devoted solitude."

Garug-Caroch laughed. "A gnome in that situation would not have been interrupting anything, I can assure you, though he might have been the occasional target of an ale crock headed in his direction."

Knarry thought about this for a moment and then replied, "Well then, perhaps we were the ones who were being protected, though an ale crock in flight would have hardly done much damage to us. But I must admit that I don't think the gnomes go in there very much anymore. The passageway has become very congested over the centuries through neglect. Even we gnomes are on the skids, more or less. But, in any case, the congestion is not a problem for us, and we can make our way through it without too much trouble."

Garug-Caroch, thinking of the brush-choked path leading towards the main entrance of the Library, remembered from his excursions with Knarry into the Southern Hill Country that a wood-gnome could walk directly through the most entangled thicket without much difficulty at all. His mind returned to his initial source of wonderment. "Is anything besides the medical library usable?" he asked.

"I don't know. We use only one alcove on the main floor, on the right-hand side of the central scriptorium as you come in. There is a whole sequence of mezzanines and balconies above the scriptorium and several tiers of archives below it.

"Nobody ever ventures into these levels, though the recent custodian is a curious and reclusive rascal who, for some reason, likes to explore the collection, especially in the subterranean vaults. His name is Twigbottom, and he comes from the hornbeam clan—a hot-headed and stiff-necked lot if there ever was one. But none of this is of interest to us as medical practitioners, you understand."

"In any case, Knarry, why do *we* need the Library?"

"You have expressed interest in words, some words anyway—isn't that correct?" Knarry replied.

"Yes."

"Well, words are what you find in a Library. If you are looking for words, where else could you find them but in a Library?"

"But Knarry, you can find words anywhere!"

"Surely, words that are around now. But in a Library you can find memory—memory of words, memories that are recorded in words, memories in books, memories that are forgotten but can be made alive again."

"Books?"

"Yes. Big collections of words. Really, Garug-Caroch, don't you college people know anything? But that's what you need, if you are ever to plumb the mystery of the Gate-Tower and of the strange words you spoke there."

Garug-Caroch nodded wearily. "I know what books are, Knarry. I was just surprised by hearing someone actually use the word for them. I was surrounded by them when I was a child. It's books that made me want to come to the College of Wisdom originally. But here nobody has any use for them. The only reason, I imagine, why the Library and its books are not being used as a source of fuel during these winters is that the protective wall is too difficult to get over. Anyway, the students are afraid of the Library and think it is haunted by some strange spirits."

Their talk turned to other matters. They knew that the Library could not be entered until the spring, when the snow had melted away from the buildings. In the meantime, Garug-Caroch agreed to accompany Knarry to the Woodlands of Morbihan and give what aid he could to the gnomes, limited as his own healing powers were. Knarry's description of the situation in the Woodlands moved him deeply. The worst of the matter was that those who contracted the plague and were cured by the gnomes did not seem to develop any immunity to the disease and were quickly reinfected.

Departure for the Woodlands would be in the morning. Garug-Caroch retired to his sleeping nook; Knarry stayed in the main room next to the hearth and, like all wood-gnomes, slept standing up.

The following morning was cold and overcast. Although the storm was spent, the sky had not cleared. It was a dull, featureless gray from horizon to horizon. The snow was piled in mountainous drifts; every path the Junior Masters had laboriously shoveled clean the previous day had vanished. Nothing moved anywhere in the bleak snowscape.

Garug-Caroch, with a disconsolate expression on his face stood at the small window that looked out at the College grounds. The view was dismal. The fire in the hearth was dead and the room was cold. A pot of pumpkin porridge had been heated over a glowing brass brazier for breakfast.

"Having second thoughts about going with me?" Knarry asked as he scooped the last few bits of pumpkin porridge out of his bowl with a thick, barky finger.

"Not really," Garug-Caroch answered. "It will be good to get away from the College, away from the endless nights of worry. Perhaps a hard trek through the snow and a month's worth of trying to heal the sick will clear my brain. I will ask the Steward of my chambers to pack us some provisions—it won't be very good, but it will help us. He is a helpful fellow, unlike most of the College staff."

Later that morning, Garug-Caroch exchanged his blue ceremonial robe for a large, fur-lined burlap cloak with a warm, tight-fitting hood. He gathered some medical implements and ointments into a leather satchel and took his walking staff out of a closet. He was ready for departure and was glad Knarry would be leading the way, slicing a path for him through the dense snowdrifts.

Knarry exited the chambers bearing his haversack, which now bulged with the provisions packed by the Steward, and Garug-Caroch locked and sealed the entrance to his chambers with a powerful incantation, notifying the Steward once again that he would be gone for a month or so. The Steward bowed politely and promised to take care of everything. He liked Garug-Caroch and was glad to be of service to him.

The movement of the Master Sage and the wood-gnome across the snowy quadrangle and out the service portal in the eastern wall was scarcely noticed by anybody except for a student who was tossing snowballs at his own reflection in a window. Fortunately, the window was of thick leaded glass and the student's aim was poor, so the window did not break.

The student stopped for a moment to watch the travelers pass by. Since he was in his first year, he was not yet familiar with many of the faculty, so he wondered who they were and especially why a wood-gnome was on the College grounds. Soon he resumed throwing his snowballs, chuckling each time one managed to splatter against the heavy windowpanes and blotted out his own image.

In the larder, the cook was busy plopping several large dollops of rancid-smelling moose butter into a bubbling cauldron of pumpkin and garlic mush and paid scant attention to the Master Sage or the wood-gnome as they passed through his kitchen.

Traveling was as difficult as they had anticipated. While pushing his way through one particularly dense snowdrift, Knarry looked around at Garug-Caroch and muttered, "In a situation like this, one would appreciate those snow-slats the Hill people use. Everyone laughs at them because they like to slide around and especially downhill on those slats. But I wouldn't mind a pair of those slats right now."

Garug-Caroch, struggling through the snow and out of breath as he tried to keep up with Knarry, mumbled his agreement. Several leagues later, out on the plains, Garug-Caroch turned to look again at the College, now little more than a dull ashen smudge in the distance. It had been his home for most of his life; whether it would still feel like his home when he returned, he was unsure.

Around him, Oval-Earth lay in the half-light of the overcast morning: motionless, featureless, fading away in every direction into the faint, almost transparent haze that hovered over the landscape and obscured the distant peaks of the Golden Mountains.

Sage and gnome set off again. Behind them, a sullen breeze obscured their tracks as they, too, faded into the distance over the snowy plains.

Chapter III

The Custodian

G arug-Caroch returned to the College of Wisdom in the early spring.
He had not intended to stay away from the College for such a long
time. He wanted to help Knarry in the Woodlands of Morbihan
for a month or two before returning to explore the holdings in the College
Library. But the plague ran before them like fire in a wind, and they ran
with it from hamlet to hamlet, from sickbed to sickbed, from funeral pyre
to funeral pyre. They burned the dead to keep the plague from spreading,
even though the villagers wanted to put the corpses out to freeze in the snow
and then bury them in the spring, when the ground had thawed.

Spring brought little hope for reprieve. Violent rains, combined with the
copious winter runoff, eroded the fields, silted up the wells, and drowned
the early plantings. Food would be scarce again the following winter.

In the late spring, the rains stopped abruptly, and the sun began to bake
the ubiquitous mud until it flaked off in a fine dust that hung in the air like
a brown fog. Often the peaks of the Golden Mountains were scarcely visible
through the dusty haze, while scabs of yellowish sludge settled down and
undulated over the milky waves of the Midland Sea.

Garug-Caroch trudged on foot across the parched fields of Oval-Earth,
the sun searing his face and cracking his lips. His lean, stooped figure bent
under the weight of the burlap cloak that was now wound up into a bundle
and strapped to his shoulders. He carried in his hands his staff and the empty
satchel that had held his former medical supplies.

As he marched across the withering plain, his vision was befuddled by an
endless spiral of images conveying sickness, starvation, and despair—memories

of his winter work with Knarry. Now there was dust in his eyes, in his nose, and in his mouth; he could feel its fine grit between his teeth, and his white beard was streaked with ruddy stains.

In the distance, he could see the College, a brown blot on an almost destitute brown landscape. The few trees that dotted the College pastures drooped in the noontide heat.

When he arrived at the College, he made directly for the service portal in the eastern wall and walked through the larder and out into the quadrangle. It was empty. The heat had driven masters and students alike into the cool, dark cellars of the old College buildings. Garug-Caroch stood once again in his familiar surroundings with a strong and sorrowful dread in his heart. He found his way into the first set of cloisters and mounted the narrow, winding stairs to the Grand Master's chambers.

His return, once it was noticed, caused a brief stir on the campus. During his absence, a few of the Junior Masters, under the guidance of the mean-spirited Arfla and despite the futile protestations of the Steward, had tried to break the seal on his chambers; since they could not break it, they knew that he was still alive somewhere.

Among some of the students, it was conjectured that Garug-Caroch had perished somewhere—frozen in a snowdrift, perhaps, or stricken by the plague, or devoured by one of the ferocious winterbeests known to have been driven by hunger from their high mountain feeding grounds into the lower valleys and foothills during the winter.

In any case, his absence, along with the knowledge of his resignation, had spurred endless speculation about whether a suitable candidate could roll a full cycle at the annual tournament of the Game of Spheres and claim the Chair that Garug-Caroch was to vacate at the end of the summer.

Garug-Caroch himself had rolled the full cycle several times during his tenure at the College. Some of the other Master Sages had reached the sixth spiral on many occasions, but attaining the seventh spiral, the *Darii*, was immeasurably more difficult.

Early in the morning on the day following his return, Garug-Caroch donned once again his blue Grand Master's robe, left his chambers, and set out for the Library. He wanted his work to be well underway before the

midday heat made most activity impossible. But he felt no little awkward-
ness about all of this.

What sort of work did one do in a Library?

What did the inside of a Library look like?

Was there a special way of acting?

Should he be bringing something with him into the Library—such as
a vial of ink and a stylus and a roll of fresh parchment? How quaintly old-
fashioned that would be! It brought back memories of when he was a child
and trotted off to grammar school similarly equipped. For now, he would
have to be content just to find his way into the Library and see what it looked
like inside and how it was organized, if it was organized.

He turned the corner from the cloister into the quadrangle and was
somewhat startled to find that many of the students and Masters were already
lying about on their gray and brown robes. They basked indolently in the
morning sun before the heat of the day would drive them down to the cellars.

One student had managed to squeeze himself into the basin of a dried-
out fountain; only his arms, legs, and head were visible—his legs drooped
over the side of the fountain, and his arms and head were occupied with the
dreary playing of a murkweed flute.

Another student was lying flat on the ground nearby and had his face
buried in a swatch of particularly loathsome weeds that had popped up
through the pavement. Exactly what he was doing and why he was doing
it were unclear.

Garug-Caroch made his way around the bodies strewn on the dusty lawns
and paths, trying not to step on them. A few students pointed contemptu-
ously at him and snickered; none bothered to greet him.

After crossing the quadrangle, he passed through the refectory, larders,
and service portal, exited the College, and followed the wall of the College
until he arrived at the Gate-Tower. Briefly he looked above the archway
where he had once seen the curious carving that had flickered and danced
before his eyes. He assumed it was still there, but now ivy vines and bird
nests hid it completely.

He glanced down the walled-in alley that led from the Gate-Tower to the
Library. He had not remembered how clogged it was with briars and broken

stone. Centuries of neglect had effectively obliterated the narrow passageway. He knew it would never have occurred to wood-gnomes to clear a path; briars were no obstacle for them. But he despaired of clearing a path for himself.

He began working his way up and around the broken stones, freeing himself from the briars' thorns as they caught in the folds of his robe. Above him on either side stood the walls that barred the access to the Library from the quadrangle.

On the other side of the walls, he could imagine the Masters and students spread out on the quadrangle grounds like white maggots occasionally squirming in the early sunlight. He could hear the dreary flute being played in the quadrangle fountain. He could understand why the walls had been built; decaying masonry had made the walkway dangerous.

It took Garug-Caroch nearly twenty minutes to push his way through the briars, but, in the end, the Library rose before him, five or six stories high, ancient and dilapidated. Above him, at the top of a badly cracked and tilted mound of stairs, the Library's carved oaken doors waited, bleached to a pale, delicate gray by centuries of rain and sun.

Garug-Caroch hobbled up over the crooked fissures of the broken stairway and pushed gently on the door. Oddly, although the doorjambs appeared twisted and bent, the door swung open easily and flawlessly. He stepped across the threshold.

A beam of dazzling sunlight flooded through the door from behind, his towering shadow at the center, and preceded him into the darkness of the interior. The doors, just as silently, swung closed behind him, cutting off the beam of sunlight and leaving him, without a shadow, in a great domed and vaulted rotunda that loomed darkly but benignly over him.

He stood in awe, adjusting his eyes to the darkness and holding his breath as if it were improper to make even the slightest disturbance in such a hallowed space. He felt mysteriously as if he had come home. He was vaguely aware that he might be the first human being to enter the Library in more than eight hundred years.

Silence and dust greeted him. Small, soiled windows high up on one side of the rotunda cast golden slits of sunlight into the shadowy interior. Overhead, rising higher and higher into the central, conical dome of the building, were bands of balconies and mezzanines, each encircled by their own rounds of alcoves with narrow windows, so that the dusty air was riddled by dozens of thin rays of light slicing through the darkness and playing off the heavy masonry on the supporting walls.

On the ground floor, tiny, red-eyed, black-skinned moss-mice with red stripes on their glossy backs scurried back and forth over the stone pavement, chirping anxiously. Clearly, they were surprised by the unfamiliar presence of the intruder. Piles of broken trestles and stools littered the floor, indicating that the base of the central vault was once a scriptorium.

At the far end of the rotunda, facing the entrance door, a single high-backed desk stood on a raised platform. Tilted on the rim of this desk was a flat clay oil lamp with a little wick that burned eerily in the darkness.

Garug-Caroch peered through the dim light and could make out thousands of books that filled the shelves in each alcove. He wondered how he should proceed. He stood motionless for a minute, mulling over his thoughts and gazing in the direction of the high-backed desk with its little clay lamp.

Something was behind that desk making little scratchy sounds. At first, it sounded to Garug-Caroch like a moss-mouse scraping together some straw for a nest. But then he concluded that it sounded more like a sharp stylus whose markings were quick, frantic, and oddly compulsive as it moved across the surface of a parchment.

Suddenly the scratching stopped.

There was silence.

A chair was shoved back, followed by the thump of heavy boots hitting the ground. The thump echoed through the rotunda. There was another silence. A second later the silence was pierced by a thin, high-pitched wail from behind the desk.

"Well, what is it ye would be wanting?" it screeched with extreme irritation.

Garug-Caroch was surprised and baffled. "I don't know what I want," he answered. He knew it was a stupid answer, but he did not know what else to say.

"Then be getting out with ye! Best to going away if ye're not clever enough to be a using a library!" the voice shot back.

With these words, a small figure popped out sideways from behind the desk. Garug-Caroch's mouth dropped. It was a wood-gnome, shorter and scrawnier than most, his skin like grisly bark, his berry eyes deep set under a woody brow, his ears like autumn leaves, sticking straight out from his head.

Like all wood-gnomes, he had dark, stiff hair; but, unlike any gnome that Garug-Caroch had ever seen, he had let his hair grow straight up above his head and had pulled it together with a piece of straggly vine into a single tuft a foot or more high.

Around the gnome flowed a silky, though tattered, floor-length robe, green, tastelessly splattered with gold and purple stars, half-moons, triangles, trapezoids, pentagrams, and other assorted geometric designs; and from beneath the garishly embroidered hem of the robe, two enormous tips of what were surely the largest bark boots in Oval-Earth rose in grotesquely delicate curls.

After a moment, Garug-Caroch managed to speak. "I'm looking . . . I'm looking for a book," he stammered.

Even as the words tumbled out of his mouth, he knew again that they had been an inordinately stupid thing to say. The gnome rocked forward and upward on the curled tips of his gigantic boots, his berry eyes glinting in his head and his tipping forward giving him just a bit more height.

"Well," he trilled in his high-pitched voice, "how most clever of ye to be coming here to find one! Now, is it for ye that ye would be wanting it? Know ye how to be reading a book? *No, of course not!* Do ye know *which* book it is ye be wanting, or will it be *any* book that'll do? Do ye be knowing mayhap what a book be?

"Ay'll be warning ye that if ye be looking for something to be throwing at one of ye fellow students, a brick or a stone would be much better'n a book. Which of ye Masters been having the presumption to be sending ye here?"

"I have no master. I am Garug-Caroch, Master Sage, and occupant of the Grand Master's Chair—until the end of summer anyway." Garug-Caroch figured it might be time to assert some appearance of authority before this wayward gnome, though he doubted it would have much effect. As a rule, wood-gnomes has little respect for human ranks or privileges; this gnome would be even more contrary than most.

"Aha!" retorted the gnome, rocking back on his boots and feigning admiration at this announcement with a huge, delirious smile. "Ay be always wanting to be meeting someone of ye lofty preeminence. No wonder ye remarkable intelligence been so overwhelming for me! No wonder Ay been so stunned by ye imposing presence. My pardon for failing to be recognizing such an illustrious personage!"

He swept his garish gown aside and bent over double in a long, obsequious bow that caused the upright tuft of hair on his head to cut a shallow furrow in the dusty floor. He looked up again sarcastically, his tuft bobbing up and down and tipped now with a ball of dust.

"And Ay be Twigbottom, of the not-so-illustrious hornbeam clan. Now that ye be mentioning it—ye did mention it, didn't ye? It seems that Knarry—of mutual acquaintance, no doubt—sent me a note about ye. Yes, it been coming only several days ago, carried by one of those tumble-shrub gnomes—such nasty creatures they be, wouldn't ye be agreeing? So, there's some sort of research ye'll be wanting to do? Research? Be ye knowing the meaning of the word? *No, of course not!* But Ay be having full confidence in ye abilities to be a-carrying on this project, whatever it may be. Ay be *so admiring* of decisiveness in a human. But please don't let me be in ye way. On the other hand," he added maliciously, "don't be in my way either."

He vanished behind the desk. After some jostling and pushing and scraping of a chair, the remorseless scratching sound began again, and Garug-Caroch noted the tip of Twigbottom's dusty hair-tuft waggling just above the rim of the desk.

Well, Garug-Caroch thought, he is as eccentric as a gnome ever gets. Knarry had said that Twigbottom had served as custodian in the Library for over a hundred fifty years and that probably he had not even left the Library for the last third of that time. Isolation can make a person mad. But there was more than eccentricity involved here, Garug-Caroch suspected. Something dark and fitful seemed to play around the petulance of Twigbottom. The Master Sage shuddered.

Garug-Caroch began his exploration of the Library. Just enough light came through the upper windows to make this possible, but he knew he would have to bring a lantern in his future forays. Thirteen alcoves arranged in an oval surrounded the central rotunda. Each was filled from floor to ceiling with books. He had no idea where to start or even what exactly he was looking for.

He walked into the first alcove and started randomly pulling some books off the shelves. Books about the geomorphology of Oval-Earth, about the evolution of the river systems, about movements of the glacial plateaus, about the rotations of the twin lavender moons of Oval-Earth around one another and around Oval-Earth itself! And such multitudes of books!

Other alcoves revealed other subjects: books of law, books about plants, about animals, about planets and stars, about the building of bridges and the rotation of crops!

A rush of deeply inexplicable nostalgia came over him—and a sadness. The Sage felt as if he had returned to a place where he should always have been. He wanted to read all of these books. Yet he knew that his time was short.

By noon, Garug-Caroch was exhausted. He made his way back to the gnome's desk, behind which the gnome was hidden, although the obsessive scratching sound continued unabated, disturbing the high-vaulted stillness of the central rotunda.

"Just how is the Library organized?" Garug-Caroch interrupted Twigbottom, not expecting to get much of a response.

There was a long pause while the scratching of the stylus continued, and then a silence. "Be ye turning around, my illustrious Master dear, and ye will see!" came the acrimonious reply from behind the desk.

Garug-Caroch turned around. Set directly above the entranceway into the central rotunda was a large, flat stone, the chiseled edges of the markings that covered it partially erased by centuries of dust. Garug-Caroch tried to read what he could, for much of the lettering had been worn away, whole words were missing, and the rotunda had not much light; the inscription had obviously been set in place when the Library was originally dedicated.

> *In accordance with the . . . will of Ospeth,*
> *We, Esril, Emperor of Oval-Earth . . .*
> *do hereby dedicate this collegiate Library,*
> *that we and our subjects and all who follow us*
> *in generations to come may grow in wisdom,*

> *and in so doing never forget that such wisdom is*
> *our only … against such sleep and dreams and*
> *so remembering, wake, and in waking,*
> *in this generation and every one that follows,*
> *hear and sing the Song of the Eternal Aeons*
> *that we may be delivered of the …*
> *So given this day by our word,*
> *Esril, Son of Ospeth, Emperor of Oval-Earth.*

There followed a long list of names — probably those who had contributed to the design and construction of the building. After this was a description of the building itself. From this, Garug-Caroch gathered that there were many levels, seven of which were subterranean.

His heart sank. Without luck or guidance, he might spend years in the Library without finding what he wanted. He directed his attention back to the inscription and read it several times over. Several phrases in particular almost seemed to take hold of him.

A sudden impulse came over him. He swung himself back to the desk. The gnome had recommenced his scratching.

"What's all of this about sleep and dreams?" he asked.

The scratching stopped.

"What's this about a song?" he asked again.

Silence.

"Why would a song be so important? What was special about this song that is mentioned in the inscription?"

Some rustling and pushing from behind the desk.

"What is this Song of the Eternal Aeons?"

A sigh.

He felt his excitement rise. He struggled with the desire to reach around the desk and tug the gnome out from behind it by grabbing his foot-high tuft of hair. Instead, he shouted, "The song, Twigbottom! *Where do I find the words of the Song of the Eternal Aeons?*"

A faint, quivering voice came from behind the desk. "No song here. No sleep. No dreams. Just books."

After a long pause, the gnome slid down from his chair with a thump and emerged from behind the desk. He was pale and looked as if he were engaged in some struggle within himself.

His face reminded Garug-Caroch vaguely of the faces of the Masters as they bent over the Game of Spheres in the annual tournament. Each face was a mask of furious concentration as it struggled to control the gemstones spiraling to the center of the board.

But behind the mask was something deeper, a desire or lust powerful enough to keep the player from wholly focusing his mind.

Garug-Caroch often wondered what his colleagues wanted so badly. He suspected that they harbored some irrational hope that each time they rolled the stones, they would unlock some powerful secret that would give them the control they desired over their own destinies and the destinies of others.

"Ay be sorry," Twigbottom said abruptly, recovering himself and becoming strangely tame, even courteous. "What be it, exactly, that ye would be wanting?"

"As I said earlier to you, I don't know what I want. That's part of the problem," Garug-Caroch responded. He was pondering why he had become so excited and why he had asked the questions he had put to the gnome.

He launched into a detailed account of his fears about the decay of Oval-Earth. The gnome looked distracted while this account was being given, as if it were difficult for him to concentrate or as if he knew all of this already and was not really interested in hearing about it. Garug-Caroch concluded his account with the inquiry: "Do you know of any books that will tell me about that?"

The gnome shook his head and spoke slowly: "There be no catalogue. The former patrons of the Library not be having a need for that. Ay been working for years on a catalogue for the medical collection — but Ay never seem to be getting much of it done. Ay work and Ay work, and then all of my work be unraveling itself somehow. Ay don't understand.

"As for a book about decline — well, maybe back when this Library was still being used, they didn't be knowing about this decline ye be speaking of and therefore couldn't be writing about it."

The gnome disappeared again behind the desk, trailing his green, be-spangled robe in the dust. Moments later, in the strangest falsetto voice, he trilled from behind the desk, "But Ay might be able to be finding something for you. It may take time. The time … the time, yes, be short. And Ay don't be having much time. In the meanwhile, continue ye own search."

The scratching of the stylus on parchment started up again.

Garug-Caroch returned to the alcove he had been working in, looked at the shelves he had yet to examine, and decided that lunch was in order. Lunch meant pushing his way through the briar-filled avenue in the midday heat and an unpleasant hour or so with his colleagues in the College refectory. But he went nevertheless.

He did not return to the Library that day but ambled back and forth across the College pastures, gazing out at the foggy Moor-Plains and the domain of the Gethsarbim, and muttering to himself: "What's all this about a song? Why did I get so worked up? Why did I demand the words of a song?"

The following day, Garug-Caroch had his Steward pack a lunch for him. He made a point of opening his private cache of Hill wine and bringing a decanter of it along with him. It would be refreshing, but it could also be useful in making Twigbottom a bit more cooperative. Wood-gnomes were known to be fond of Hill wine. Once again, he pushed his way through the briar-entangled lane. The Library was astonishingly cool during the day, and Garug-Caroch could plan on spending all his waking hours there.

Waking … yes, he thought, I'm waking up.

This routine became regular for him. All through the late spring and into the summer, he continued his work in the Library, having decided to forgo his usual summer sojourn in the Southern Hill Country. He had too much to do. He was astounded by the range of subjects those ancient scholars had studied, and he was beginning to understand why they did so and to share their enthusiasm for all those aspects of things that they so reverently described in their works. Often, he lost whole days at a time when he became sidetracked on matters that fired his curiosity or absorbed his attention.

Even his relationship with Twigbottom prospered after a fashion; their conversations, although infrequent, were friendlier, a condition often enhanced by sharing the decanter of cool Hill wine at lunch.

But the gnome remained something of a mystery, and especially so whenever Garug-Caroch broached the subject of his research. There seemed to be a struggle going on inside the gnome from which he could tear himself away only with great effort and which was triggered by any request Garug-Caroch made for information or direction.

But since those requests were uniformly fruitless, Garug-Caroch did not make them often, and his relationship with the gnome seemed tolerably comfortable. He arrived early each morning at the Library, worked until lunch, shared his wine with the gnome, and worked on until the dinner hour at the refectory.

The spring weeks passed in that fashion. Garug-Caroch ignored events at the College and eventually took to dining alone in his chambers, rather than enduring the painful and dreary gossip of the dinner hour.

In the searing months of the summer, the College was vacated by the students and the faculty as they flocked to the few ramshackle beach resorts left on the shores of the Midland Sea, where they treaded water all day long and their disheveled heads bobbed aimlessly on the surface of the milky water like fried cubes of turnip pulp floating in bowls of paddle-fish chowder.

To be sure, Garug-Caroch missed his summer vacation in the cool Southern Hill Country, but the vacancy and quiet of the College buildings somehow made the heat more endurable.

Even when the students drifted back to the campus in the early autumn, Garug-Caroch continued his new routine. He barely noticed how much his life at the College had changed.

The Game of Spheres had lost its last feeble attractions for him. From time to time, he would sit dutifully at the board, trying to focus his mind on the gemstones. But it was hopeless; the game, Garug-Caroch decided, was just dull.

His mind would always wander back to the Library, back to the books and their contents and to the few clues he thought he had discovered about the decline of Oval-Earth.

He found it curious that none of the old books ever mentioned anything about the Brotherhood of the Drowsers on the Isle in the Midland Sea.

By the early fall, though Garug-Caroch's resignation had become official, he continued to occupy his chambers because no other occupant had come forward or had presented the right qualifications to displace him. This state of affairs was soon to change.

Early one autumn morning, the time for the annual tournament was announced by the enormous brass gong mounted over the Hall of Games. Garug-Caroch, despite his change of heart, felt himself obliged to attend, although the sorry roster of participants for this year's tournament inspired little anticipation of interesting performances on the board.

One of the more prominent among these participants was Arfla. Garug-Caroch had long since discovered Arfla's easy shifts from groveling flatterer to petty backstabber. What worried him most about Arfla, however, was that even Arfla, who was now considered one of the better gamesmen of the Junior Masters, was not nearly as skilled as the weakest of the Senior Masters. And none of the Senior Masters in residence at the College could approach the level of a Master Sage.

Yet Arfla oddly had the appearance of skill, as if he could delude a group of observers into thinking that he played a skillful game. He was also making strange and presumptuous claims that he would soon be Grand Master, skipping over the ranks of Senior Master and Master Sage altogether. A lot of students laughed at him for this, and Arfla would not, in the end, forget their derision.

The tournament began with its customary opening rituals and dreary preliminaries. Such rituals were long, pedantic, verbose, obtuse; litanies of facts about the Game of Spheres were repeated endlessly. Each Junior and Senior Master present had the opportunity to incant several of these litanies, and the process was lengthy and tedious.

The opening ceremonies were followed by a sequence of pompous, self-serving remarks delivered by those who presided at the tournament. Erendroop, Senior Master and Dean of the Hall of Games, was, as usual, unforgivably dull.

Garug-Caroch took the chance afforded by Erendroop's vacuous speech to let his eyes wander about the Hall of Games. Despite the fact that he had spent a substantial part of his life in this building, he had never really noticed much about it, except for the inscription over the entrance.

His eyes came to rest finally on a stone balcony nearly fifty feet above him. It ran around three sides of the Hall and looked as if it would give an observer a remarkable view of the proceedings below. Never, in his tenure at the College, had Garug-Caroch seen anybody using the balcony. In fact, he had the impression that the stairway up to the balcony had been walled up ages ago and that it was not possible to climb up there anymore. Yet now, for the first time, he wondered what it would be like to stand up there, looking down on the Masters involved in their interminable games below.

Meanwhile, Erendroop droned on. Garug-Caroch gazed at the balcony again and again. His head became suffused with a slightly vague feeling … he felt as if, somehow, he was up there … yes, actually up there … watching from above … taking note … listening … *he could see and hear that the Masters gathered below were withering in the Unsong of the one who spoke unsinging meaning, their own unsinging unweaving into the unwhole. The Unsong gathered slowly around about them, pulsing and rolling slowly as they unsang it. But on the balcony where he stood, there was stillness and space, a vast counterpoint to the intricate stone carvings that wound their way around the walls, remembering, as stone does, the hands that once shaped it, the minds that once embodied in it an intense passion and then perished, leaving the stone to stretch into the unimaginable future, a fugue too slow and deep for human ears and minds. . . .*

The blunt thud of Erendroop's gavel brought Garug-Caroch back to his senses. His head hurt, and whatever it was that had filled his mind moments ago had faded away. For a moment, he tried to retrieve it, but it slipped away like a thought that has been momentarily captured in some crystalline phrase and yet gets lost.

Erendroop announced the order of players. Garug-Caroch rose and left the Hall, shuddering at the thought of the brainless frenzy that would now impact the sequence of games, of the students and Masters running back and forth as rumors flew through the Hall, and of the ogling and cheering and flattery that would accompany anything that looked like a halfway competent performance.

On the steps outside the Hall of Games, he sat down and watched the dust and withered leaves of a barren autumn swirling in the wind. His head hurt, and still he could not quite remember what it was that had been going through his mind before Erendroop began calling the first round of participants to the board. In the end, Garug-Caroch walked back to his chamber, his cloak pulled up over his mouth and nose to keep out the dust that blew in scorching yellow clouds across the empty quadrangle.

On the following day, Garug-Caroch ignored the tournament and returned to the Library, where he had been working recently in the eighth alcove. He had discovered an obscure and largely unintelligible book about mathematics. In one of the final chapters of the book, he plowed through an almost incomprehensible discussion of the nature of numbers; he thought that the author was claiming that numbers had some sort of existence outside of mathematics, and as he struggled to the end of the discussion, he came across a startling remark:

> And so what is common to all is the Song of the Eternal Aeons, and it is there that the Eternally Real manifests itself. It is there that numbers themselves are original, as is all else. Mathematics is thus no more than the bringing to the focus of the mind one of the infinite aspects of the Song. The study of mathematics thus is to be recommended to all, and especially to the young, as an antidote to that sleep of the mind in which the Kingdom of Darkness waits dreaming, and from which decay and ruin emerge to possess the forgetful.

The Song again! And a mention of a Kingdom of Darkness! And of ruin and decay?

Garug-Caroch scrambled off to the gnome's desk at once, book in hand. He went up to the back of the desk and thumped loudly on it three times. It was one of several odd little gestures he had evolved recently to communicate with Twigbottom without disturbing his privacy.

As usual, there was no immediate answer.

Then the gnome staggered from behind the desk. His face was contorted with anguish. Without waiting for Garug-Caroch to speak, the gnome began: "It be soon now. He be grown powerful, but not so powerful that Ay not be able to be winning some knowledge from him. Go to the tournament that ye may see evidence of his strength. *Be certain to return.* If Ay be not here, flee! Flee from the College! Go to the Southern Hill Country! Hide yeself! They be not there yet! If Ay be here when ye return, we will be seeking what ye need in the levels below. Go! *The time is short!*"

Garug-Caroch was speechless. But, as he began to ask if the gnome was ill, what he meant, and how he knew what had been wanted, and as a multitude of other questions tumbled through his mind, the gnome raised his hand weakly.

"Go, human! Go now!" he said as he vanished behind his desk again.

Garug-Caroch stood, astonished, for a moment. And then, because he did not know what else to do, he ran from the Library and thrashed his way as best he could through the briar passageway towards the Gate-Tower. His head buzzed with questions:

Who is "he"?

Who are "they"?

What's happening to the gnome?

What's going to happen at the tournament?

He imagined in distaste the futile efforts that would be made to roll the sixth spiral to attain the rank of Master Sage and the seventh spiral to be eligible for the Grand Master's Chair. The Hall of Games would be crowded and hot, the Junior Masters in their gray robes scurrying here and there, running errands for the black-robed Senior Masters or jockeying for a better view of the main boards; the brown-robed students variously bored and exhilarated by what was happening.

As the brambles caught in his robe and sent him stumbling over broken paving stones, he began to see in his mind's eye, as he had once before, the view from the balcony. He saw beneath him the Junior Masters thronged like hungry wood lice around the Senior Masters, each one barely distinguishable from the other.

At the board he could see that attention was focusing on one Master in particular, one who did not deserve to be there, an imposter! But he was doing well, it seemed, and the crowd of onlookers gasped with admiration. As Garug-Caroch thrust through a particularly thick patch of briars, the vision faded. He was at the Gate-Tower.

The great brass gong above the Hall of Games began to toll — seven slow peals, the traditional announcement of the election of a new Grand Master.

That can't be so, Garug-Caroch thought, and he began running for the service portal. But perhaps it was.

Something had changed, and very much for the worse.

He was aware of some looming image of corruption, some dark shadow spreading its arms to embrace the College. He bolted through the service portal and into the quadrangle. There he stopped abruptly.

At the end of the quadrangle, the doors of the Hall of Games were flung open, and a great crowd of Masters and students spilled out onto the steps. Flashes of color from the Masters' ceremonial hoods mingled with the massed oily brown and gray and black of the undulating robes.

Arms waved tumultuously back and forth; voices shouted and cheered. The crowd oozed slowly down the steps, revealing a single figure, arms raised high in triumph, standing at the top of the stairs.

Garug-Caroch was stunned, but he could not recognize the figure on the steps. He began walking forward, slowly now.

It was the tradition of the College that when a new Master assumed the Chair of the Grand Master, his predecessor handed over the insignia of the office in a ceremony especially designed for that purpose. But those small matters had obviously been dispensed with.

"Nonetheless," Garug-Caroch said to himself, "I shall mount the steps and congratulate him, whoever he is; it is my duty to do so."

While he was pressing through the crowd near the foot of the stairs and looking up, he finally recognized the new Grand Master. It was Arfla, and over him, Garug-Caroch sensed immediately, hung some dark and terrifying power.

Still, he continued to push through the crowd and began climbing the stairs. The crowd grew silent. On the step below Arfla, Garug-Caroch spoke.

"My congratulations to the new Grand Master. I see you have already assumed the office. I will return to my chambers and remove the official blue robe and the scarlet hood of the Grand Master. My Steward can brush them off and press them and bring them to you as soon as they are ready."

Arfla glanced at the robe and noticed momentarily the burrs and twigs and crumbled shards of stone caught in its folds. His brief curiosity about the condition of the robe was quickly displaced by querulous impatience.

Garug-Caroch had difficulty making out the expression on Arfla's face; it seemed to change each moment, almost like a candle flame flickering in a draft. Arfla smiled, his thin lips cutting a quivering slit in his bloated face, and Garug-Caroch shuddered.

"You are not wanted here, old man," Arfla proclaimed with a smirk, his reddish, swollen eyes blazing with hatred. "Your chambers are now my chambers; your robe is now my robe. I will have you barred from the College. Leave now. You are banished."

He turned from Garug-Caroch back to the crowd, raising his arms once more: the crowd resumed its coarse cheering.

Suddenly Garug-Caroch found himself rocked back and forth by two burly College gendarmes. His robe and hood were stripped off, leaving him in a threadbare tunic. The robe and hood were deposited into the hands of Arfla, who raised them high above his head; he basked in the adulation of the crowd.

Garug-Caroch was shocked. "You can't do that," he said. "It's against all the rules of the College." He was about to protest further when Arfla turned and laughed.

"I am the rules of the College, old man. I am the Grand Master. Go!"

"The Grand Master protects and cherishes the rules; he doesn't make them!" Garug-Caroch retorted.

Arfla laughed again. The students laughed. They screeched and rollicked in laughter; they bent over in laughter, falling to the ground and rolling in the dust and pounding one another until tears came to their eyes and blood spurted from broken noses and cheeks gouged by dirty fingernails.

Garug-Caroch found himself shoved down to the base of the steps. He turned and pushed his way back through the wildly hysterical crowd. His mind was blank; he seemed to have no will of his own.

As he passed through the crowd, the power faded. He began to walk as quickly as he could, without attracting attention, back towards the service portal.

Behind him he could still sense the darkness that cloaked Arfla. He could feel his own stomach knotting up in fear.

Once outside the service portal, he ran along the wall to the Gate-Tower. In the distance, across the college pastures, he could see small knots of students fleeing the College—enemies of Arfla, he presumed, scoffers, skeptics, those not easily deceived by appearances.

He entered through the portcullis and shoved and tore his way through the briars to the Library as fast as he could. When he arrived at the Library, he burst into the central rotunda.

"Are you here? What's happening?" he shouted, and the sound of his voice surprised him as it reverberated in the stillness of the Library. The gnome appeared, not from behind the desk, but from the door that led down to the subterranean collection. He held a sputtering torch in one hand.

"Quickly," he called, "the books ye be seeking lie far below us. We must go now, while his power be directed elsewhere." Without waiting, he turned and began the descent.

Garug-Caroch ran after him, crying out, "Who are you talking about? Whose power is directed elsewhere?"

The gnome replied as he hurried down the steps: "Ye have seen Arfla. My adversary. Myself. Quickly now! Ye life be at risk if we delay, and more than that for me." The gnome hurried on, his torch flickering precariously, his oversized boots clumsily thumping on the stairs as he descended.

Garug-Caroch could hardly keep up with the gnome's irregular pace. He stumbled several times, saved only by the landing at the bottom of each flight of stairs. He was in a dream, he thought, a nightmare. The shadows from the gnome's eerie robe and grotesquely curled bark boots flowed and twisted across the walls, polymorphous and menacing. Around them, the mossy stonework of the ancient subterranean passageways and archives glimmered damply in the torchlight.

On the fifth level down, their pace slowed suddenly. Garug-Caroch could feel a sudden pressure on his mind, a will directed against his own, an insistence that he go back. The gnome stumbled, almost as if he had been struck.

"He knows! He be coming! Hurry!" Twigbottom wailed.

Now there were no questions in Garug-Caroch's mind. Something was coming, or already waiting. He had a sense of a presence slowly filling the cellars below. Vague images flashed through his mind—images of things he was glad he could not grasp clearly. They were laced with a hunger, a craving he could feel like thick, ropy worms writhing in his stomach. He wanted to gag and run. But he and the gnome finally hurried down to the Library's bottom floor.

The gnome, his torch raised as high as possible, his face pale with fear, pointed to the shelves on a nearby wall. "Those be ye books," he cried, "there be too many there to be taking with ye or making a choice. Just grab as many as ye can be carrying and run!

"He has called the ptoloch. He has possessed it. It be coming."

A ptoloch? Was this some kind of perverse gnome joke? He had not heard this word "ptoloch" since he was a child and his mother read him nursery stories. It was an innocent enough creature, even if the most repulsive in Oval-Earth, according to the nursery stories, but this one apparently was both real and, in some sense, "possessed."

Meanwhile, Garug-Caroch saw, in Twigbottom's torchlight, a set of what looked like about eighty huge leather-bound volumes lined up on some shelves. In a moment's decision, he lunged at the first books in the set, grabbed six dusty tomes from the shelves, and stacked them frantically in his arms. It was as much as he could carry.

Deep under the stone floor of the Library, something was forcing its way up through the earth. Garug-Caroch could feel the floor swaying and lifting beneath his feet. He grabbed the last book even as he felt the floor beneath him buckle.

When he began running towards the stairs, the first of the great stone slabs in the floor reared upward like a monstrous trapdoor. He saw that he was too late. A second stone, directly in front of the stairs, was thrust violently into the air.

A shapeless black hump bulged out of the opening, a mass of slimy flesh, foul, rotting, and fetid. The stench was intolerable. Spiny hooks and tentacles twisted out of the side of the slimy mass and groped blindly around, searching for something to grasp.

A thousand little lipless mouths opened like tiny slits over the entire surface of the flesh and began alternately sucking at the air and puffing out unspeakably foul aromas. Some of the mouths distended into wide, dripping cavities, revealing channels that reached down deep into the flesh of the monster.

Garug-Caroch was almost bent over with nausea; he felt like dropping the immense weight of books and erupting into violent and compulsive vomiting. To be drawn into one of those pulsating cavities would be to perish amid a foulness that was beyond the worst nightmares one could have.

For a moment, Garug-Caroch forgot his own situation and began looking for Twigbottom. He saw him backed into a corner at the other side of the ptoloch.

A fearful struggle was going on there: Twigbottom was trying to save himself from being physically enveloped by the slimy flesh of the monster even as he was attempting to fight off another power, emanating from the beast, that was exerting all its energy to tear the gnome free of his ties with the earth and to absorb his earth-power into itself.

Garug-Caroch knew that the ties of a wood-gnome went deep. Like the roots of a great tree, they plunged down into the heart of nature. Garug-Caroch could feel, in the depths of even Twigbottom's irascible soul, the nurture of plants bursting into life in the spring, the warm rich loam of the forest in the summer, the sap of centuries-old trees sinking into their roots as the chill of autumn settled over them, and more; beneath the seasonal rise and fall of life, he sensed a deeper, heavier rhythm, an ancient and slower song of soil, rocks, and water. The gnome was rooted in all of this, and the dark power with which the gnome struggled was trying to tear the gnome away from it and claim it as its own.

Twigbottom, with a harsh shriek, reached beneath him into the fullness of his earth-power and thrust the intruder from his mind, but not without exhausting every shred of physical life force he had left in him. As he collapsed into one of the dripping cavities of the ptoloch, he cried out to Garug-Caroch: "Run, fool! This be death!" The last that Garug-Caroch saw of Twigbottom was the wiggling hair-tuft vanishing into the palpitating black slime of the beast.

And Garug-Caroch ran. He grasped the six heavy volumes in his arms, held his breath, and scrambled up the slippery hump that was quivering up through the floor in front of him. As he slid back and forth on the greasy mass, he could sense hundreds of little mouths sucking and tugging horribly at his tunic.

The tiny tentacles likewise plucked at him, but these gave him something to get footholds on, and he was able to mount to the top of the hump. There, one mouth began to stretch out as a wide, slavering gill poised to engorge him, but one of the ponderous books toppled out of Garug-Caroch's arms and into the gill, momentarily choking it and giving Garug-Caroch time to slide down the other side of the hump.

He landed on the floor at the bottom of the stairs, his books scattered in every direction. He picked himself up and collected his five remaining books. The beast rolled and moaned behind him, caught up in a series of painful contractions; then, with a convulsive heave, it spat out the sixth book into the darkness below.

As Garug-Caroch groped his way up the stairs, he could hear behind him great blocks of stone falling and breaking. A quick backward glance showed that even Twigbottom's sputtering torch had been swallowed up.

The stairs shook, and the entire Library seemed to be grinding on its foundations. But Garug-Caroch kept moving steadily from one level of the subterranean vaults to the next, fumbling through the darkness. He felt as if his bones were going to break under the strain. He yearned for the light of the sun squinting down between the narrow yellow cornices of the scriptorium. Around him in the darkness he could hear the moss-mice scurrying in panic, squealing and flailing against the walls, as if they, too, knew the terror below. At last, Garug-Caroch bolted from the stairwell door into the rotunda and out through the main doors of the Library. There he collapsed on the steps, panting, still clutching his precious books.

He realized he was alone, that the gnome was dead, sealed up beneath the rock, entombed inside the monster that had been called to rise from underneath the Library. He also realized that the presence that had filled the lowest vault of the Library was the same presence that had cloaked the newly elevated Arfla in power. Perhaps it, too, had been snuffed out temporarily in the avalanche of stone and had wasted itself in trying, in vain, to take possession of the earth-power of the gnome.

But it would muster its power again; it would return.

Garug-Caroch gathered up his books, exited the Library, and pushed his way through the briars until he passed through the Gate-Tower and headed back to the service portal. He was sure now that somehow Arfla posed no threat to him, though he didn't know how long that might last. He was right. The Steward stood by the door, mystified by what was going on. Inside his chambers, Garug-Caroch saw that Arfla, fresh from his triumph and yet oddly depleted in energy, had just taken possession of the rooms. Arfla sat in the Grand Master's chair, desperately trying to roll something better than a second spiral on Garug-Caroch's private game board. He looked weak and pathetic and gazed at Garug-Caroch with fear in his eyes.

"Fool!" Garug-Caroch said to him. "You don't know the price of your folly! When your true masters return, they will consume you! Now leave these chambers until I have had the chance to clear out my things!"

Arfla whimpered and scuttled out the door like a large, wounded beetle, knocking over the game board as he went and sending the gemstones flying all over the floor. The Steward gaped at him as he hurried down the hall. Then he turned to help Garug-Caroch make his preparations for departure.

They packed up the books taken from the Library in old leather cases, wrapped up the game board in burlap, collected the scattered gemstones and secured them in a small velvet pouch, and piled his clothing, what little there was of it, in a traveling basket. Outside, Garug-Caroch could hear songs and laughter from the Ale Hall. College life was resuming its normal pace. The ale-hour had begun.

On the following day, Garug-Caroch, with the help of his loyal Steward, visited several local villages in the vicinity of the College and was finally able to purchase a moose and a two-wheeled moose-cart from a farmer for a reasonable price. The moose, named Collielava, was a feeble old creature with rather sagging, yellowish antlers, his tall legs a bit crooked with age, but he was still serviceable for light drawing before some generous owner would retire him and put him out to pasture. The cart itself was a rickety affair, supported by two large wooden wheels that tilted so far inward under the wagon that it was a wonder it could stand upward at all. But it was the best that Garug-Caroch and his Steward could find.

They wasted no time in bringing the moose and the wagon back to the College and loading the wagon with the books and clothes basket and a small supply of wine and food. Garug-Caroch hesitated before he added his Game of Spheres board to the mound of items on the cart. But he tossed it on and placed the small pouch that contained the gemstones in a pocket of his robe. He had lived too much of his life with the Game of Spheres to abandon it now. He gave a goodly carafe of Hill wine and a few silver coins to his Steward and thanked him for his steadfast service.

Finally, he mounted the wagon, took up the reins, and guided the lanky moose and the creaky cart gently down the path that led away from the service portal. He took a quick look backward at the Gate-Tower and its barely discernable inscription. After that, the cart rounded the College buildings and rolled unsteadily up the ramp to the raised bed of the Eastern Arm of the Radial High-Road.

Garug-Caroch never looked back at the College as it faded from view behind him. He knew that he would never see it again. He felt little regret over that knowledge, yet he did feel regret, even a deep chagrin, over his own apathy about leaving behind him a life's work that had, in the end, meant so little to him.

Chapter IV

The Journey to the Hills

The itinerary from the College to the Southern Hill Country led first along the Eastern Arm of the Radial High-Road System in the direction of the Capital. Since all four arms of the System met in the Imperial Plaza of the Capital, one could simply turn left at the great intersection and follow the Southern Arm of the System along the western edge of the Midland Sea and over the wide, rolling plains towards the Hill Country at the southernmost tip of Oval-Earth.

Such a journey would have once been pleasant and relaxing, if one could have made it several centuries earlier. At that time, small inns, situated at regular intervals along the Radial High-Roads and part of the imperial hostel network, still tendered to the needs of travelers at affordable prices.

The four arms of the system, each built up from the surrounding plains on raised dikes, were almost as straight as arrows and were frequently bordered on both sides of the roadway by long rows of trees, which spread their boughs over the pavement below and provided shade in the summer and windbreaks in the winter. A multitude of stone bridges had straddled the small rivers and streams that flowed from the mountains and through the countryside. The prosperous commerce of former times made abundant use of the Radial High-Road System, which was but the central axis of a web of regional roads that wound their way through all the hills and valleys of Oval-Earth.

The view from the Radial High-Roads was ever lovely: in all directions along the distant horizon, the Golden Mountains shimmered and sparkled in the sunlight. As the four arms of the Radial High-Road System converged at the Capital, which was situated on a rise overlooking the Midland Sea, they afforded a superb vista of its milk-white watery expanse and of the round, bright-blue island at its center.

In the intervening centuries, the roads had been allowed to decay. Most of the inns were closed; the remaining few, often in sorry condition, had raised prices and lowered services to the point at which most travelers preferred to spend the night in the open somewhere, living off the provisions they had brought with them for the journey.

The shade trees that had lined the High-Roads had been felled by farmers desperate for firewood in the winter; others had died and rotted by the side of the road. As a result, the roads, deprived of shade, blistered in the intensity of the midday heat. Their pavement became cracked and broken, while sizable chunks of the roads were gradually dislodged by heavy rains and toppled off the side of the dikes into the ditches below, leaving behind them huge, dusty potholes. Few of the bridges survived. The now infrequent travelers had to ford the rivers and streams as best they could.

But the loveliness of the view, when the now capricious weather permitted, remained and compensated, just a bit, for the inevitable hardships of the journey. As Garug-Caroch's moose-cart lumbered slowly over the deeply rutted pavement of the roadway, his eyes ranged over the Golden Mountains, now in their autumnal grandeur — over the yellows, reds, and earthy browns that blanketed the mountains' lower slopes, and then up across the deep, ruddy crimson that brightened into the red-tinged golden hues where the highest of the mountains, the glittering jewels of Oval-Earth, pierced the iridescent blue of the sky. "It's refreshment for the soul just to gaze upon them," Garug-Caroch thought, "and I need that."

He also needed sleep. He had spent the final night at the College in his chambers poring over the five heavy tomes that he had hauled off with him in his escape from the Library. He understood very little of what he read. The books were old and moldy — their leathern covers peeled and flaked with age. Some of them had moss-mice holes chewed directly through them. The writing on the parchment was faded in many places, and the language was filled with archaic words and phrases that Garug-Caroch did not understand.

But he had grasped one essential point: the books were the initial section of an extensive Commentary (from what he could now presume was that eighty-volume set he had seen in the lowest vault of the Library) on the Song of the Eternal Aeons.

The Song was never quoted, as if the ancient writer assumed that a perfect knowledge of the Song was part, if not the core, of what any well-educated person would know by memory. The text of the Commentary was replete with references to the Song. "I have a job ahead of me," Garug-Caroch had mumbled to himself. From these initial volumes, he figured he might be able to reconstruct at the least the opening lines of the Song.

Garug-Caroch was one of the few travelers on the Eastern Arm of the Radial High-Road System that day. It was unseasonably hot for autumn, and the road was dusty and dry. Collielava, the gaunt, droopy-antlered moose who drew the wagon, was already showing signs of fatigue by mid-day; he looked longingly at the cool waters of a nearby farmer's pond for a drink as well as for a prolonged dip among its reedy banks. He swung his head around as far as he could and looked at Garug-Caroch, who was sitting on the wagon.

Garug-Caroch was only too happy to oblige. He had already developed an affection for this great, gentle creature. Garug-Caroch pulled the unsteady, two-wheeled wagon over to the side of the road and cautiously down the bank of the dike. When he brought it to a stop, pleased that it had not overturned on its way down the bank, he clambered from the wagon and unhitched the tackle and reins from the moose. Collielava immediately sloshed cautiously across the swampy rim of the pond and plunged, with a satisfying sigh, into the pond itself.

Garug-Caroch sat down to have lunch in the shade of a parkaberry bush and to watch Collielava wallow luxuriously in the sunlit waters. It was fun to look at him. The moose tossed and splashed his wide-spanned antlers. Then he stood up, dripping with water and weeds, and munched on large wads of swamp grass.

Garug-Caroch similarly gnawed on a stale hunk of turnip bread, which he washed down with some cool Hill wine. He also cut off several slivers from a small wedge of moose cheese that the Steward, in a last sympathetic gesture, had slipped into his pack. The cheese added some flavor to the tasteless turnip bread.

Garug-Caroch thought of Arfla and felt some pity for him, despite his nastiness. Whatever power was at work at the College would toss Arfla aside like a broken toy once it had used him up. He thought of Twigbottom, too. He choked on the bread and stopped eating for a moment.

Granted, Twigbottom had not been the most agreeable sort of personage, or gnome, as the case might be, but he had, in the end, given his life in the face of some remorseless evil. Garug-Caroch honored him for this sacrifice and sorrowed for him. Twigbottom, whatever else one might want to say about him, had, in the end, used his earth-power as a wood-gnome both to defend his own spirit and to set in motion what could very well be the defense, in its dire distress, of Oval-Earth itself.

With such somber thoughts, Garug-Caroch packed away the remainder of his lunch and, coaxing Collielava out of the water, rehitched him to the wagon. The shimmering moose, now refreshed and revitalized, hauled the creaky wagon up the steep bank to the High-Road, and they were on their way again.

The two-day journey to the Capital was uneventful. In the evening of the first day, Garug-Caroch could not find an inn that was still intact and open for business, so he led his moose wagon down into a ravine by the side of the road. The ferocious heat of the day gave way abruptly to a frigid night. Encamped in the ravine, Garug-Caroch kindled a small fire to cook his sparse victuals and watched the binary lavender moons in their picturesque traverse across the sky as they slowly spiraled around each other as if in a ceremonious dance; then, wrapped in his burlap cloak, he slept under the autumn stars, close to the moose, whose warmth he welcomed in the chill night.

Collielava had begun to return Garug-Caroch's affection and insisted on laying his head close to Garug-Caroch's head; this would have been fine if the moose's antlers didn't occasionally wake Garug-Caroch up by jabbing him now and then and thrusting him to one side or another. Despite these minor interruptions, however, Garug-Caroch slept better than he had for years.

At the end of the second day of travel, he found an inn, or what one might once have called an inn; it had been originally part of the Radial High-Road hostel system, as was made clear by the remnants of the imperial insignia on a wood carving over the entrance gate. Most of the main building had fallen down, though a large stone chimney stood amid the ruined timbers. But a few stables still were standing, and one of these served as a shelter and dining hall for the guests.

Garug-Caroch unhitched Collielava and led him to one of the other stables for the night. He made sure that Collielava had plenty to eat and a good bed of hay to sleep on. He returned to the guest stable in time for dinner. Five fellow guests were seated at a long wooden trestle. Two of them were tiny wood-gnomes, of the kumquat clan, with bright orange hair and puffy little orange noses. They were constantly giggling and whispering to each other. Next to them sat an enormous, dour peat-digger whose clothing was liberally besprinkled with the product of his trade. He seemed to be the object of the gnomes' amusement, though he ignored it by staring vacantly at a large, gaping hole in the stable wall.

On the other side of the dinner trestle, a middle-aged woman and her teenage daughter were engaged in a muted power struggle over "proper table manners." The mother insisted on poking her daughter with an angry finger and hissing constant exhortations at her. Such exhortations were being ignored, as the girl squirmed away from the rasping lips and fended off the mother's jabs with swift motions of her elbow.

The matron, embarrassed by her daughter's obstinacy, was quick to inform Garug-Caroch, after he sat down next to her, that she was taking her daughter to a "finishing school" in the Capital. She was confident that such a school would inculcate in her recalcitrant offspring the "deportment appropriate for a young lady in polite society."

Garug-Caroch couldn't imagine what sort of "finishing school" could still exist in the Capital and that there was anything like "polite society" left in Oval-Earth. He also wondered what there was to "finish" anyway, the young lady in question obviously being the sort of maiden who spends much of her time embroiled in fistfights with village urchins, as evidenced by her missing her two front teeth and by a sizable scar under the right side of her chin.

But he chose not to press the issue and agreed that the mother was looking out for the best interests of the child; he also suggested that an immediate visit to a teeth-crafter might well advance the project she had in mind. The matron approved of his advice, though it occurred to Garug-Caroch that the only teeth-crafters left in Oval-Earth were wood-gnomes and they rarely resided in the Capital.

Meanwhile, the slovenly innkeeper, wearing an unspeakably filthy apron, limped awkwardly around the table and slapped thick clots of marsh-spud pudding from a wooden ladle into the shallow wooden basins that served as eating vessels for the guests. Fruit sauce, normally served with such a pudding to mollify its bitterness, was not provided, and there was nothing else to eat and no other way to eat it except by tearing apart the thick paste of the pudding with one's hands and stuffing it into one's mouth.

When the matron made the mistake of asking for something to drink, she was met with a stream of abuse from the innkeeper, who castigated her for fancying that she was a guest at the palace of the Imperial Viceroy. The peat-digger momentarily shifted his stare from the hole in the wall and glared angrily at the innkeeper, who immediately desisted from his tirade and vanished into the kitchen. The kumquat gnomes stopped giggling, and both broke out into fits of violent hiccups.

Dinner did not last long; the guests had little to say to one another and disappeared into makeshift niches along the side of the stable, where straw-covered pallets would serve as beds for the night. Garug-Caroch knocked on the kitchen door and asked the innkeeper if he could purchase a candle. The innkeeper treated this request with a great deal of suspicion; but, after rubbing his grimy hands against his apron, he agreed to the purchase at a very high price and went to fetch the candle. It was not much of a candle.

When Garug-Caroch asked that the candle be lit for him, he was again charged a small fee, but the candle enabled him to withdraw into his niche, recline upon his straw pallet, and spend some of the night studying the books of the Commentary. He did not make much progress with it. Reconstructing the Song and coming to some real understanding of the Commentary was going to take a long time. Anyway, the candle stub quickly burned out.

Garug-Caroch reached the shore of the Midland Sea about noon of the third day. It was sweltering, so he let Collielava enjoy another romp in the water. It was strange to watch the tall white beast dive and splash around in the shining white waters of the Sea.

Out in the center of the Sea lay the Isle of the Drowsers. Garug-Caroch gazed at it with intense curiosity. As he observed the darkly solemn blue spruce trees that covered the island, he remembered that he had found several references to it during the previous night's study of the Commentary. If he was interpreting the mysterious allusions in the text correctly, the island had once been called the "Eye of the Universe" and had been home to some sort of mystic seers. They were of interest to him because, as best as he could gather from the obscure pages of the Commentary, they—and they alone in all of Oval-Earth—chanted the entire Song each morning as they rose to watch the sun's ascent over the Golden Mountains. They were considered to be a Brethren of the "wakeful," of the "watchful," of the "vigilant."

They, more than anyone else in Oval-Earth, had been most awake, most alert both day and night as they gazed from their island solitude into the far depths of the universe. How things change, Garug-Caroch thought. It struck him that the entire Midland Sea, with its oval shape, its white waters, and the round blue island with its round black marble tower in the center, was the perfect image of an eye—an eye looking upward, outward, beyond itself.

The Drowsers now occupied the island and, as far as anyone knew, rarely arose from their slumbers. They dreamt out their lives in the deepest of sleep. "What dreams, what extraordinary dreams, they must have!" Garug-Caroch supposed; nevertheless, if a copy of the Song had survived in some forgotten nook of the island dwelling, it would be well worth a trip to the island someday to find it.

But Garug-Caroch was not ready yet for such a journey; it was too dangerous to approach the unknown without further inquiry. No one could even guess what dire results a visit to the Isle of the Drowsers could bring down upon the unprepared traveler.

When the worst of the noontide heat was over, Garug-Caroch summoned the moose out of the water and hitched him again to the cart. They proceeded quickly along the remainder of the Eastern Arm of the Radial High-Road, which passed through the walls of the Capital and led to the Imperial Plaza. Here they could make the left turn onto the Southern Arm.

Garug-Caroch wanted to make his stay in the Capital as brief as possible, but there was no escaping the inevitable and tiresome encounter with the imperial officials of the Ministry of Travel, who set up their registration booths at the center of the Plaza. All visitors from every direction were required to register and, of course, to pay the High-Road toll as well as the visitors' tax. The officials also routinely inspected all wares being transported along the High-Road System and charged capriciously imposed import-export duty fees.

The decay of what had been once a proud imperial city was all too obvious. The municipal walls were in dismal shape. A noisy and ill-kempt platoon of guards patrolled along its overgrown battlements from time to time, but, for the most part, the walls were unattended and the gateway through the eastern wall, though still crowned on top by the ancient imperial insignia, had only a pair of rusty hinges where the massive gates had once swung open to the east.

The approach to the Imperial Plaza was equally dismal. As the four arms of the Imperial High-Road System entered the Capital, the names of the roads were changed to "boulevards." On both sides of these once spacious and elegant boulevards were quarters of the city that had disintegrated into loathsome slums filled with trash and abandoned buildings.

Here and there, above the squalor of the houses, could be seen an occasional palatial building that may have once served as an urban residence for some great landed gentry of former ages or as an imperial center for a service or a benefice made available for all the denizens of Oval-Earth. Such buildings were now empty shells, monumental walls of windows and doors with no dwellings left behind them; it was said that they had been destroyed during the War of Desolation. The ancient quarters that surrounded them exuded nothing but the stench of refuse left by an idle populace and by the innumerable predatory rodents and other vermin that spawned uncontrollably in the clogged sewers of the city.

In recent times, another plague had arisen in the city as well — an especially large and noxious insect of a bluish color with luminous orange streaks on its body and with grotesque, hairy wings. It was called the hairy-winged fly and was the size of a human fist. These flies bred in the swamps that bordered the city walls and that received the sundry effluvia that washed out of the city streets after a heavy rain.

Despite their largeness and their dank, hairy wings, these flies could buzz around the city streets with enormous speed. Their wings emitted a loud grating sound as they whizzed by. They bit animals and humans and sucked on plants and bored into the thick skin of wood-gnomes. They were almost impossible to kill, and only the well-aimed blow of a hefty stave could bring one down, though the black bloody splatter of the swatted fly was a bad as the fly itself. To have one's house, or room at night, invaded by a hairy-winged fly was an invitation to madness.

Garug-Caroch directed his moose-cart up the Eastern Boulevard towards the Imperial Plaza and tried to ignore what he saw around him. He had seen it many times before in his previous journeys to the Hill Country. Usually, he traveled southward in the late spring and northward in the late summer, not in the autumn, as he was doing now, and he was surprised at how empty the city seemed to be. Perhaps the unseasonable heat was keeping everyone indoors. Gradually he approached the cluster of large government buildings that encircled the Imperial Plaza.

As he crossed the Imperial Plaza, Garug-Caroch saw that some good had come of the unpleasant heat; the lines at the booths set up by the Ministry of Travel were much shorter than he remembered from his previous visits, though still long enough to cause a serious delay in the journey.

He expected a two-hour wait at the most, but time dragged on as he stood in line. Collielava grew impatient and shook his antlers back and forth as his huge black nose dripped profusely from the torrid heat of the Plaza.

At one point, a hairy-winged fly buzzed into the Plaza and alighted on his back. Garug-Caroch swatted at it with the long sleeves of his robe before it had a chance to bite the moose, and the fly, in turn, buzzed directly into Garug-Caroch's face, making him fall down and then bolting in and around the other persons in line as they flailed helplessly at it until it finally flew off into the western quarter of the city.

A long time ago, the center of the Plaza had been occupied by a magnificent fountain, which cooled and freshened the air with its high-spraying jets of water and provided both personages and beasts of burden with icy spring water piped in from the glaciers of the Golden Mountain. But the pipes had decayed, and the fountain had become so dilapidated that it was finally torn down.

Now the center of the Plaza was marked by the soiled canvas booths, where a particularly decrepit group of functionaries preyed ceaselessly on all the travelers who had to funnel through their officious lines and who had to meet their countless and arbitrary rules, which changed from day to day without notice.

As the delay extended into the late afternoon, rumors began to spread down the line. Apparently—so the story went as it passed along the line—someone up front had been detained and was being questioned on the suspicion of espionage. The questioning was taking a long time and absorbing all the attention of those who were on duty.

"Spying?" Garug-Caroch asked incredulously of an elderly woodchopper who was next in line. "For whom?" The woodchopper shook his head and waggled a finger—the only finger that remained on his right hand—to show his lack of certainty. He said that it was for an unnamed power beyond the Golden Mountains. Garug-Caroch scowled, "Of course, it's an 'unnamed power.' We don't know anything about what lies beyond the Golden Mountains."

A stocky woman in a vermilion cloak standing several persons in front of him—a widow, he had gathered, and of some wealth, since she had been prattling on all afternoon about a large plantation she owned close to the Capital—turned around and eyed him with suspicion. She muttered things about the Kingdom of Darkness and, as was usually done, mentioned the War of Desolation.

She also made some thinly disguised references to "people who might be interested in someone like you," so that Garug-Caroch grew silent and turned away from her. He knew he must keep his opinions to himself. Feeling just a bit triumphant, the woman focused her attention on the front of the line again and wrapped herself ever deeper in her garish vermilion cloak, which she wore despite the searing heat of the Plaza.

Garug-Caroch knew that informing on fellow citizens was a major pastime in Oval-Earth, especially at the Capital, even if there was no basis for informing at all. The Capital thrived on its dejection and fear. He also knew that no jail in the Capital could hold him for long with his powers of sealing and unsealing, but he didn't want to waste time by getting entangled with the authorities.

The waiting line finally began to move as another rumor passed through the crowd to the effect that the whole espionage incident had been a ploy used by the Ministry of Travel functionaries to extort money out of a well-to-do miner from the region of the Western Rock-Falls. It had worked; the miner had to pay a handsome fee to be cleared of the charges.

At least Garug-Caroch, with his frayed, weather-beaten robe, did not have to worry much about extortion, though he realized that a fuss could arise about Collielava. White moose were once abundant in the wilderness regions of Oval-Earth and had been domesticated only in fairly recent times, replacing a former animal that resembled it and that likewise had been used for riding and pulling. But it was now extinct and forgotten; the moose were following the same path, and, as they grew scarce, they became more valuable. Collielava was old and might not arouse too much attention.

Still, when his turn came, Garug-Caroch had to work his way through the long line of querulous officials burrowing through baskets of forms and slips and snapping at the travelers as well as among themselves. They examined the moose and the moose-cart and all its contents. They scoffed when they saw the Game of Spheres board, and one of them did a silly imitation of a student intent upon playing the game.

They were puzzled by the books. "What are these?" a functionary brayed as he shook one of the volumes to see what was inside it. He had a long unshaven jaw that protruded far out from underneath his mouth and that was besmirched with sweat and dust.

"Books!" Garug-Caroch answered.

"Do you have a permit for these ... these ..."

"Books."

"Books? What do you do with them?"

"Read them."

"Read them? Do you have a permit?"

"No one has ever needed a permit for books before."

"No one has ever had books before."

"So, when did a permit become necessary?"

"It became necessary now." The lips of the unshaven jaw stretched back in a malicious grin to reveal a row of enormous jagged yellow teeth on the bottom of the mouth and concealing the teeth of the upper part of the mouth, if there were any.

"And how do I get one of these permits?" Garug-Caroch asked sarcastically, since he knew how this was going to be done anyway.

The functionary scooped up a crinkled green slip from one of his baskets, wrote on it "Permit for Books," and took a wooden stamp, dipped it into a jug of oily black ink, and slammed it down on the green slip, splattering ink all over the front of his uniform as he did so. "Twelve coppers is the price for the permit," he added.

Garug-Caroch dug into his sleeve pockets and dropped twelve coppers onto the functionary's table. The long, slimy jaw again bristled into a toothy smile. Garug-Caroch took up the permit and led his moose-cart away from the booths. He looked back momentarily. Several functionaries were gathered together and were quarreling about how to divide the twelve coppers. He also noticed that the mother and daughter he had met at the inn the previous evening had just entered the Plaza and were standing at the back of the line. He waved at them in a friendly manner, but they were too occupied jabbing and elbowing one another about something to see him.

In the early evening, having made his way through the "infernal bowels" (as he put it) of the Ministry of Travel, Garug-Caroch thought briefly of taking a room in one of the inns in the Capital since it was now rather late to be venturing out on the Southern Arm of the Radial High-Road System.

He changed his mind about this. He did not like the city and did not get along well with any of the imperial officials, who swarmed about the bedraggled streets at unusual times like gangs of thugs. He was also worried that Collielava, who was regarded with no small degree of covetousness in the Imperial Plaza, might end up as a particularly large joint of broiled meat to assuage the insatiable appetites of the Imperial Guard.

And the city itself! Ospeth, the great emperor of legendary renown, built the Capital, it was said, as the shining diadem of Oval-Earth, a joy to all its peoples. If there was any truth in those stories, it was no longer true of the ill-kept city filled with ruined buildings — theaters, concert halls, dance pavilions, parks and bridle paths and racecourses, museums with magnificent marbled colonnades crumbling now into heaps of shards and dust.

At these majestic reminders of a once glorious past, the citizens of the city would sadly shake their heads and think upon the War of Desolation. No one could even remember what purpose many of these ancient buildings had served.

Garug-Caroch had no desire to sit with the weary populace at their street cafés for hours in the evening and share their lamentations about the shabby condition of the city. A night spent under the stars somewhere along the Southern Arm of the Radial High-Road was much more to his taste and to his and Collielava's safety, even if his departure would be late.

The Southern Arm was somewhat more picturesque than the Eastern Arm, and at one point, it ran right along the banks of the Midland Sea, where both he and Collielava could go for long refreshing swims now and then. He spent one night in an old fishing village by the Sea, where the fishermen regaled him with some "decent" seafood — milk-white shrimp sautéed with leeks and quince in sizzling moose butter — and with frightening stories about the Isle of the Drowsers, most of which he only half believed. Where did the fisherman get such outlandish ideas about strange presences, evil forces, born of dreams, of sleep? But the shrimp were tasty, especially after the food he had eaten recently.

On the morning of the fourth day out from the Capital, after passing through league after league of crumbling villages and desiccated fields, he led his moose-cart upward from the plains of Oval-Earth and into the low foothills that skirted the Hill Country proper.

Here the ravages of the past seasons did not seem so marked; the vegetation was thicker, the fall colors richer, the heat less oppressive. In the early evening, Garug-Caroch and his moose-cart approached Cantanteroff, the last village on the Southern Arm of the Radial High-Road and the southern terminus of the High-Road itself. At this juncture, a regional road wound up into the high slopes and forests of the Hill Country.

The moose-cart creaked and tilted along the rutted main street of the village until it came to the far end of the village, where a low, dome-shaped earth-house stood beneath a grove of shady trees. Knarry was sitting on a rock in front of the earth-house, resting from a busy day of examining sore throats and picking lice out of the ears of screaming children. Next to him was curled up Bomsiell, his large four-eared forest cat. Both he and the cat looked up as the moose-cart ground to a halt. Collielava shook his antlers back and forth as if in greeting, and Bomsiell stood up, arched her back, and stretched out her lithe, gray-furred limbs.

Bomsiell was larger than most dogs, and her four, sharply pointed ears — two facing forward and two backward — twitched nervously, as always. Meanwhile, the Master Sage climbed down from the cart and was about to speak, when he was addressed by the rough voice of the wood-gnome.

"I have received your message, Garug-Caroch," Knarry said directly and without salutations. "There is much to discuss; there is evil stirring and working at places other than the College."

Garug-Caroch sighed. "Can it wait for just a moment, Knarry?" he replied. "I need an hour or two without worry. And I need a bath."

Knarry nodded. "After supper, then. It's time to rest."

Knarry stood up, showed Garug-Caroch where to bed Collielava down for the night, helped him to unpack a few items from the wagon, and led him into the fragrant earth-house.

These earth-houses of the wood-gnomes always intrigued Garug-Caroch. Knarry's was typical except for the front section, which was devoted to his medical practice — a waiting room, an examining room, and a dispensary — all laid out in a very human fashion to serve the human needs of the patients.

But once one left the front of the house, the floor plan shifted to something Garug-Caroch could never fathom. The rooms were small and on varying levels; the floor of one might be a foot or two higher than that of an adjacent room. Hallways could fork unexpectedly and slope up or down; walls rarely met at right angles, and, most baffling of all, ceilings often sloped or even curved in a bewildering array of directions. Many of the rooms were empty of furnishings and had no ostensible purpose. No gnomes had ever been able to explain to Garug-Caroch why they built their houses as they did. They did not understand it themselves.

Despite his curiosity, Garug-Caroch was content to follow Knarry through the maze of the earth-house to a small, low-raftered room where a capacious wooden tub awaited with its steaming hot-spring waters. There Knarry left Garug-Caroch to soak his travel-weary limbs for a while. Later, in a fresh robe woven of mountain flax, Garug-Caroch joined Knarry in the galley, where Knarry opened and poked around in a warm open-hearth stove that emanated the most delectable aromas. "Baked balloon-fish!" Garug-Caroch exclaimed. "Now, that could raise anyone's spirit!"

"It should," Knarry answered. "Those fish are hard enough to catch, even for a gnome." He had spent part of the morning with a long-handled net, making pass after pass at the fish as they floated up and down in the air at the edge of a waterfall in a valley just east of the village. Their ability to inflate themselves made waterfalls their perfect habitats and also made their flesh especially light and tender.

Knarry served up this finest of freshwater catches with almonds, creamed marsh-root, and parkaberry sauce. Even Bomsiell received a handsome slice of balloon-fish, which she gobbled down, delicate little bones and all. A jigger or two of gnome-spirits concluded the meal. Garug-Caroch sat for some time, slowly savoring the pungent, faintly sweet liqueur.

Knarry broke the silence. "Why don't we walk up to the gazebo? We have stories to exchange and plans to make."

Garug-Caroch always loved to sit in Knarry's hillside gazebo and watch the sunset over the western mountains, but he was not ready yet to discuss the problems they needed to resolve. He agreed, nevertheless, and they were on their way—Garug-Caroch with his long, nervous strides and Knarry, just a bit shorter but stubby and very strong, moving easily alongside him. Bomsiell stayed behind to guard the house and keep Collielava company in the moose-shed.

Knarry and Garug-Caroch arrived at the gazebo and, sitting at their ease on the benches, watched the sun go down over the Golden Mountains in the west. Stars flickered over the entire span of Oval-Earth, and the twin lavender moons bathed the Midland Sea in a pearl-like glow.

Their conversation turned to serious matters. Garug-Caroch recounted his experiences in the Library in some detail. Knarry listened closely, interrupting frequently with questions and comments.

"A *ptoloch*, Garug? A *ptoloch*? And you say this ptoloch was *called*?" Knarry inquired at one point.

"You gnomes know of ptolochs, then?"

Knarry snorted and shook his head. "They are part of our legends, yes — the stuff of which our bardic Gno'menai make their songs and poems. They are portrayed as dark creatures of the lower depths, monstrous, huge, many-legged, insatiable in their hunger, fetid in their abominable smell, implacable — yet harmless. I don't know that there is a wood-gnome in Oval-Earth who would believe anymore that such things exist. But we now have evidence of them — direct and incontrovertible, unless you were subject to some kind of delusion at the time.

"But tell me more about the struggle to tear Twigbottom's mind free of its ties to the earth. The picture you gave of Twigbottom's mind reaching down into the earth like the roots of a tree — that's just what it is like to be a wood-gnome."

Garug-Caroch repeated his description. Knarry seemed to hang on every word, and his agitation increased as the story proceeded. He sprang from his bench and landed with an enormous thump, then paced back and forth across the gazebo in short ponderous steps. With a gruff snort, he stopped and spoke to Garug-Caroch. "What are your plans?"

Garug-Caroch answered, "I'm going to the cabin where I spend the summers in order to figure out what I can about the Song. There is some great power connected with it. You remember what happened to me at the Gate-Tower? That stone carving was an illustration of part of the Song, and the words it induced me to utter — those are the words from the Song that the carving illustrates. The effect of pronouncing them aloud was very great indeed. Further, I've found what seem to be other parts of the Song referred to in the five books I saved from the Library. Maybe the Song has power that can defeat whatever it was I met in the Library, whatever it is that is deforming the seasons."

"Have you tested it? Have you recited out loud the words you know?" Knarry asked.

"No. I'm too ignorant of the effects to take the risk — I haven't any clear idea of what might happen. The impression I have from the Commentary is that the Song was an object of great reverence, something one would proclaim only in very special circumstances. I am not sure what those circumstances were. I have no intention of repeating those words until I really know what I am doing."

Knarry looked thoughtfully at Garug-Caroch, but before he could say anything, the Master Sage continued.

"I think the Song played a pivotal role in the life of the College, very probably in all of Oval-Earth. A fellowship of mystic seers on the island in the Midland Sea once devoted their lives to it.

"But the Song was lost. The Commentary doesn't look as though it has been touched for centuries, maybe even for millennia. How could something like that be forgotten? What could make us forget it?

"But I'm going to reconstruct what I can of the Song from the initial five volumes of the Commentary, line by line, however long it takes me. Even a few lines may be enough to stem the tide of what endangers Oval-Earth. It should be quiet and safe at the cabin; I can do my work there."

Knarry listened to this account and shook his shaggy head morosely. "I don't think so, Garug-Caroch," he said, "there may be no safe places. But I've got something better. A little less than a day's journey south and east of here, up in the mountains and well away from any road, there's an abandoned earth-house.

"An old friend, Gnarl-Oak, lived there. He was tougher and wiser than most gnomes, but he has been gone to the Taiga five years now. The house is as solid as a fortress, and almost no one knows it's there. In any case, the place is a lot more rugged than your summer cabin, and remember, you will be spending the winter. Best of all, it's only fourteen leagues from Tundra-Bear and Fox-Foot's village. That's where you should go."

Garug-Caroch looked out into the darkness now covering Oval-Earth. He turned back to Knarry and said: "Agreed. Perhaps Tundra-Bear could lay in a supply of firewood and some provisions; if we had to haul them from here, we'd need a small caravan. I don't think my moose, Collielava, could pull too heavy a load up the Regional Road."

"No difficulty," Knarry answered. He added, "The Hill people will look after you. Tundra-Bear and Fox-Foot can supply you with wood for the approaching winter, and you will have ample provisions for food."

Knarry leaned forward, "I think you are going to be in great danger. When the winter snows come, you will be cut off from all help and defense, even from Tundra-Bear's village. The winterbeests from the high glaciers of the mountain rim are venturing deeper into the highlands and the valleys each year. Anything powerful enough to 'call' a 'ptoloch,' can also 'call' a winterbeest. Even Gnarl-Oak's massive front door could not resist a winterbeest's claws for very long. Further, I have resolved to send Bomsiell with you to be your friend and protector."

"Your forest cat? But she's been your companion for years!"

"She and her kind are the ancient enemies of the winterbeest. They are too agile for the winterbeest to catch, and they move with astonishing speed over the most treacherous ice and snow. Their extra set of ears, their remarkable sense of smell — nothing could give you earlier warning of a winterbeest. Besides, Bomsiell is a very intelligent cat and will provide company for you during the long winter nights. She also loves to explore. Maybe she will help you find your way through the rambling underground mazes of Gnarl-Oak's house. Gnarl-Oak's is a particularly complex one. At the very least, she will be able to lead you back to the main chamber if you should get lost."

Knarry ended with the rough, guttural chortle typical of ponderosa wood-gnomes. After a moment, his mood changed, and he turned towards Garug-Caroch, looked him steadily in the eye, and solemnly announced, "Now I have things of deep import to tell you."

Garug-Caroch looked back. "I don't want to hear it, but I must."

"A great evil has befallen the wood-gnomes."

Garug-Caroch stood up and walked to the far side of the gazebo. He gazed out over the starlit expanse of Oval-Earth for a moment. The idea that the gnomes might be at the mercy of whatever adverse powers stirred in Oval-Earth disturbed Garug-Caroch as nothing else did. They were the heart of Oval-Earth, its unchanging center. They endured, aeon after aeon, like the great forests where they went for their final metamorphoses.

"What evil, Knarry?" he asked finally. Garug-Caroch returned to his bench and sat down again, leaning forward with his elbows on his knees and looking anxiously at Knarry.

Knarry stood up, pulled a flint-stone from his pocket, and struck a light in a small lantern that hung from the center of the gazebo. Moving over to the side of the gazebo but still standing in the flickering glow of the lantern, he began to speak.

"The power of the wood-gnomes is rooted in the earth itself, in the very rhythms of its life. Such power can be very great, and consequently, we use it cautiously and never to our own advantage. This is why most of us are physicians, teeth-crafters, healers of plants and animals. After our metamorphosis into trees on the Northern Taiga, our power becomes much greater, but at that point, our stationary mode of life as trees confines the use of the power purely to the maintenance of the natural cycles of life. For we are the primary agency through which earth-power is channeled into the climatic conditions of Oval-Earth.

"Only one other creature in Oval-Earth has a profounder connection with earth-power than we do; this is the rock-gnome. Rock-gnomes are never seen or heard. They live in caverns deep under the earth. Nobody knows exactly where. They have some special connection with the great Rock-Falls of the western perimeter and with that region known as the Barrows in the north-west corner of Oval-Earth, but nobody knows what this connection is.

"The power of the rock-gnome is rooted in the very primeval depths of the earth itself, in the immeasurable forces inherent in minerals and in the mysteries of the mineralogical kingdom that reach out to the planets and stars beyond us. Thus, they grasp things differently than we do. They do not even perceive time or space or matter as we do, but instead they apprehend all three as aspects of some deeper unity.

"Now, I think you can see the perplexity in which the wood-gnomes are cast. The deterioration of the weather in Oval-Earth has been going on for some time, but very slowly—nothing that isn't consistent with the thousand-year cycles the weather goes through. Then, two years ago, shortly after your experience at the Gate-Tower, as you yourself noticed, the climate of Oval-Earth began to deteriorate in the most drastic way. Widespread devastation has come upon the land; and within a few more years, if the weather continues as it has, we can expect famine and disease so rampant that even the healing powers of the wood-gnomes will falter. We are already overworked.

The people everywhere are suffering. Only the Hill people, who never seem to be affected by anything, have continued in their usual habits of life.

"At our Gathering of the Clans last year, the subject was brought up before the Council of Elders. There was naturally some reluctance to discuss the matter. The malaise that has affected the Oval-Earth populations since the War of Desolation has had its consequences even among us. And then—"

"The War of Desolation?" Garug-Caroch interrupted.

"Yes, I—"

"But all our ills are traced to it, yet we know nothing about it. Knarry, even you—"

"I know. I invoke it like everybody else. I don't know what else to do. But I must go on with my report, Garug."

"Proceed. I won't interrupt you again."

Knarry nodded. He resumed his account of the Gathering. "The Council of Elders hedged and dodged for days, but the issue could no longer be ignored. Everything pointed to only one conclusion: something had gone wrong on the Northern Taiga. Something had happened that distorted the normal working of those ensouled trees of that great woodland.

"Our first thought was to appoint a delegation to go to the Northern Taiga in order to investigate. There was some bewilderment about how to go about it. After all, nobody goes to the Northern Taiga and then actually comes back! One goes to the ancestors only at the time of the final metamorphosis. Once there, what would one do? It is not as if anyone knows his way around there, or what one does while there, or if there is anyone to talk to, or even how one gets back. But we did appoint a delegation nevertheless."

Knarry fell silent, his eyes fixed on Garug-Caroch's face. "Garug," he continued, "a delegation of twelve wood-gnomes was sent. Twelve! But, Garug, only three returned! Of those three, *two are hopelessly insane!*"

"Wood-gnomes—insane! That's impossible. Wood-gnomes don't even get physically unhealthy!"

"Remember Twigbottom! That was strange enough. He was on the verge of insanity, if I read you right about his behavior and what he went through in his final moments. But these two really are insane. The Council of Elders has assigned some physicians of the sassafras clan to care for them. They are good with mental illness—well, at least among humans. What they can do for gnomes, only time will tell. They have no prior experience with such a matter."

"What about the third one—the one who didn't go insane! Has he told you what happened?"

"He doesn't quite know what happened—at least to most of the delegation. He never fully got there, if you understand me. It was an ill-fated enterprise from the start. Against my explicit warnings, the delegation insisted on taking the Radial High-Road through the Capital. Well, you know about the registration problem there. The delegation ran immediately into trouble, for the officials from the Ministry of Travel declared that they could not issue permits for entry into the Northern Taiga. Why? Apparently, such a permit had never been requested before, and hence there were no slips made up upon which such a request could be recorded. Thus, it was impossible! Why not make up such a slip? Because the Ministry of Imperial Paperwork was closed for the week!"

"Knarry, they can make up those slips at a moment's notice, using anything at hand upon which they can smack those filthy stamps. I just experienced that."

"I know. But they give wood-gnomes an even harder time than they do humans, especially when there is a whole mob of them. They think that wood-gnomes are 'well-heeled' and can cough up as much money as one wishes to extort from them. In any case, the delegation was not detained very long by this. The right palms were crossed with copper coins, and soon the delegation had all the papers it needed and even a few it didn't need.

"Beyond the Capital they discovered that the Northern Arm of the Radial High-Road was in savage disrepair and that the surrounding plains had been flooded recently by furious squalls of unprecedented dimensions. Gnomes' ability to float on water was helpful under these circumstances; in fact, I don't know how they would have managed without it. But the real troubles started when they reached the steep escarpment that rises from the plains in the far north to form the high plateau of the Northern Taiga.

"There is a path up that wall, steep and narrow, but accessible only to gnomes. *Kyn Ardagh* it is called in the old tongue—the 'Road to Heaven.' It was gone, Garug, gone. Parts were washed away; other sections were blocked by stones the size of houses perched dangerously over the precipitous drop.

"Anyway, the delegation decided to chance the climb. As a safety reserve, they left one member at the foot of the escarpment, a certain Rough-Bark of the juniper clan, a relatively young fellow and inexperienced, but nimble enough if help was needed. The rest of them, all eleven, began clambering up the perilous ascent. Rough-Bark says he waited patiently for three days at the foot of Kyn Ardagh for something to happen and finally, losing his patience, began the climb himself when it didn't.

"Halfway up, scrambling over the rocks and abutments, he found the two gnomes I told you about curled up in a shallow cave that had been eroded out of the surface of the escarpment. Both were mad and whimpered and quivered like seedlings. Neither could talk. They still can't.

"Now, you know, as you just said, that wood-gnomes don't go mad, or at least you thought, and we all thought, we knew that. Well, we were wrong. We were too certain of our place in the world. Anyway, somehow Rough-Bark brought those two crippled gnomes back down the cliff by lowering them on long, stringy vines.

"There's one other thing, maybe more important than anything else. Rough-Bark claims that, as he approached his fellow gnomes, something attacked his body from behind and invaded his mind, tearing at it, trying to uproot it from its earth-ties. He spun around to face an ungainly beast that looked at first like a winterbeest but later looked like the puffed-up specter of a wood-gnome or, better, an amalgam of wood-gnomes indistinguishable by clan but distorted hideously; at other times, it looked like a human whose swollen face and fiery, lustful eyes were half hidden by a dark cowl. The beast swung a huge, bristly club.

"Rough-Bark fought back by evading it—by darting from boulder to boulder, tipping loose stones from the cliff and rolling them down on the beast. His very inexperience was a help, as was the fact that the junipers are accustomed to cliffs and rocky surfaces. Anyway, he tumbled and fell and scrambled over the boulders that lay in the path, sometimes almost dropping from the escarpment itself, but clinging at the last moment with rooty fingers and swinging himself up again. The beast finally sank in exhaustion on a precarious ledge.

"But the spiritual fight was not over yet; Rough-Bark resisted the intruder in the end by summoning up the remnants of his earth-power, but not before he had some kind of vision. In the vision, he saw the Ancestral Tree hanging limp and broken, with a hideous gash in its dense bark, as if some thin but long strand of wood had been torn from its side.

"The vision was over as soon as he ejected the demonic force that had held him in its grasp. Rough-Bark immediately had to attend to the two impaired gnomes, and that was difficult enough to do, especially since the beast was gradually recovering its energy and preparing to attack again. When he had lowered the gnomes to the base of the escarpment, he sought the help of a local wood-gnome settlement nearby — the domicile of the primitive Orugug wood-gnomes. There he put the injured gnomes temporarily into the care of an Orugug elder named Branch-Knot. It was not easy for him to communicate what was happening to Branch-Knot or to any of the Orugug gnomes, for they do not speak our language, and Rough-Bark does not speak the primeval gnome tongue.

"He was going to climb Kyn Ardagh to find out what happened to the other nine members of delegation, but Branch-Knot somehow deterred him. Instead, Rough-Bark was urged to deliver his report to the Council of Elders, which he did, and the injured gnomes, by order of the Council, were borne away on litters from the Orugug settlement to the sanatorium run by the sassafras clan.

"All of this is terrible enough, Garug, but, if Rough-Bark's vision is accurate, we are in the greatest danger of all. The Ancestral Tree is the root, the ancient source of earth-power in Oval-Earth. Whoever managed to wrest that strand of wood away from the Tree and has it in its possession has prodigious power, very likely enough to deform the seasons."

Knarry and Garug-Caroch sat for a while without talking. After a few minutes, Knarry added, "No further delegations have been sent. It will be up to the next meeting of the Council of Elders to decide what to do. But the matter is urgent, as you can see. Oval-Earth may be on the verge of another..."

"Another War of Desolation," Garug-Caroch declared somewhat impetuously.

"It seems so." Knarry continued.

"And with whom is this war to be fought?" asked Garug-Caroch.

"With the Kingdom of Darkness."

"And where is this Kingdom of Darkness?"

"It has always been said that the Kingdom of Darkness lies beyond the Golden Mountains."

"And what do you think these 'powers' are that struggle to overwhelm the body and enter the mind and take possession of it, producing prodigies of monstrous force and danger?"

"Emissaries of the Kingdom of Darkness … the forerunners of the invasion … the reconnaissance … the vanguard of doom. What else can I think? What else is there that provides even a glimmer of explanation?"

Garug-Caroch shook his head for a few moments and said, "All of that, Knarry, is speculation of the vaguest kind. It would help if we actually knew something about it. Our legends are no better than ill-founded rumors. We don't even know where the legends come from. And what do they tell us? They tell us that we were invaded by the warriors of the Kingdom of Darkness. They were powerful and almost destroyed Oval-Earth. Did we finally defeat them? What made them go away? What made the War stop? We don't hear of a victory, but we do hear of a threatened return.

"We blame most of the ruined buildings in Oval-Earth on the War, but we don't make any effort to rebuild them because we think it will happen all over again. Yet there are no defenses. The Imperial Viceroy, a petty despot and usurper, surrounds himself with hirelings and functionaries, but there is no army; there isn't even a constabulary to control petty crime. Why isn't there a border guard to watch for the approach of an alien host from across the mountains?

"Yet people get arrested for trumped-up charges of espionage! Have you ever seen pictures of the War of Desolation? Why are there no battlefields that tourists visit with little maps and accompanied by guides who show them that this happened here or that happened there? Why do we have no idea what their warriors looked like, what they wore as armor, what kind of weapons they carried?

"And our own warriors — who were they? Were wood-gnomes involved? Did they serve as massed infantry carrying great staves with thorns, while moose-mounted human cavalry staged gallant attacks against the foe? Human memory has retained nothing of this—not even the memory of the wood-gnomes has anything to say! Why, Knarry?"

Knarry was unable to answer.

"Do you realize, Knarry," Garug-Caroch went on, "that we have lost all of our history? *We have no history. We cannot write our own history.*"

The twin moons had set behind the mountains. Except for the brilliance of the stars, it was very dark. Knarry extinguished the lantern, and the Sage followed him back through the shadowy woods to the earth-house. Somewhere in the darkness a widowbird began her nightly lament, and the gnome could sense the nocturnal comings and goings of the smaller creatures of the hills. Bomsiell greeted Knarry and Garug-Caroch as they approached the house. Collielava thumped his heavy hooves in the shed in welcome.

Back in the earth-house, Knarry lit a single candle and led Garug-Caroch to his room at the end of a curiously tilted, zigzag hallway. "I think you're right about the Song," Knarry reflected as they walked down the hallway. "It is the key to the defense of Oval-Earth. But, Garug! *We* are not the only ones who know that.

"The despoiling of the Ancestral Tree may have taken place in response to your accidental discovery of some words of the Song. And I think that they—whoever or whatever they are—know that the recovery of the Song is in your hands. Be wary, Garug! You are in great danger. I think—"

Garug-Caroch interrupted. "Enough, Knarry. I'm too tired. I need a good night's sleep more than anything else. I'm sure you are right about the danger. But I don't understand the situation very well. Let me sleep on it; perhaps the morning will bring light to our minds as well as to the world outside your house."

Knarry turned to go. "Don't you need the candle?" Garug-Caroch asked.

Knarry chortled. "You know we can find our way in the dark."

"That's right," Garug-Caroch said, and as he wearily closed his door, he added, "I'm sorry about what happened to the gnomes, Knarry. But I fear it is only the beginning of our grief."

Chapter V

The Winter Storm

A utumn in the Hill Country was resplendent with color as Garug-Caroch and Knarry slowly made their way up the steep, winding road that led into the highlands. The moose-cart rolled laboriously behind them. The abundant streams from the mountains had helped the Hill Country escape the worst effects of the summer drought, and its autumn glory was rich and varied. Knarry stomped steadily forward; he carried a sizable pack on his back. Garug-Caroch strode rather gingerly, given his advanced age. He bore his staff in his right hand and hung on to a leather strap of a small sack with his left. His robe often fluffed about him in the cool mountain breezes. At times, Bomsiell would sleep uneasily on a pile of baskets loaded somewhat loosely in the cart; she yowled when the cart jolted over an occasional stone in the road or dropped suddenly into a rut. At other times, she bounded alongside the cart, sometimes running ahead, circling back through the woods, disappearing for a quarter of an hour, and reappearing well down the road and dashing to catch up with astonishing speed. In one especially large rut, the cart lurched to the side, almost tossing out Garug-Caroch's elaborately carved game board. Knarry tucked it back into place with a wry grimace and said: "Why do you bother with this thing, Garug? I've never seen the point of it."

Garug-Caroch was hard-pressed to find an answer. After all, he had lost interest in the Game himself. "A force of habit, I guess, Knarry, just a force of habit," he said.

The travelers continued on in silence, Garug-Caroch admiring the landscape and wondering why he had never spent an autumn here. "Always in a rush to get back to the College after the holidays; always in a rush to get back to the annual tournament," he mused.

The Regional Road wound ever higher into the forested uplands. The journey was difficult but rewarding, and Collielava, too, seemed to enjoy the bracing mountain air. He liked to stop and nibble on the grasses that grew by the wayside. Eventually the travelers reached an old cart-path that led eastward from the Regional Road and through a dense forest. They followed it through the woodland and down though a ravine and back out again into a series of highland pastures. At the far end of one pasture, tucked into the side of the hill, was a sturdy earth-house with its timbered roof-dome blending almost perfectly with the surrounding groves. It had a massive front door made of thick oak planks with two narrow windows on either side. Under each window was a small bench where an inhabitant could sit in the evening and watch the sunset over Oval-Earth.

The earth-house had already been prepared well for their arrival, for the rooms were swept clean and tidy, the larders were filled with baskets of produce from mountain pastures and gardens, and the woodshed was stacked high with abundant firewood. Clearly, Knarry's advance message had arrived in Tundra-Bear and Fox-Foot's village and had been acted on with the dispatch and thoroughness typical of Hill people. All he and Garug-Caroch had to do was unload the cart and bring in the various personal items that Garug-Caroch had salvaged from his College chambers. Many of these were stored in Gnarl-Oak's old, rough-hewn cupboards. Afterwards Knarry showed Garug-Caroch through a small portion of the intricately designed maze of the earth-house, most of which was built deep into the hillside.

Garug-Caroch was impressed by it all but admitted he would really need only the front room with its capacious fireplace and its two small windows on either side of the door looking out into the pastures and forests. Bomsiell restlessly explored the more accessible parts of the dwelling, scampering up and down its zigzag passageways with delight.

Meanwhile, with Knarry's help, Garug-Caroch set up a large table in the front room and stacked the five volumes of the Commentary on one end of the table. There he unpacked a considerable store of candles, parchment, ink, and pens, which Knarry, with the help of a few wood-gnome associates, had been able to muster up for Garug-Caroch's use. On a smaller table under one of the narrow windows by the door, Garug-Caroch set up his Game of Spheres board. "Only for recreation," he assured Knarry, who looked at it somewhat dubiously.

As Garug-Caroch and Knarry emerged from the earth-house to see if anything was left in the cart and to see to Collielava's needs, they noticed two figures watching them from a distant rise. The figures waved at them and quickly descended the grassy slope in their direction. It was Tundra-Bear and Fox-Foot.

As always, Garug-Caroch was astonished by their remarkable appearance—their tall, lean, supple bodies, the bronze hue of their skin, the bright green of their long, flowing hair contrasting with the deeply shaded purple of their eyes. They wore thigh-length tunics made of pale-green linen and gathered up around their waists by white hempen cords. On their feet, simple straw sandals were attached to their legs by thin leather straps that crisscrossed over their shins as high as their knees. Finely wrought longbows and quivers of brightly feathered arrows were strapped to their shoulders.

Like all married couples among the Hill people, they were almost mirror images of each other, a masculine and feminine form of one person; and they moved in perfect consort together, their bodies slightly touching much of the time. Tundra-Bear was larger than Fox-Foot. He had powerful shoulders and arms.

Fox-Foot was strong but delicate and moved with the grace of a young deer. Her dark green hair fell loosely over her bronze shoulders and over the light green tunic to her waist.

It was said in the lowlands that the Hill people never altered; and indeed, for all the disastrous changes that had taken place in the recent ages of Oval-Earth, the Hill people were least affected by it. They remained as they were—remote, undisturbed, serene in their ways and in their character.

When Tundra-Bear and Fox-Foot arrived at the earth-house, they inquired about whether the preparations had been satisfactory. It would have been easy for Garug-Caroch to be effusive in expressing his gratitude, as his gratitude was indeed boundless—after all, this work had been provided out of no other motive than that of sheer generosity; since he knew that Hill people were deeply embarrassed by expressions of gratitude, however, he merely uttered his simple contentment with how he had found things. That was quite enough to say. Tundra-Bear and Fox-Foot, taciturn as usual, were supremely happy with such an acknowledgment. Meanwhile, Knarry was delighted to see his old friends, and Bomsiell cavorted around and purred as she rubbed herself against their legs.

After a brief repast, Fox-Foot accompanied Garug-Caroch on a long, leisurely walk and introduced him to a number of the delicacies that grew wild in the neighborhood — the mushrooms, nuts, edible flowers, and various barks that could be brewed into wholesome teas. Such foraging would hardly be necessary, for there were already plenty of provisions for the winter, but Fox-Foot thought that Garug-Caroch might enjoy his spare hours during the final months of autumn by wandering through the wooded uplands and collecting fresh supplies to garnish his daily fare. She also assured him that she and Tundra-Bear would come to visit him as often as they could, though, during the worst of the winter months, such travel would become difficult and dangerous.

While Fox-Foot enlisted Knarry's help in sorting out a basket full of fresh mushrooms that she and Garug-Caroch had just culled from the near hillside, Tundra-Bear invited Garug-Caroch into the earth-house. He opened one of the cupboards and drew a wide straw valise from it. He opened the valise: inside was a crossbow and several bolts lined up in a small leather case. He made an effort to explain the basics of self-defense against a winterbeest.

"This will be more useful to you than a longbow — the tension can be left pre-set, and the bolt will be in place. It takes much less training to use this weapon at short range; a longbow is difficult to use, though more effective if you know how to use it," Tundra-Bear explained.

He looked at Garug-Caroch with his deep-purple eyes and wondered if Garug-Caroch could understand what he said. Lowlanders, in Tundra-Bear's view, were good at understanding complicated things but not good at understanding simple things.

He explained, "All you need to do is aim and pull the trigger. But it's no use hitting a winterbeest with one of these, Garug, unless it knocks the beast down and takes away its spirit. One blow from its foreclaws can rip open a man's chest, and a winterbeest needs only a few seconds to give such a blow.

"What you must do is burst the beast's heart with a single bolt. When the beast comes in for the kill, it will rise on its hind legs. At that point, and not before, you must strike. The bolt must enter directly between the forelegs in the center of the chest, and at close range. Only then will the beast die instantly."

"And if I miss?" queried Garug-Caroch.

"There are no second chances. It is not marksmanship that counts in this matter, Garug. What is wanted here is courage. Hold fast with the crossbow until the target is no more than three or four paces away. If you do that, you will be victorious.

"Remember, too, Garug, that you will have Bomsiell with you. She will not only give you advance warning; she is also equipped by nature to attack a winterbeest when necessary. Forest cats do not prefer to do that, but they will do it when cornered. They circle the beast and attack from the back by leaping up to the head and clawing at the eyes from behind. Their speed and the sharpness of their claws will sometimes — not always — bring a winterbeest down, especially if it is surprised by the attack."

Garug-Caroch lifted the crossbow and aimed it at the door, through which, presumably, a winterbeest would burst its way. He lowered it and looked carefully over the weapon. "I am not confident in my ability to do this, Tundra-Bear," he remarked, "but I will try."

In the late afternoon, Tundra-Bear and Fox-Foot said their farewells, promising to visit Garug-Caroch at regular intervals, weather permitting, and warning him about loud poundings at the door, which could be a winterbeest. They gathered up their bows and quivers and departed for their village. Knarry and Garug-Caroch watched them as they disappeared into the woodlands.

Knarry spent the night at the Gnarl-Oak's earth-house. The following morning, after a few last admonitions addressed to Garug-Caroch, he hitched Collielava to the moose-cart and prepared for the journey back along the Regional Road and down to Cantanteroff in the foothills. Garug-Caroch was sad to see them go.

He said farewell to Collielava, who snorted affectionately and rubbed his long nose against Garug-Caroch's arm. He had decided not to have Collielava sold but, rather, to be put out to pasture at a farmstead close to Cantanteroff, where the final years of a moose life could be lived out in tranquility and safety. Knarry knew a local merchant who would be glad to put up Collielava in exchange for the moose-cart, such as it was.

As a parting statement, Knarry told Garug-Caroch that, if it was necessary to get a message to him, he could tie a small band and a packet to Bomsiell's neck and pronounce Knarry's name several times. The forest cat would understand and bring whatever message was sent. Bomsiell had often carried both messages and medicines through trying weather and would be up to the task. And nothing could catch a forest cat when it was in full stride.

Garug-Caroch thanked him for the advice. He watched long and hard as Collielava pulled the old cart, Knarry walking at his side across the highland pastures and along the woodland path, until they were out of sight. He knew they would soon turn onto the Regional Road and descend into the lowlands.

Autumn passed. Garug-Caroch arose one morning and went outside to sit on a bench and have his breakfast tea when he encountered a sharp chill and a thin wisp of snow. Bomsiell followed him out and seemed to be aroused by the light snowfall, as thin as it was, and was now alert and active, crossing back and forth on the open field in front of the house, sniffing and listening and making sharp prints in the snow.

In the distance, Garug-Caroch could see heavy masses of coal-black clouds gathering over the Northern Taiga. He knew that beneath those clouds there was nothing but white—deep, white snow driven by menacing winds. It looked foreboding and angry. He shivered and retreated into the earth-house, shut the door, and crossed over to the large stone hearth. Bomsiell had entered with him; she was sufficiently domesticated to want to avoid the first great onslaught. In moments, the fire was crackling and blazing and Bomsiell was dozing at the edge of the hearth. Garug-Caroch settled down to continue his work.

The winter fell upon Oval-Earth like a famished hover-owl seizing a moss-mouse in its talons. Snow piled up and drifted in enormous dunes across the landscape. Since the Radial High-Roads were closed almost immediately, all transport and communication ceased. In the Capital, the officials of the Ministry of Travel dismantled their booths at the center of the Imperial Plaza and retreated into their chilly corridors and offices, heated only by blazing smoky brands, and fretted nervously over their filing baskets, shifting slips and forms from one basket to another and back again to their original baskets.

At the College of Wisdom, students and faculty huddled ever closer to the blazing hearths in their rooms and boiled their turnip beer into a hot, sudsy foam that singed the throat and filled the rooms with rancid steam. The villages and farms throughout Oval-Earth were buried in snow; the people had to dig tunnels from house to house and even to run shafts upward to let in light and air and to allow the smoke from their chimneys to escape into the dark, tumultuous skies.

In the Hills, snow was packed deep in the valleys and covered the ridges in bizarre formations. Streams and waterfalls were frozen over. The villages of the Hill people were now isolated from one another, and all the animals of the forests lay in coverts and burrows deep in winter hibernation.

Only here and there, the large white bulk of a solitary winterbeest, driven down from the high glaciers in search of food, groveled across the icy surface, its porcine snout grunting and rooting in the snow and its foot-long claws scratching for tubers and other edible vegetation.

Now and again, a winterbeest would wander into a Hill village and begin tearing at the doors or walls of one of the houses, mad with the scent of fresh meat inside. But the Hill people had long since mastered the art of dispatching a winterbeest with crossbow or longbow, and, among them, death from a winterbeest was very rare. They roasted the winterbeests they killed, and used their pelts to make the great white cloaks that they wore in winter and that were so much coveted elsewhere in Oval-Earth.

Soon the winter solstice came around. A storm had darkened the entire day, and it was evening. Inside the warm earth-house, Garug-Caroch was patiently pursuing his research. At the far end of the room, the flickering fire shed abundant warmth. The large, crudely hewn wooden table at the center of the room was covered by books, rolls of parchment, and a group of candles aflame with light and caked with melted wax.

At this table Garug-Caroch worked most of the day. On the other table under the window lay the Game of Spheres board, which Garug-Caroch had planned to use only for recreation; but up until now, he had not used it at all, and it was covered by a fine dust of ashes from the hearth. Bomsiell slept by the fire with all four ears twitching whenever a particularly harsh gust of wind swept past the house. Over the fire stood an iron trivet upon which a pinkish-orange marsh-root porridge bubbled in a copper pot.

Garug-Caroch's work was painstaking and laborious. He read carefully through the huge tomes, making notes and lists of words scrawled on tiny pieces of paper. He would spend hours arranging and rearranging these scraps of paper like bits of a puzzle to see if they would make sense among themselves and with the books that were a commentary upon them. Often, he would work through the entire night, sleeping only now and then. He had to exercise a careful discipline upon himself as he proceeded, for the books he studied were filled with much marvelous and profound lore, and he could concentrate only with great difficulty on the particular and specialized task he had before him — to draw from the text the actual words of the Song itself.

Garug-Caroch was driving himself, and he knew it. But he felt the urgency of the task grow as each of the winter's cruel days passed. He knew that in the villages of the lowlands there would be starvation and plague and shortages of firewood.

Behind the sufferings of the villagers loomed the vague but threatening power that was possessing Oval-Earth. As the winter wore on, he watched, through the narrow windows by the door, storm after storm roll down over Oval-Earth from the Northern Taiga, and his conviction grew stronger that the power of the gnomes had indeed been usurped.

Whatever now controlled the weather was greater than any power he was familiar with in Oval-Earth. The recovery of the Song was the last hope of men and gnomes and plants and animals alike.

The work had progressed. By the solstice, he felt that he knew what the first two verses of the Song might be. Further, since the volumes of the entire Commentary were elaborately cross-referenced with one another, he already had an idea of what some of the individual words of later verses were.

Garug-Caroch felt content, sitting at the great wooden table and looking over his work. In a mood for some relaxation, he walked to the hearth and heated some Hill wine laced with spices and herbs.

As in the days at the College, he rested by the fire in an old armchair, sipping the hot wine. Bomsiell stirred uneasily and stared into the glowing embers of the hearth. Garug-Caroch's mind wandered back to the College, to the many nights like this when he had spent his time musing before the fire, and to Knarry and how he had appeared in the middle of the snowstorm.

Bits of conversation from happier times and images of faces he recalled affectionately floated through his mind. For some time, he sat, half-dozing in the warm light of the fire. How good it was to dream, to sleep, but only after the mind had been vigorous and purposeful … to rest from one's labor, when that labor had connection, had meaning in the whole organic scheme of things, when it resonated with the earth, with the stars, with something beyond the stars. The Song was teaching him that.

He was awakened by the steady increase in the intensity of the storm outside. The wind howled and screeched over the hillside, as the nearby trees groaned with their bending and swaying. The snow whirled up in furious gusts, pushing with wild ferocity against the small, dark, frost-covered windowpanes.

Bomsiell sat up suddenly, eyes wide open and all four ears quivering at attention. She was hissing softly.

"A winterbeest?" Garug-Caroch asked himself. "Not in this fury, Bomsiell," he said aloud. He snatched a candle and a knife from the table and ran to one of the small windows next to the door. With the knife he scraped away the frost, but he still could see nothing.

Bomsiell, meanwhile, had become aroused into a frenzy; she paced back and forth across the room, her teeth bared, her claws variously emerging and contracting. Garug-Caroch turned to take the candle and the knife back to the table; but, as he did, he heard behind him a deafening scratch of claws on the surface of the door. Bomsiell yowled.

For a moment, Garug-Caroch was frozen with fear. He bolted to the bed at the other side of the room and drew the crossbow from beneath it. He gasped in momentary relief; Tundra-Bear had loaded it on his last visit.

Garug-Caroch knelt behind the table, resting the crossbow on a pile of notes and aiming it directly at the center of the door. Images of the winterbeest arose in his mind. It would be taller than a man when it reared up on its hind legs; he could see the forelegs raised from the beast's heavily muscled shoulders, ready to strike and kill. Its porcine nose would slaver; its long rodent teeth would drip with a frothy saliva. For a moment, he thought of hiding deeper in the earth-house, but he recalled Tundra-Bear's terse admonition. "What is wanted here is courage," he had said.

Garug-Caroch gritted his teeth and sighted down the crossbow shaft. "I can't miss as long as I don't fire too soon," he announced. Bomsiell seemed to approve. She moved to the side of the door, poised to attack from behind—to leap onto the head, as forest cats did, and tear at the monster's eyes.

The clawing continued as the Sage remained positioned behind the table, his muscles tensed. Abruptly, a long, curved, razor-sharp set of claws managed to find their way through the many-layered door, spewing splinters of wood through the room. Garug-Caroch drew a sharp breath and tightened his finger around the trigger of the crossbow. The forest cat snarled, ready to spring. The massive oak door bulged as the winterbeest pressed against it.

Suddenly it backed off, giving forth a deep, coarse growl of frustration and fear; a shoving of snow and a thump against the door signaled that it had turned around.

And it was gone!

An icy sluice of wind blew snowflakes through the hole that the beast had made in the door.

For some minutes, Garug-Caroch did not move, uncertain about what had occurred and what would happen next. Bomsiell stood stiffly poised for some time, her curious purring indicating that she did not understand the unusual behavior of the winterbeest.

But she relaxed finally and returned to stretch out by the fire. After observing Bomsiell's relaxed demeanor, Garug-Caroch rose, stiff and shaking. Shivering in the cold draft, he made his way to the door, but he could see and hear nothing.

"I've got to block this hole, Bomsiell, or we'll freeze to death," Garug-Caroch informed the cat. Taking a piece of cloth and some soft wax from around one of the candles, he attempted to plug the hole. The jagged, splintered edges caught the cloth and held it in place, but, despite the wax that he pressed in around the sides of the cloth, the cold air continued to seep in. Still cold, Garug-Caroch returned to the fire. He left the crossbow on the table. He might need it again.

Once more he sat down by the fire, troubled by the winterbeest's inexplicable retreat. "Why did it leave?" he muttered repeatedly. "Why should I be worried that it left?" he asked himself.

But the warmth of the fire slowly soothed him, and he ladled out for himself a wide wooden bowlful of the porridge steaming over the fire. Savoring its tart aroma, he sat eating peacefully for some time. Once again, the storm began to increase its fury. The trees outside moaned, and the snow swirled around the earth-house. He shuddered in his deep, warm chair and continued to stir the hot porridge.

Again, the cat sat up, her eyes alert, her ears all twitching and dithering. Garug-Caroch sat up, too, and, after replacing the bowl near the hearth, he stood and paced back and forth across the room, his burlap robe drawn tightly around him and his arms folded. "I should get back to work," he said to himself. "Then I will stop thinking about danger—whether real or imagined." He went to the table and observed for a moment the crossbow covering some of his notes and the volume he had been studying. He changed his mind. "The Game of Spheres," he thought. "I haven't played it since I have been here. Maybe it will help. Maybe it will get my mind off my fears."

He brought two candles to illuminate the Game of Spheres board and placed one on either side. He used a piece of linen to wipe off the layer of ash that had accumulated on it. The great board was carved with hundreds of narrow channels that formed circles within circles, and ovals and ellipses of various kinds, all of which crisscrossed and wound around one another in thousands of complex patterns.

Along the side of these channels were engraved elaborate sequences of numbers and symbols that defined the mathematics of each curve and its potential transformations as it intersected with others. Each channel of Garug-Caroch's board was highly polished; he had rolled, he recalled, a myriad of gemstones through them. "And learned less from all that than from a single page of one of those books in the Library," he declared loudly.

From the small leather pouch at the edge of the board he drew a handful of brightly colored gemstones — an agate, a topaz, an emerald, a ruby, a sapphire, an amethyst, and another stone, a fiery blue diamond, playable only in an attempt on a *Darii*. He smiled to look at them. How early in life he had mastered the extraordinary rhythms of the game!

The diaphanous glow of the gemstones reminded him of his school days at the College of Wisdom when the Game of Spheres was just beginning to unfold to him the boundless formations it could produce out of seemingly random conjunctions let loose by a skillful hand and an adept mind.

The mystical power of the Game, its utter fascination, its hypnotic spell lay in the sheer, though only apparent, fortuitousness of its beauty, its absolute whimsicality, the depth of its ephemeral capriciousness, all of which were, in fact, controlled by tens of thousands of mathematical calculations made in fractions of seconds as the gemstones whirred through the circuits.

With a well-trained movement of the fingers, and with just the precise impetus, he sent an agate spinning off through the channels. He could sense its motion, almost as if he were the stone; he knew its possibilities intimately.

At the first junction he transformed its curve with only the slightest touch of his mathematical power. The topaz followed, and the emerald, and the ruby, all glittering and shining at first in the candlelight and soon blazing and glowing through a hidden inner power of their own as they spun through the circuits and gyrated past each other, flashing on and off, colliding and separating, weaving in and out, whirling again and again through multitudinous patterns.

The Mind is the Cosmos, thought Garug-Caroch, repeating for himself the motto of the Hall of Games: *The Game is the Mind. Power over the Game is power over the Cosmos.*

What nonsense!

Then he saw what he had never quite seen before. For the first time in his life, he recognized that there was a deeper structure of which the stones in their whirlwind gyre were only a reflection. He plunged his mind in, without restraint, trying to see the whole of the pattern, trying to grasp its inner dynamic. But the deeper he sought, the more elusive it became. It seemed to recede into an unfathomable distance — a great and inconsolable emptiness.

In his excitement, he cast the sapphire, followed almost immediately by the amethyst. Desperate to see deeper into the game, he picked up the final stone, the fiery blue diamond, rolled it about in his fingers, and with a practiced flex of his wrist, loosed it upon the board.

It whizzed with unsurpassable speed past the other stones and through the circuits, the complex pattern of a *Darii* emerging with a perfection that he had never thrown before. The seventh spiral glittered with light as the diamond spun around it.

But the vast emptiness behind it grew, and in it something stirred, something old and evil. It reached out lazily to touch Garug-Caroch's mind, and he knew the ages it had waited, the cold but all-consuming lust that possessed it, its devious and terrible attractiveness, its invitation to a drowsiness, a sleep beyond all sleep, a cessation, a death . . .

For a moment, his soul hung in the balance.

Suddenly a strange, inexplicable rage overwhelmed Garug-Caroch. Before he could even begin to account for what he was doing, he swept the board so violently from the table that it flew across the room and was dashed into the fire. The gemstones rolled wildly about the floor. Bomsiell sprang back from the fire in alarm and looked questioningly at Garug-Caroch, who now stood immobile, his face pale, but his vision clearing with understanding. "No, no. That I will not have or be. Not now, not ever!"

And then it came—a sense of a yawning, disconsolate absence, drawing up space into itself, of a perverse will turned against his own. The Library cellars flashed through his mind. But this was different: here there was a weighty power, a force more palpable and direct than anything he had encountered in the Library. His awareness of the power grew.

A moment later, the earth-house lurched violently, as if shaken by some giant hand. Garug-Caroch was thrown to the wooden planks of the floor. Dishes, books, candles, wine, and porridge were scattered throughout the room. Bomsiell was wide-eyed with terror. Picking himself up, Garug-Caroch stepped quickly to the window. The wind and snow were whirling now in unparalleled rage.

Something was out there.

Something was out there, and this time it was not a winterbeest. Whatever it was, it had frightened away the winterbeest. As his eyes focused on the amorphous shapes that whirled before them in the snowstorm, Garug-Caroch saw it—a misty, nebulous figure standing tree-high about two hundred paces from the earth-house. It shimmered with a ghastly, sulfurous incandescence, swollen and undulating and livid. It had a vaguely human form, but without discernible features.

Garug-Caroch bolted from the window and seized a narrow piece of parchment and several smaller pieces from the table. He turned quickly and called Bomsiell to him. He stuffed the pieces of parchment into the small gemstone pouch and, attaching the pouch to the cat's neck with a leather thong, looked Bomsiell straight in the eye and said, "Go to Knarry, Knarry, Knarry."

Bomsiell's muscles tightened, and her fur bristled. She knew exactly what was being asked of her.

Garug-Caroch unlatched the heavy wooden door and flung it open. A blast of wind thrust itself through the door, hurling him sideward and blowing out the candles as it tossed parchment and books up into the vault of the arched ceiling. Garug-Caroch clutched the door frame and pulled himself out into the surging storm. Bomsiell scudded past him, brushing past his legs and darting off at an angle into the snowy drifts. She disappeared swiftly into the darkness.

Garug-Caroch looked again at the towering image that faced him. Its arms were raised high above its head. Its eyes were fiery slits of yellow light. In the glow of its body, the Sage could discern a massive Staff made of gnarled wood that twisted and convulsed in its grasp, as if it, too, knew the horror that held it.

Suddenly the monstrous specter lowered the Staff and pointed it directly at Garug-Caroch. A sparkling greenish-blue beam of dark fire slithered out from the end of the shaft and writhed its way through the storm towards the Sage.

But even as the enormous specter was lowering the Staff, Garug-Caroch had begun chanting—yes, chanting the initial lines of the Song of the Eternal Aeons. He knew the words, and he knew that the words were right and true:

> *Out of the radiant garland*
> *of stars,*
>
> *Out of the primordial*
> *beauty of old . . .*

Suddenly the area surrounding the earth-house was irradiated by a brilliant light of startling intensity. The air trembled and thundered.

The beam of fire and the words of the Song met halfway between the giant specter and Garug-Caroch in a violent implosion, everything sucked inward with stupendous velocity and then bursting outward again in a blast so thunderous that the nearby mountains were jarred to their roots in the ground.

The whole of Oval-Earth shook from east to west, from north to south.

In Cantanteroff, Knarry's medical cabinets fell over and spilled their contents on the dispensary floor. In villages throughout Oval-Earth, walls cracked and roofs buckled and people were thrown out of their beds. In the Capital, baskets of forms and slips of paper were pitched off shelves and blown through the drafty corridors of the vacant offices. At the College of Wisdom, huge blocks of stone in the foundation of the Library slipped a little more, and the massive joists in the upper floors groaned and creaked.

Deep down inside the great subterranean dormitory under the Isle of the Drowsers, a single member — just a single member — of the Brotherhood awoke and, with wide, clear eyes, looked around at his slumbering brethren in astonishment and dismay.

The winter storm at once abated.

A soft, gentle snow fell on the shattered remains of Gnarl-Oak's earth-house. The scattered coals from the fire were dampened and went out; a scorched half of the Game of Spheres board still lay among them. It was soon covered with snow.

Everything else was gone.

The specter was gone.

The Staff was gone.

Garug-Caroch was gone.

Snow drifted quietly down over the ruins.

The Search

Chapter I

Fragmented Spring

Knarry waited for the upland snows to melt before making his departure from Cantanteroff into the Hills. He was not in a hurry. He knew that something momentous had happened at the time of the winter solstice, something perhaps unparalleled in the history of Oval-Earth. He knew that, whatever it was, it might take a while to figure out, but also that, in some way difficult to explain to himself at the present moment, it had had results at least temporarily beneficial for the denizens of Oval-Earth.

For the cataclysm that had shaken the expanse of Oval-Earth in the midst of the storm was followed, curiously, by a tempering of the weather: soon after the event, milder winds and gentler conditions made life easier for the populace. The winter months followed more or less their normal course, and the signs of an early spring held forth the promise, however slender a promise it might be, of renewed life and restored productivity.

One could only draw the conclusion that some victory, partial but with its own kind of finality, had been wrested from those forces whose ill omens threatened such imminent calamity.

Of course, having received no further messages from the hills after Bomsiell's arrival in the stormy night, Knarry realized that whatever victory may have been achieved involved a dreadful cost. But nothing could be done now about whatever had occurred; energy and resolve had to be reserved for what was yet to come. And Knarry knew, to the depths of his earth-power, rooted in the sources of life itself, that what was yet to come would make the highest demands on his discernment and perseverance.

As soon as he received word that the Regional Road was open, Knarry made arrangements with a young terebinth-gnome recently moved into the locale to maintain his medical dispensary and practice. He closed up the rest of his earth-house and wondered if he would ever return to it. Then he packed up a commodious haversack with dried fish cakes and pumpkin muffins, rolled up a shaggy woolen blanket, and gathered various items he would need for the journey—a knife, a tinderbox, and the leather pouch containing the shreds of parchment that Bomsiell had brought to him during the winter storm.

He heaved the haversack over his shoulder, and with a farewell glance at his earth-house, he trod with heavy steps to the Regional Road and began the ascent into the Hills. He looked around for Bomsiell as he left, knowing that she would soon join him. Sure enough, when he was less than a league from his house, Bomsiell bolted out of a covert of brush and, tail lifted high and all four ears twittering in the morning air, bounded alongside him on his journey.

It was a glorious spring of the kind that used to come to Oval-Earth before the weather had changed two years earlier. Green foliage burgeoned in the woodlands, and brightly hued wildflowers bloomed over the pastures and beside the brooks. The air was thronged with birds twittering and flying among the treetops. A gentle, sweetly aromatic breeze wafted over the coun-tryside, picking up a touch of coolness as it passed through some shady valley just awakening from under its coverlet of snow. The streams and waterfalls rushed through gullies, and balloon-fish sparkled as they drifted in the air along the rims of torrents and dallied in the welcome sunlight.

As Knarry strode steadily upward along the road that wound before him through the deep forests, Bomsiell bounced sometimes ahead of him, and at other times lingered behind to watch a moss-mouse scurry into a burrow or an angry starling chirp at her from a nearby branch. The Regional Road climbed gradually higher into the uplands. Far beneath the two travelers, deep valleys and gorges echoed with the dim roar of melted snow flowing down into the lakes and rivers of the central plains. The white water of the distant Midland Sea in the distance shone like mother-of-pearl as it received the freshening torrents from the mountains. Overhead, a rare, amber-feathered highland falcon soared among the peaks of the Golden Mountains.

In midafternoon, the travelers turned from the Regional Road and followed the path that led through the deep wood and the ravine and out again into the highland pastures. At the end of the first pasture, where the slope of the hill ascended steeply, they saw a large, jagged crater that looked like a wide hole scooped out of the hillside. Bomsiell yowled and loped forward over the pasture. They had arrived at the place where old Gnarl-Oak's earth-house once had been.

Knarry unloaded the haversack from his shoulders and sat on a boulder for a while, resting from the steep climb into the Hills and gaping at the great wound in the mountainside. He felt little astonishment and great sadness at what he saw.

The events in the depth of winter—the explosion that had toppled the vials of medicine out of his medical cabinets, the arrival of Bomsiell with the leather pouch—all had intimated, all too clearly, what had happened. Now he had only to learn the details—and that, he knew, would not be easy. Under any circumstances, it was important for him to be calm and methodical in his investigations and to restrain the profound sorrow that occasionally threatened to overwhelm him.

After a sufficient rest and a cool drink of parkaberry juice, Knarry approached the ruins cautiously. He did not know what he might find. He saw quickly that the entire upper section of the earth-house had been blown off—it was difficult to tell how much of the lower chambers and tunnels might still be intact because the entrances into them were clogged with debris. He noted bits of broken glass almost hidden by the profuse wildflowers that had just begun to bloom. Pieces of wood were scattered here and there. He entered the empty cavity torn in the hillside and, picking up a shattered piece of floorboard, used it to poke around in the rubble.

Bomsiell, meanwhile, had ventured deeper into the crater and began to scratch at the debris. She meowed to Knarry, who came over to see what had caught her attention. Knarry leaned down and drew a half-burnt Game of Spheres board from the mixture of coals and rubble that had covered it. Strange, he thought, this looks as if it might have been thrown into the fire before the explosion occurred. It is half-burned. Why would Garug-Caroch throw his most treasured possession into the fire?

Further probing with the floorboard revealed an iron trivet and a copper pot. The pot was empty except for a single ant that was busy scouring out whatever might be left in there to eat. It looked angrily at Knarry, scurried out of the pot, and disappeared into the debris. Knarry felt sad at heart as he examined these few remains. He remembered helping Garug-Caroch bring these things up to the Hills.

Then a glint of something in the dust caught his eye. He leaned over and, with knotty fingers, sifted through the debris until he plucked a blue diamond gemstone out of the ashes. Diamond! he thought. Was Garug-Caroch trying to roll a *Darii*?

Knarry glanced over at Bomsiell, who was now sitting calmly, her eyes patient but alert. "You would know, if only you could tell me," Knarry told her. She meowed in return. Knarry continued to search through the ruins. He found a few more gemstones, a crossbow bolt, and some pages from one of the books of the Commentary. He dropped the gemstones into the leather pouch. Everything else was gone.

It was approaching evening now, and the sun was descending over the Golden Mountains. Knarry found a sheltered grove nearby and began preparations to spend the night. He rolled out the woolen blanket, unpacked his haversack, and started to gather wood for a fire. Bomsiell watched all his movements with curiosity and especially eyed the tin container that held the dried fish cakes.

At the same time, both Knarry and Bomsiell became aware that something was moving in the distance. Turning their eyes to the crest of the hill, which was aglow with the ruddy tints of twilight, they saw the silhouettes of two figures looking down at them. Both were dressed in winterbeest pelts, for the weather was still cold at night, and bore great longbows and quivers on their backs. Knarry waved at Tundra-Bear and Fox-Foot.

By the time they descended from the crest of the hill, Knarry had enkindled the campfire and had drawn up some logs for seats. The two entered into the circle of firelight, the brilliant greenness of their hair, their bronze skin, the deep translucent violet of their eyes, and the whiteness of the winterbeest pelts lit up by the flickering glow of the flames. Knarry was always amazed at the ability of Hill people to see, like wild animals, in the darkness of night or in the shade of the forest, even though wood-gnomes could also move through the dark, but by the powers of extraordinary tactile sensation rather than by sight. Meanwhile, Bomsiell greeted the two as old friends. She rubbed herself against Fox-Foot's pelt and purred as Fox-Foot stroked her furry head.

Tundra-Bear and Fox-Foot removed their longbows and quivers and rested them against a nearby tree. They came to sit by the fire. Knarry offered them a single cup of wine, for he knew that married couples among the Hill people always drank from the same cup and ate from the same platter. The two watched him in silence with their deep purple eyes. Hill people were never quick to speak.

When the cup of wine had been passed back and forth several times between Fox-Foot and Tundra-Bear and the fire had died down a bit, Knarry spoke: "Tell me what happened. Tell me what you know." Inducing Hill people to speak at any length was always an achievement, but Knarry hoped that the unusual circumstances might alter their usual reticence. Bomsiell sat by the fire and seemed to be listening.

Tundra-Bear stared into the fire for a few minutes before answering: "We know little of what happened, Knarry. This was the first time we know of that a person from the lowlands decided to spend the winter in the Hills. He must have had special reasons to do this, about which we did not ask. We were well acquainted with the Master Sage from his previous visits to the Hills. He was a good man. And he was your friend, Knarry. We tried hard to see that he had all that he needed. I put in a supply of wood that would be adequate for the severest of winters. His supply of food was plentiful. Much of it came from Fox-Foot's garden."

Fox-Foot nodded in agreement. She added, "We visited him many times in the autumn, and he would tell us interesting things and show us those things he called 'books' that he had brought with him. He also had his board with many carvings on it. In past years, during the summer at his cabin, he would play games on it by spinning colored stones into the carvings. It was wonderful to watch, for the stones would glitter like little fires, but we always thought it was a child's game and did not know why he played it and why he thought it was so important. But this time, in Gnarl-Oak's house, he did not seem to play it—or anyway, we never saw him play it."

Both were silent for several minutes and stared into the dying embers of the campfire. Tundra-Bear continued: "The winter came, and our village was snowed in by drifts so deep that we could not cross them. As the darkest time of year approached, we heard reports from the signal towers farther up the valley that winterbeests were moving towards our village. As you know, I had left a crossbow with the Master Sage; I taught him how to use it, and I loaded it for him. Also, the forest cat would give him warning. Still, I was fearful for his safety."

Fox-Foot interrupted: "Then came the time when the night is the darkest and longest. That is when I thought we should attach snow-slats to our feet and cross the hills, no matter how difficult that would be, so that we could be certain of his safety. We did this and departed.

"It was difficult to walk, even with the snow-slats. We had to keep our bows strung and our arrows ready, and this slowed us down too. The night came very early, and the storm was fierce. When we were only two leagues from the dwelling of the Master Sage, we saw a large winterbeest hastening from that direction in great fear. It is not often that we see a winterbeest so full of fear. It rushed right past us, as if we were not there, though we had both gone down on one knee and drawn our bows. Then ... but you tell it, Tundra-Bear."

"We saw an unnatural light that shone brightly from near the earth-house. Then we heard a rushing noise like the thunder-squalls that come over the mountains. A moment later, there was a flash of lightning and a thrust of air that threw us down into the snowdrifts and made us roll many times over and over down the hillside. I was worried for Fox-Foot, but she was all right."

Tundra-Bear impulsively clasped her hand as he said this, as if he were reliving the experience.

"When we picked ourselves up," Tundra-Bear went on, "it was difficult to move over the snow because our snow-slats were broken. We did try to approach the earth-house. We could see through the darkness of the night but not through the mist and smoke that surrounded the dwelling. We returned to our village that night and tried again during the following days, but we were not able to approach the dwelling of the Master Sage.

"For a long time, a thick mist hung over it that made it impossible for us to find our way there. When the mist blew away, we came to see what had happened, though we could not see much. A soft snow had buried everything, and not much seemed to be left. There was no sign of the Master Sage and no sign of Bomsiell either. Close to where the earth-house had been, we found something very strange."

Tundra-Bear was silent again.

"What was it?" Knarry asked after a minute, wondering why he was being kept in suspense.

Fox-Foot turned to Knarry and said, "Come to the village, and we will show it to you. We found it about a hundred paces from the earth-house. It lay on the grass, for all the snow had been melted for two or three paces around it and a strange warmth came from it that made the grass grow and some flowers come up, even though it was the deepest winter and very cold. At first, we were cautious about touching it, but then we picked it up, wrapped it in a piece of winterbeest fur, and brought it to the village. Come and see it, Knarry, for we cannot describe it. We don't know what it is."

"But it is dark now, and there is a long way to go," Knarry said.

"We will show the way; it will not take much effort," Fox-Foot answered with a smile.

Knarry glanced at Bomsiell and said, "Looks like dinner will have to wait, Bomsiell!"

Bomsiell purred, sprang to her feet, and was ready to go. Knarry rolled up the woolen blanket, gathered up his belongings into the haversack, extinguished the fire, and followed Tundra-Bear and Fox-Foot through the dark woodland. Bomsiell ran ahead, since she already knew the way. They hiked quickly and smoothly over the hills on old, well-worn footpaths until they descended into a small valley. Here they could see the lights of the village at the end of the valley. Soon they were walking through the gates of the village stockade and down the main street.

Knarry was familiar with the village. He always admired its delicate fountains, colorful shrines, and beautifully carved wooden houses, tall and steeply gabled and adorned by intricate balconies that hung over the street and that, in season, drooped their long flowers over the side of the balustrades. The main street was illuminated by flaming torches placed at regular intervals among the houses. The small, leaded, many-colored windows of the houses were also ablaze with cheerful light. Knarry could hear the sounds of laughter and singing. Many Hill people thronged the streets, greeting their neighbors and welcoming Knarry, while dogs of a dozen breeds darted around through the crowd and barked warily at Bomsiell as she passed by; and sleepy cats in doorways stood up, arched their backs, and stared at her in amazement.

"We are having our Spring festival," Tundra-Bear observed, somewhat belatedly, as was his custom.

"You are always having a festival," Knarry commented.

"It is good to have festivals," Fox-Foot replied. Apparently, she felt that no further explanation was necessary.

They arrived at a house at the far end of the village and entered through a finely carved cedar doorway. As lovely as the doorway was, however, it was tall and slender and well conformed to the usual occupants of the household, so that Knarry had to turn himself sideways to squeeze through the door. The interior of the house was warm and fragrant with herbs and dried fruit hanging from the rafters of the ceiling. A cheerful fire burned behind the grate of a large clay stove in the corner. It was bordered with tiles and painted in dozens of intricate designs and colors. The walls were hung with finely woven wool blankets, shimmering fur pelts of various kinds, and various brass implements necessary for life in the mountains.

In the center of the room was a long wooden table with a tallow lamp hanging above it. Five children — two boys and three girls — of different ages and heights, were sitting around the table working with leather, stitching linen tunics, or carving wooden utensils. Their bright green hair glittered in the lamplight. "Hi, Momma! Hi, Poppa!" they shouted to their parents. They knew that their parents were intending to bring Knarry home with them, so they were not surprised to see him, and, after all, he had been a guest in the past. Still, they were, as ever, stunned by his thick, shaggy appearance; after some momentary shyness, they greeted him as well. "Hi, Knarry!"

They welcomed Bomsiell too. They were familiar with forest cats in the wild as fearsome, unapproachable creatures. Bomsiell was, as ever, an object of rapt attention for she was the only domesticated forest cat they had ever known. The family dog—a somewhat aging moorland rover with black fur—moved over to the side of the room and sat upright on his haunches, staring at Bomsiell and thumping his tail rhythmically against the floor. It always took a little while before they could approach one another, touch noses, and renew their old friendship.

Fox-Foot asked the two oldest children, a boy and a girl, to fetch for Knarry a bowl of hot soup and a loaf of bread. The other children squeezed together and made room for Knarry at the table. They left off their carving and leather trimming and gazed at him. Moments later, the boy and the girl emerged from the kitchen with a steaming tureen of soup and a large oak platter that held a loaf of dark bread. Knarry set the dense, grainy mountain loaf in front of himself and sliced off a large wedge of it. This he dipped into the steaming tureen, soaked up some of the broth, and slurped it into his enormous mouth with obvious glee.

In the meantime, the girl returned to the kitchen and brought Bomsiell a cup of fresh moose milk and several slices of smoked glacial fish. Bomsiell wasted no time in lapping up her delayed evening meal and chewing her way carefully through the tough but succulent flesh of the fish. As a gesture of friendship, she picked up the final sliver of fish, trotted over to the dog, and dropped it at his feet. He licked her head in gratitude, right between her four ears, then dispatched the sliver of fish with a single gulp.

While Tundra-Bear and Fox-Foot busied themselves in another room, shedding bows and quivers and changing into their village garb, the children continued to stare at Knarry while he ate; they rarely saw anybody from the lowlands and even more rarely did they see a wood-gnome, though Knarry was a figure familiar to them from his annual visits. Knarry looked up now and then at this circle of slender, green-haired admirers with their delicate purple eyes; once he winked at them and emitted a soft, deep chortle, at which the younger ones all giggled and hid their faces.

Fox-Foot entered the room and announced that the children could go up the street to attend the festival dance in the village square. With a shout, they scrambled out of the house, followed by the elderly moorland rover, who scampered after them as best he could. Tundra-Bear came into the room and sat at the table opposite to Knarry for a while.

After a lengthy silence, he explained to Knarry that the mysterious object that he and Fox-Foot had told him about was not in the house but was kept in an old chest on the top floor of the village signal tower. Fox-Foot was putting away some of the leather work; she said, "We thought we should put the thing—it seems to be a very precious thing—in the safest place we knew. And that was in the tower, Knarry." They would have to go there to see it but would have to pass by the festival dance on the way. Knarry agreed. He was eager to see what they had found.

At the festival dance, they stopped for a moment to gaze at the dancers. Tundra-Bear and Fox-Foot could not resist joining in for a round. It was an astonishing sight. The dancers moved in the light of the great bonfire at the center of the square; strange reedy instruments and drums beat out a sprightly melody as each member of a couple moved in emulation of his or her partner's motions.

It was a cheerful but restrained form of dancing; their feet tapped the surface of the square in rhythm with the music, and their bodies leaned first one way and then another, off to the side, then back and forth, and each couple, though seemingly fully self-contained, fully like one person, moved in perfect harmony with all the other couples around them. This included even the very old and the young who were dancing. Knarry always took pleasure in noting that the elderly Hill people possessed great dignity as their features matured and their hair turned into a mellow amber-brown. Even the children danced, for at an early age they knew who their later spouses in life would be, and the deeply rooted pairing instinct of the Hill people was already evident in them.

After several turns through the dancing crowd, Tundra-Bear and Fox-Foot detached themselves from the dance. They returned to him flushed from the dance and happy. Knarry wondered if there was anything that could make people like this unhappy. He looked around the festival tables laden with neatly piled stacks of fresh spring roots, cut into thin little slices and baked with fruit preserves and honey. The children especially loved these delicacies and snatched them from the tables to eat between the dances.

Vats of Hill wine, having now aged properly from the previous year's grape harvest, were on display, and small wooden goblets of the sweet beverage were passed around from hand to hand in the merry throng. Many of the vats would be shipped off to the lowlands later in the spring in exchange for metallic goods and other items difficult to make in the Hills.

"Let's go to the signal tower," Fox-Foot said.

They left the music behind, and, for Knarry's sake, Tundra-Bear took hold of a burning torch from one of the street-arcs. Holding it high above him, he led Knarry and Fox-Foot up to the village gates, along a ramp bordering the inside of the stockade, and up a steep rise to the signal tower. Knarry observed for a moment the carved gables of the village below them in the darkness. They looked like a flotilla of little ships with ornate prows. Then he looked up at the lithe wooden signal tower that reached into the starry night.

One by one, they entered the portals of the tower and ascended the circular stairs that spiraled up the tower. They arrived shortly at the top floor, which was a small storage room. Only the open observation deck was still above them; there, the villagers would watch for winterbeests and for signal fires from neighboring villages when news was circulated through the Hill Country.

The storage room contained neatly stacked piles of arrows, a rack lined with highly polished longbows, a number of formidable crossbows suspended from the rafters, and bins of tar, winterbeest tallow, and various pots and other implements used in the elaborate system of fire signals used in the Hills. Carefully fitted into a corner and partially concealed by a blanket was an old wooden chest, carved with the Hill people's elaborate designs.

As Tundra-Bear held the torch, Fox-Foot gently slid the blanket to the side, opened the chest, and removed several layers of linen cloth. Knarry crouched nervously over the chest. Fox-Foot gradually uncovered a small casket adorned with little jewels.

"We put it in here," she said. "This casket has come down through my family from many generations. It is said that it was a gift of a lowlander to one of my ancestors." Knarry recognized in the casket the exquisite but long forgotten craftsmanship of the Gethsarbim who lived in the Moor-Plains. Such an object would be a rare antique these days in the lowlands, if anyone were to have any interest in antiques.

With careful movements of her slender fingers, she opened the lid of the casket. There, against a velvety purple lining, as purple as the eyes of the Hill people, lay a long, thin splinter of wood.

It moved and quivered softly in its velvety bed. It was alive.

Knarry leaned closer and gazed upon it.

"What is it?" Fox-Foot asked.

Tundra-Bear brought the torch over the casket and waited for the reply.

"From the Northern Taiga ..." Knarry whispered, his voice husky with awe and reverence. "It's a fragment ... a splice ... a splinter ..."

"Yes, Knarry," said Fox-Foot, "finish what you were saying. A fragment ... a splinter of what?"

"Of the Ancestral Tree," he said. He watched it twitch and curl at the ends even as he said this. A strange warmth seemed to rise from it. He turned his head around and looked at Tundra-Bear and Fox-Foot. "I am descended from the Tree to which this belongs; all wood-gnomes are descended from this Tree," he said, "and I must bring it home again."

Chapter II

The Gathering of the Clans

Plans for the imminent departure of Tundra-Bear and Fox-Foot from their village in the Hills was met with curiosity and consternation among their neighbors and townsfolk. Separation among the Hill people was seldom regarded as being difficult; prolonged hunting excursions into the deep forests or up the slopes of the Golden Mountains were common, and the people were so intimate with one another that physical separation was perceived as inconsequential—even apart, they always felt themselves to be together. Those who stayed behind were absorbed into the care and trust of others around them. The only concern for those who left arose from the possibility of danger—that they might find themselves the victims of a rare avalanche, or of a fall into some mountain ravine, or of a winterbeest whose approach had been swifter than the ability of a Hill hunter, man or woman, to respond to it.

In Tundra-Bear and Fox-Foot's case, the curiosity arose because they were to descend into the lowlands, where Hill people rarely went. What possible reason could there be for wanting to venture into such unfamiliar terrain? The consternation arose because, even though they were to travel in Knarry's company, the dangers of the lowlands were unknown; and the dangers must be considerable, for Knarry's request that they accompany him was made in the awareness that he needed, even desperately needed, their help.

Knarry would be their protection against all that was unfamiliar and unpredictable to them about life in the lowlands; and they, as hunters of the ferocious winterbeests in the high mountain fastnesses and with their expertise in the use of the longbow, would be Knarry's protection against potential threats to his life and well-being.

Of course, the Hill people knew very little about the lowlanders; contacts were often limited to the occasional hunters and fishermen, sundry vacationers, and others who wandered up into the Hills, usually during the summer. Some simply came to enjoy the beauty and repose of the landscape; Garug-Caroch had been one such person.

The Hill people took delight also in those lowlanders, increasingly rare in recent times, who passed through their villages, enjoyed their hospitality, and studied the local animal and plant life—a subject about which the Hill people were pleased to be informative and helpful, though they often were amused by the scrolls and pens these genteel naturalists carried with them to record their observations. Wasn't memory good enough?

But other lowlanders were sometimes troublesome visitors—particularly the unwary and greedy prospectors looking for gold and gems among the higher mountain passes, whose lack of circumspection, of the forethought and the forbearance that any well-brought-up child should have, often resulted in their ending up as all-too-delectable repasts for the perpetually famished winterbeests.

Knarry's immediate plan was to go to the great plateau of Claha-ain, located just to the north and west of the Hill Country. There, at the time of the spring equinox, the wood-gnomes of Oval-Earth gathered to meet with their clans and to attend the Plenary Session of the Grand Council of Elders. Knarry was held in high regard among the wood-gnomes; indeed, his prospects for becoming eventually a member of the Grand Council were considered especially favorable by those wood-gnomes, whose opinions carried some authority among the others.

At this year's session, Knarry planned to present what he knew of the troubles besetting Oval-Earth. He would tell them about Garug-Caroch, about the untimely demise of Twigbottom, about the events leading up to the winter storm. Tundra-Bear and Fox-Foot would bear witness to the truth and to the importance of his observations. His presentation would be climaxed by lifting up the jeweled casket before the eyes of the presumably awestruck assembly and showing to it the Splinter of the Ancestral Tree. It would be a dramatic moment, one that could not help but affect deeply every wood-gnome gathered there.

Of course, there was a flaw in this plan, and Knarry was well aware of what it was: his presentation would not have been listed on the official agenda or program, and there was no time or opportunity left to arrange for that. His presentation, therefore, would have to be an abrupt intervention in the proceedings. Such unannounced interventions were seldom tolerated at the Plenary Session and could backfire on the intervener, resulting in his ostracism and in the ruin of his political aspirations, if he had any. But that was the last thing Knarry was concerned with at present. He would have to take the risk involved and submit to whatever consequences ensued.

Knarry had other reasons for wanting Tundra-Bear and Fox-Foot with him, reasons that he was not quite ready to admit to himself. He needed their courage—for he knew, in his knotty heart, that he was afraid. In ordinary times, it was possible to know how wood-gnomes might respond to certain challenges; in these troubled times, wood-gnomes were not fully themselves anymore. Their actions, even their sentiments, might be unpredictable.

The steadiness of the Hill people, bred into them over the generations by withstanding the sudden assaults of winterbeests, could be a valuable support for him in an emergency. Also, he had need of Tundra-Bear and Fox-Foot's curious ability to read others' characters. Though the Hill people were far from possessing advanced intellectual or sophisticated reasoning capacities, their pristine integrity as well as the independence and clarity of perception bred by their isolation allowed them to see through, and not be taken in by, the frequently warped complexities of lowlanders.

Tundra-Bear and Fox-Foot were apprised of Knarry's plan, and after much discussion and explanation, both with Knarry and among themselves, they agreed to cooperate as fully as they could. Much of what Knarry had told them about Garug-Caroch, about the College of Wisdom, and about other matters was beyond their ability to understand. But they did know that there was a very great distress present in Oval-Earth that they must help to alleviate.

Their own people, thus far, had been largely immune to it; but this condition might not last much longer. They thought of their beloved children, of their fellow villagers and countrymen, of their beautiful and fragrant hills and forests, and decided to venture into the lowlands to help Knarry ferret out and dispatch what they were inclined to call the "winterbeest in the heart of Oval-Earth."

The departure took place two days after the disclosure of the Splinter in the signal tower. Tundra-Bear and Fox-Foot's children understood their parents' leave-taking as being not much different from the annual hunting excursion they always took after the snows had melted in the spring.

The oldest daughter, Swallow-Flight, was put in charge of the household. She was already a young woman of sixteen whose marriage was planned for the following year. Her future husband, Badger-Claw, would come to visit her each day from the neighboring village and would help her with the work. The two of them were already excellent archers and would soon embark on hunting expeditions of their own. The work of the household would not interfere with their daily workouts on the archery range near the village. Moreover, Fox-Foot comforted the family by conjecturing that the separation would not be long.

On this occasion, however, Swallow-Flight detected a tone of unusual somberness in her mother's voice; this journey was to be much more than an ordinary pursuit of the mountain quarry. Tundra-Bear likewise made sure his oldest son, Red-Wolf, now thirteen, would look after the moose stable in the back of the house. The cow moose needed to be milked each day and led out to pasture on the nearby hillside, where the village pasturing grounds were located. Red-Wolf would also train the frisky young bull-moose to help him bring firewood from the upland forests. Early spring was wood-gathering time, so that the wood could season properly for the needs of the next winter. Red-Wolf, brandishing his little axe with some bravado, assured his father that he would find a plentiful supply of fresh wood on his return.

On a cool but pleasant spring morning, Tundra-Bear, Fox-Foot, and Knarry waved goodbye to the children and to the villagers who had gathered to see them off and began the trek down to the lowlands. Knarry had his haversack tossed over his shoulder; in it was carefully bundled the jeweled casket. Tundra-Bear and Fox-Foot had decided not to wear the winterbeest pelts into the lowlands, where, Knarry had told them, the climate would get very hot before too long; instead, they were garbed in the light, pale-green, knee-length tunics that they ordinarily wore during the warmer months.

Their long bronze arms and legs were bare, and their dark green hair swung freely around their heads. Both carried longbows, sheaths of arrows, sleeping blankets (which could also serve as cloaks in cold weather), and satchels for food and other necessities. Behind the three travelers, Bomsiell trotted along with tail lifted high and eyes alert for any moss-mouse foolish enough scurry across her path.

There was little traffic on the Regional Road. At one point, a woodsman leading a moose loaded up with fresh-cut timber hailed the travelers as they passed. Later, they saw a small band of fishermen carrying nets and baskets to a local waterfall. The men seemed in high spirits, although Knarry wondered how they would be feeling after an hour or two of trying to net balloon-fish and tumbling, as often happened, into the waterfall itself. Balloon-fish were never easy to catch, as Knarry knew from experience. Also, the spouts of spirit-jugs protruding from the baskets did not portend any sustained success in the fishing venture; a few swigs from those jugs would be enough to impair the delicate balance on slippery ledges needed to bag the evasive balloon-fish.

Knarry mused on how good everything looked. The weather of Oval-Earth had certainly improved. Whatever had happened in the great storm of the winter solstice, the evil that was growing in Oval-Earth had received a setback. Some of its power was gone. If the Splinter he bore in the jeweled casket on his back was any clue to the devastating event that had occurred, then the strand of the Ancestral Tree that Rough-Bark had envisaged in his mad reverie on Kyn Ardagh was involved.

The powers of evil, whoever they were, had used that strand of the Tree as an enchanted staff to alter and control the weather. The Splinter had been torn off and left behind in the great implosion of the earth-house.

Where was the rest of the staff? It could no longer be in *their* hands!

Was it possible that Garug-Caroch, wherever he was, if he was still alive somewhere (which seemed so unlikely), held it in his possession?

And what had Garug-Caroch done—except to sing, perhaps, the two verses of the Song of the Eternal Aeons that he had obviously deciphered from the ancient books and that had arrived in the winter storm scribbled on the parchment that was attached to Bomsiell?

Yet even to possess a tiny strand of the Ancestral Tree was to possess a talisman of incalculable power. Knarry could feel the warmth of the Splinter through the side of his haversack. What could he do with it, if the need for preternatural assistance should arise in the course of their journey?

In the evening, the four travelers arrived at Cantanteroff to spend the night in Knarry's earth-house. Knarry showed Tundra-Bear and Fox-Foot around the earth-house, recalling with some affection, as he did so, Garug-Caroch's ever lively wonder at the curious configurations of its chambers and hallways. But Tundra-Bear and Fox-Foot were uninterested. They were considerably more interested in the spacious bathtub and its hot-spring waters. Knarry left them to splash around in it, as he, amused by their delightful and often childlike simplicity, examined the medical facilities. The young terebinth gnome left in charge was maintaining good order in the dispensary—he had obviously left for the day. Then Knarry entered the galley to prepare the evening dinner. Bomsiell sat on the floor of the galley and stared up at him with big eyes and all four ears erect. She was waiting for her evening fish cake.

Over dinner, Knarry and his guests deliberated about the itinerary to the Claha-ain Plateau. Knarry urged that the Radial High-Road System be avoided. He did not want to run accidentally into any functionaries of the Imperial Viceroy. The presence of Hill people in the lowlands would be regarded as highly suspicious. Tundra-Bear and Fox-Foot agreed, without exactly knowing why they agreed, and Bomsiell looked up for a moment from gnawing her somewhat stale fish cake as if to add her own consent to the idea.

Knarry left the table and entered his dispensary, where he found an old map he kept as a guide when making medical visits into the hinterlands of Cantanteroff. Returning into the dining chamber, he cleared a space among the platters and cups and spread out the map. With his finger, he traced a path that led, somewhat indirectly, to the foot of the Claha-ain Plateau. Tundra-Bear and Fox-Foot followed the movement of his big knobby finger over the surface of the map.

When Knarry withdrew his finger from the map, they continued to follow it. Knarry realized that they did not understand what a map was. He rolled it up quickly. Tundra-Bear and Fox-Foot looked curiously at him and at each other, but Knarry did not feel inclined to explain.

After dinner, they all walked up the nearby knoll to the gazebo, where Knarry and Garug-Caroch had once conversed. Here they watched the sun go down over Oval-Earth and the twin lavender moons arise from the Golden Mountains like two great luminous eyes, like the glowing purple eyes of a Hill Country maiden.

The annual gathering of the clans was still several days away, so Knarry attended to various matters pertaining to his medical practice, conferred with the terebinth gnome during dispensary hours, and consulted with him on several difficult cases. The terebinth gnome, like a number of other wood-gnomes, was not planning to attend the annual gathering because there was too much medical work to be done. Meanwhile, Tundra-Bear and Fox-Foot explored the surrounding country. On the first morning, after a simple breakfast, they strapped their longbows over their shoulders and walked out of Cantanteroff to the neighboring villages.

They were puzzled by the shabbiness and disarray of the villages. Gardens were overrun by weeds; many had not been replanted yet for the new growing season. Roofs of houses had partially caved in, yet the inhabitants sat idly by, doing nothing to fix them. Instead, they stared at Tundra-Bear and Fox-Foot with dazed and indolent expressions.

The roads from village to village were rutted; manure-stained cattle and moose wandered over meadows where rare tufts of thin grass sprouted from arid, sunbaked soil; and ill-kempt children squabbled with one another in dusty yards. A few children noticed Tundra-Bear and Fox-Foot as they passed by; one undernourished-looking boy approached them and seemed to implore them for help with his sad eyes. Fox-Foot took his hand, and together they went off into a nearby grove where she found some berries and mushrooms for him to eat. She wove a little basket for him out of reeds to gather the fruit.

Meanwhile, Tundra-Bear stayed behind and prodded a moose out of a vegetable garden whose fence had collapsed on one side. He propped up the fence by carving several saplings into posts to support it. Moments later, he witnessed a disheveled man attired in ragged livery being driven across the village square by a hail of stones and barking dogs. "Tax collector!" the villagers shouted at him. The tax collector trundled swiftly down the road past Tundra-Bear, eyeing him suspiciously as he went by.

By late afternoon, Tundra-Bear and Fox-Foot were glad to get back to Cantanteroff and to Knarry's earth-house, for at least here was order and good measure to things, even if it was all quite zigzaggy in a wood-gnomish sort of way. They told Knarry about the events of the day. They told him especially about their effort to locate the pasture of Garug-Caroch's elderly moose, Collielava, and how pleased they were to find him well taken care of and in good health.

Knarry, in turn, instructed them in the use of money by taking out a satchel of copper coins and spreading them on the table. Tundra-Bear and Fox-Foot found it all funny and laughed to think that one could buy a moose with twenty-four coppers or a crossbow with sixteen. After all, the copper itself was not good for very much, except possibly for making arrowheads—and they would not be particularly good arrowheads.

On the following morning, the four travelers set off for the Claha-ain Plateau, giving themselves a day and a half to reach their destination. The journey was not arduous, even though the path twisted back and forth from one little valley to another, and the landscape was scarred by a multitude of thin gorges and narrow, jagged ridges roughly parallel to one another. Since no inns were available and the villages were not especially hospitable, the night was spent in the woods.

The next morning, they came to the foot of the Claha-ain Plateau; but because they had approached it from the back, rather than from the direction commonly taken by the wood-gnomes, they had to climb up its rock face on a makeshift, uncharted, and largely unknown path used by the local inhabitants during the summer months to bring their goats to and from summer pasturage. The goat-path led up over a small hillock at the far end of the plateau.

When the ascent was finished, Knarry, Tundra-Bear, Fox-Foot, and Bomsiell stood on the hillock and looked down over the plateau. It was already covered at the far end by the colorful tents of the clan chieftains; beyond them, a spacious, dazzling pavilion had been erected for the Grand Council of Elders. The fairgrounds swarmed with multitudes of wood-gnomes, all dressed out in their finest and most peculiar attire.

Knarry groaned as he gazed at the distant assembly; in years past, one could look forward to this annual event with pleasure. Old friendships were renewed, gnome-lore was traded back and forth, the bardic recitations of the Gno'menai were heard, and prized possessions of the gnomes were loaded into the tents to be judged in the many contests held during the fair. But this year, it would be different. Knarry could already feel the tension.

The four companions descended the hillock, crossed the intervening meadows between the hillock and the fairgrounds, and passed through the vast encampment of the gnome clans. The crowd was one great hubbub of greetings and chortles, animated talk and poundings of stakes for the tents, and the clatter of cooking utensils as victuals were basted over ovens of stones heated by the scalding geothermal shafts that arose here and there on the Claha-ain Plateau.

Several gnome bands were playing in various quarters. They played a bizarre thumping, squeaking music with their clay instruments, variously known as hooters, glips, duck-pipes, wing-snappers, snoodlehorns, and the large concave drums called whangbocks. gnome-spirits, ordinarily consumed only in the evening after dinner and in great moderation, had obviously made the rounds already, and a certain lightness of mood masked the grimness that lay underneath.

As they threaded through the crowd on the main fairway, Tundra-Bear and Fox-Foot stared with wonder at the many sizes and shapes that wood-gnomes came in. Tall, elegant gnomes gathered around the tent of the elm clan; stubby, flamboyant gnomes dusted off the official banner of the palmettos; sweet-faced, gentle-eyed gnomes of the sugar-maple clan put finishing touches on the flat-cakes they were famous for, the more so because of their curious custom of pouring sticky brown sap over these flat-cakes.

There were also oaks and eucalyptus, banyan and rhododendron and baobab, juniper and laurel and puddlepot and yum-yum and hornbeam and the pariah thornbrush, whom everyone took a certain pleasure in avoiding and who, in turn, took a certain pleasure in being avoided. Each clan had its own heraldic banners and colors, its own distinctive cuisine, its own peculiarities of dress and behavior.

Knarry led his companions directly through the crowd to the tent of the ponderosa clan. There he introduced them to many of his clansmen. It was a sturdy, husky group of gnomes who milled about in the tent, powerfully built like Knarry and full of vitality and good humor. Tundra-Bear and Fox-Foot were impressed. But the ponderosa gnomes, who ordinarily had the highest trust and pride in Knarry, were somewhat taken aback by his introduction of these extraordinary looking green-haired strangers into what was always regarded as a privileged event for wood-gnomes. They regarded Bomsiell as well with misgivings and wondered if one or several of them might be utilized as temporary scratching posts by this enormous four-eared feline with her fearsome claws.

Knarry realized quickly that his unusual guests only intensified a suspicion of which he, apparently, was the object. There was a strangeness in the atmosphere; the usual dignity of the ponderosa clan members seemed to be marred by an insidious resentment permeating many in the group, and, though perhaps the majority of the ponderosa clan carried on in their usual hearty and robust way, parts of the tent were seething with muffled rumors and whisperings. Small clusters of gnomes here and there huddled together in little "groves," as it were, glancing to the sides, looking suspiciously at one another and at Knarry. One gnome, a certain Needle-Frond, reputed to have an especially ugly disposition, snubbed Knarry as he passed by and refused to extend his greetings.

But the message was clear, and the atmosphere was potentially explosive. As soon as he could draw Tundra-Bear and Fox-Foot to the side of the tent, Knarry warned them that they should make plans for a sudden escape from the plateau—should one be necessary. Such plans were hastily discussed. Tundra-Bear, Fox-Foot, and Bomsiell would withdraw to the hillock at the far end of the plateau and would wait for news from Knarry. The goat-path would be the escape route, if a sudden escape should be necessary. The wood-gnomes, who used the main entry to the plateau, would probably not know of its existence.

After the discussion, Knarry returned to mingle with his fellow clan-gnomes in hopes that he could learn more about the rumors that were being spread around in such secrecy. Meanwhile, his companions slipped out through a side-flap in the tent and made their way back to the hillock.

Shortly after the noontide feasting was finished in the clan tents, five towering gnomes of the redwood clan, having mounted a platform in front of the pavilion of the Grand Council, lifted huge wooden tubas to their lips. A deep, mournful sound floated over the plateau and echoed from the Golden Mountains. It was the summoning of the clans.

Gradually a host of wood-gnomes began to stream up the fairway to the pavilion. They approached with great noise and commotion, as marshals of the hickory clan cried out over the din, directing the crowd to proper areas for seating. The colorful banners of the clans flapped in the breeze. Once again, the redwood summoners blew their mournful tubas over the multitude. At the signal, the gnomes became silent and seated themselves to observe the proceedings.

The annual convocation began with the Primate of the Grand Council arising to speak. It was Rivenbranch of the cypress clan. He delivered a pompous, formal speech that assured the multitude that "everything was fine," but there were "some problems" that needed "urgent attention," and "those invested with the proper authority" were doing "everything in their power to make sure that the appropriate measures" were being taken "to bring matters to a speedy and satisfactory conclusion." The other members of the Grand Council, seated in a semicircle on the platform behind the speaker's rostrum, nodded their assent periodically throughout the speech.

One old, wizened member of the Council sitting at the far end of the semicircle was from the willow clan and seemed rather close to the time of his metamorphosis, for he ignored Rivenbranch's speech altogether and studied at length a leaf that had just sprouted from his little finger. The willow clan was not noted for the quickness of its intelligence.

The conclusion of the Primate's speech was met with a combination of muted, bored applause and annoyed mutterings; and as Rivenbranch attempted to return to his seat in the semicircle, he tripped over his own feet and fell headlong over the seat and into the pavilion behind the platform. The redwood tuba players ran to help him up, as wave upon wave of chortles flowed back and forth through the multitude, chortles perhaps not so much amused as sardonic and bitter.

Verdant-Tuft, Secretary of the Grand Council, now rose to open the business meeting. All across the gathered clans, banners were lifted for recognition. Verdant-Tuft pointed his herald's staff at the chestnut banner, and a member of the chestnut clan leapt up and shouted: "What's happened about the situation on the Northern Taiga? Where is Rough-Bark? What about the delegation? What's going on? Why don't we get any information about it?" Chestnut clan members were famous for getting directly to the point.

"I am glad you asked that question, most esteemed member of the chestnut clan. Appropriate investigations are being made into—" Verdant-Tuft began.

"No … no … no!" arose from various parts of the crowd.

"Let him speak!" others cried out.

The multitude dissolved into a mutinous uproar. Hickory clan marshals moved swiftly through the crowd to restore order. Verdant-Tuft resumed his answer: "As I was trying to say, we have appointed a commission to investigate the matter. The commission has not yet concluded its report, and, until such time as—"

The crowd again broke into angry shouting. Banners were waved frantically back and forth. The hickories ran up and down the aisles, shaking their wands over the multitude and threatening to expel any rowdy intruder. Among the ponderosa clan, a brief scuffle took place for possession of the banner. Out of the scuffle, Knarry stood up, brandishing the banner high over the crowd and calling for attention. With trembling hands, Verdant-Tuft pointed the herald's staff at him. The crowd fell silent.

"I ask permission to mount the rostrum." Knarry declared. This was an unusual request. The crowd murmured. Members of the ponderosa clan looked at one another in alarm. What was Knarry up to? Whom did he represent?

"Permission granted," replied Verdant-Tuft anxiously, though he was relieved to be able to step away from the rostrum. Under ordinary circumstances he would not grant such permission, unless it had been prepared for by a petition presented prior to the assembly. A small chorus of angry voices in the back of the crowd was lifted in virulent protest, but Knarry strode down the central aisle in the assembly and mounted the rostrum. His haversack was strapped over one shoulder.

He gazed imperiously out over the crowd with his great hazel eyes and shaggy brows. The crowd grew still. "Most honored Primate of the Grand Council, honorable Elders of the Grand Council, clan chieftains, and assembled wood-gnomes of Oval-Earth, I have news of the greatest import to tell you." Another murmur ran through the crowd. Angry voices at the back of the crowd again rose and fell. Several hickories were dispatched to the rear in order to quell the uproar.

He continued: "Never has Oval-Earth been in greater danger. Never have the lives and destinies of the wood-gnomes, and of all the Oval-Earth peoples whom we serve, been so jeopardized. We face a peril whose extent is unknown but whose presence every day grows among us. Never before in our history has it become so incumbent upon us to muster the fullest resources of our ancient earth-power to heal the imponderable wound that has beset us in every way of life."

The crowd broke into another uproar. Banners were shaken wildly back and forth; gnomes shouted at each other and at the speaker; more scuffles broke out here and there in the crowd. Marshals of the hickory clan moved once again through the multitude in order to restore silence.

Knarry went on, "Wood-gnomes, hear me! The Ancestral Tree has been violated!"

Another roar welled up from the crowd, as wood-gnomes jumped to their feet and started pushing one another back and forth into the open spaces between the clan groups and into the ranks of the fellow clans. The hickory marshals were overwhelmed momentarily but managed to calm things down after a minute.

Knarry raised his powerful arms on the rostrum and shouted over the crowd, "Hear me! The vision of Rough-Bark was correct. A strip or shard of the Ancestral Tree has been torn from its side. I don't know how big that shard is, but it is perhaps big enough to fashion a Staff of colossal power — a power that can be used for evil if it is in the wrong hands. The Staff, purloined from the Ancestral Tree, has been used to deform the weather of Oval-Earth. Nothing else can explain what has happened in the last few years."

A voice came from the front of the crowd: "Where is it now? Where is this purloined Staff?"

"The question? What was the question?" came from the back of the crowd.

"Let me speak! I will explain everything that I know!" Knarry shouted back over the rising din.

"Where is the purloined Staff? Answer us now!"

"Let him speak!"

Knarry raised his voice again: "I don't know where it is. I believe that—"

"Why don't you know? Why are you addressing us if you don't know?"

"Why won't you let me speak? I believe that the purloined Staff is now out of the hands of the evil powers that used it. The weather has already improved."

Voices cried out from every direction. "What evil powers?" "How do you know all this?" "What's your proof?" "Why should we believe you?" The mood in the crowd became ever more contentious, violent, and sinister.

"Order, order!" shouted Verdant-Tuft, waving the herald's staff over the multitude.

"Let Knarry have his say," one of the ponderosa gnomes roared, even while the malicious Needle-Frond was pulling at his cloak and attempting to silence him. Other gnomes echoed the sentiment. "Knarry must be allowed to speak; only he can tell us!"

"What powers? What powers?" a group began to chant.

"I do not know what powers. The powers of the Kingdom of Darkness perhaps," Knarry replied loudly. "According to Garug-Caroch—"

"Who is Garug-Caroch?" shouted many voices, as an angry commotion at the back of the crowd broke out again.

"He was a Master Sage and the Grand Master at the College of Wisdom. He was studying the problem when—"

The commotion at the back of the crowd became so fierce that a squad of hickory marshals were again dispatched to try to manage it. The hornbeam banner waved frantically in the rear.

Knarry knew that further effort to deliver the long, carefully reasoned oration he had planned would be futile. What he had to say was lengthy and complicated, and what the crowd wanted was something simple and quick. He was appalled that the normal reasonableness of wood-gnomes had been so utterly overthrown. He reached into his haversack and pulled out the jeweled casket.

"Here I have my proof!" he cried out over the crowd.

Therewith he opened the casket and lifted out the Splinter and held it high in the air above him. It snapped and wiggled in his fingers and glistened in the sunlight. An immense power seemed to emanate from its small, narrow frame that fixated the attention of everyone present. "A piece of the purloined Staff! A shred of the Ancestral Tree!"

The crowd was speechless with awe for a moment, just long enough for a member of the hornbeam clan to scream out loudly and sharply from the back of the crowd: "Accomplice to murder!"

Pandemonium spread through the multitude. The hickories stormed back and forth, trying to restore order, but the hornbeams were mad with hysteria and shoved and pushed one another and all those around them. "Conspirator with Garug-Caroch!" the hornbeam gnome shrieked. "He is an accomplice to murder! He helped Garug-Caroch to plot the murder of our Twigbottom, who did nothing in this life to deserve such a fate except tend a musty old Library!"

"This accusation is absurd," Knarry shouted back. "Please attend to the business at hand. I assure you that your information is founded on rumors and gossip. I have a piece of the Ancestral Tree here in my hands—" He was drowned out.

"Violator!" other voices cried. "You are the violator; you are the one who has violated the Ancestral Tree! You have the proof of your violation in your hands!"

"No! I am trying to serve you! We need to send a new delegation! We need to find the purloined Staff and return it and this fragment to its proper place! We need to return earth-power to its proper function! Please heed my words!"

"Violator! Agent of the Kingdom of Darkness! Spy! Extortionist! Thief!"

"No, no, listen to me!" Knarry protested.

Other voices rose in his defense, but to no avail. The meeting dissolved into a riot. Clans clashed, banners were torn down and re-erected, wood-gnomes pushed and trampled one another in frantic charging and counter-charging. Verdant-Tuft commanded the hefty redwood tuba players to apprehend Knarry for questioning and to deliver the Splinter of the Ancestral Tree into the keeping of the Grand Council.

The redwood gnomes clambered up onto the platform to do as they were bid, as Knarry slipped the casket back into the haversack without its contents. He looked at the Splinter. "Now, old friend, I will find out about your powers," he murmured to it. "If my cause is just, I know that you will serve me in a way that is just. I will point you in whatever direction I need your help. The rest is up to you."

He pointed the Splinter at the redwood gnomes who were about to grapple with him. Struck by a ferocious impact, they flew backward on the platform, sweeping Verdant-Tuft and many of the Elders with them as they crashed over the railings and onto the ground behind the platform, landing in a tangled, squirming heap. Only the willow gnome remained stationary throughout all of this commotion, sitting on his bench and still obliviously concentrating upon the leaf on his little finger.

Knarry leapt down from the side of the platform and rushed away from the crowd by circumventing the pavilion to its rear and avoiding the knot of Elders and redwood gnomes still trying to disentangle themselves from one another at the base of the platform. He made a wide circle around the milling, struggling crowd until he reached the fairway. He hoped that the confusion would last long enough to assist his escape down the fairway and out across the pastures to the hillock beyond them. But a gesticulating, riotous gang of hornbeams accosted him as he rounded the crowd and was heading into the fairway.

Again, Knarry pointed the Splinter. It convulsed in his hands. He could feel the energy burst out of it. The hornbeams in its trajectory of force stood transfixed for a moment and suddenly were knocked and toppled over in a dozen directions as if struck by a gigantic but invisible rolling ball. Knarry was no less astonished by the effect of the Splinter. That would make an interesting sport, he thought for a moment as he bolted down the fairway. A moment later, he was galloping across the grassy fields of the plateau as fast as his knotty legs could carry him.

From the hillock, Tundra-Bear and Fox-Foot had been straining to watch the distant proceedings, though even with their keen eyesight, it was difficult to make out what was happening. Bomsiell, however, was agitated and stared intently in the direction of the pavilion. She had been able to detect the voice of Knarry as it shouted over the multitude and, by crouching in an attack position and extending her long, razor-sharp claws, showed that she recognized the peril Knarry was in. Tundra-Bear and Fox-Foot were mystified by the tumult that ensued, the swirling mass of gnomes that charged in every direction and back again, colliding, falling down, and renewing their efforts in a wild scramble and disarray.

They looked at each other as if searching out an explanation. Then they saw Knarry break loose from the tumult and dash away from the fairgrounds and across the meadows towards them. Seconds later, a thin stream of pursuers flowed out on the fields after him, railing and tripping over themselves.

Tundra-Bear and Fox-Foot looked at each other again, wondering what they should do. Bomsiell did not hesitate; she bolted down the hillock in long, loping strides of astonishing speed, sped across the pastures, circled behind Knarry, and covered his retreat by following behind him and intermittently whirling and snarling at the pursuers, though the frenzied mob was still quite far away.

On the hillock, Tundra-Bear and Fox-Foot reached for their longbows, carefully strung them, drew several wad-tipped arrows from their quivers, used in most ordinary situations for sending fire signals, and knelt in a firing position. Fox-Foot dipped the arrows into a vial of winterbeest tallow, while Tundra-Bear struck a flurry of sparks from his tinderbox. They ignited two of the arrows. Tundra-Bear and Fox-Foot drew back the flaming arrows in their bows and released them simultaneously with a powerful twang.

The arrows arched upward from the hillock and high over the plateau, and then, nosing downward, they plummeted into two of the clan tents. Several more flaming arrows followed in the same manner, and the fairgrounds were rapidly swallowed up in a raging conflagration. Steep columns of fire arose from the clan tents while the pavilion was enveloped in black swirling smoke.

The front line of Knarry's pursuers, noting the flaming arrows high above them, slid to a stop on the grassy pastures while the following mob piled into them. The mob disengaged themselves and turned back to rescue their possessions and to put out the fires. Gnomes, by reputation, were terrified of fires, and both Tundra-Bear and Fox-Foot regretted having to resort to such a method to turn them back.

Knarry crested the hillock, exhausted but flushed with excitement. Bomsiell loped up behind him. "They've gone mad," Knarry said, breathlessly, "the whole lot of them, except the hickories maybe." He looked back over the plateau, which was now a chaos of fire and alarms and running wood-gnomes carrying prized possessions to safety. Only the hornbeams, who recovered slowly from their collision with the Splinter's earth-power, continued to prowl through the smoking havoc of the fairgrounds, searching for Knarry. Meanwhile, redwood constables barricaded the main entry to the plateau to prevent Knarry's escape.

On the distant hillock, the companions hurriedly prepared to leave. Tundra-Bear and Fox-Foot unstrung the longbows and slung them over their shoulders. They put the tinderbox and vial of winterbeest tallow back in their satchels and bound up their sheaths of arrows. Knarry removed the jeweled casket from his haversack and wrapped the Splinter carefully in its velvety lining. "This will be very useful to us," he sighed, "but I never thought I would be using it in this way."

He closed the lid of the casket, replaced it in the haversack, and swung the haversack over his shoulder. Led by an eager Bomsiell, the companions turned their steps once more to the hidden goat-path and descended rapidly into the lowlands of Oval-Earth. In a clearing at the foot of the plateau, Fox-Foot stopped and asked, "Knarry, why are we running away? It is not our custom to run away from danger."

Knarry thought for a moment. "Yes, Fox-Foot, I understand that. But sometimes one must step aside and let a danger go past — such as avoiding an avalanche in the mountains by climbing onto a ridge and allowing it to roll past. Anyway, we are perhaps a greater danger to the gnomes than they are to us. We can only help them now by being about our business and staying out of their way."

Fox-Foot seemed to accept this explanation, though she was still puzzled. Knarry did not know how long it might be before one of the gnome authorities examined the hillock and discovered the footpath, so he expressed the need for haste. He explained that a return to Cantanteroff was impossible. The main roads to Cantanteroff would be put under immediate surveillance, and Knarry's earth-house would be watched, if not impounded.

Furthermore, he acknowledged that bringing his three companions into the gathering was a tactical blunder, although the fire-arrows arching over the pasture would have betrayed them anyway. Officials would now be on the lookout for a Hill couple in the lowlands. Who else could loose arrows like that and at such a distance? And then there was Bomsiell!

There would be danger involved in any direction they decided to go. Staying far away from inhabited areas would be necessary. Fox-Foot was saddened that she would not be returning at once to the village. But they decided to discuss the matter as soon as they were sufficiently far away from the plateau to make camp for the night.

Before they left the clearing, Knarry could not refrain from asking, "How did the two of you come up with the idea of shooting fire-arrows at the tents? I thought you Hill people used fire-arrows only for sending signals."

Fox-Foot glanced at Tundra-Bear and turned to Knarry: "You spoke, Knarry, of an avalanche and we are sure you are right about what you say; but at that moment of which you speak, we saw something different. In the mountains sometimes, after a dry spell or during a lightning storm, a great fire will begin that can destroy many leagues of the forest. We try to stop the fire and save the forest and all its animals and birds by shooting tallow-dipped arrows from a distance into mounds of brush. In this way, the new fire may help to put out the old fire by taking away the fodder that nourishes it and the air it breathes.

"When we saw what was happening on the plateau, it looked to us like a great woodlands fire. We wanted to do something. What else could we do? We were not happy to do it, and we are sorry to burn down the tents of the clans. We hope that nobody was injured."

Knarry responded, as he made ready to resume the flight, "You did the right thing. I don't think any of the wood-gnomes were hurt by your action. Gnomes are fearful of fires, but they are experts in knowing how to put them out and how to use salves and ointments in the treatment of burns, if such should occur. In years to come, if we are fortunate in our quest, they will thank you for your action. But they will not feel too thankful right now. We must be on our way."

Chapter III

Hrudan the Smith

"We have, I presume," Knarry announced several hours later, while bathing his wedge-shaped feet in a cool stream that flowed out of the Golden Mountains, "the status of criminals."

The Claha-ain Plateau was already ten leagues to the south of them. Smoky columns could still be seen rising from its crest. The four travelers had stopped to rest after a rapid trek through tangled woodlands where it would be hard either to follow or to track them successfully. Knarry sat by a brook, his bark boots, scarlet-rimmed socks, and haversack reposing on the mossy bank next to him. Tundra-Bear and Fox-Foot sat nearby on a rocky outcrop by the brook and listened to him. Overhead, a grove of tall sycamore trees sheltered them from the midafternoon sun. Bomsiell, perched high on a branch of one of the trees, served as a lookout.

"Criminals? What are criminals? I don't understand," Tundra-Bear replied.

"I don't think there is much of a question of understanding involved here, Tundra-Bear. It doesn't make any sense at all," Knarry sighed as he shifted his feet in the icy stream. "What is clear is that I stand accused of crimes — several of them, and heinous crimes as well. I am accused of conspiring to murder Twigbottom. The actual murder, according to the unfounded presumption of guilt, was carried out by Garug-Caroch. Further, I am even accused of being the one who has violated the Ancestral Tree. Imagine what that makes me responsible for: all the catastrophe that has beset Oval-Earth these last several years, to say nothing of whom I might be in league with — the forces of the Kingdom of Darkness no less. Yes, I, Knarry, master of espionage, double agent, saboteur extraordinaire! What a figure I must cut, or has been cut out of me! Now, if you can work out the reasoning processes that led to such a remarkable set of conclusions, please let me know what, in heaven's name, they could be."

Fox-Foot shook her head. "I don't think that I can work that out," she said, genuinely disappointed not to be able to provide an answer to Knarry's question.

Knarry smiled. "Fox-Foot, I really didn't expect you to have an answer. I am just … just asking a question that has no answer. People, and even gnomes, do that all the time."

"Why do they do that?" Fox-Foot asked. She added immediately, "But I do not expect an answer to that." She laughed. "Now you see I did that too!"

Knarry laughed.

Tundra-Bear resumed the discussion. "How serious are these accusations, Knarry?"

"In a way, not too serious," Knarry said. "They were not formal in a purely legal sense. They were not the results of an official inquiry, nor were they advanced in accordance with proper procedure; instead, they were shouted at me by anonymous members of a crowd. But, in an atmosphere of such hysteria, accusations like that tend to stick. There was no way to fend them off with reasonable discussion. Hysteria among wood-gnomes! The shame of it! One would never believe such a thing could happen."

"But why did you say 'we' a while ago?'" asked Tundra-Bear. "Are Fox-Foot and I criminals as well?"

"Well, I admit it may be just a bit too soon for the wood-gnomes to have drawn that particular conclusion. But they will. Once the fires are out and the hickories have restored some semblance of order, they will remember your brief appearance among the tents, and they will know just what sort of archers could shoot arrows the way you did. Just look at what you have done, my hapless accomplices! You have thwarted the long 'branch' of the law by helping me to escape and by burning down, in the process, the clan tents of the gnomes—including, if my eyes served me well, the pavilion of the Grand Council of Elders itself. This is the first time in the history of Oval-Earth that such a calamitous thing has happened and that the gathering of the wood-gnome clans on the Claha-ain Plateau has ended in such mayhem. It will be blamed on me—and, of course, on you. I'm sorry about that."

Knarry stirred his large, wedge-like feet in the stream. They were still hot and sore after the long run over the plateau and down the goat-path. The ten-league hike made in haste had not been helpful either, but the icy water felt good as it rippled between his stubby triangular toes. The physical exertion seemed to have no effect on the Hill couple, who were accustomed to much longer and more strenuous endeavors.

"The question is now: What do we do?" Knarry queried.

"We can return to the Hills," Fox-Foot answered. "There you will be protected. No one will come to find you, and, if they do, we will hide you. The Hills are full of secret places and backwoods trails that only our people know about."

Knarry was silent. He removed his feet from the stream, dried them with his blanket, and pulled on his scarlet-rimmed socks and his shaggy bark boots. He turned to Tundra-Bear and Fox-Foot.

"I don't think we should do that. I would rather not draw the Hill people into this. It could turn into a bitter conflict. Further, simply hiding will only make everything worse. The last thing we need is gangs of imperial functionaries tromping all over the Hill Country, upsetting your way of life and rooting through your lovely villages as they search for us. Furthermore, we must take more positive action. I had counted on the help of my fellow gnomes, but I see they have been deeply affected by the evil afflicting Oval-Earth. The only thing we can do is to undertake on our own the task that I had hoped they would be willing to organize and carry out. A concerted effort by a large group of wood-gnomes could be a formidable thing, but obviously they are in no condition now to make such an effort."

"What do you have in mind, Knarry?" Tundra-Bear asked.

Knarry shook his head. "I really don't know where to begin. We have the Splinter. It may somehow tell us."

"And has it told you anything yet?"

"No. But my instinct is, as I said several days ago when you revealed the Splinter to me in the signal tower of your village, to bring it home. Maybe there is something that will follow from that."

"Then we shall go to the Northern Taiga?"

"Yes."

Tundra-Bear and Fox-Foot looked at one another. They never imagined that they had embarked on such an extraordinary journey. Nobody but wood-gnomes ever went to the Northern Taiga, and even they went only at the time of their metamorphoses.

"We shall gladly accompany you, Knarry, for what you are doing is right," said Fox-Foot. "But let us not delay. We must move swiftly, for we cannot be away from the Hills too long. Anyway, I think there is little time. You have told us that whatever it is that wishes evil for Oval-Earth is provoked into greater fury by anything that opposes it. Like a winterbeest's, its strike shall be swift and deadly."

"You are not afraid?" asked Knarry.

"Are you afraid?" said Tundra-Bear.

Knarry hesitated. "We have the Splinter—it possesses unusual degrees of earth-power. It derives from the source of earth-power itself. I have already seen a little bit of what it can do. And we have two verses of the Song of the Eternal Aeons. That is even more powerful, for, if my inference about what happened in the winter storm at Gnarl-Oak's dwelling is correct, Garug-Caroch's incantation was able to wrest the purloined Staff from the forces of evil. Earth-power is good and strives to be on the side of the good. But evil can try to possess it.

"That is exactly what the force of evil is trying to do: it flies through the night, through the storm and the shadows; over the course of aeons, it strives to absorb and claim for its own the creative energy innate in all things—in the earth, in human beings, in gnomes, in all creatures, in the very seismic rhythms of the universe itself.

"Its goal is the exercise of sheer power for its own sake—aimless, uncreative extinguishing of all that is good in life, of life itself. It is the tasteless, formless, emptiness of the Kingdom of Not-Be, knowing no other passion but its own remorseless passion for annihilation.

"Garug-Caroch learned in the Library that only the Song, which, from what little we know about it already, is a love song for the goodness of creation, can stand up to and surmount such a relentless force. In the winter storm, two lines of the Song destroyed the hold that evil had over the purloined Staff. Of course, we do not know where the Staff is now. But the main purpose of our pilgrimage is to find the words of the Song. That would be the greatest power of all."

The companions sat in the stillness of the woodland for a minute and listened to the murmur of the brook as it gurgled down through its many little pools and channels and over tiny cascades. Fox-Foot tightened her arm around Tundra-Bear's arm and moved closer to him.

"There is much of what you say that we cannot understand, Knarry. We do not even understand the words you use. How can there be a Kingdom of Not-Be? How can 'not-be' be?

"But I wish we could help," she said. "I wish we knew the words of that Song you are talking about, or even part of it. But we do not. Yet it seems familiar to us, this Song, in some way. Because our lives are a song like that, a song that makes things come together, a song that, I think, if I can use words like your words, makes 'be' be, or at least makes 'more be' be.

"Tundra-Bear and I are like two tones in that song, like two tones played on a mountain lute when the strings are in harmony and are plucked together. Through we are different from one another, yet we make a oneness together. And we are part of a melody that embraces our children and our kinsfolk and our villagers and everyone else we know, and the flowers and birds and sunrises and snowflakes. I think the Song of the Eternal Aeons would be like that."

"I know these things about you," Knarry acknowledged. "That is why I want you to accompany me. The words of the Song somehow live inside the two of you, even though you don't know them. How could I do without you? There's Bomsiell, too. And there is the Splinter—which I think may point the way. What more could I ask?"

"Let's be on our way," said Fox-Foot.

They arose, hoisted haversacks, quivers, and longbows over their shoulders, and motioned for Bomsiell to jump down from the tree. The journey had begun.

The group traveled northward from the region of the Claha-ain Plateau and along the western fringe of the Golden Mountains. It was formidable terrain—hilly and forested, with dense outcrops of rock and precipitous stony canyons eroded into the sides of the mountains. Many small rivers cut narrow gorges through long, parallel ridges that rippled across the landscape.

Often the travelers had to traverse these gorges on vine-suspended bridges that were old and in disrepair and that swayed back and forth over deep chasms as they were crossed.

Villages and farmsteads were rare in this section of Oval-Earth; it had never been densely inhabited because the ground was too difficult to farm. In earlier centuries, a prosperous mining industry had thrived in these regions; but now many of the mines were closed and the old mining stations were abandoned.

Earlier times also had seen a flourishing tourist trade, particularly in the region of the most prodigious and spectacular natural wonder in Oval-Earth — the Great Rock-Falls. This was a broad expanse of ridge, several hundred paces high, over which a steady flow of boulders perpetually avalanched downward into a wide opening in the earth. The noise of the Falls could be heard from twenty leagues away. In the days of tourism, visitors had to approach the Falls with thick earmuffs so that they would not be deafened by the roar; still, the sight was so impressive that many journeyed to see it at least once in their lifetime.

At night, many colored sparks and flashes created by the colliding rocks of the Falls looked like a cascade of flickering stars. Inns had been built on hilltops and at other locations at some distance from the Falls in order to take full advantage of this extraordinary sight. But those days were gone, and the tourist inns had decayed and fallen down. Most of the miners were gone too.

As the travelers worked their way northward across the ravines and through the dense woodlands, Fox-Foot remarked several times on the isolation of the countryside. At one point, she asked Knarry if many wood-gnomes made their home in this region. He said that they generally didn't but was unsure why this was so.

After some further thought on the subject, he commented: "This is inhospitable land for a wood-gnome, despite the many forests that grow here. There is a presence here that is, somehow, too much for us, too big, too overwhelming, perhaps too 'unearthly', if you'll pardon the expression. We cannot detect what it is, but it has something to do with what people call the 'rock-gnomes.' We have never seen them; as far as I know, no one in Oval-Earth has ever seen them. But we know somehow that they are here and that they somehow are not here. They live somewhere under Oval-Earth, but their power is most apparent in this region. Other than this, we know nothing about them." Knarry fell into a long meditative silence.

Fox-Foot avowed, "I should like very much someday to see a rock-gnome."

Knarry rejoined, "Fox-Foot, if there is anyone in all of Oval-Earth who will ever see a rock-gnome, I believe it will be you."

The travelers moved northward. Knarry took note of the extraordinary and forbidding landscape they traversed. Abounding cataracts plunged down from the jagged spurs of steep precipices, spraying the narrow footpaths with torrential currents and making them muddy and treacherous. Swags of stunted trees overhung the misty chasms below that echoed with the howl of whirlwinds channeling their way through yawning rifts and ledges bristling with wild thistle and gloomy heather. Here and there, deep fissures cleaved the earthen crust and emitted the steamy, sulfurous breath of geothermal energy, posed to spew the embers of its cataclysmic brood into the sky. It was no place for a human being; it was no place for a wood-gnome either.

By dusk of the second day, they entered a more welcoming terrain and began to look for a campsite for the night. They were ready to prepare a clearing in the woodland when they heard in the distance the steady, powerful clanking of metal against metal. Knarry listened for a while.

"I would guess by that sound that we are close to a village of some sort," he said. "It must be a smithy, though I admit that I have not heard the sounds of a smithy since I was a mere sapling—I mean, stripling. Anyway, a smithy usually means a village nearby. We need not be anxious about entering it because I'm sure we are far ahead of any news that could be concerned with us. And, frankly, we need some provender for tonight and for our journey tomorrow. We must take the risk."

Several minutes later, the group entered a small, run-down mining settlement. Not more than a dozen old ramshackle houses, each one leaning precariously against the other, comprised the full extent of the settlement. The houses looked deserted: their windows were broken or boarded up, and many of their doors, loosely slung on twisted hinges, swung out on dilapidated porches whose posts were toppled over, whose floorboards were mostly pulled up, and whose former railings had long since disappeared. Some of the doors slammed back and forth randomly with the wind.

A house at the far end of the village was larger than the rest, but its second-floor balcony had partially collapsed, and a large sign dangled aslant from the roof. It said: "General Store." Clearly, the store was no longer in business. In the middle of the village was a house that showed some sign of life, for a dim lantern flickered beside its door. It was a tavern with a battered shingle swinging over its entrance in the late evening breeze. It read: "The Red Ruby Café." The faded image of a ruby gemstone could just barely be made out beside the words. Many of the windows were partially boarded up, giving the place a squinting, sneering appearance. Knarry asked the others to wait for him outside as he entered the tavern to inquire about lodging for the night.

Inside it was dark and particularly gloomy: a single oil lamp hung above an old wooden bar shedding an uneasy yellowish-red glow over the rough-hewn tables and chairs. The bar itself was built at a curious downward angle, as if it were a chute of some kind. An unshaven, bedraggled-looking man with a bullish lump of a head and a patch over one eye sat behind the bar and was wiping out some ale mugs with an oily handkerchief—presumably the same rag used to clean off the oil lamp when that was necessary.

"Mine host, I presume," Knarry exclaimed to him cheerfully, assuming the attitude of a boon traveler looking for good fellowship and a fine dinner in a local inn.

"What!" the barman growled back. His single eye rolled around its grimy socket and fixed Knarry in an angry stare.

"Ah, the innkeeper, I presume," Knarry continued in his cheerful mode, "My friends and I seek your gracious—"

"No vacancy!" the barman cut him off.

"No vacancy? But there's not a soul in—"

"No vacancy!"

"Sir, I ask only for a night's—"

"Be off with you! Clear out! No wood-gnomes allowed!"

The barman rolled his eye back to his mugs and his oily handkerchief, even as he raised a thick, hairy arm and pointed to a sign over the bar. "Wod nooms not welcom heer" was spelled on it in clumsily painted letters.

Knarry meditated on how easily he could take this poor excuse for a human and wipe off the filthy counter with him. Instead, with gentle words of farewell, he retreated from the tavern and stepped out into the street again.

"No use going in there," he said to his companions.

"I thought so," said Tundra-Bear. "But let us follow the sound we hear. One who can swing a hammer like that has a spirit such as we have not yet seen in the lowlands. Let's go and see."

As the travelers walked up the lane past the remaining houses in the settlement, a small band of ragged miners, all packed and leaning together, stumbled by them, singing loudly and veering unsteadily back and forth from one side of the path to the other. It managed to maneuver its way up to the front door of the inn, crowded up against it, and seemed to fall through it all at once. The door swung shut behind it. The singing, now muffled by the closed door, turned into a medley of croaking and baying, punctuated by the sounds of ale mugs sloshing and sliding down the wooden ramp of the bar and slapping into the miners' impatient hands.

Beyond the settlement, a lane wound up a hill and through a grove of trees. There, in the evening light, the group could make out a large, powerful dwelling made of tree-length logs fixed together with black iron fittings. It had several sections to it; the central section was a tall, wide house, three stories high with a majestic balcony on its third floor. A cheerful light glowed from its sturdy windows. A smaller section to the right was a single-story shed whose doors opened in the front. To the left, a commodious barn with attached corrals and outbuildings could just be made out in the half-light of the evening.

The companions made their way up the hill and looked into the shed. A blazing fire lit up its interior. There, a bearded man of huge proportions swung a weighty hammer against a red-hot slab of steel laid out on an anvil. They watched in awe. None of them had ever seen a sight quite like this before.

In a pause between the blows, a woman's voice suddenly called out, "Hrudan!"

"What is it, Illyria?" he answered as he rested the hammer.

"We have visitors," she shouted back. The group turned around and saw a slender, elegant woman leaning from the balcony in the upper section of the house. She was dressed in a well-fitting purple robe gathered neatly around her. Her auburn hair hung in two long braids over her shoulders.

After Hrudan had laid the hammer on the anvil and replaced the red-hot metallic plate he had been working with into the mouth of the furnace, he emerged from the smithy and walked towards the visitors. His rough leather tunic and powerful limbs glistened with sweat. Black wavy hair and a dense, curly black beard framed a majestic face with piercing blue eyes. He was covered with coal-black soot from the smithy. The strange company of a wood-gnome, two Hill people with their green hair, and a forest cat aroused his immediate curiosity. He greeted them heartily and asked what they wanted.

"Victuals and a place to spend the night," replied Knarry.

Hrudan looked at them steadfastly for a moment. He wondered why they were traveling through this region. No one had been by for years, except for the occasional prospector and the unruly bands of miners who were more of a nuisance than a real threat. As he hesitated, Illyria called from the balcony, "Have them come in. They are welcome."

"By all means," echoed Hrudan. He led them to the door and ushered them into the house, where Illyria had descended from the upper floors and was waiting for them. Hrudan returned to the forge, extinguished the fire, poured a bucket of cold water over himself, wiped himself off and came back to the house.

The travelers had never been in such an impressive domicile. It was built like a fortress, with whole trees fitted perfectly into place. The front room was a large hall-like edifice, two stories high, with an interior balcony that encircled the entire room. A massive carved staircase at one side of the room led up to the interior balcony. A series of rooms seemed to lead off from the balcony at regular intervals.

Intricately woven rugs were draped over the railings of the balcony and tapestries bearing ancient heraldic symbols hung from the walls. Some of these symbols showed curious animals of various kinds. At the far end of the hall, a huge stone fireplace blazed with logs. A long iron spit traversed the fire and sizzled with roasted eels that were suspended like thin strips from the spit. On a table in the center of the room was a loaf of black bread and a steaming cauldron of broth.

Illyria invited the guests to the table. "We were just about to have our evening meal," she said. "We are delighted to share it with you." The travelers deposited their various accoutrements on an oaken chest and sat down at the table. Bomsiell crouched down by the chair at the head of the table and waited.

Hrudan disappeared for a few minutes up the staircase and into one of the upper chambers. Later he reemerged, cleansed of his smithy's smoke and grit and dressed in a fine white linen robe that came down to his feet and was bound at the waist by a wide leather belt with a shimmering brass buckle. He bore himself regally to the head of the table and sat down in a magnificently carved oaken chair. Bomsiell peered up at him with astonishment.

Meanwhile, Illyria had exited from a side door at the far end of the hall to go to the stables behind the house. She reappeared shortly afterwards, accompanied by a young man of about sixteen years old. He was tall and dark-haired with strong features, and large, dark, glowing eyes. Illyria introduced him to the guests: "This is our son," she said. "His name is Erudan." Erudan sat down at the table looking rather closely at Tundra-Bear and Fox-Foot. He had never seen Hill people before. His gaze rested upon Fox-Foot for a moment; women of the lowlands rarely possessed such startling beauty.

The meal was eaten initially in silence as Hrudan presided, while Illyria served the hot broth and bread. Hrudan then asked the guests questions about their homelands and families. Erudan was fascinated with Bomsiell and wanted to find out everything about her. When the first course was finished, Hrudan went to the hearth and tended to the roasting eels. When he had basted them for a final time, he brought them to the table. He sliced off one generous portion of eel and extended it to Bomsiell. She stood up on her hind legs and eagerly pulled it down to herself on the floor. She gazed at it for a while, waiting for it to cool.

The visitors, who had never seen or tasted eel before, were puzzled at first about how to eat these long, spiny slabs of meat, but they watched the deft movements of their hosts in detaching the succulent flesh from its wiry skeletal cage and were soon able to imitate them. Bomsiell, however, when the slice of eel had cooled, ate her entire portion, bones and all. The food was delicious to the travelers, who had been almost weak with hunger.

After the meal was finished, Hrudan invited the guests to sit by the fire. Illyria and Erudan joined them. Hrudan asked them what sort of journey they were making. Knarry looked briefly at Tundra-Bear and Fox-Foot, who nodded approval at his implied request. Hrudan and his family clearly could be trusted.

Knarry turned back to Hrudan and declared, "We are fugitives."

Hrudan seemed to be completely unmoved by this startling utterance. He pronounced rather solemnly, "There is nothing to run *to* in Oval-Earth. Therefore, those who are running *from* something must be going, more or less, in the right direction. And whatever your situation is, to have brought you to such a remote outpost of human habitation and to have brought Hill people out of their blessed isolation, it must be sufficiently urgent to merit the deepest interest. Therefore, do proceed, and have confidence in us."

Knarry once again turned to Tundra-Bear and Fox-Foot. They were a bit taken aback at the formality of this speech. But it also comforted them. Knarry looked at Hrudan again and continued. Before the flickering glow of the fire, he related all that he knew: the story of Garug-Caroch, the Splinter of the Ancestral Tree, the riotous outcome of the gathering of the clans.

Hrudan, Illyria, and eventually even Erudan, interrupted him with many questions; sometimes Fox-Foot inserted some detail or other that Knarry had overlooked, and Tundra-Bear occasionally offered a further explanation of a point. When the storm of the winter solstice was related and Bomsiell's name was mentioned, she yowled and wiggled her four ears. How Knarry wished she could talk so that she could tell the full story.

Hours later, as the fire burned low, Hrudan sat in silence, thinking about all that had been told him. "I wish I knew how to help you," he began. "Here in Oval-Earth we have lost our history. Nothing makes sense to us, because we don't know how things got to be the way they are. We attribute everything to the War of Desolation, about which nothing is known. Other than that, there is no history.

"Many generations ago, my forebears moved out to this remote region of Oval-Earth in order to be away from the disaffection of the Oval-Earth peoples. It was like leaving a plague-ridden city, even though we have occasionally returned and found there exceptional persons, men and women whom we have brought back here to be our spouses and to perpetuate the family line. Now there are left only myself and my wife, who is from one of the old manor families of the Downs, and my son. Soon my son must venture out to seek a wife for himself.

"Over the generations, we have become ironsmiths—welders and molders of axes and plows, saws and picks, and other instruments used by the miners of the region and by the timbermen and farmers of the nearby districts. The need for these implements, however, has fallen off in recent years, though I still make them in hope that one day Oval-Earth shall recover its soul and shall know once again the love of shaping things and making them grow."

Knarry looked around the great hall as Hrudan spoke. He had never before seen a lodging built with such craftsmanship. He wondered why the hall was built as it was and what the meanings of the tapestries were. Finally, he asked Hrudan about these.

Hrudan replied that he did not know. There was much that had come down to him through the family line that he did not understand. At this moment, Erudan suddenly interjected, "Show him the Battle-Axe, Father! That is the best of all!"

"Run and bring it to me," Hrudan answered. Erudan leapt from his seat, bounded up the carved wooden staircase, and vanished into the darkness of the upper chambers. He returned holding something large and heavy, wrapped in a linen coverlet.

"Reveal it," said Hrudan, with a magisterial tone of command in his voice.

Erudan unfolded the linen coverlet. The visitors peered down at an enormous Battle-Axe. It was glaringly bright and ornately designed. Its double blade was etched on both sides with an ancient script that none of them could read; and its handle was coiled with sturdy threads of bronze intricately designed and wound around each other. Knarry picked it up and turned it over in his grasp. Despite his considerable strength, he found it difficult to wield. But he could sense some deep power latent in the Axe—not a power like that of the Splinter, but more like—well, like some infinitely greater power, perhaps like the power of the Song. He wondered vaguely if the inscription on the glimmering steel of the Axe was, in fact, the Song of the Eternal Aeons. He asked Hrudan to say more about the Axe.

Hrudan explained, "This Axe has been passed down through generations of my family. We do not know what it signifies or how it was originally used. It is said to predate the War of Desolation—that is all we know."

Tundra-Bear now handled the Axe. "What a beautiful thing," he said. "I have never seen a thing fashioned by human hands that was finer than this. And what power tingles in its heart! Against this Axe, no winterbeest would stand, even the most gigantic and ferocious of them. If only I could have one like it."

Hrudan laughed, "But that is impossible. The Axe has been made with a skill of metals and a skill of smithing that goes beyond anything we could ever dream of in our time. It is like some of the ruined buildings made by Ospeth in the ancient Capital—yes, even like the Library and the Gate-Tower at the College of Wisdom. We do not possess anymore the knowledge to make such things. We do not even know how to repair them. My recent ancestors have become smiths for no other reason: to emulate one day the skill it took to make this Axe. But we are far from achieving such a consummate goal."

"What did your ancestors do before they became smiths?" Fox-Foot asked.

"I do not know what the ancestors did," Hrudan replied.

"I, too, will be a good smith," said Erudan.

Illyria smiled. "And I think it is now a good time for everyone to take his rest. It is late. We will have provisions ready for you in the morning. Your journey to the Northern Taiga will be difficult, but tomorrow we can give you help to find the right way."

As Bomsiell curled up by the dying embers of the hearth, Illyria led the guests to the upstairs rooms. Carrying a candle, she mounted the stairs in front of them and proceeded along the balcony until she had come to the appropriate doors. In each room she lit candles for the use of the guests.

Never had they anticipated, or even seen before, such luxurious accommodations. Each room had a fine large bedstead with carved posts and beautifully woven canopies. Brightly hued carpets of symmetrical floral designs covered the floors. The walls were made of carved wooden panels depicting scenes of various kinds—perhaps an Oval-Earth of another age with proudly armed moose riders galloping down well-paved roads, fishermen hauling in heavy catches of fish, farmers harvesting abundant crops, a fine city with magnificent buildings, and tiny gondolas navigated by the miniscule Gethsarbim through the misty waterways of the Moor-Plains. Knarry even recognized the College of Wisdom depicted in one of the panels: in the carving, the Gate-Tower stood firm and strong, and the Library was not surrounded by a retaining wall.

There were mysterious pictures as well. One of them showed a princely personage sitting on a throne and holding a lyre on his lap. He was dressed in magnificent regalia; yet the top of his body was doglike in form with flippers for arms, and the lower part was that of an aquatic creature with a long tail and flamboyant tail fins. His flippers seemed to caress the strings of the lyre. Another picture showed heavily robed men standing on top of a tower and staring into the sky. Yet another carving depicted a group of men and women dressed in bird feathers.

Knarry asked Illyria about these pictures. She explained, "The meaning of many of these carvings has been lost. The picture of the men on the tower most likely depicts the ancient Brethren of the Wakeful. Now, of course, they are known as the Drowsers."

She turned to the images of the doglike creatures with fishlike tails. "The figure of the prince with the lyre is unknown, but old legends in the Downs, where I came from, spoke of several lost races of intelligent creatures. One of them was the Hydro-Sylph creatures, who lived, it was said, in underground rivers that flowed beneath the Golden Mountains. On various festive occasions during the year, they would emerge from their caves and swim down the River N'ea to join in the Oval-Earth celebrations. It was also said that they were lovers of poetry and spent much of the day reciting poems to themselves and others."

Illyria pointed at the carvings of the people dressed in feathers. "Another race was the People of the Wind, who could tame birds of whatever kind and dressed in garments woven of feathers. Whereas no account of what happened to the Hydro-Sylphs has survived, it is said that the People of the Wind left their ancient home in the Woodlands of Morbihan by migrating over the Golden Mountains.

"This is strange because we do not know of any way to cross over the mountains. But perhaps the People of the Wind found such a way, because they made many forays into the remotest parts of the mountains in their efforts to tame the great scarlet eagles that used to roost there on the highest peaks. But these are all folktales. We do not know the truth of them."

"And what is this creature here?" Knarry asked as he pointed to a carving of a tall, four-legged creature with a broad arched neck covered with a mane of long hair. "It looks like a moose, but it has no horns, and it is much more noble-looking. Some of the tapestries downstairs also depict animals like these."

Illyria was puzzled for a moment. "It is called a 'horse,'" she said. "I am often surprised when people don't recognize it, because it has been a common enough word in Oval-Earth, at least in the Downs, though the creature has been extinct for many aeons. I tend to forget that few know what it actually looked like. But yes, that is a horse. It must have been a beautiful animal. They were not all of the same color, as is the moose. They were black and brown and white, and ruddy colored and tan, and there were many kinds of them. Herds of horses used to roam the Downs."

Knarry was lost in thought. "It is strange, Illyria, but during the winter storm, when Garug-Caroch sent me two verses of what I take to be the Song of the Eternal Aeons, he included other scraps of parchment in the leather pouch he tied around Bomsiell's neck. On many of these scraps were written a single word, as if they were pieces of a puzzle that he was trying to fit together. On one scrap of parchment, he had written prominently the word 'horses.'"

Illyria commented, "It must be a word in that Song you talked about at supper."

She left the guests to care for themselves. Knarry admired the bed in his room but did not need it. He removed his bark boots, blew out his candle, and stationed himself in the middle of the room on his huge, wedged feet, still encased in their scarlet-rimmed stockings. Soon he was asleep.

Tundra-Bear and Fox-Foot did not need their candle at all. In the darkness, they tumbled down into their bed together and laughed in surprise when they found themselves sinking into a soft coverlet. Their idea of a comfortable bed was a wooden board with a flaxen cloth stretched over it. In the winter, a winterbeest pelt might be added to that. But they were soon accustomed to the pliant bedding and even rather enjoyed it as they bounced up and down in it, still finding it to be immensely funny and laughing themselves to sleep. Why would anyone need something soft to sleep on? Wouldn't it be bad for the bones and twist them all out of shape?

Downstairs, Hrudan helped Illyria and Erudan clean up after the evening meal. He carefully wrapped the Battle-Axe in its cover. Erudan began to carry it to the foot of the stairs when a loud pounding was heard against the door.

"Some drunken miners," murmured Hrudan, "looking for something to drink, I suspect."

He walked to the heavy wooden door, unbolted the fastenings, and swung it open. In the darkness, the swollen, bullish head of the innkeeper from the Red Ruby Café leered at him with his one eye. Beside him stood a ragged man in a torn-up imperial uniform—a tax-collector without doubt! A crowd of drunken miners pressed up from behind them. Some of the miners were chanting, "Reward! Reward!"

The innkeeper from the Red Ruby Café spoke first. "You got that wood-gnome in here?" he bawled.

"He came in this direction. We saw him! Those two with the green hair —we saw them too! They all came in this direction," several voices shouted from behind.

"And a huge cat, a lynx maybe, something, but with four ears," another voice shrieked. "What kind of critter could have four ears? It couldn't be up to anything good."

The tax collector burped and rubbed his eyes. He had obviously been loitering for a while at the Red Ruby Café before he managed to work up the courage—or the arrogance—to fulfill his presumed duty. "It's a crime, you know," he mumbled, "to harbor fugitives from the law." The exertion of making this declaration practically caused him to fall over the doorstep into the front room. He added, "I will have to take them into … into … yes, into [burp!] custody."

The crowd of miners cheered his little performance and began once more to chant, "Reward! Reward!"

Hrudan replied, "Who my guests are is a matter that concerns only me. Further, as long as they are here, they are protected by guest rights, and I am the one whose civil duty and responsibility it is to guarantee those rights."

The innkeeper shouted back, "We'll see about that!" With a powerful shove, he pushed his way through the door. The tax collector and the crowd of miners cascaded through after him. In another powerful shove, they found themselves ejected backward out the door in a rolling heap of arms and legs. The tax collector seemed to drop out of nowhere directly on top of them, followed by the innkeeper. The door slammed shut behind them.

Hrudan turned to Erudan, who stood close by, still holding the Axe, and told him to warn the others.

But Illyria intruded. "Let them sleep," she said. "We have handled this kind of situation before and can do so again. I will make sure that the rear doors are sealed and that no ground-floor windows are open. I will secure all the internal shutters."

She ran off to the rear of the dwelling while Erudan handed the Axe to his father, who unwrapped it. Its deep inner powers quivered in Hrudan's hands. "I don't think we will need this," he said to himself, "but I want to be sure."

He followed Erudan up the stairs and climbed another stairway up to the third floor, where a door led out to the exterior balcony. Below him he could see the drunken crowd weaving its way back to the settlement. They were swearing and complaining and rubbing sore limbs. They would certainly fortify themselves with additional ale at the Red Ruby Café, he thought, but they would be back.

Erudan took over the watch on the outside balcony, while Hrudan went below to work out a strategy in case the crowd should return. Peculiar noises could be heard from the settlement. Boards and timbers were being stripped from some of the abandoned houses, and a great deal of thumping and banging indicated that something was being made out of them. Illyria joined Erudan on the balcony.

She remarked, "I wish they could put that kind of effort into repairing some of the buildings in the settlement, instead of tearing them down and building whatever it is they think they can use against us!"

An hour later, Erudan whispered from above that the crowd was again making its way up the path to the house. They carried with them a make-shift wooden scaffold or ladder. It was a wide, loosely constructed web of boards, ropes, and vines, all supported on two long wooden beams. Hrudan instructed Erudan to keep him informed of exactly what was happening. Illyria, meanwhile, fetched two long poles from the interior of the house.

The crowd, led by the innkeeper and the tax collector, swayed and tottered up the path, this time more unruly than ever. With a great deal of pushing and bickering, they managed to stand the scaffold straight up in the air directly in front of the house. It was about two and a half stories high. With a heave, they brought the scaffold smacking down against the third-floor balcony. Then they began to climb onto the scaffold and to scramble like beetles up the viny webbing. Erudan called down to Hrudan to ask if they should try yet to push the scaffold over from above. Illyria and he braced the poles against the two long beams but could not budge it.

"You won't be able to do that now, not with all that weight on it," Hrudan proclaimed from down below.

Hrudan waited a moment, unbolted the door, looked to see if the time was right, and rushed out through the door. Two miners, who had not yet mounted the scaffold, ran off as soon as they saw him. The rest were over his head on the slanted scaffold. The innkeeper, who was at the front of the mob, had practically reached the level of the balcony. Hrudan swung the Axe around his head. It began to glow in the darkness of the night. Then, with two whizzing swings in each direction, Hrudan cut clear through the base timbers of the scaffold. The lower ends of the long beams flew off into the distant woods with a crash.

A cry arose from the climbers as the scaffold abruptly jolted downward and landed upright on its new base, closer to the house but wavering slightly back and forth. Gradually, as the mob panicked, the scaffold began to tilt backward until finally, with a firm nudge from Illyria's and Erudan's poles, it hurtled downward into the grove of trees in front of the house. Many of the miners grabbed at branches as they fell through the thick foliage. Others hit the ground with thuds, cracking sounds, and screams of pain. The innkeeper, meanwhile, dangled from the railing of the balcony; Erudan politely loosened his fingers, so that he fell straight down in front of the door, where Hrudan caught him, whirled him about by one leg, and tossed him clear over to the grove of trees, where he knocked over the tax collector, who was just picking himself up.

The squirming mob managed to disentangle itself with much effort and scurried back down the lane to the settlement, many limping and moaning or grasping elbows or heads or broken noses. Several of the more irate and still intact miners started punching at the tax collector (for "dereliction of duty," as they drunkenly bellowed), and the bullheaded barman had lost his eye patch, revealing a cavernous reddish pit that matched the bloody hole in his mouth where several teeth had been summarily knocked out.

Hrudan reentered the house, wiped off the Axe, and wrapped it in linen again. "That's it for tonight, I guess," he called up to Erudan and Illyria. "Let's go to bed. That's all the power that the settlement can muster at present. But, in a few days, it will be different. We need to make plans; we are now involved with the destiny of our guests, whether we like it or not." During the entire episode, the guests had not awakened. Even Bomsiell purred softly by the hearth with an occasional twitching of her ears.

The following morning, the visitors arose early. Erudan went off to the moose stables to fetch fresh milk for breakfast, and Illyria mixed fresh berries with honey to make a delicious fruit compote. After breakfast, Hrudan and Knarry conferred for more than an hour. Hrudan was familiar with the western regions and could show the way to the escarpment that fringed the Northern Taiga. He was also concerned about the information that Knarry had imparted to him the previous evening and desired to participate in the task that the travelers were carrying out.

After the conference was over, the whole group came together and discussed the plans. Hrudan, it was agreed, would accompany Knarry, Tundra-Bear, Fox-Foot, and Bomsiell on their journey to the Northern Taiga. Illyria and Erudan would seek refuge in the Hills in Tundra-Bear and Fox-Foot's village. They all recognized that the Hill Country might be the last place to hold out if the crisis in Oval-Earth came to a head. It would need leadership and links with the lowlands. With Tundra-Bear and Fox-Foot's consent, Illyria resolved to use their village as a base to organize a defense of the Hill Country against any force that set out to destroy it; and Erudan would be useful in setting up communications with the lowlands, if necessary.

"Don't worry about your lodge," Knarry said to Hrudan and Illyria. "With the earth-power of the Splinter and what I learned about sealing from

Garug-Caroch, no one will be able to enter this dwelling without possessing some extraordinary source of unsealing. You will even be able to put your moose herd out to pasture without worrying about their being molested. But leave them here. If you travel with them, you will attract too much attention. We now know how quickly news can travel, even under the present conditions in Oval-Earth."

Fox-Foot assured Illyria and Erudan that they would be welcome in her village and in her house. She gave them a message to carry to Swallow-Flight and elaborate directions about how to get there. "Be sure," she instructed them, "to pass behind, not in front of, the Claha-ain Plateau. Don't pass through Cantanteroff, and don't use the Regional Road. Ascend directly into the Hills at the southwestern base. There are hunting trails there that the Hill people of the area can lead you through." Her sense for the stratagems demanded by the task ahead of them was maturing quickly.

Tundra-Bear found a Hill longbow among the small arsenal of weapons in the upper room where the Battle-Axe was kept, and he trained Erudan in its use. Erudan learned quickly.

"It will take time," Tundra-Bear told him. "When you get to the Hills, be sure to practice each day." Erudan was also equipped with a large quiver full of bright, sharp arrows. "Such bows are made to combat winterbeests and other fearsome creatures. To use them against a fellow human being is never to be done," Tundra-Bear warned him.

After a sufficient stockpile of provisions was made, the house submitted to a final check, and all the necessary traveling gear hoisted over shoulders or attached to leather belts, the group exited the house by the front door. There they saw the makeshift scaffold of the night assault lying partially shattered in front of the house. Hrudan lifted the entire mass of wooden beams, boards, and vines, and flung it over the side of the hill. After that, he closed up the smithy and the other sheds. Knarry lifted the jeweled casket from his haversack, brought forth the Splinter of the Ancestral Tree, and sealed the main door of the magnificent lodge. Hrudan tried with all his strength to pull it open and could not. Meanwhile, Erudan released the moose herd from the stable to let them run free in the neighboring pastures and woods, where they would be able to care for themselves.

Hrudan drew Erudan and Illyria aside to bid them farewell. He embraced both of them and spoke with them for a long time. After Erudan and Illyria had said goodbye to the others, Hrudan accompanied them for a few hundred paces as they began their southward journey towards the Hill Country.

He returned alone. His face was deeply shadowed by grief. He wrapped a large black cape around his shoulders, attached the Battle-Axe to a strap that he slung around his right shoulder, and hoisted a huge pack of supplies over his left shoulder. With a brief gesture bidding them to follow him, he led Knarry, Tundra-Bear, Fox-Foot, and Bomsiell down through the settlement and past the Red Ruby Café. In the early morning light, its boarded windows seemed to squint even more than they normally did.

There was no sign of the miners or of the previous night's activity, except for remnants of boards, vines, tools, and other paraphernalia involved in building the scaffold that lay littered across the street. Hrudan displayed little interest in that. He knew the countryside well. He chose a path that led northward from the settlement. The companions resumed the journey to the Northern Taiga.

Chapter IV

Kasyan of the Barrows

Towards noon of the second day's trek northward from Hrudan's lodge, Tundra-Bear noticed that Bomsiell was detecting some unusual sound; she would now and then halt in her stride and stand rigid, pointing in a west-northwesterly direction; the tips of her four ears were trembling. Soon he could detect a faint but unbroken vibration in the air. Fox-Foot whispered to Tundra-Bear that she, too, heard a humming in her ears that resembled the buzzing of glacial bees as they entered and exited their icy hives. They mentioned this disturbance to Hrudan. He observed, "Your ears are good, for even though we are still many leagues away, we are approaching the Great Rock-Falls. We will need to prepare for safeguarding our ears from the roar it makes as the cascade of boulders plummets into the earth."

A few hours later, the steady tremor in the air had become noticeable to everybody. Since the itinerary northward would draw them close to the Falls, they wanted to be protected from its thunderous clamor. As they rested for lunch, meting out once again the provisions that Illyria had so well packed for them, Hrudan gave instructions about how to weave headbands from vines wrapped around with leaves and pine needles. Large clumps of heavy moss were attached to cover the ears. Fox-Foot fashioned a small head covering for Bomsiell, who was growing ever more agitated by the distant rumble.

After lunch, the travelers secured the headbands around their ears. Knarry looked particularly outlandish in the crown of branches and knots that surrounded his knobby head, but he took the laughter of Tundra-Bear and Fox-Foot in good spirits. Hrudan was too preoccupied with studying the landscape before him to pay much attention to the amusement of the others, while Bomsiell twice scratched Fox-Foot's covering off her head and flicked it away with one of her paws before she would finally consent to wear it. When everyone was ready for departure, Hrudan showed them several hand signals he would use to lead them safely past the Falls.

Within a league or two, they entered territory curiously lacking in all animate life: there were no signs of birds, moss-mice, or other small animals of the forest. Even the streams ran empty of fish; and the occasional dark-green dragon-beetles and tangerine butterflies of the region no longer paddled through the tremulous air. The travelers tightened their headbands. The air shook with the roar of the Falls; the surrounding forest trembled and throbbed with its vibrations. Knarry wondered how even trees and shrubs could live amid this perpetual uproar. Hrudan shouted, through the rising din, that from this point on, the travelers would no longer be able to talk to one another and would have to communicate with one another by using the hand signals he had taught them.

After crossing over several more hills, and the thin chasms that separated them, the travelers came to the edge of a tall cliff that bordered on a deep abyss. There they stood and gazed across the abyss. On the other side and slightly upward from them, a torrent of brightly multicolored boulders—more like colossal translucent gemstones than like boulders—leapt out of a yawning gap, over half a league wide, in the Golden Mountains and rocketed into the depths of the abyss below.

Knarry knew there could be no natural explanation for such a spectacle. The speed of the falling boulders—the glowing and flashing of their mineral essences even in full sunlight, the dazzling reds and greens and amethysts and deep cobalts and yellow quartzes, and the spinning and colliding of the boulders on their downward plunge—reminded him somehow of the times when he watched Garug-Caroch play the Game of Spheres.

Yet the Game of Spheres was tame in comparison with the power and splendor of the Falls. For the Falls were a living, vibrant force of almost infinite complexity: vast sheets and shifting veils of plunging rocks formed irregular internal patterns within the larger flow of the Falls. Boulders shattered on impact and burst into towering fountains of tiny glowing flakes that arced upward against the surface of the Falls, before drifting downward again with the flow.

The torrent raged and surged and twisted in titanic eddies, while a mist-like haze of mineral dust hovered over the abyss and glittered with sunbeams and the sparkling inner light of the boulders themselves.

What was even more astonishing, in its way, was the realization, within five or six minutes of watching the sight, that the same boulders and shifting patterns of boulders were spinning past again and again at gradually modulating intervals, so that something under the earth was hurling them at immense speed back up through the mountain, out once more into the sunshine, and into their precipitous dive back into the abyss. It was a perfect circuit, a perpetual circular movement of the most extraordinary power. One could be dazzled; one could be lulled forever by the glory of such a sight.

Except for the ear-shattering noise!

Bomsiell took no interest in the spectacle at all. She sat back on her haunches, held her paws over her head, and meowed in pain. Others, as awestruck as they were by the titanic play of force and brilliance before them, were grasping their aching heads and were eager to leave.

Hrudan signaled to the others. He led them along the side of the abyss for two or three hundred paces until they came to the head of a narrow, stony path that crisscrossed sharply down the face of the cliff to a ledge that then circled around one end of the abyss and entered a cavern in the flank of the mountain. They negotiated the path with some difficulty, though Tundra-Bear and Fox-Foot, with their balance perfected by a lifetime of mountain ascents and descents, were able to help Hrudan and Knarry. Bomsiell needed no assistance; indeed, she loped down the twisting pathway with ease and vanished into the mouth of the cave long before the others arrived.

The cave issued into a tunnel that ran behind the Falls for its full length. A section of the tunnel beside the Falls was open and formed a kind of natural window. Here the travelers could look out through the window at the cascade of boulders as if it were a shower of colossal jewels forming a curtain of many-colored light with the brightness of the sunny sky beyond them. But here the roar of the falling boulders was even more unbearable. They groped quickly through the rest of the tunnel.

Towards the end of the passageway, Hrudan made a point of stopping his companions and motioning for them to gather around him; he pointed his arm at the mouth of another narrow cavern that exited from the passageway and appeared to wind down into the depths of the earth. He indicated that he would have something to say about that cavern later on. They continued through the passageway, emerged from beneath the Falls, and ascended the nearby heights. They entered the trembling woodlands once again.

Three hours later, they were relieved to shake the headbands from their ears. Bomsiell tugged off her ear covering with her claws and tossed it into the air, whereupon she chased it, caught it, and playfully ripped it to shreds. Knarry was especially pleased to dislodge the branchy crown from his head. He put it ceremoniously on the peak of a small fir tree and said, "Here, you wear it." The tremor of the Falls, meanwhile, was still in the air, but it appeared muted and distant in comparison with what they had experienced. Fox-Foot announced, "They were right in the old days when they said that everyone should see the Rock-Falls once in a lifetime. It would be hard to go back there again."

The others agreed, though Hrudan added that the spectacle of the Falls at night was even better when the boulders glowed and flashed in the darkness. He had been to the Rock-Falls many times in his life; despite the discomfort, he admired its power and beauty. Meanwhile, Knarry fumbled around in his haversack for a vial of ointment. This he administered to the travelers by putting a drop on the forehead of each. It rapidly cured their headaches. Repacking the vial, he asked Hrudan about the cavern under the Falls.

"It is one of the many things in Oval-Earth we don't understand, Knarry," he answered. "I know that some adventurers in the old days tried to explore it. But they found that the cavern turned gradually into a narrow shaft that seemed to have no terminus. Other shafts trailed off from this shaft, and it appeared to them that an entire maze or network of underground passageways branched out through the depths of Oval-Earth. They were, naturally, afraid of getting lost. Further, the explorers would run out of candles or lantern oil or whatever it was they were using to give them light.

"But most intimidating of all were some stories about occasional encounters with large shapeless creatures that filled up the shafts with an oily, oozing bulk, blocking the way and sliding lethargically along through the shafts. They were so gruesome and repellent that one simply had to flee from their presence, though otherwise they appeared to be harmless. As a result, the explorations were given up, and we don't know where the shafts go."

"This creature, Hrudan, the shapeless bulky thing, what was it called?"

"My memory does not serve me well here, Knarry. It is a strange word—that is all I remember."

"'Ptoloch'? Could that be the word?"

"'Ptoloch,' did you say? That word is strange enough, but it sounds familiar in some way."

Knarry stared at the ground for a few moments. He thought of Garug-Caroch and Twigbottom in the Library. Hrudan pressed him for more information. Knarry demurred for the moment. "We will have time for all these things," he assured Hrudan.

Fox-Foot interjected, "I would certainly not like to go through that tunnel; nor would I like the meet one of those things, those ptolochs, even if they are mainly harmless, as you say."

The travelers spent their third night in a tall, deep pine forest. They were now far enough away from the Falls to enjoy the woodland silence once again. Bomsiell chased a tangerine butterfly (which evaded her), and a moss-mouse leapt onto Knarry's bark boots, exchanged glances with him for a second, squeaked, and scampered away. The forest floor underneath was a thick mat of pine needles. High overhead, through the dense forest canopy, they could see the stars. They made a fire and prepared their evening meal. Tundra-Bear and Fox-Foot broiled some dried eels over the fire and served them to the others with a slice of branmeal cake.

The two of them retired early to sleep together in a small covert of forsythia brush, and Bomsiell clawed her way up to a fork in a nearby tree and curled up there for the night. Conversation at dinner had been sparse, as if the travelers' ears still vibrated with the power of the Falls.

After the others had retired, Knarry sat by the fire and asked Hrudan about what came next on their journey. Hrudan gathered his cloak around himself against the chill of the night. He answered that he was uncertain, for they were entering a region that was once famous, if not infamous, throughout Oval-Earth for its peculiar landscape of small, rounded mounds spread more or less evenly over its surface.

He had heard a rare and unusually enterprising prospector talk about it on one occasion; it was a hollow, desolate, arid land that could be viewed from some nearby hilltops and that seemed to be deserted and devoid of much life except for the thin and thorny scrub one might expect to see in a wasteland of that sort, though dense coppices of chaparral dotted some of the flat areas between the mounds. Even its potential for mineral wealth had not lured explorers into its wilderness of nubs and gullies; or, if it had, these explorers had not come back to tell about it.

The region was not only gloomy in appearance; a legend, current among miners and prospectors about the War of Desolation, associated it with a great "last stand" made by someone or other, and the scarred, hideous aspect of the region was attributed to the intensity of conflict that had taken place there. The land stood, for some reason, accursed; it was known as the Barrows.

"That's the first time I have heard something specific about the War of Desolation, even though it's a legend," Knarry suggested. "A last stand. What could that have been? It sounds dramatic."

"Only a legend," Hrudan repeated.

"Can't we avoid it? Do we have to enter these Barrows?" asked Knarry.

"We could avoid it," answered Hrudan, "but it is, I think, the shortest distance between us — that is, from where we are now — and the conjunction of the Golden Mountains with the western side of the escarpment that borders the Northern Taiga. If we are to enter the forest of the Northern Taiga, as you have urged, Knarry, we must ascend the escarpment.

"Obviously, we don't want to ascend the escarpment at Kyn Ardagh. From what you have told me, Knarry, that approach would be too dangerous. At the edge of the mountains would be our best approach, for, if the escarpment is too steep, we can edge our way up the side of the mountain and cross over into the Taiga at the appropriate elevation. A direct route across the Barrows would take us there. If, instead, we circle around the Barrows, our journey would be longer and we would be pushed over into more populated areas and closer to the Northern Arm of the Radial High-Road.

"The bailiffs of that entire region might well be looking for us by now. I know that is unlikely, and, in any event, we do not need to be afraid of them. But we just don't need the unpleasant incidents and unnecessary delays they could cause us. Further, I do not wish to injure any of them. They are what is left, as little as it is, of respect for law in Oval-Earth."

Knarry nodded his agreement. "But it will be dangerous," he added. "We have no idea what we will find there."

"Unpredictable, and therefore dangerous, I grant. But it is a risk I believe we must take," Hrudan conceded.

On the following morning, the companions mustered their belongings and continued their trek, Bomsiell—as usual—sometimes in front and sometimes behind, Hrudan leading the way, Tundra-Bear and Fox-Foot in the middle, and Knarry bringing up the rear with his heavy tread. By midmorning they emerged from the pine forest and saw before them a wasted, desolate countryside consisting of what seemed to be an infinity of small, rounded hills, baking hot and white in the morning sun. They stood at the edge of the sandy waste and checked their supplies of water and food. Hrudan enjoined them to cross over the edge and into the desert. Immediately they advanced into the parched landscape of the Barrows.

The journey was toilsome and frustrating. Their feet sank into the sandy ground, and dust arose in thick clouds around them, blinding their eyes and choking their mouths and nostrils. The heat was almost unbearable. At times, they stopped and passed cups of water and juices among themselves. Bomsiell lapped water from Fox-Foot's hand, and Knarry wiped dust out of the eyes of Tundra-Bear and Hrudan. But the shimmering heat, the monotony of the endless mounds, and the barren, featureless aspect of the desert turned the journey into a nightmare of aimless wandering.

They even had a sense of hallucinating, for strange shadows passed as bundles of tumble-brush scudded by them across the desert floor, and eddies of wind and dust whirred about them, wiping out their tracks in the sand and giving them the impression that they were standing in one place even as they trudged.

Within several hours, the band had lost its bearings. The mounds were just high enough to block their vision of anything in the distance, so that all they could see was the small circle of mounds immediately around them. Since the mounds were all identical to one another, it was impossible to get any sense of forward motion. Further, it was impossible to climb the mounds. Their cindery flanks provided no foot- or handholds and simply gave way under the effort to scramble up them; and the scar left by the effort was quickly filled up with new sand, so that no identifying mark could be left behind on a mound. The band had the sense of moving in ever-narrowing, ever-more-aimless circles; and, by the late afternoon, they had to admit that they were thoroughly, hopelessly lost.

In the evening, they settled down for the night amid a growth of desert chaparral that grew between two mounds. The gnarled branches of the chaparral provided them with some cover from an unpleasant, dusty breeze that blew steadily over the Barrows. Some deadwood in the area could also be used for making a fire. The travelers sat down together and draped their blankets over two arched pieces of deadwood to erect a makeshift windbreak. Their fire cast an eerie glow over the circle of mounds around them. Here they crouched together and talked. They had to make a plan to get themselves out of the Barrows.

Hrudan admitted to the others that his idea of passing through the Barrows had been mistaken. He simply had not realized how difficult it might be.

Fox-Foot was as cheerful as ever. "We will find a way out," she exclaimed. She came up with a plan. "We will use our arrows as markers to create straight lines by embedding them in the sand at intervals," she suggested.

"Will the arrows stand up in this sand?" Tundra-Bear wondered aloud. He withdrew an arrow from his quiver and plunged it into the sand. Soon it drooped over to the side but was still visible.

"It may work," Knarry said. "We need to try it. We need to try anything." Fox-Foot, Tundra-Bear, and Hrudan all thought it should work and were eager for the morning and a chance to try it out. They had no sooner expressed their confidence in the plan than they heard, uttered in a strange, hoarse voice addressing them out of the darkness: "It won't work."

"You just said it would work, Knarry," said Tundra-Bear, startled by this comment.

"I know I said it would work," Knarry replied. "I didn't say it wouldn't work."

The strange voice grumbled again, "It's an ingenious idea, of course; that I grant you. But, if we look at this logically, it won't work."

"Who said that?" Tundra-Bear exclaimed. The travelers all looked at each other when they heard:

"I said it, obviously. Logically, it would be impossible for anyone else but myself to have said it, given that I expressed a view contrary to what all of you expressed, and I, at least, should hardly allow myself to contradict what I just said; *ergo* ..."

Tundra-Bear and Hrudan sprang to their feet, pushing aside the shelter of blankets, and peered through the darkness in the direction of the voice.

They were immediately joined by Knarry, Fox-Foot, and Bomsiell. A figure sat by the edge of the chaparral cluster. At first, only Tundra-Bear and Fox-Foot could see clearly; but Knarry brought over a flaming brand of the campfire to give some light.

There they saw a large, shaggy dog reclining against a chaparral bush. He was recognizable at once as a Moor-Plains Retriever with golden fur, a black nose, and white tips on his tail and legs. But his forelegs were folded behind his head and his hind-legs were crossed in a distinctly human fashion. A leather pouch was strapped across his shoulders.

And—this was more than they could believe, and for a moment, they thought they were the victims of one more hallucination for the day—he was puffing on a pipe. Yes, smoking a large, curved, blackbriar pipe! And looking very casual and self-satisfied for all that! A fragrant cloud of bilberry smoke rose over him.

"A dog!" Fox-Foot gasped.

"I beg your pardon," the dog protested calmly. "I am not a dog. I am Tristan-Phoros, philosopher and logician, at your service."

"But you look like a dog!" she said.

"Appearances are deceptive," he countered. "That is why we need to exercise our rational faculties."

Tristan-Phoros, bringing one paw from behind his head, removed the pipe from his mouth and, cradling the bowl of the pipe in his paw, pointed the mouthpiece at Fox-Foot. He cleared his throat and said, "Now, can dogs speak?"

"No," said Fox-Foot.

"Can I speak?" said Tristan-Phoros.

"Yes."

"Now, if speech is not a property of being a dog, can a creature possessed of that property be the same sort of creature as one not possessed of that property?"

Fox-Foot pondered for a moment. Her purple eyes glowed in the dark. "You use strange words," she said. "Though I do not understand this word 'property,' I think what you say is right."

"*Ergo*, I am not a dog." Tristan-Phoros returned the pipe to his mouth and puffed on it with satisfaction. His tail, tucked up behind his rear legs, wagged just a bit before he brought it to a rigid halt.

Fox-Foot pondered for another moment. She held up her hand to prevent the others from entering the conversation. "Do all dogs have tails," asked Fox-Foot, staring at the tail.

"Yes," answered Tristan-Phoros, removing his pipe and unable to conceal a slight tone of alarm in his otherwise doggy voice.

"Do *you* have a tail?"

Tristan-Phoros hesitated. He looked down disdainfully at his furry appendage. "I suppose one could call it that."

"What else could one call it?" she asked.

"I grant it is a tail," he conceded.

"*Ergo* (whatever that word means), you are a dog," Fox-Foot concluded with a delighted smile. She was pleased to have resolved this issue.

Tristan-Phoros took several more puffs on his pipe, pointed the mouthpiece at her again, and said, "Do cats have tails?"

"Yes."

"Are cats dogs?"

"No."

"Therefore, not all things that have tails are dogs?"

"Well ... that much is clear."

"*Ergo*, I am not *necessarily* a dog. Dogs may have tails, but, conversely, having tails does not—if you will excuse the expression—'entail' doggyness."

Fox-Foot was confused by this word "entail." How can something "entail" and not have a tail? She was ready to reply when Knarry grunted, "Enough of this! Who are you, and what are you doing here?"

"And why do you object to our plan of getting out of the Barrows?" added Hrudan.

Tristan-Phoros snuffed out his pipe and put it neatly away in his pouch. "I would be glad to discuss these matters with you—but over dinner. It has been a terribly long time since I have had a proper dinner, and what you have brought looks sumptuous—at least to my eyes, since it has been, well, a few days, or perhaps a few centuries, since I have last consumed something of any substance whatsoever, which is to say, consumed anything at all."

The group quickly ushered him into their makeshift tent of blankets and chaparral boughs. In a very doglike fashion he walked on all fours into the shelter. Bomsiell accompanied him. She wanted to be friends and was glad to have another four-footed creature in their company. She brushed against his leg. Tristan-Phoros jumped slightly to the side. "I conjecture that this forest cat, this Bomsiell, as I have heard you calling her, mistakes me for being a fellow animal. She must be disabused of such a notion." Bomsiell looked hurt by this remark and settled down into a sulky crouch at the far end of the shelter.

At the fireside, Tristan-Phoros once again assumed a human sitting position. He was served some dried eel, which he gobbled down with true canine gluttony, ecstatically crunching the wiry bones. Tundra-Bear offered him a small broth bone that he happened to have in his pack. Tristan-Phoros looked away with a mortified expression on his face. "You forget, my dear . . . ah, Tundra-Bear, is it? that my situation is not altogether unequivocal," he pointed out. "This is not to say that I find that little bone you offer wholly unattractive. But I shall not surrender to my impulse to gnaw on it, as strong as that impulse may be."

"Sorry!" Tundra-Bear responded, though he was not too sure he understood what Tristan-Phoros had said.

Knarry raised his questions once again. Tristan-Phoros answered: "I regret that I can tell you really very little. I remember being here in the Barrows, and I can't remember much about being anywhere else. Yet I seem to know a great deal about the rest of Oval-Earth, and I don't understand how I know it, because I don't remember ever having been there. Moreover, I know somehow that I am a philosopher and a logician. Yet it is all in a strange void. Where did I learn to be this? Where did I come from? Why do I have this curious … whatever you want to call it … shape? I mean this appearance that has manifestly caused all of you to mistake me for a dog.

"As for getting out of the Barrows," he elaborated, "you might as well know that I have bent all the resources of my mind for as long as I can remember to solve that problem. The plan you proposed a while ago will not work for reasons I should be glad to explain, for it is a matter of simple mathematics.

"The fact is, my friends, that the Barrows does not exhibit the same kind of time and space coordinates that we are accustomed to under normal circumstances, though how I happen to know what normal circumstances are is a mystery to me. Until we learn how it works, we will never make our exit.

"My charming green-haired interlocutor here (is it Fox-Foot by name?) has proposed maintaining straight lines by lining up arrows. But it behooves me to inform you that in the Barrows, and this much I *have* figured out, straight lines are curved lines. Please do not look at me as if I were daft. The geometry with which we are familiar (I don't know why or how I am familiar with it) doesn't work here. It just doesn't work."

"So, we could be here until we meet our death," said Hrudan.

"Ah, my dear Hrudan, death implies change, and change implies transition from one state to another. Transition from one state to another implies time. Now, there is time here in the Barrows, and there isn't," Tristan-Phoros professed.

"We will not die here, for time in this derelict domain does not operate like that. I do not know how long I have been here in the Barrows — it might be five years; it might be three hundred years. There is little long-range sense of time here at all. Even as space is curiously *bent* here in the Barrows, so is time. And it dilates — it opens and closes, bends and twists, comes back on itself like … like a … a dog … ahem … chasing … ahem … his own tail, if you will pardon the expression."

Tristan-Phoros was embarrassed by his own analogy and wished he hadn't brought it up. He glanced furtively at Fox-Foot and was worried that she might be impelled to continue the tail discussion. But she wasn't paying much attention to him at all. She was impatient for simple, practical answers.

Meanwhile, Knarry thought of the rock-gnomes. This is what the old stories said about them. Somehow the Barrows were part of their dominion—a place not without time but where time had an entirely different meaning; and not without space but where space, too, had an entirely different meaning.

"How will we get out?" asked Fox-Foot.

Tristan-Phoros fetched his pipe out of the leather satchel, loaded it with dried bilberry weed, and picked up a twig from the fire with which to light it. "I hope you don't mind if I have an after-dinner smoke," he said. After several long and meditative puffs, which filled the shelter with sweet, heavy fumes, he began: "I think there is a way. But what we need is a guide."

"A guide!" said Hrudan.

"Yes, a guide. Now the Barrows is, as far as I have seen it, a very empty place. Its emptiness is so profound, so absolutely pervasive, that the presence of one single creature in it becomes—should I say?—remarkable, extraordinary, inescapable. But remarkable to whom? For something to be remarkable, there must be, logically speaking, someone to whom that thing is remarkable. Now there is something remarkable—a presence in this forsaken desert. And to whom is this presence remarkable? Well, the answer, of course, is to me. Hence, there must be at least two of us in this dreary wasteland.

"Now, something *really* extraordinary has happened. The group of you has entered the Burrows—who knows why? Perhaps you will explain eventually—and here we are, all sitting together. We are virtually the biggest crowd to assemble in the Barrows ever in its peculiar non-history. We are, in effect, a teeming multitude, a nation of nations, countless tribes encamped over the desert wastes. Naturally, as such, we are bound to attract a certain attention. If the Barrows has an inhabitant other than me, that inhabitant assuredly has taken a great interest in us. After all, I found you quickly enough."

The travelers looked around a bit nervously. Knarry inserted, "You said, 'if the Barrows has an inhabitant'?"

"Which, of course, it does," Tristan-Phoros went on. "It's probably the most obvious thing about the place. If an empty place shows constant signs that someone is about, that someone is, inevitably, a very important personage. And that someone belongs here in a way I don't, or at least has been around a lot longer, even though the word 'longer' does not always make sense here."

Hrudan asked, "All of this is fine, Tristan-Phoros, but what's the point? Should we find this creature? And how do we find him?"

"Find him?" Tristan-Phoros remarked. "We don't need to find him, my dear Hrudan. He is watching us right now. He has followed you all day, darting from one mound to another and gazing at you with what I presume to be his beady little eyes. After all, I have never seen him directly. But he has been following me around for days, years, centuries, or whatever. He is a terribly curious creature. He has found us. We, on the other hand, need to *catch* him!"

"And that's our solution?" asked Fox-Foot.

"That *may be* our solution," Tristan-Phoros corrected.

"And how shall we catch him?"

"With the proper lure."

"And what will that be?"

"I would think that practically anything would do. You see the Barrows are devoid of all human artifacts. Our inhabitant, if we may call him that, desires some kind of human or even gnome-made thing. I do believe, for example, that, in all his pursuit of me, what he has really been interested in is not me but my pipe, for when I smoke it, I hear the surrounding chaparral rustle and the dust stir just a bit more resolutely than usual.

"Now, I suggest that we just leave something for him — anything that will attract his attention — in the middle of some little gully ringed by mounds. When he attempts to seize the object, we spring from behind the mounds and capture him. It is good that there are many of us, for he is fast, and we will need to block every exit that might be available to him. He runs with the speed of a wind-funnel darting over a desert."

Knarry and Hrudan agreed that the plan sounded excellent. Tundra-Bear and Fox-Foot began to search through their satchels for something suitable as a lure.

Tristan-Phoros cautioned them, "It has got to be good, for we have only one chance at this. If it doesn't work, we may have lost our sole opportunity to escape this infernal wasteland. In that respect, I would like to hazard a proposal."

"Speak, then," said Hrudan.

Tristan-Phoros turned to Hrudan. "The artifact must be the best artifact we've got, for that will be most effective in drawing our hapless inhabitant into the trap. And I rather think you are the one who has it, Hrudan."

"What do you mean?"

"That large object you carry over your shoulder — it must be very important."

"The Battle-Axe!" he exclaimed.

"If that is what it is, then fine; we must use it."

"But what if I need to use it? What if the inhabitant is dangerous?"

Tristan-Phoros cleared his throat and looked attentively at Hrudan. "If something is dangerous to us, do we mean that it is harmful?"

"Assuredly."

"And if something is harmful to us, it is because *its* own well-being to some extent depends on the deprivation of *our* own well-being."

"I agree."

"Now, given that there have been only two inhabitants of this distasteful wasteland, if one was dangerous to the other, then that one would have in some way attempted to deprive the other of its well-being."

"It would seem natural to assume that."

"And since one has nothing here (except one's pipe), the only well-being that one could be, in any substantial sense, deprived of is either one's life or one's pipe."

"I can think of nothing else."

"But have I been deprived of my life?"

"Not that I can see."

"Or my pipe?"

"Obviously not."

"If he were dangerous, I, or my pipe, would not be here now. But I am here now. And so is my pipe. *Ergo*, he is harmless. Of that I am reasonably sure."

Tristan-Phoros's proposal occasioned some debate. Knarry shuffled his thick bark boots in the sand and wondered how they could catch such a swift creature as this who could run "like the wind." He thought of the "hallucinations" they had seen in the desert and imagined that perhaps some of these had been the figure itself scurrying past them with enormous velocity. Fox-Foot and Tundra-Bear suggested a variety of coils and catch-strings they could make from their longbows.

Tristan-Phoros, of course, brandishing his pipe, raised all his "logical" objections and reminded the company to keep their voices down since their potential "raptee," as he called the mysterious figure, was most likely nearby and could hear much of what they, the potential "raptors," were discussing.

Eventually a plan was devised that sounded reasonably effective. In order to begin baiting the trap, Hrudan unwrapped the Axe. After polishing it prominently in the firelight, he went out into the darkness, where the Axe glowed with a strange iridescent light. He swung it around his head several times, sliced through a gnarled bough of chaparral as if it were a wisp of flax, and brought both Axe and bough back to the fire. He wrapped the Axe in its cover and tossed the bough on the fire.

"Very good," said Tristan-Phoros. "Our mysterious stranger has certainly seen it, and nobody could fail to be impressed."

Bomsiell suddenly sat alert and wiggled her ears. They all heard the sound of a soft thump on the sand and scurrying away. "There he goes, the poor fellow. Let's hope we see him tomorrow morning," said Tristan-Phoros, "and this time, face-to-face."

With this final comment, Tristan-Phoros curled himself up, quite doglike, with his tail folded up around his nose, and went to sleep. The others soon were asleep; only Bomsiell stayed awake, examining the dying embers of the fire and watching the shifting sands of the desert as the lavender moons rose and fell over the Barrows.

Dawn rose austerely over the mounds. In the early light, only the tops of the mounds shone with the sun; the rest of the Barrows lay in shadowy darkness. The travelers arose, breakfasted, and quickly dismantled their windbreak and collected their supplies. They knew that to go in any direction at all would be pointless, but they would have to beguile the inhabitant to believe they thought otherwise. They marched off in a determined fashion with Tristan-Phoros at the front, studying the conformations of the mounds as he went, and Hrudan placed strategically at the back of the small caravan.

After an hour or two (as it seemed) of trekking around and through the dusty mounds, they reached a spot that Tristan-Phoros signaled to the others was ideally suited for the trap; five mounds, closely spaced with narrow passages between them, encircled a small depression in the desert floor. The companions traversed the small depression.

Hrudan, still walking behind them, allowed the Battle-Axe to slip from its linen covering and land behind him in the center of the depression. He stumbled forward, as if glad to have been relieved of this heavy burden on a journey that now exhausted his body and spirit.

The travelers passed between the two mounds at the far side of the depression. They quickly assumed their positions. Knarry and Hrudan hid themselves behind these mounds, as Fox-Foot and Tundra-Bear circled around behind the two mounds at the side. Tristan-Phoros, with Bomsiell trailing along beside him, waited with Fox-Foot behind one of these mounds until he saw a thin, wispy figure hop impulsively into the depression; then he and Bomsiell slipped behind the mound in the rear. Now every exit was covered.

Tristan-Phoros peeked out from behind one side of the mound, his floppy ears momentarily erect; Bomsiell peeked from the other side, her ears a-twitter and her eyes big and bright. The figure in the depression had crouched down beside the Axe. "It has worked beautifully," thought Tristan-Phoros. "Now we must catch him."

"Now!" he shouted, though it came out more as a bark than a human shout. Bomsiell sprang; Hrudan and Knarry, with their massive bodies, blocked their passages; Fox-Foot and Tundra-Bear held their longbows sideways to keep anyone from passing through the narrow apertures between their mounds.

Nothing happened. Bomsiell sat on her haunches looking down on a crumpled figure prostrate at the center of the depression.

They stood at their positions for several moments longer. Then they converged in a run. An astonishingly lean, birdlike man, covered with be-draggled red feathers, arms and legs seared deep brown by the glare of Barrows sunlight, and thin white hair sticking straight up on his head, was doubled over in the middle of the shallow pit. The front of his head was pushed into the sand before the Battle-Axe. He shuddered and trembled, and he seemed to be sobbing.

Tundra-Bear and Fox-Foot stepped down into the pit and gently lifted him up. He had a narrow face with a long, beaked nose and a wispy white beard, and indeed, as Tristan-Phoros had supposed, his eyes were small and beady and intensely dilated with fear. His fragile, bony frame shook violently from head to toe.

"You need not be afraid of us," said Fox-Foot.

He looked at her and around at the others. His eyes fixed on Hrudan especially. With some effort, the bird-man opened his mouth, revealing a complete absence of teeth, and tried to speak.

"Your maj-maj," he muttered helplessly, chin and beard shaking, his toothless gums thumping against one another. He gaped at Hrudan with awestruck eyes.

"Quiet now," said Fox-Foot. She helped him to sit down by the side of the pit. The others gathered around and sat as well, putting down their haversacks and blanket-packs and listening carefully. Tundra-Bear offered him some water from a small birch-bark cup, which he lapped up frantically, spilling some of it over his white beard and scraggly red feathers. Fox-Foot asked, "What is your name?"

He looked around again, his tense little eyes darting from one person to another but always back to Hrudan. He tried to say something, but his speech was incoherent. His lips stammered uncontrollably. Once again, he tried.

"Kas-K-K-Kasyan. My n-name is K-Kasyan."

"Kasyan?" she repeated.

"K-Kasyan." The effort to say this exhausted him. He tucked his narrow face into a cage of bony hands. His feathered garment trembled, and as it did, a fine, choking dust arose from it that Tundra-Bear attempted to waft away by fanning him with a swag of chaparral brush.

"Have you been here a long time, Kasyan?" Fox-Foot asked.

"N-no. Y-yes, l-l-long time. I think. No time. No, l-long time," he stuttered as he looked up again.

"What were you trying to say to that man there … to Hrudan?"

Kasyan looked at Hrudan and back again to the Battle-Axe, which still lay on the sand of the gully.

Hrudan bent forward, picked up the Axe, wiped the dust off its blade with a cloth, and pronounced solemnly, "It belonged to my ancestors."

Kasyan continued to shake. "Axe … G-G-Great Axe. Imp-Imperial Axe. Em-Emperor. Y-your maj—"

Hrudan gazed at the Axe and back at him.

Knarry interrupted. "Kasyan, how did you come to the Barrows?"

Kasyan turned his attention to Knarry, who knelt down beside him. "P-people … my people … a long time ago … left … I … I left … left behind … my people …"

"Your people? And where were they going?"

Kasyan lifted a long, stick-like arm covered with his feather garment and pointed a bony finger to the Golden Mountains. "Over there … over there."

"Over there! Over the Golden Mountains!" Knarry cried out. "But that's impossible! Nobody can cross over the Golden Mountains!"

"They cross over, over there … ages … and ages ago … yesterday … ages ago."

Knarry drew a small bottle from his haversack and leaned closer to Kasyan. "I have something for you, Kasyan. A gnome ointment, made from a sap blend rich in earth-power. It will be good for you. Take some." He helped Kasyan lift the small vial to his parched lips and imbibe the sweet, sticky fluid. Another birch-bark cup of water was offered, and Kasyan was quick to gulp it down. In just a few moments, the gnome ointment settled Kasyan's trembling and made it easier for him to speak.

Knarry proceeded with his interrogation. "Why did your people leave Oval-Earth?"

"Because it become e … vil … evil … place."

"And what was making it evil, Kasyan?"

"Because peoples for … get … forget …"

"Yes … forget what?"

"W-w-words," Kasyan stuttered.

"Words?"

"W-w-words, words, the Song. They for-forgetting the w-w-words of the Song."

Knarry stood up and drew Hrudan to the side while Fox-Foot and Tundra-Bear tended to Kasyan. Bomsiell and Tristan-Phoros sat uneasily together at the side of the gully and didn't know what to do with themselves.

Knarry informed Hrudan of what he had been suspecting for a while and now felt he knew. They were in the presence of a living fossil of the ancient civilization of Oval-Earth, a relic preserved by the space-time dilation of the Barrows.

But if it were true that Kasyan was a living fossil, he was also partially mad — his body desiccated, and his mind burned out by the endless heat and desolation of the Barrows.

If only they could bring him out of the Barrows, heal his troubled brain, restore him again — what might they learn, what incalculable secrets about the history of Oval-Earth would be revealed!

Tundra-Bear began talking to Kasyan. "Why did you not cross over the mountains with your people, Kasyan? Why are you still here?"

Kasyan trembled violently once again. "I … afraid. I cannot do it. I left behind."

Tundra-Bear pressed him to explain.

"There a p-pass … a pass through mountains. Narrow, thin, called 'Needle.' So thin called, yes, called 'Needle.'"

"Why is the 'Needle' something to fear, Kasyan?"

"Be-because of 'the Eye.' Must get through 'the Eye' of the Needle."

"An eye of a needle? You mean some opening at the end of the pass, a defile or an arched passage through the rock, or something like that?"

"Yes, that … th-th-that … b-but more."

"And … what is that more?"

"An Eye."

"An Eye? What do you mean, 'an Eye'?"

"Nothing so fearful in Oval-Earth as th-th-the Eye. I saw it. I first to see it. I fled. But my people not afraid. They fought it. And they p-p-passed over the Golden Mountains. I come to Barrows … here ever since."

Kasyan wrapped his arms around his head and rocked back and forth, moaning and quivering. "I fled. I fled. They fight. They are brave. They scale c-c-cliffs, get behind it. But I flee. It come after me, come out of archway, and I flee."

Everyone remained silent at hearing this remarkable confession. Knarry thought once more about the Midland Sea and the Isle of the Drowsers. He remembered how Garug-Caroch told him that the old Commentary on the Song had referred to the island as the Eye of the Universe. But what was this "Eye" that Kasyan had so feared and his people so bravely fought?

Kasyan, as if hearing Knarry's thoughts, murmured partially under his breath, "When g-good Eye close, e-evil Eye open."

"What did you say!" Knarry exclaimed, but Kasyan seemed not to hear and persisted in mumbling to himself, "Someday they come ... come back ... rescue me. I fled ... but I draw it out ... drew it out ... made it.... That day ... my rescue ... be soon."

Knarry looked about distractedly at the others. "Of course, he's mad. We must remember that. Anything he says could be suspect."

"I do not suspect him, Knarry," Tundra-Bear said. "I do not know what this 'Eye' is of which he speaks. But it was a great force of evil. And Kasyan was braver than he thinks he was. If I understand him aright, he was the first of his people to see the 'Eye,' and his flight made the 'Eye' chase after him, drawing it out of the archway, where it blocked the way and was safe from attack. Kasyan made it possible for his people to fight the 'Eye.' He is a hero, and he knows, in a way, that he is. That is why he knows his people shall return someday to find him."

Tristan-Phoros intruded, "A brilliant inference, Tundra-Bear! I wish I could have done as well myself."

"No infer-er-ence, or whatever you said, at all, Tristan-Phoros," Tundra-Bear replied. "It is simple. A hunter of winterbeests knows how simple it is."

Hrudan was eager to pursue other matters: "Did your people migrate before or after the War of Desolation?"

Kasyan looked at him numbly. "War of Desolation? What War of Desolation?" he said. "No War of Desolation."

"Presumably before," Tristan-Phoros whispered to Hrudan, as if to answer for Kasyan. "He has never heard of it."

"And what can you tell us about a place called the Kingdom of Darkness?" Hrudan went on.

Kasyan blinked and shook his head.

"Were your people not fearful of a Kingdom of Darkness that lay beyond the Golden Mountains?" Hrudan added.

" 'Eye' try to keep my people in, not to keep others out."

"Who were your people? What was their name?"

"My people … People of the Wind. Tamers of birds. Red-feathered Riders of the Imperial Dawn."

Hrudan remembered the old carved panel in his lodge and Illyria's legends about such a people who once lived in the Woodlands of Morbihan. And Kasyan, as bedraggled in attire and as wasted in appearance as he was, was dressed, true to the depictions in the panel, in a cloak of roseate feathers.

Hrudan asked further, "Have you ever heard of the Hydro-Sylphs?"

Kasyan gaped at him with his toothless mouth, "Hydro-Sylphs? I know Hydro-Sylphs. M-makers of poems, g-gliders under the mountains. They know what happens … no longer surface in River N'ea. We make migration then, our people—"

Knarry interrupted loudly, "This is madness, *madness!* … Really … I mean, it goes against everything we have ever been taught. Though," he added, "we have not been taught much of anything."

He jumped to his feet and asked Hrudan to join him for a short walk. They strolled around the closest mound. Tristan-Phoros trotted behind, eager to be party to this deliberation. Knarry turned to Hrudan. "We must put him to a test to see if there is anything to what he says. I am going to ask him whether he knows the Song. We must all be alert, for really strange things could happen now." Hrudan agreed to the course of action, Tristan-Phoros nodded his consent, and the three returned to the pit and sat down again.

Knarry resumed the questioning. "Kasyan, now listen to me: Can you tell us the words of the song—the Song of the Eternal Aeons?"

Kasyan flicked around his birdlike head. "You m-m-mean you don't know it?"

"Of course we don't. We know a small part of it—just two verses. If it were possible, we would like to know all of it."

"But why don't you know it? You have it w-w-with you!"

"What do you mean?"

"I know what he means," Tristan-Phoros said. But Kasyan did not give him time to speak further.

"It's w-w-written on your Axe. D-d-don't you see it!" he chirped.

Hrudan seized the Axe at the same moment and gaped at the ancient script etched across the blade. Knarry wrested it out of Hrudan's hands and studied the script.

"But we can't read the charactery!" Knarry shouted back.

"Neither c-can I!" screeched Kasyan, his arms waving back and forth like a stork readying himself to fly.

"Then how do you know it is the Song?"

"Axe known through Oval-Earth to have song words upon it. Only other place . . . on p-p-parchment guarded by Brethren of Wakeful on Eye of Universe in Midland Sea! G-good Eye."

"What is this Axe?" cried Hrudan.

"Im-Im-Imperial . . ." Kasyan stammered. He bounced up to his feet and began hopping around in little nervous steps.

Tristan-Phoros suddenly lurched up from his repose. "Do you know the Song, Kasyan?"

"No, not yet! Let him speak of the Axe!" Knarry barked.

"We need to get out of the Barrows!" Tristan-Phoros snarled back. "That's the one thing we really need to know right now!"

Kasyan was agitated and dazed and happy. His feathers tingled all over him, and he seemed ready to dance some curious bird dance. He bounced in little circles around the rim of the depression. He cawed, "I remember only two verses. They—"

"Wait! wait!" Knarry growled as he rummaged around in his haversack for something to write with. The jeweled casket flew open of its own accord, and the Splinter popped into his hand. Knarry flipped open a small vial of ink with his woody thumbnail, and the Splinter instantly arched over from his fingers and dipped itself into the ink while Knarry flattened out a shred of parchment with his other hand.

Kasyan twittered and somersaulted and hopped around and opened his toothless mouth to sing:

> *Shone forth the aurora,*
> *The thunderous dawn*

> *Shafts aflame*
> *In the brilliant-hued night —*

At once, the Barrows was suffused with strange rosy dew and the fragrance of flowers in bloom. The travelers all sprang to their feet as Knarry wrote wildly on the parchment.

Fox-Foot gasped, "Look!"

Before them stretched a straight path leading to the north directly out of the Barrows.

They pulled their gear together as quickly as possible, but not before Kasyan, in a dazzling leap, had taken advantage of their distraction, seized one of Tundra-Bear's arrows, and catapulted himself across the shallow pit. Tundra-Bear lunged after him and dove headfirst into a dusty mound while Fox-Foot made an effort to catch hold of Kasyan's feather garment. But he slipped away with the speed of a barn swallow and disappeared into the mounds. Fox-Foot was left grasping a few tattered feathers in her hand.

"Catch him!" Hrudan commanded. "We need him."

"Forget about him!" yelped Tristan-Phoros in return. "We need to get out of the Barrows. Run! Run for it! It's our only chance."

Knarry and Hrudan and Tundra-Bear and Fox-Foot hoisted their gear over their shoulders and ran pell-mell down the path through the Barrows, with Tristan-Phoros and Bomsiell loping somewhat casually and cheerfully behind them. Within what seemed both a moment and a long time, they found themselves tumbling down in fatigue at the borders of the wasteland.

From there, they looked back and saw the path close up swiftly behind them. All that was left to their sight was the vast, desolate vista of the mounds stretching out into the dusty haze. They wondered where Kasyan had gone, though it was unlikely that he could have gone anywhere at all.

Their faces, their clothes, and their gear were caked with dust. As they turned from the Barrows, they entered a narrow stretch of forest. Here a slender waterfall purled gently down from ledge to ledge on a towering cliff at their side. It collected in a cool, shady pool at its base. The companions took turns bathing themselves in it and washing their clothes. They dusted off their longbows and haversacks and blanket straps and other equipment.

Hrudan meditated curiously on his mighty Axe and used a linen cloth to polish its shimmering blade. Finally, Bomsiell and Tristan-Phoros sported in the pool, lapping its refreshing, crystal-clear waters.

When everyone had settled down to rest, Fox-Foot expressed her sorrow for Kasyan and for his exile in the Barrows. Knarry consoled her: "He was not ready to leave the Barrows yet, Fox-Foot. For he could have done it at any time, if he had so wanted. The verses of the Song gave him that power. He didn't want to return to Oval-Earth. His people had their reasons for leaving it. And he is confident that one day his people will remember him and come back to rescue him. Meanwhile, he was able to make off with some object of human craftsmanship—an arrow, but I can't imagine what he will do with it."

Knarry leaned back and scanned the cliff that towered high above them. "Does anyone know where we are?" he inquired.

Hrudan answered, "Our destination has been reached, Knarry. You should be familiar with it, though we have taken an unusual approach. We have arrived at the great escarpment of the Northern Taiga."

Chapter V

The Northern Taiga

After a lengthy consultation around the fireside in the evening, in which the puzzling events of the Barrows and the even more puzzling conversation with Kasyan were submitted to interpretations and reinterpretations, plans were made for the course of action on the following day. The project was to climb the escarpment, enter the Taiga, and find the Ancestral Tree.

Knarry could not help but express his anxiety. For a wood-gnome to venture into the hallowed forest while still in the prime of his pre-metamorphosis life was certainly a violation of ancient custom. But it was not unthinkable, and certainly the Grand Council of Elders had resolved upon such a course of action when they sent Rough-Bark's delegation to investigate what had happened to the Ancestral Tree.

What was unthinkable — at least until now—was that humans, and other (as it were, analogous) creatures, could, or would, make such an entrance as well. Knarry, though distraught and truly unsettled, perhaps for the first time in his gnome-life, still had the ability to search through his prodigious memory for any reasons, precedents, or other considerations that would debar his companions from the proposed excursion.

He had to admit that he could not think of any obstacles to the venture. It was just one of those things that, to his knowledge, had never come up in the past, and hence, no one had ever thought about it before.

To all of these somewhat convoluted deliberations, of course, Tristan-Phoros was quick to append his invariably "logical" inferences and deductions, while Tundra-Bear and Fox-Foot saw to the more practical concerns of logistics and movement over what would certainly be difficult terrain.

Only Hrudan was intimate with some of the geographical difficulties that would have to be surmounted.

The most immediate and preliminary problem was the approach to, and the potential escape from, the Taiga. Knarry reminded his companions of the tragedy that had taken place on the Kyn Ardagh in the previous year. This meant that the main approach to the Taiga might be closed or otherwise impassible and that, in any event, some fearsome peril awaited there to block the way.

The best procedure would be to enter the Taiga from the western end where it abutted the Golden Mountains and by directly scaling the escarpment and circling into the forest from behind. In this way, they would evade whatever evil presence was "guarding" the ancient woodland at the high end of Kyn Ardagh. Since the nature and extent of the peril was unknown, any advantage the group could have would be of considerable benefit.

Knarry also resolved that, after the visit to the Ancestral Tree, the descent from the Taiga should be made down whatever was left of Kyn Ardagh, unless some emergency arose that drove them directly to the escarpment, in which case a rapid descent of the sheer cliff would be very dangerous indeed. But Knarry figured, with a bit of "logical" help from Tristan-Phoros, that the alien presence in the woodland might very well be incapacitated once the group had made contact with the Ancestral Tree.

Hence, the way to the crest of Kyn Ardagh and its subsequent descent would now be open. But it was conceded that this might be wishful thinking. Fox-Foot informed the group that she and Tundra-Bear could leave a web of vines suspended over the part of the escarpment where the ascent had been made so that a rapid descent would be possible from there.

Knarry had other motives as well. He informed his fellow travelers that he was acquainted with the wood-gnome Branch-Knot, whose earth-house was situated not far from the base of Kyn Ardagh. Branch-Knot belonged to the primeval clan of the Orugug wood-gnomes, who lived close to the Northern Taiga and who still spoke the ancient tongue.

Since the Orugug wood-gnomes rarely went to the meeting of the clans on Claha-ain Plateau, Branch-Knot most likely would not be aware of the charges brought against Knarry and would not be hostile to him. But even if he had heard the news, Branch-Knot was an old and trusted friend and not one who, under any circumstances, would jump to conclusions and be susceptible to irresponsible gossip. If the descent of Kyn Ardagh were successful, Branch-Knot's hospitality and his snug earth-house would provide a welcome refuge from what assuredly would be the day's challenges and perplexities.

Further, the companions decided that Tristan-Phoros and Bomsiell should not make the ascent but should follow along the base of the escarpment until they arrived at the foot of Kyn Ardagh and there await the return of the others. Tristan-Phoros did not particularly appreciate what he interpreted as being grouped with Bomsiell as a "four-footed" creature unable to make the ascent of the cliff, but he was content not to have to face some disagreeable adventure, especially since he was still recovering from his unpleasant "sojourn"—as he called it—in the Barrows.

He was also glad to have some time to think about all that he had learned from Knarry and the others about the situation in Oval-Earth. Hrudan gave detailed instructions about the journey that Bomsiell and he would have to make, and he told Tristan-Phoros to entrust himself to Bomsiell's instincts in following old paths hidden by brush and finding suitable defiles for crossing through gorges and over ridges.

In the morning, Tundra-Bear and Fox-Foot foraged through the surrounding woodland and returned with armfuls of twisted vines. With the help of Knarry and Hrudan, they straightened out the vines and coiled them into long, tensile ropes knotted at intervals and joined firmly to one another by further slipknots and self-tightening knots woven into the beginnings and ends of the vines. Tundra-Bear and Fox-Foot were accustomed to scaling large, sheer cliffs on their spring hunting expeditions and knew the lore of vine climbing in detail. They instructed Knarry and Hrudan on how to move over the face of the cliff and how to handle the vines as supports and promised to guide them as carefully as possible until they had acquired some practice. They also devised hoists for pulling up the equipment and provisions behind them.

Farewells were exchanged. Tristan-Phoros and Bomsiell trotted off on their journey eastward along the base of the escarpment towards Kyn Ardagh. The others explored the cliff face in a westerly direction until they could discover a promising route up the cliff. Within half an hour, Tundra-Bear noticed a long, thin fissure that twisted up the face of the escarpment. He signaled to the others and, uncoiling the first vine rope behind him, made preparations to start the climb. Both he and Fox-Foot removed their tall linen boots, revealing long, slender feet with somewhat extended and tensile toes. No wonder they preferred to climb barefoot!

Meanwhile, all the climbers attached ropes to the makeshift safety harnesses that Fox-Foot had woven. Tundra-Bear was the first to enter the fissure; he moved upward carefully and quickly. Hrudan entered directly behind him, and Knarry followed. Fox-Foot came last in order to rearrange and secure the vines for a possible emergency descent, as well as to watch for the safety of Hrudan and Knarry just above her. The provisions were left in a bundle at the base of the cliff with a rope attached. The bundle would be drawn up and deposited at various levels as the climb progressed.

Movement inside the fissure was fairly easy: the parallel abutments along the cliff face provided numerous rocky ledges for secure handholds and places to rest the feet. Only Tundra-Bear, as the leader, sometimes had to take risky stretches of the arms or legs to gain new positions ever and ever higher on the cliff. Once in position, he could attach the vine ropes to outcroppings so that the followers could use the knots on the ropes to straddle difficult sections and circumvent overhangs. Although Tundra-Bear had never before attempted a climb of such long duration, he was accustomed to the work he was doing and had excellent balance. The others followed without much of a problem, though Hrudan felt uneasy at times and kept his eyes diverted from the greater and greater depths below.

Knarry, despite his heavy bulk and clumsy appearance, moved effortlessly—his strength, his balance, the curious block-like shape of his feet all helped him cling to the rock face with singular ease. Fox-Foot was as nimble as a mountain-fawn on the cliff and watched especially for Hrudan. Naturally, they took turns climbing, the stationary ones securing those in motion.

Eventually, Tundra-Bear reached a large outcropping and decided to make this their first resting place. He anchored the top vine rope to a bony sprout of granite, and sitting down and bracing himself against the outcrop, he helped to draw in the others. With the strength of Hrudan, the provisions were hauled up from the base of the cliff. The four climbers sat on the ledge and looked outward. They could see below them the Barrows with its arid mounds extending off to the horizon. Fox-Foot imagined for a second that she could see an isolated figure among them, darting aimlessly like a jittery little flea. "I hope he will not be alone for too much longer," she said.

Tundra-Bear entered the fissure again, and the ascent advanced by similar stages all the way up the escarpment. Gradually the climbers could see more and more of Oval-Earth beneath them. They could see beyond the Barrows to the Rock-Falls in the west; later, the Midland Sea, with its white waters and blue island, rose into distant view; and, finally, even the tips of the Golden Mountains of the southern rim could be seen just barely cresting over the far horizon. Knarry viewed the vast landscape with fondness and sorrow. "What a beautiful domain it is," he proclaimed. "What a proper home for us to dwell in, and yet how full of anguish and decay and desolation!"

Towards the top of the escarpment, the fissure narrowed to a thin chimney and disappeared altogether. The last few hundred paces had to be climbed over a bare rock face. Tundra-Bear and Fox-Foot were undaunted by this challenge; from their final resting perch on a protruding shelf of striated pink porphyry, with their longbows they shot vine ropes attached to specially designed cambered arrows over the top of the cliff.

It took several tries, but finally one arrow caught in a stony cleft high above them and, with the rope attached, provided a sturdy brace. Tundra-Bear tested the rope, and with Fox-Foot locking in the lower end of the rope as well as attaching another rope to Tundra-Bear's vine harness, he made a solo climb over the remaining rock face. Once on top, he used several sturdy pinnacles of rock to devise a system of pulleys with the ropes hanging back down to the final way station. Now, with Tundra-Bear pulling from the top and Knarry from the bottom, it was possible to haul Hrudan right up to the top of the cliff. Then he and Tundra-Bear similarly hauled Knarry up the sheer rock face from above. Fox-Foot needed no help — after preparing the final stage of the escape apparatus, she scrambled up the vine ropes with lightness and speed.

As soon as everyone had assembled at the top of the cliff and all the provisions and gear were in place, Fox-Foot and Tundra-Bear instructed the others in the way to descend the web of vines now drooped over the escarpment. At this point, Knarry turned towards the deep, solemn forest that rose over them. He said, "Until now, no human has entered the Northern Taiga, and no wood-gnome has penetrated its hallowed depths until his time of metamorphosis has come. But we must enter—we must find the Ancestral Tree."

The group outfitted itself as a hunting party. Tundra-Bear and Fox-Foot strung their bows and readied arrows for immediate use. Knarry removed the Splinter from the jeweled casket and placed it inside his leather vest. Hrudan slipped the Battle-Axe from its cloth covering and slung it across his chest. They entered the forest.

Knarry had never imagined how vast and deep the forest was. Rank upon rank of solemn trees stood in majestic silence. There was no underbrush, and no animal life stirred in the forest. The stillness was unlike anything the travelers had ever experienced before. The sounds of their footsteps on the fine, grainy soil almost seemed to echo among the lofty treetops. When they spoke to one another, they felt compelled to whisper.

Overhead, the forest canopy arose in jeweled splendor; the leaves seemed to have the brightness of gold-rimmed emeralds. Many of the trees were hung with dazzling fruits and berries suspended like bright globes among their dense foliage; other trees bore lovely crowns of fresh blossoms that opened their petals to the skies. The entire woodland was alive with tender breezes wafting a dozen varied fragrances through its vaulted depths. The trees murmured softly with a strange kind of life.

Knarry could feel the presence of the gnome-souls in them. He could feel them through their silence, their serenity, their deeply contemplative rootedness and kinship with the earth and its rhythms.

But he could also feel an ineffable sadness emanating from the trees—a sign, a call of distress, a muted melancholy causing the boughs to droop and the leaves to sag. League upon league, the travelers wandered through the great forest; one type of tree after another towered above them in sorrowful resignation: sycamore and birch, oak and elm, sumac and persimmon, willow and bilberry and ponderosa and catalume and raisinbill and lollyboly and hickory.

Gradually the travelers entered deeper and older sections of the forest. Beyond these venerable groves, they saw what looked like a clearing. They realized they must be close to the center of the woodlands. After passing through a narrow valley and over a slight rise, they entered the clearing. In the middle rose the shaft of a mighty, towering Tree that stretched far above them into the heavens. It had thick boughs that extended in every direction high over the forest canopy. Its gnarled bark and its powerful limbs with their great fountains of leaves glittered in the noontide sunlight.

But its boughs were drooping, and its enameled, jewel-like leaves were slowly being shed to the ground. Many of them already lay in withered clumps scattered about the clearing. The bark of its trunk showed a thin, deep tear—an open, trembling scar out of which a steady stream of sap oozed and wound its way down the side of the trunk to the forest floor.

Knarry, awestruck by the sight by the great Tree, whispered reverently, "It is the Ancestral Tree." Knarry approached the Tree and placed his shaggy hands gently against the torn bark with the practiced touch of a healer. He remained in this posture for some time, his head bowed in thought. The scar in the truck of the Tree quivered gently under the pressure of his touch. Hrudan wondered if Knarry was somehow trying to communicate with the Tree. Knarry pronounced, tenderly and sadly, "The Ancestral Tree is dying."

The travelers put down their fighting gear and gazed at the Tree.

Tundra-Bear broke the silence and asked, "What will we do?"

Knarry was hesitant to answer. He turned from the Tree and asked the others to join him in a circle. They sat down together. "Now we know that some of our guesses have been confirmed," he said somberly. "The Ancestral Tree has been violated. It must have taken unusual force—and yes, unusual malice—to have done that."

Fox-Foot asked, "But why would someone do it?"

Knarry shook his head. "The only reason I can think of is that whatever wishes to dominate and destroy Oval-Earth felt that a Staff made from the Ancestral Tree would have reservoirs of immense earth-power stored in it. The possession of this Staff would enable the evil forces to weaken Oval-Earth even more than it has already been by deforming the seasonal changes."

"And that worked," Hrudan interjected.

"For a time it worked," Knarry corrected him. "But now the seasons have been restored somewhat, though not completely, to normal. They cannot be fully normal when the Ancestral Tree is languishing and perishing the way it is. So, things can get only worse from this point on, as the life-sap flows out of the gash in the Tree's bark."

"Meanwhile, the Staff . . . ?" said Tundra-Bear.

"Yes, the Staff!" replied Knarry. "The Staff is somehow, somewhere at large. The forces of evil must no longer possess it. But where is it? Garug-Caroch used the Song—that is, the two verses he knew—to remove the Staff from the hands of the enemy. But Garug-Caroch has disappeared and is presumably dead. And the Staff is gone too."

Another long silence ensued as Knarry thought about what should be done. He knew that only by finding the Staff and rejoining it to the Tree would the wound be healed. But how would one go about either task? Then he thought he might do an experiment. "Look," he said to the others, "let's try to rejoin the Splinter to the Tree."

The others were willing to help, but they had no idea of what to do. Neither did Knarry. They all stood up and watched Knarry. He fetched the Splinter out of his leather jerkin and approached the Tree again. The Splinter convulsed violently in his hands, and when Knarry fitted it up against the wound, the entire Tree heaved and trembled to its roots, and its branches shook, bringing down a small shower of dying leaves. But the Splinter refused to stay in place. Knarry tried some sealing techniques he had learned from Garug-Caroch, but these had no effect. As a last resort, he tried gnome-lore healing practices; these also affected nothing.

Fox-Foot interrupted the proceedings. "How about the Song?" she queried. "The Song might be the answer! We have four verses now. It would be very powerful."

"And very unpredictable," said Knarry, who was reluctant to use it yet. "We need to know more about what the Song is capable of before we can invoke it properly."

Suddenly, without warning, Knarry, Tundra-Bear, Fox-Foot, and Hrudan were thrust by some powerful force across the clearing and up against the trees on the opposite side. They sprang to their feet and looked in horror.

On the other side of the clearing stood a creature that, at first sight, seemed to be a winterbeest except that it was larger—much larger—and its skin was covered with craggy, bristling bark. It had huge clawed hands and ferocious, burning eyes that bulged out of a low, bony forehead. It bore a club almost as large as a full-grown tree; out of the club grew great spiky thorns. The gush of air created by the mere swing of that club had tossed the four travelers across the clearing.

Knarry could feel immediately that the demonic creature in front of them had once been a gnome, or was perhaps several gnomes ingested into one, and that some force had reshaped it into the image of a winterbeest and tripled its size. It was nearly twenty paces tall with shoulders four paces wide. Knarry could barely stand to look at its face, for he could recognize in it the horribly deformed visage of a wood-gnome. Its jaws had been stretched forward more than a pace long, filled with the rodent-like teeth of the winterbeest but somehow rehinged. The jaw swung back and forth, slack and loose, while a gigantically distended tongue flapped about inside the mouth like a dying balloon-fish.

But the eyes!

It was the eyes that Knarry knew. They were gnomes' eyes, and trapped in them were gnomes' spirits, horrified at what they had become and at what they were doing even at this moment. The thing bellowed and drooled and shambled awkwardly towards them.

Knarry could not move, his mind locked in horror. But Fox-Foot, followed closely by Tundra-Bear, reacted with blinding speed. Years of combat with winterbeests had accustomed the couple to act with unflinching courage and to move in quickly against their foe.

Even the monster was surprised to see them dart to their bows in the center of the clearing, to arm and take aim, and to discharge two quivering arrows directly into its chest. The action was so fast that it seemed a single movement. But the monster stood fast, gawked downward at the arrows projecting from its chest, and with its free hand, flicked them off, emitting at the same time a thick, grotesque chortle. It went on to slobber in the disfigured accents of a wood-gnome:

"No little human things hurt *me*. I will hurt *you*, tear you to pieces." It continued to speak, but the words deteriorated into grunts interspersed with the sound of the saliva-dripping tongue slapping against the roof of its mouth, sucking in some of its own drool and spewing out the rest in a dense, malodorous spray. It raised its club for another blow.

Tundra-Bear and Fox-Foot leapt to either side of the clearing so that the blow swooped down through empty air, once again causing a powerful gush of wind to bluster through the clearing. Fox-Foot shouted to Knarry as he held on to a nearby tree to keep from being toppled over by the blast. "It's not flesh!" she cried out. "It's made of wood!" Once again, she and Tundra-Bear aimed and discharged their arrows, but with the same effect. The monstrosity saw the arrows coming this time and merely brushed them away.

Knarry, who still thought he held the Splinter of the Ancestral Tree in his hand, faltered and stumbled. If only he could use the Splinter, but he discovered that it had dropped from his hands and landed on the ground at his feet. Knarry was frozen; he could not reach over to retrieve it. Immediately, the monster stomped heavily and slowly across the clearing in the Knarry's direction; its block-like feet sank into the mossy soil, kicking up stones and sand and clumps of moss as it went. Looking at its feet, Knarry realized more clearly that the creature was a wood-gnome, but hideously morphed into the shape of a ravening beast.

The Splinter, meanwhile, buckled and squirmed on the ground. Knarry grew weaker. A force from the monster seemed to reach out and want to absorb him, to uproot him from his earth-ties, to draw him into some dark abyss of enslavement and horror. The story that Garug-Caroch told about Twigbottom in the Library flashed through Knarry's mind; he remembered what Rough-Bark had experienced in the vision when he tried to recover the remaining members of the delegation that had gone to the Taiga.

Knarry felt his own disintegration taking place inside himself, and he struggled to resist it. He also sensed that the monster lusted after the Splinter and was out to seize it. The Splinter twisted and writhed on the ground, its own agony reflecting the inner struggle that Knarry was experiencing.

Knarry felt himself weakening.

The beast now stood directly over him and was raising its club for another blow. Knarry could do nothing to help himself. He was paralyzed. A sap-like sweat poured profusely over his helplessly inert body. His limbs trembled in every joint, trying to respond to his will, but his strength was gone. He bent his head in horrified resignation as he waited for the club to come smashing down upon him. He knew that Tundra-Bear and Fox-Foot could not help.

Suddenly there was an unearthly cracking sound, and the creature reeled backward with an ear-shattering roar. The enormous thorn-club dropped out of the creature's uplifted hands and thudded into the ground behind it.

Planted deep in the monster's chest was the Battle-Axe of Hrudan, and attached to the Axe was Hrudan himself, who grasped the bronze-corded handle. With one leg braced against the monster, Hrudan wrenched the powerful Axe out of its chest, swung it backward in a wide circle, and brought it smacking downward into the chest of the monster again, splitting the creature along its front like a huge log of wood.

The monster toppled backward like a felled tree and crashed over its own immense club, whose thorns now tore into the monster's woody fibers. Shards of wood and whirling splinters flew in every direction through the clearing. Hrudan wasted no time in mounting on top of the fallen hulk, hacking its limbs off with the Axe. Arms and legs and paws and head were lopped off with astounding speed, as the Axe whirred and hummed through the air.

To Hrudan's surprise, it lit up with a dazzling inner light as it hewed and thrust, and the lettering on its blade sparkled and danced in the half-light of the woodland glade. Again, Hrudan heaved the Axe into the middle of the monster's chest, this time splitting the body in two. As the halves fell asunder, a thick ruddy vein of poisonous resin smoked and reeked at the core of the creature.

Almost at once, the limbs of the monster began to assume different shapes — the shapes of wood-gnomes. Hrudan stepped back from the scene of the combat and, along with Tundra-Bear and Fox-Foot, watched with amazement as the battlefield litter consolidated and transformed itself into a small crowd of limp, struggling wood-gnomes.

Just as rapidly, these wood-gnomes, who now lay strewn and helpless over the surface of the clearing, commenced their metamorphoses into trees. Their feet grew into roots that took hold in the firm soil, and their arms spread upward into the sky; their bodies lifted from the ground and narrowed into thin, straight trunks, and their fingers splayed outward in a mesh of dozens of interlaced tendrils, while their heads, of many shapes and colors, turned into dense, leafy fronds. But they were happy, burgeoning, and thriving, and they seemed to cry out in mute gratitude to Hrudan.

Meanwhile, as they did this, Knarry could sense his own strength slowly returning. He recognized who these wood-gnomes were—they were the members of Rough-Bark's delegation that had failed to return to Oval-Earth. Something had absorbed them; some being had enfleshed itself in their substances and taken on the form of a gnome-like monstrosity—borrowing the beast-like shape and deforming it in a material extracted from their future destiny as trees.

Now these gnomes had returned to what they were supposed to be—even if prematurely and tragically passing through their metamorphoses long before it was their proper time to do so. They would have but one consolation for a life cut so short: they would spend the rest of the ages in the shadow of the Ancestral Tree. This itself was an honor and a distinction. But it was an honor and a distinction that would matter little if the life of the Great Tree could not be preserved.

Tundra-Bear and Fox-Foot helped Knarry repossess the Splinter, if not also his composure, and led him back into the clearing that now sprouted eight new trees. All remnants of the monster had completely vanished. An evil vapor seemed to linger in the clearing for but a moment, only to waft away maliciously through the nearby groves and into the forest towards the escarpment. It was returning to the lowlands. At the other side of the clearing, Hrudan stood wiping wood sap off his Axe and studying it with amazed concentration.

Hrudan slung the Axe around his shoulders. He bore his head high; his eyes blazed dark and grim beneath his brows like the eyes of a mountain eagle.

Nobody seemed inclined to talk. They collected their haversacks and equipment and outfitted themselves once more as a hunting party. Further troubles might lie ahead, though the travelers were convinced that the great peril of the Taiga had been met and defeated.

Knarry turned to the Ancestral Tree, which he had tried to heal. The wound still gaped on its barky flank. But there was one change—the flow of sap seemed to have been stemmed just a little. Perhaps the action of the Splinter against the Tree had helped. He did not know. He shuddered inside himself as he realized how close he had come to being absorbed into the wood-gnome prodigy and, with him, his earth-power and his strength.

With a last look at the Ancestral Tree and a promise uttered in his soul that he would one day be back with the purloined Staff, he led the others out of the clearing and into the depths of the forest.

The band moved silently over the gently rolling hills of the Taiga. In a few hours, they came to the edge of the escarpment and looked out over the broad expanse of Oval-Earth. It was late afternoon, and the sun was beginning to set beyond the Great Rock-Falls in the west. Admiring the beauty of Oval-Earth from the height of the escarpment, they hiked along the brink until they arrived at the head of Kyn Ardagh. The ancient roadway was, as Rough-Bark had reported, in devastating disrepair. But it would serve as a way to leave the Taiga without the need of vines and climbing techniques.

Just before the travelers began to descend over the rubble and boulders that lay strewn over the path, Knarry noticed a warped little hornbeam shrub that was perched precariously on the edge of the cliff. He smiled. "Thank goodness," he thought, "Twigbottom made it after all."

The four weary travelers arrived at the foot of Kyn Ardagh at nightfall. Bomsiell heard them coming from afar and raced to them through the underbrush with welcoming meows. Tristan-Phoros was so delighted to know they were safe that he jumped up from the tree he was sitting against, dropped his pipe on the ground, barked, and started to gallop in their direction. But he screeched to a stop, his front paws digging into the turf of the woodland, and arced back to retrieve his pipe.

Soon he, too, was bounding through the forest, wagging his tail mightily, and feeling the compulsive and inexplicable urge to jump up on his friends and lick their faces. This, in the end, he successfully resisted. The others, for their part, were also delighted at the reunion and patted Bomsiell and greeted Tristan-Phoros but were careful not to pat him because he would certainly be deeply resentful of that.

Knarry now led the group eastward into the woodlands at the foot of Kyn Ardagh and along the base of the escarpment. Not far off they saw an earth-house in a small clearing close to the cliff. Behind it was a deep recess carved out by erosion in the cliff. Out of the recess, through the boulders and the slag, flowed an icy little steam. A cluster of boulders fallen from the escarpment made a kind of wall or redoubt in front of the recess. "A natural fortress," Knarry remarked to the others. "We must remember it in case we ever need it."

As they approached the earth-house, Knarry turned to the others and filled them in on some of the lore about the Orugug wood-gnomes. Old legends conveyed that they were the first wood-gnomes to evolve out of the seeds of the Ancestral Tree in the Age of the Beginnings. They still lived in their original homeland, close to the Taiga, and had little commerce with the rest of Oval-Earth. They spoke the ancient gnomish tongue but also knew some of the modern tongue — or at least enough to be hospitable to the few strangers who came their way.

Knarry was well-acquainted with them and with their colorful dialect and archaic gnome-ways, for his wide traveling through Oval-Earth in search of medicinal herbs had frequently brought him to their territory and to the earth-house of his old friend Branch-Knot.

The Orugug gnomes were especially known among their fellow gnomes for having preserved the most ancient formulas for herbal remedies, many of which were distilled from exotic plants available only in their region. Branch-Knot had an especially large collection of such distillates displayed on shelves in his dispensary. Knarry had once acquired from Branch-Knot's inventory a vial of rhubarb-osier ointment to cure an outbreak of moose-grange in his area.

The companions approached the earth-house — a strange, jagged mound of soil and roots, unlike the smooth domes of the normal wood-gnome dwellings. It had the usual central door with narrow windows on either side, though the door was sawed unevenly, being wider at the top than at the bottom, and the windows were tilted inward towards the top of the door. Knarry went to the door and knocked firmly against its heavy wooden panels.

A moment later, the door was nudged open a bit, and a gnome with a curiously wide head and flat face peered out. The top of his head looked like a little bush because small leafy branches covered it instead of hair. His bark-like lips were smiling. A round green eye was located directly in the center of his chin, surrounded by a little crater of concentric woody ridges. It was Branch-Knot.

Knarry spoke, "*A te eru, a te d'eru anca t'ath?*"

Branch-Knot's eye looked out at the others and back at Knarry. His eye closed; his head revolved around in a full circle and came to a stop; his eye opened again and he said, "*D'eru anca noh' atu t'ath.*"

Knarry turned to the others. "He welcomes us. He is honored to offer hospitality."

Branch-Knot ushered the travelers into his earth-house, showed them about the dim interior with his little lantern, and found places for them to bed down for the night. It was the usual, oddly designed earth-house, though some items—pieces of furniture and the like—were unaccountably positioned upside down and affixed with wooden pegs directly to the ceiling.

After the tour, conducted in a cheerful gibberish no one but Knarry could understand, Branch-Knot enkindled a cheerful fire in the hearth, jostled about in his galley for a while, and served up a hearty repast of hot millet broth and lacy wintergreen salad. He could follow only patches of the conversation that went on during dinner; Knarry translated the more important points for him. He often spun his head around and smiled his strange smile, showing teeth-like protuberances that resembled little brown mushrooms.

At one point, Knarry asked him if he had heard of what happened at the meeting of the clans. Again, he revolved his head in a circle, and all of his charming little mushrooms glowed as he smiled. "*Can'aha drulo't rama't, Knari, a' tha'lu,*" he said. He sputtered out some clipped, raspy chortles, the bush on top of his head waggling back and forth and the eye in his chin winking merrily. "*Mat'a dan'u watabi, gnomenie lenta n'a.*" Knarry chortled too. Branch-Knot had said that he heard that Knarry was now an outlaw but that he didn't believe a word of it. The gnomes, Branch-Knot had added pointedly, must be nuts—*lenta*, as he called them.

When dinner was over, Tristan-Phoros lit up his pipe and summarily claimed possession of Branch-Knot's big old tattered armchair, where he sunk back into the speckled cushions and emitted several fulsome clouds of smoke. Here the fire from the hearth sporadically lit up his golden floppy ears and his big black nose. Branch-Knot found Tristan-Phoros especially amusing, though he had never expressed—indeed, had never felt—surprise at Tristan-Phoros's extraordinary deportment.

"I've been thinking," Tristan-Phoros finally declared to the others in a somberly meditative tone.

"Oh, really," said Hrudan playfully. "Now, that's unusual for you! What have you been thinking about?"

"I've been thinking … thinking a lot … thinking about the Kingdom of Darkness."

"The Kingdom of Darkness?"

"Yes."

"Can it wait for morning?"

"Well … I guess it can."

"Good," said Hrudan. He was tired after his fight with the monster on the Taiga; and he was brooding deeply about Illyria and Erudan. What could the future hold in store for them, and for Erudan's future bride and children, when Oval-Earth could spawn such ungainly and terrible monstrosities as the one he had encountered in combat earlier in the day? He resolved to make Knarry's quest his quest as well. The band would need the protection of his Axe and of his ability to wield it. He was glad that Illyria and Erudan would be safe among the Hill people.

Gradually everyone arose from their chairs, wished one another good night, and retired to various rooms in the earth-house to sleep. Knarry slept, as usual, standing up; and Branch-Knot, as was the custom among the Orugug wood-gnomes, slept standing upside down, the bush on his head spreading out like surface roots over the jagged floorboards. Bomsiell curled up close to the dying fire on the hearth. Only Tristan-Phoros stayed awake, sitting in the armchair and puffing slowly on his pipe. He was thinking.

Chapter VI

The Capital

"Our enterprise calls for—how should we call it?—*research*," Tristan-Phoros remarked, as Knarry flipped some fresh lindenberry cakes on a heated flat-stone over Branch-Knot's hearth. It was morning, and the early sun cast bright beams of light through the narrow windows of the earth-house. Tristan-Phoros had spent much of the night settled back in Branch-Knot's tattered armchair, puffing on his pipe, dozing off for a bit at times and awakening with a jolt, and turning over and over again in his mind the dilemmas of the situation that he, and his newfound companions, found themselves in.

"Now, just what do you mean by 'research'?" Knarry grumbled as he tipped and jostled the hot flat-stone to spread the batter for a new round of cakes. Bomsiell stood close by, fascinated by the batter as it bubbled and popped each time a lindenberry became too hot and burst its skin, emitting a tiny spurt of purple juice. Branch-Knot was busy bustling about the galley and mixing up another bowl of batter. He enjoyed his guests and was having fun listening to their animated discussions, only a little of which he could understand.

"I mean," Tristan-Phoros resumed, "that something must exist—something, somewhere—that tells us about this so-called Kingdom of Darkness. It is difficult to imagine that such a widespread perception of an incalculable threat to Oval-Earth could have been, and still can be, fostered without any apparent shred of historical evidence. There must be something—a document, a testimony, an archive, a deposition of some sort—that we can consult. Someone must have known something about it in the past and written down whatever was known. The problem is: Where would we sniff out—uh, I mean, discover such a document?"

Knarry tossed the latest batch of sizzling flat-cakes onto a platter of birch bark and passed them around to Tundra-Bear and Fox-Foot, who sat on one side of the rough-hewn wooden trestle that served as a table. Bomsiell rushed over to them and stood up on her hind legs, curling one front paw over the edge of the table. Tundra-Bear slid a flat-cake in her direction, and she hooked it delicately with a single claw and pulled down to the floor. She crouched, looking at it, and as she usually did, waited until it cooled. Fox-Foot bent down and added a capacious dollop of moose butter to the cake, which Bomsiell lost no time in licking with her long, scaly tongue.

"I don't know that anything of the sort you are describing actually does exist, Tristan-Phoros," Knarry replied, "but if it does, it can be in only one place. I know it sounds strange to mention such a place, and most people do not even know there is such a thing; but it is the Ministry of Historical Records."

"Ministry of Historical Records? In the Capital?" Hrudan inquired. He had already taken a walk through the surrounding fields and copses that morning and had finished the breakfast Knarry and Branch-Knot had made for him.

"Yes."

"Then we must go there!" Tristan-Phoros yapped. Tundra-Bear and Fox-Foot looked up from their breakfast, and Hrudan exclaimed, "How will we do that? We are most likely considered to be fugitives; we cannot enter the Capital. We can be certain that by now the Viceroy's assorted thugs and hirelings have been alerted about us throughout the length and breadth of Oval-Earth."

"And even if we could enter the Capital, we would not have access to the Ministry of Historical Records," Knarry added. "Like all the ministries, it is closed to the public unless special permits have been issued. Also, I have reason to believe that the Ministry of Historical Records is especially debarred from all public admittance. The records are carefully guarded — if, in fact, it still does have any historical records, and those records are organized in such a fashion as to enable a person to find what he is looking for."

Branch-Knot revolved his head around in a full circle because he felt a certain inclination to agree with Knarry, even though he did not quite understand what Knarry had said. The green eye in the middle of his chin twinkled with amusement. "*M'iana ha'idahan, Knarri!*" he gurgled merrily between his mushrooms, urging Knarry onward towards whatever it was he needed to be doing.

"Tell me, Knarry," asked Tristan-Phoros, "from everything I have heard from you regarding the situation in Oval-Earth in the past few days, the question arises: Is anything, by and large, done correctly in Oval-Earth?"

"It is doubtful," he muttered.

"Does 'to do something carefully' mean the same as 'to do it correctly'?"

"I would generally think so."

"Then, to say that the records are 'carefully' guarded is the same as to say that they are guarded 'correctly.'"

"Agreed."

"But haven't we conceded that it is doubtful anything is done 'correctly' in Oval-Earth?"

"To be sure."

"*Ergo*, it is doubtful that the records are 'carefully' guarded."

Knarry consented with a somewhat abrupt and cautious nod.

Tristan-Phoros continued, "Indeed, I would regard it as axiomatic that the Imperial Government is ineffectual in everything it does. It will be ineffectual in keeping us from the records. It will be ineffectual in apprehending us in the Capital. If it does apprehend us, it will be ineffectual in detaining us for long. *Ergo* ..." He hesitated.

"*Ergo* ...?" the others echoed, impatiently.

"*Ergo*, it behooves us to enter the Capital and to do our 'research.'" Tristan-Phoros paused for a moment after making this sage pronouncement and declaimed, "Anyway, I need to visit the Capital in order to find a pipe shop. I need to replenish my supply of bilberry weed."

"Ah, the indomitable persuasiveness of self-interest!" Knarry observed.

"Self-interest? Scarcely self-interest in the narrow sense, my fine-notched friend! How do you expect me to think without my pipe? You do want me to think, don't you?" Tristan-Phoros objected.

"Of course we do, Tristan-Phoros," Fox-Foot interceded, "but how are we to enter the Capital? Must we approach under the cover of darkness and then find our way out again while the city sleeps? We don't want to hurt the people of Oval-Earth. We are trying to help them. We want to avoid them as much as possible."

Fox-Foot's reservations occasioned a long silence among the companions. Branch-Knot shuffled over to Knarry. "*La'ha la'lois moha'ba te'ten ta,*" he whispered into Knarry's floppy, leaflike ear. All the little shrubs on the top of his head trembled with delight. Knarry looked at him; he was a bit surprised, both by the suggestion and by the fact that Branch-Knot had understood somehow the issue they were discussing.

"*Moha'ba?*" he asked Branch-Knot in disbelief.

Branch-Knot's head spun around in two little circles — first to the left and then to the right. "*Moha'ba!*" he repeated, as his tiny green eye winked in slightly devious pleasure.

Knarry turned to the others. "*Moha'ba* — disguise! Branch-Knot thinks we should go in disguise!"

"*Moha'ba! Moha'ba!*" Branch-Knot clucked; his mushrooms glittered.

"Disguise is the only method," replied Tristan-Phoros. "Branch-Knot has supplied the obvious solution. Since my task as philosopher and logician is solely to seek the truth, however, I shall leave working out the details of this rather ungainly descent into deception to others."

Knarry chortled. "I don't think any of us should necessarily be more skilled in that matter than you would be, Tristan-Phoros. After all, you insist that you are not a dog, and consequently you either are in disguise yourself, or else you suffer from some curious delusions about your identity."

"Really!" Tristan-Phoros huffed. "Now, I admit that there are things I don't understand. But that doesn't mean I will not understand them someday."

"No matter," Fox-Foot interceded again, "we will all figure something out."

Plans were proposed, argued about, rejected, and proposed again. Tristan-Phoros puffed meditatively on his pipe, Knarry waved around his shaggy hands, Hrudan glared through the sunny windows of the earth-house with his aquiline eyes as he brooded over the alternatives, Tundra-Bear and Fox-Foot offered their simple but invariably practical advice, though the idea of disguise was so foreign to them that could not fully understand what was being proposed.

Branch-Knot just kept nodding and spinning his bushy head around as if he agreed with everyone, no matter how different their opinions were.

Bomsiell spent her time following an indigo-backed bally-beetle as it ambled aimlessly around the floor until it vanished under a loose floorboard.

Hrudan and Tundra-Bear occupied the remainder of the morning foraging in the neighboring villages for attire suitable for disguises. The small amount of coin that Hrudan carried in his haversack was sufficient to purchase garments of various kinds. The villagers were glad to have currency, though the strange appearance of Tundra-Bear startled them somewhat and the magnificent stature of Hrudan compelled their immediate admiration. In addition to the garments, they purchased a small two-wheeled draw-cart that Hrudan could pull easily behind him by grasping the two long poles attached to the front.

Later in the day, Knarry made an effort to train and coordinate everyone in the roles they were to play. Tundra-Bear and Fox-Foot were especially difficult in this regard, for they did not understand the idea of a masquerade and of assuming an identity one did not really have. How could one person be two people at once?

Tristan-Phoros, through elaborate logical demonstration, finally convinced them that it could be done, though he deftly evaded their questions of how one species could be two different species at the same time. He did note, and this he made clear to his slightly bewildered green-haired friends, that their names — Fox-Foot and Tundra-Bear — were only names and did not indicate that either she or he were actually what the words ordinarily pointed to.

With a bit of Knarry's help, Tristan-Phoros was also helpful in composing some documents that could be used in potential confrontations with imperial officials, should the need arise. His disguise, as it turned out, would be very simple: he would be disguised, much to his satisfaction, as a dog, the implication being, of course, that he was not really a dog after all.

By the following morning, the bizarre pageant had been outfitted. It departed from the yard in front of Branch-Knot's earth-house. Branch-Knot was pleased to see his suggestion materialized in quite such an extravagant form; he smiled with his glittering mushrooms, his little eye twinkled in his chin, and his head whirred about as he waved goodbye to the procession. He was also glad to have provided the group with an abundant store of nourishing provisions for the difficult days ahead.

The caravan headed south along the local cart-paths until it reached the tip of the Northern Arm of the Radial High-Road. Here it advanced southward along the abysmally torn-up and fractured surface of the road.

Fox-Foot was decked out in a flowing amber robe embroidered with flowers; she was to play the role of a well-to-do landowner, though in ill-health, seeking out the respite of a medicinal spa and making, in the meantime, the rounds of some of her far-flung properties. A blue hood drawn well over her head concealed her green hair, though her deep amethyst eyes and green eyebrows could still be noticed in the depth of the hood. She sat on the front of the draw-cart, which Hrudan, grasping the two long poles attached to the front of the wagon and arrayed in the frayed tunic of a peasant drover, jostled along behind him over the bumpy road.

On either side of the rickety cart walked Tundra-Bear and Knarry; their job was to help move the cart along and to keep it from tipping over on the tilting surfaces of the broken pavement. Both of them had heavy cloaks gathered about them. Knarry assumed the character of the personal physician of the wealthy lady — since "Madam," as he called her, was ever suffering from one or another ailment and needed his constant attention and medications.

Tundra-Bear posed as a student on leave of absence from the College of Wisdom who was temporarily enlisted in the lady's service as secretary and scribe. A tattered academic hood was drawn well over his face. As he had been instructed to do, he constantly mumbled short (and to him, meaningless) mathematical formulas taught him by Tristan-Phoros, who was familiar, for reasons he himself could not explain, with the Game of Spheres.

Bomsiell perched on the back of the cart, partially hidden by the blankets which were pulled over the small heaps of baggage. It had been agreed that there was no satisfactory way to disguise a forest cat; she would simply have to stay out of sight.

Under the blankets were collected the haversacks of the companions, Branch-Knot's provisions, as well as the longbows, the quivers of arrows, and the Battle-Axe.

Knarry carried the Splinter of the Ancestral Tree in the leather jerkin under his cloak.

Finally, Tristan-Phoros trotted behind the group. As it turned out, he was not entirely happy with his role, for it emerged that he was to act as the lady's pet and was enjoined to display, at times, appropriate pet-like behavior by wagging his tail, panting, begging for a cookie, and the like. His pipe and bilberry-weed pouch had been tucked into the baggage on the draw-cart.

Further, he was strictly forbidden ever to talk or to engage in philosophical dialogues with strangers, an onerous injunction he consented to only by securing in return the promise from everyone that some limits must be observed and that no one should pat him on the head or scratch behind his ears and say to him, "Good doggy!" Most of all, no one should throw a stick and expect him to retrieve it.

By the late afternoon of the following day, the band approached the Capital. There had not been much traffic along the Northern Arm, except for the armed platoons of hirelings who trundled quickly along the road as if in pursuit of someone. The hirelings would wobble by the group in disorderly fashion, jabbering in constant disagreement while their rusty and bent halberds clunked noisily against one another. They seemed not to have any commanding officer and no clear sense of where they were supposed to go, though they were in a great hurry to get there.

They assumed, apparently, that whatever was hiding would be hidden in remote places and certainly would not appear in full daylight on the Radial High-Road System. Except for the occasional coarse remark as they squeezed past in some narrow spots, they paid little heed to the wealthy landowner and her curious entourage.

Other than that, there had been little to break the monotony of the journey. The surrounding landscape, recovering from recent floods, was bleak and lonely, and little desolate villages, built on rises over the flood-plain, showed few signs of life. Here and there, a white moose, scraggy with famine, pulled on a stray sprig of vegetation that had broken through the muddy surface of the plain.

Towards evening, the band entered the run-down, trash-strewn boulevards of the Capital; the Northern Boulevard was in particularly bad shape, and the quarters that bordered it on either side were sunk into a dingy, musty decrepitude. There did not seem to be a single window that had not been broken, and only a few had been partially repaired by stretching mats of swamp reeds over the openings.

Tundra-Bear and Fox-Foot could scarcely believe what they were seeing; both of them choked on the foulness of the air, but they made a fullhearted effort to maintain their disguises.

At one point, an orange-streaked hairy-winged fly buzzed out of a slimy back alley and dived down at Tristan-Phoros, biting him viciously on his tail and tearing out a sizable tuft of white fur from its tip. Tristan-Phoros whirled around, his teeth bared and snarling, and lunged at the monstrous fly, but it had already whizzed off into the alley again. He was about ready to pour out a volley of verbal abuse when Knarry prevented it by glaring at him; Tristan-Phoros yelped and tucked his tail between his legs. The few stragglers along the boulevard merely stared vacantly at the group, without giving it much thought.

The band of travelers finally reached the Imperial Plaza. Here they took in the dismal spectacle of the once-great Capital square, now mostly in ruins. The shells of enormous, burned-out buildings stood around them. At the southern end of the Plaza stood the Imperial Court—a massive palace lined with huge columns and porticoes and crowned by a tall dome overhead. Fox-Foot noted rather particularly how soot-stained the windows of the dome were; one window was even shattered. The Imperial Plaza was empty except for a few early-evening strollers, who idly observed the group and several of whom condescendingly patted Tristan-Phoros, who, for his part, endured it with little impatience.

The band was soon accosted by the functionaries of the Ministry of Travel. It was the end of the day for them, and they were preparing to pack up their boxes and stamps when the group entered the Plaza. Nevertheless, as annoyed as they were by this delay in their departure, they took pleasure in thinking that they could wrest a few more coins from some hapless travelers. They directed the group to line up in front of the booths until permits could be stamped and the proper fees paid. But a caravan of this size was odd in this age of Oval-Earth and required a great deal of processing.

Knarry, acting as the official representative of the wealthy lady, declared that her purpose in traveling was to visit the "waters" of the Down country for her health. Her entourage was all a necessary part of her travel, since she intended to stop at a number of farmsteads in her ownership to collect rents and to settle accounts. She also intended to remain for a day or two in the Capital to visit old friends. Fox-Foot glanced furtively at Knarry while he spoke and gave little nods now and then as if to approve of what he had said.

The lazy, ill-tempered functionaries examined the group with some curiosity. One unshaven lout with a long, dusty jaw capped by a lower row of jagged yellow teeth noticed what he thought were purple eyes under the lady's hood. He approached Fox-Foot and extended a long, grimy hand towards her face in order to slide her hood off her head. What happened then was as much a surprise for her as it was for him and for everyone else who observed the incident.

Trained by years of instantaneous and unhesitating response to the sudden affronts of dangerous glacial creatures, she swung her heavily robed arm around in front of her and slapped his hand away. The sound of the slap resonated through the Imperial Plaza. The functionary gaped at his grimy hand in sheer astonishment; it dangled loosely from his wrist and was bright red from the force of the blow.

Everyone else stared at the functionary. Then the other functionaries began to laugh. They pointed at him and howled with glee. When he turned to them angrily, they laughed even more and began to dance about in a merry little jig, kicking up their legs and squealing and flailing their arms about over their heads.

They imitated Fox-Foot, slapping at one another's hands and leaping up and down and finally slapping heads and backs and faces. The slapping rapidly transformed into smacking one another's noses with closed fists. The scene quickly disintegrated into an ugly brawl with the functionaries rolling over one another on the tables and the ground, kicking and punching and swearing as the tables toppled over and the filing baskets spilled their contents of forms and slips to be blown about by the evening breeze.

Suddenly, a head functionary emerged out of one of the soiled booths, stood imperiously in the tent opening, and bawled at his subordinates to stop. They disentangled themselves from one another, picked themselves up off the ground, and shook the dust off their torn livery. The churl with the long jaw had lost a tooth, and a thin line of blood curled down from his mouth through the gritty stubble on his chin.

The head functionary eyed the band of strangers with malicious contempt. He was a short man in boots with tall soles that made him stand almost a pace higher than his natural stature would allow. His livery was stained with turnip beer. He gazed at the strangers through a monocle that had a long string connected to the one remaining button on his jacket. After a protracted silence, he moved to the main table — the only table still left standing — and looked over the various documents spread out on its surface. He removed the monocle and addressed himself directly to Knarry.

"This all seems to be in order, wood-gnome," he said. "But, of course, there will be fees. And, ahem, there is a matter of the appropriate . . . consideration."

Hrudan bristled with anger; he stepped up to the head functionary and spoke forcefully to him: "This is a disgrace. As one privileged to work for the public good, it is your unremitting obligation to present to the public a character whose principled demeanor shall set an example to —"

The mouth of the head functionary dropped open with amazement. His hands began to shake, and he cowered backward towards the booth. The other functionaries trembled, their eyes diverted from the stern visage that confronted them. Knarry grasped Hrudan's arm and pulled him away. He spoke quietly to Hrudan for a moment.

When he had calmed him down, Knarry turned back to the functionaries; he dislodged some coins from his sleeve pockets and dropped them on the table. The functionaries' frightened grimaces melted into obsequious smiles. The proper stamps were affixed to the documents. The full sum of an appropriate "consideration" could be waived this time, considering "Madam's" sensitive health.

Furthermore, the functionaries' greed was consoled by the thought that a more lucrative "consideration" could be demanded from the lady on her return trip, once her rents had been collected and her affairs put in order. In any event, the band was permitted to pass through the Plaza and was on its way to an inn at the far end of the city.

The functionaries, meanwhile, made a half-hearted effort to clean up the tables, baskets, and paperwork strewn over the Imperial Plaza. But they soon gave up and figured that a brisk night wind would certainly take care of what they had no inclination to sweep up.

As the band plodded through the jumbled streets of the old quarter in the eastern part of the city, Tristan-Phoros kept watch for a pipe shop that might still be open. When he saw one, he induced Tundra-Bear to enter it and purchase a packet of fresh bilberry weed.

He burrowed into the mound of materials on the draw-cart where his sack and pipe were hidden and produced a single tiny nugget of gold — his only find in the Barrows, so he said, through all that "timeless time" — which he gave to Tundra-Bear. Tundra-Bear entered the shop. He stayed in there for what seemed an inordinately long time. (Tundra-Bear had never been in a shop before and did not know precisely what to do in one.) But the purchase was made, and Tundra-Bear came out of the shop bearing both a packet of bilberry weed and a big grin on his face. It had been a new experience for him; it had also been a new experience for the shopkeeper, who peeked out the door after him and wondered who or what he was.

The inn, which had once been one of the old baronial residences of the city, was a shabby quagmire of rotten beams and falling plaster. The band checked in at a counter in the large entrance hall that showed the shattered remains of elegant, marbled walls and fine old balustrades. In the meantime, the group unloaded their various possessions and roped the draw-cart to a moose rail outside the inn.

The innkeeper was a jolly enough fellow — a heavy man with tiny eyes, practically no nose at all, and an enormous smile. He offered them the special: the "baronial suite" with free dinner and breakfast at a modest price — four coppers per night for the whole group. Knarry signed up for one night. He had to show the permits stamped by the Ministry of Travel before they could be taken to their rooms. While the innkeeper was studying the permits, Bomsiell darted unseen past the hotel counter and up the stairs, where she hid and waited for the others to follow.

The "baronial suite" was an ornate but now shabby parlor with two sleeping rooms attached on either side. There was practically no furniture, and the floors obviously had not been swept for months. A pair of under-garments, discarded presumably by some previous guest, lay on the floor directly in the middle of the parlor. The beds in the sleeping rooms were mats covered with a thin layer of moldy straw that served as nests for large, thriving colonies of bally-beetles.

The innkeeper, however, jovially showed them around the suite, boasted about its many "adorable" features, noted that it had a private "balcony" (where they could "sunbathe," there being no other bath available), and praised the view of the city street from its high arched windows. The view was nothing to rave about, though one could see over the rooftops, in the fading orange twilight, the distant dome of the Imperial Court.

When the innkeeper left, Knarry began to unpack his things, Bomsiell came out of hiding, and Tundra-Bear and Fox-Foot slid the protective covers off their longbows. Tristan-Phoros made a rush to retrieve his pipe and sack, and using his new supply of bilberry weed, was soon "fumigating" the room with the soft, aromatic haze from his pipe.

Hrudan, after exploring the bedrooms on his own, declared that everyone would have to sleep on the parlor floor, since the beds were unsuitable for human or feline or, presumably, canine slumber. Fox-Foot used the end of her longbow to pick up the undergarments on the floor at the center of the parlor, and, with face averted, carried them to one of the windows and tossed them out. The travelers helped one another to clean out the parlor, which they would all use as a sleeping room.

The original wine cellars of the baronial residence, so the jovial innkeeper had told them, had been converted into a restaurant that was called Ye Quainte Olde Taverne. Since dinner was included with the price of the room, the companions decided to put off using Branch-Knot's sumptuous-looking provisions for the time being, except for Bomsiell and Tristan-Phoros, who would have their dinner from that source. They remained in the "baronial suite" while the others sought out the restaurant, which was reached by descending a stone staircase that wound around a wide pillar into the tall, barrel-vaulted cellars beneath the ground floor.

In the restaurant, rank with a sordid variety of rancid odors, they were ushered to a table by a waiter dressed in a squalid smock covered with food stains. They were the only patrons, but the waiter acted as if the locale was crowded with customers and as if it was difficult to find a table for them.

After they were seated, he drew a pad of leaf-paper from his smock and a piece of well-bitten yellow chalk showing teeth marks.

"Good evening. My name is Lackey-Lick. I am your server tonight. What'll it be?" he smirked. He bore a perpetual, ear-to-ear smile, which revealed a mass of missing teeth and blackened gums as well as a throng of fat dimples squeezed up unpleasantly around his eyes.

"What's on the menu?" Knarry asked exuberantly, projecting the "good-gnome-well-met" personality that he sometimes liked to assume in public places. The last time he had done that was in the Red Ruby Café, near Hrudan's lodge. It hadn't done him much good there, as it turned out.

"Mashed marsh-root and muffins. Turnips baked with plover eggs and heaped on a steaming bed of marinated pumpkin seeds. Cabbage sautéed with garlic and served in toasty slabs of sun-dried torpel pudding. Lizard tongue in tangy brine with braised barley and garnished with a glaze of dragonweed marmalade. Grilled Midland Sea shad in season with Sauce Imperial. That's it." Lackey-Lick smirked. He had intensely salivated, even drooled, during the recitation of this gastronomical litany.

Fox-Foot and Tundra-Bear had never been in a restaurant before and didn't know what they were supposed to do. They were puzzled by the strange combinations of foods they were being offered. Tundra-Bear whispered to Fox-Foot about the "steaming bed of marinated pumpkin seeds," which struck him as an odd sort of thing to sleep on. Knarry was simply appalled by the selections, and his hearty demeanor rapidly became dour and withdrawn. Only Hrudan was able to rise to the occasion.

"That Midland Sea shad sounds interesting," Hrudan remarked. "What's in the Sauce Imperial?"

"Begging your pardon, sir," Lackey-Lick replied with a slightly sideways bow and a huge smile, "but it were better you did not know what's in the Sauce Imperial."

"I'll have the shad but without the Sauce Imperial."

"Begging your pardon, sir, but the shad may only be served with the Sauce Imperial."

"Well, I'll have the shad anyway."

"Begging your pardon, sir, but it's not in season."

"Then I'll have the lizard tongue," said Hrudan.

"Begging your pardon, sir, we're out of that too."

"In that case, I'll have the cabbage."

"Begging your pardon, sir, but we're also out of that."

"What do you have?"

"Mashed marsh-root and muffins."

"Why didn't you just say that in the first place?"

"Begging your pardon, sir, but I did say that in the first place." Lackey-Lick smirked again. His fat dimples closed over his eyes and opened again.

"Yes, but why did you bother to mention the others?"

"Begging your pardon, sir, but Ye Quainte Olde Taverne is a respectable establishment. We like to keep up appearances. We are the only four-star restaurant in the Capital."

Knarry spoke up: "Four orders of mashed marsh-root and muffins."

The waiter stuck the yellow chalk in his mouth, wetted it, chewed it, and used the moistened, masticated end to write down the order on the leaf-paper. It took a long time to perform this little operation, since he wrote down the order four separate times. He wiped the chalk on his smock before replacing it in its inner pocket.

He smirked. "While you are waiting for your orders, you may feel free to help yourself to broth at our broth-bar. Our specialty today is cream of leech soup. The leeches are pond-fresh. Enjoy." He walked away smirking.

"Good," said the others. They were hungry.

But not for long.

The cream of leech soup at the broth-bar sat in an earthenware tureen on a low trivet, where it was heated by a single candle underneath. It was surrounded by an assortment of chipped crocks and ungainly clay spoons. A soup ladle was half sunk in the broth, which looked like a grayish-green puddle of swamp sludge. Several ominous-looking ruddy-yellow strands of flesh swam around languidly in the lukewarm fluid. Obviously, the leeches were still alive.

On one side of the tureen lay a dead hairy-winged fly floating upside down on the surface of the thick soup. Another hairy-winged fly was partially submerged in the soup, its six bristly bluish legs splayed outward. Occasionally it jerked around in the soup as the leeches curled out of the brew and tugged it back and forth; they were feeding on it.

Knarry contemplated this ghastly sight for a few moments and announced, "Given that a hairy-winged fly can live on almost anything without being poisoned by it, I would consider it most perilous for any of us to touch this soup." The others did not need much convincing. They returned to the table.

Knarry was glad that Tristan-Phoros was not with them, for he would certainly have posed an objection to Knarry's prognosis, insisting that the leeches, despite the presumably baleful broth, were alive and apparently flourishing. Something could thrive on that soup.

The order took forever to arrive. As they were waiting, other customers descended the steps to the restaurant. Among them, a group of four officials arrived. They were directed to a table at the opposite end of the old cellar. They doffed their official caps, pounded the dust off them, and hung them on pegs over the table. The waiter took out his chalk and leaf-paper and told them what was on the menu. It was the same routine. He smirked, and they ended up ordering the mashed marsh-root and muffins. Like everybody else, they approached the broth-bar, only to back away from it in horror.

Then they sat at their table and spent much of their time glowering at the other customers and especially at Knarry, Hrudan, Tundra-Bear, and Fox-Foot, all of whom regretted that they had not stayed upstairs with Tristan-Phoros and Bomsiell and partaken of the wholesome staples that Branch-Knot had been so good to provide.

Another slovenly official arrived. He wore a maroon uniform with tarnished brass buttons and sported a wiry, disheveled beard. He did not wait to be directed to a table but shuffled over to the table beside them and slumped down heavily into a chair. There he gazed up absentmindedly into the barrel vaults of the old cellar. The smirking waiter approached, but the official waved him away with the words "the usual." The waiter disappeared and showed up later carrying a tankard of frothy turnip beer. He clunked it down on the table and walked away.

The official dragged the tankard over to his side of the table and, after a deep breath, buried his face in the froth and slowly lifted and tilted the tankard towards his mouth. He must have finished half the beer in the tankard by the time he thumped it back down on the table. His beard was flecked with froth. But he seemed happy now. He wiped his beard with a dirty sleeve. He scrutinized Hrudan and Knarry, and Fox-Foot and Tundra-Bear, both of whom still wore their hoods drawn over their faces.

"You are strangers," he said.

"In for a short visit," Knarry replied.

"A visit?" the official retorted. "Who would want to visit here?" He took another deep drink from the tankard and pushed it away.

"Actually, we also have some business," Fox-Foot said. Knarry motioned for her to be silent.

The official ignored her comment. "I would think that a visit to the Capital would be the last thing anyone in his, and even her, right mind would do," he averred. "Look at this wreck of a restaurant. They serve, and have served from time immemorial, only their miserable mashed marsh-root and muffins, which you will find, I dare say, practically inedible. Then there is the 'broth of the day'—'broth of the month,' one should say. At least their turnip beer is good. I don't know where they get it from. Some brewer out there in the boondocks still has some standards."

"Why don't you leave the Capital?" Fox-Foot asked. "Why do you stay where you don't want to be?"

"I would leave if I could, but I can't. I'm indispensable." He rubbed his wiry beard. "May I join you? I could use some company for a change."

"By all means," Knarry responded. The official slouched out of his chair and dragged it over to their table. He reached for his tankard and slumped back into his chair, taking another great draught.

"Who are you, and why are you so 'indispensable'?" Knarry requested of him after he was comfortable again.

"I am Toten-Haas," he blurted out through his foamy beard. "I am the head official at the most important ministry in Oval-Earth. I am not only the head official there; I am the only official there. I don't suppose you ever heard of it. It is called the Ministry of Insoluble Affairs. All things in Oval-Earth end up, invariably, at the Ministry of Insoluble Affairs."

"What do you do there?"

"I receive all matters that other ministries cannot handle, all difficulties that others cannot solve."

"Do you get a lot of business?"

"*Everything* in Oval-Earth is insoluble! The motto of the ministry is 'All the business of Oval-Earth is our business'!"

"What do you do with it there?"

"I file it."

"So, you don't try to solve it?"

"Of course not. It is the Ministry of Insoluble Affairs. If the affairs could be solved, then the name of the ministry would hardly be appropriate, would it?"

"It must be kind of sad, I mean, to have so many insoluble problems become your responsibility."

Toten-Haas looked vacantly at him. His eyes were glazed and weary. Then he shouted, "Waiter, another usual!"

Knarry stretched out his shaggy hand and patted him on the shoulder. "You look like a good sort of fellow," he said.

Toten-Haas nodded his head. "How could I know what sort of fellow I am? One makes the best of a bad situation, that's all. But I appreciate your comment.

"The Ministry of Insoluble Affairs was not one of the original ministries established by the ancient Imperial House of Ospeth. It has arisen in these latter times because, they say, the War of Desolation made it necessary. I don't know what to think about this War of Desolation.

"The Ministry of Insoluble Affairs is a kind of rubbish bin for everything that happens in Oval-Earth, and everything that has happened for a long time, and I never, I mean *never*, run into any actual records of the War of Desolation, though I suppose you could call the War of Desolation the great-granddaddy of all insoluble affairs. In any case, the Ministry of Insoluble Affairs rose into prominence in direct proportion to the failure of other ministries to carry out their original tasks. That much I think I understand."

Hrudan murmured something in response, but Toten-Haas did not hear it. He changed the subject and said, "The lady there, who hides her face in her cloak, said a while ago you have business here in the Capital. Maybe I can be of help. You are civil people, and I have not forgotten what civility is all about, as rare as it is these days."

Knarry glanced at Hrudan to see if he approved. Hrudan nodded his approval. Knarry leaned forward to Toten-Haas and whispered, "We need to enter the Ministry of Historical Records. We need to consult some documents there."

Toten-Haas blinked at him; he looked around at the others and laughed. "The Ministry of Historical Records! Certainly, my good friend, you must be daft! Nobody ever goes in there. It has a single functionary—a singularly nearsighted chap named Klorp who is thoroughly unpleasant. He keeps the place locked up as tight as can be. He doesn't even deal with my ministry—it's not necessary. History is a dead matter. Anyway, you could never get in there without a court permit."

"How do you get that . . . that court permit?" Hrudan queried, speaking directly to Toten-Haas for the first time.

"By petitioning the court, that's how. In effect, you need to petition the Viceroy himself. As you know, he is in charge of everything."

The victuals, if one could call them that, arrived. Lackey-Lick bustled officiously around the table, and even though each order was identical, he went through some effort to make sure each customer got the right one. The mashed marsh-root was a heap of warm pink slush in a bowl. The muffins were sodden and moldy. The "usual" also arrived. The waiter smirked and asked if there was anything more he could bring. Toten-Haas, meanwhile, drained half the tankard at a single lift. The waiter was assured that nothing more would be required. Puffing up the dimples around his eyes, he retired with a slanted bow and a smirk.

Tundra-Bear and Fox-Foot probed the marsh-root with their spoons. They looked at each other and put their spoons back down on the table. Neither Hrudan nor Knarry even bothered to examine the fare. Knarry persisted in his line of questioning: "What is the procedure for such a petition?"

Toten-Haas wiped his beard again with his soiled sleeve. "You must present yourself at court as early as possible in the morning. You must have a written document that states your purpose. You must obey absolutely the court protocol until you have the opportunity to present your petition to the Viceroy's chief scrivener, who will then pass it on to the Viceroy. None of this will be easy to do. Also, the fact that your request will be very unusual won't make it any easier. Much will depend on the mood of the Viceroy. Sometimes he fancies that a petitioner has done him a favor, and then he is inclined to return the favor."

Fox-Foot interrupted, "What kind of favor can someone do for the Viceroy?"

"I'm afraid that's a perfect sort of question for the Ministry of Insoluble Affairs."

Knarry added, "What about the court protocol? How do we know what that is supposed to be?"

"That's the worst part. The protocol changes from day to day. It can change halfway through the day. It can change on the spur of the moment according to the whim of the Viceroy. Whoever disobeys the protocol is ejected, often in a most disagreeable way, from the court chambers through a sliding panel in the floor. The panel leads to a chute that dumps the unfortunate petitioner on the street outside the palace. My advice is that you are well back on the line of petitioners. The first half dozen or so petitioners will all be ejected. You will learn from their mistakes what you should and should not do."

Toten-Haas took another drink and smiled bitterly at his companions. "Of course, if that fails, there is always another way here in the Capital to get what you want."

"What's that?" asked Hrudan, already suspecting what the answer might be.

"A little gift — what they call a 'consideration.' You know it always works. I doubt very much that Klorp, for all his isolation at the Ministry of Historical Records, would not find a little 'consideration' very tempting indeed, though you may still need the court permit. He is, I understand, a stickler for forms, especially since he never gets any forms."

"Do you get such 'considerations,' Toten-Haas?"

"No, I do not. No one ever requires anything of me, anyway. What comes to the Ministry of Insoluble Affairs stays at the Ministry of Insoluble Affairs. It may well be the most depressing place in the whole city — and that is to say a great deal; but one's employment there has a way of preserving, if nothing else and in some minimal way, one's integrity. If a 'consideration' came my way, I would refuse it. I do not wish to become any more of an insoluble affair to myself than I already am."

"I think it has preserved your integrity, Toten-Haas," Hrudan said, "and I don't think you are an insoluble affair." The others nodded their approval. Toten-Haas was content.

The supper was concluded, even though scarcely anything was touched. The travelers bid farewell to Toten-Haas and rose to leave their table. Ye Quainte Olde Taverne was almost empty now. The four officials across the room had already left. Lackey-Lick stood by the broth-bar, where the candle still burned unsteadily beneath the tureen of cream of leech soup. He bowed and smirked.

The companions climbed the stairs to their rooms. When they arrived at the "baronial suite," they found Bomsiell asleep on a window ledge and Tristan-Phoros cleaning out the stem of his pipe. The fragrant smoke from the pipe still drifted around the room. A single pale lantern hung from the ceiling overhead. Tristan-Phoros inquired about their dinner.

"Dreadful!" was the answer.

The group sat on the floor in a small circle, passed around some of Branch-Knot's provisions, which were eaten with pleasure, and discussed the brief conversation with Toten-Haas.

"I should have liked to meet this honorable gentleman," Tristan-Phoros remarked. "I, too, have my own kind of interest in the insoluble—certain ambiguities in logical method difficult to resolve. I wonder if Toten-Haas would be willing to discuss such matters."

Hrudan commenced the debate about the alternatives facing the group. Should an effort be made to procure a court permit, or should they go directly to the Ministry of Historical Records and try to bribe their way in? Clearly Hrudan preferred the former, the idea of bribery being upsetting to him. Fox-Foot wondered whether there was a favor they could do for the Viceroy. That solution was dismissed rather quickly as being too improbable, though Fox-Foot continued to ponder it.

Knarry got into a long argument with Tristan-Phoros about "the priorities" of either course of action until Fox-Foot suggested that they might refer the dilemma to Toten-Haas at the Ministry of Insoluble Affairs. They all laughed.

But they decided at last that Hrudan and Tundra-Bear would test their fortune at the court of the Viceroy the following morning. The others would plan to meet them at the entrance to the Ministry of Historical Records. No one, of course, was sure exactly where the Ministry was located, except that it was in the northeast quarter of the city and that it was a squat, windowless building facing out on a small square and had an exceptionally scraggly tower—both lean and leaning—that rose up awkwardly over its central front door.

The tower itself, they figured, would act as a landmark to bring them all there together, and with that confidence, they retired for the night. Only Hrudan and Knarry worked for a while into the night, composing on parchment by candlelight the court petition that would be presented to the Imperial Viceroy the following day.

Chapter VII

The Chartulary of the Kingdom of Darkness

At dawn of the following day, a chill, damp wind blew through the narrow streets of the Capital, and the sky was overcast. Knarry took care of the formalities involved in checking out of the inn; the noseless innkeeper was as jovial as ever. The others helped to pack up the draw-cart. They skipped, with pleasure, the "free" breakfast and departed the "adorable" lodging of the "baronial suite" with little regret.

The plan was for Knarry, accompanied by Fox-Foot, Tristan-Phoros, and Bomsiell, to find their way to the square in the northeast quarter of the city, where the Ministry of Historical Records was located. There they would wait for Hrudan and Tundra-Bear. Knarry would take over Hrudan's task of pulling the cart. Meanwhile, Hrudan and Tundra-Bear would venture to the court of the Viceroy. They would carry with them only the slender strip of parchment on which a petition had been carefully penned by candlelight just a few hours before. Entrance to the court with weapons of any kind would obviously be impossible.

Knarry warned Hrudan that he should be patient and that he should do everything in his power to check the indignation he would undoubtedly feel during the court proceedings; and Tundra-Bear was reminded that he should always keep his hood well drawn over his head. When the time came for the band to separate, Knarry felt assured that everything was neatly under control and that the everyone was well acquainted with their assigned tasks for the day. Hrudan and Tundra-Bear set out in the direction of the Imperial Plaza. The others, wishing to avoid the exposure of the boulevards, began to thread their way through the maze of narrow side streets towards the Ministry of Historical Records.

Fox-Foot, still garbed in her long, embroidered robe, decided not to ride on the cart but rather to follow behind it for a while. Bomsiell sat on the back of the cart, her eyes fixed on Fox-Foot, as if waiting for some prearranged signal. Up ahead, Tristan-Phoros trotted jauntily along, his head aloft as he tried to figure out how to navigate through the tangle of littered alleyways.

After a minute or two, Fox-Foot suddenly shed her long robe and tossed it onto the back of the cart. "Knarry," she cried, "we will see you later. Don't worry about us! We will see you there!" Dressed only in her green tunic and woolen blanket-cape and with her quiver, curiously empty of arrows, strapped over her shoulder, she whistled to Bomsiell, who bounded off the cart and joined her.

They disappeared into the thicket of streets, as quickly as wild deer would vanish into the dense undergrowth of a mountain forest. Knarry practically dropped the poles of the draw-cart in surprise. He wanted to call after them but knew instantly that there would be no point in trying to do that. Tristan-Phoros merely sat down on his haunches, his head tilted backward, looking over his shoulders after them and wondering what was going on.

The long entrance pavilion of the Imperial Court was thronged with petitioners that morning. They huddled up against the huge columned walls of the old palace to protect themselves from the cold winds blowing out of the north. Hrudan and Tundra-Bear took their place in the queue. Hrudan examined the palatial structure with great interest, even though it was in advanced stages of disrepair. Small flurries of paper slips and forms from the previous evening still blew in gusts and eddies across the Plaza, though the functionaries of the Ministry of Travel had not yet set up their tables and booths.

Eventually, the tall, ornate portals of the Imperial Court swung open. Two Imperial Guards dressed in tarnished armor and carrying halberds, emerged and engaged in a curious sort of jig in front of the portals, crisscrossing back and forth, hopping up and down, and periodically clanging the blades of their halberds against one another. They wore pointy helmets capped with enormous yellow plumes, and the plumes bobbed up and down as they jigged. Finally, they stopped hopping and ceremoniously stood to the side, where they began to marshal the jostling crowd of petitioners through the portals and up the stairs to the Court.

The interior of the Imperial Court was a spacious circular chamber whose ceiling opened up into the lofty dome above. It was unbearably stuffy, and only the single broken window in the ornate row of windows that circled around the dome let in a thin sluice of fresh air.

The floor, deeply worn but showing evidence of former mosaic designs, was cordoned off into two areas: a rear area, where the crowd assembled, and a front area, where several tall desks faced the assembly and where a throne stood on a dais against the wall. Above the throne was a ragged canopy of red silk adorned with gold threads. On the walls around the Imperial Court were faded murals depicting various scenes and events in Oval-Earth. The murals were very ancient, because the painting of pictorial images was a lost art in Oval-Earth.

The petitioners crowded into the assembly area of the Imperial Court and began shoving and pushing one another to get the right position in the order of presentation. Everyone wanted to avoid being among the first five or six to present a petition. When the Viceroy and his agents entered, the crowd would be required to freeze in their positions, so the struggle was largely a matter of keeping as far away as possible from the cordon at the center of the room.

Tundra-Bear and Hrudan stood in the center of the assembly area and simply did not move or allow themselves to be moved, so that the crowd jockeyed wildly around them. Hrudan had to avoid the almost overwhelming urge to call the crowd to order. Instead, he stood in utter distress, gazing over the heads of the swirling throng.

He examined the murals on the walls. To his amazement, they resembled the wood carvings in his own house. One of them even depicted a royal figure with a doglike body and a tail like a fish's and holding a lyre in its hands. A Hydro-Sylph, he thought, as Illyria would call it. There were also depictions of that noble but extinct animal remembered in some remote regions of Oval-Earth as the horse.

A gong reverberated through the hollow-domed chamber. The portals next to the throne were flung open, and the crowd froze. A double line of Imperial

Guards carrying halberds and wearing yellow-plumed helmets marched into the Imperial Court. They advanced to the cordon in the center of the court.

The lines split, one marching to the right and the other to the left; they circled back to the walls on either side, where the guards lined up at regular intervals, holding their halberds in front of them and resting the butt ends on the floor.

Next, a file of crossbow bearers entered the hall followed by a Sergeant-at-Arms carrying a particularly fine crossbow embossed with gold emblems. After a ceremonious display of marching back and forth, while the Sergeant-at-Arms performed a set of elaborate little pirouettes with his crossbow in the center, they formed into a protective semicircle around the throne.

A contingent of heavily robed Imperial Quill-Drivers, accompanied by clerks bearing file baskets and secretarial implements, entered the courtroom. The Quill-Drivers fanned out to the various desks, where they scrambled up the little ladders that led to the top of their high, narrow stools.

The Grand High Scrivener followed them, carrying the Imperial Appointment Book over his head. He climbed up the stool at the central desk and pounded the book down onto the surface of the desk, raising an unseemly cloud of brownish dust. He sneezed once or twice and readjusted his enormous spectacles.

Once the Grand High Scrivener was seated, a small army of other officials marched into the chamber: Nib-Nibblers, Tale-Bearers, Scroll-Rollers, Wax-Welders, Seal-Stampers, Parchment-Pleaters, Rumor-Spreaders, Glad-Handers, Claim-Adjusters, Lackeys-at-Large, Malicious Doodlers, and Retroactive Rubricians, in addition to an assortment of curial Blabbers, Pettifoggers, Scandal-Mongers, Back-Stabbers, and Filibusterers whose common task it was to purvey, at the Viceroy's bidding, whatever background hubbub, commotion, and general confusion might be requisite for the occasion.

They were followed by two large, brutal-looking guards armed with knotty billy clubs who tromped in and advanced directly to the cordon. They were known as the Ejectors. Finally, the Herald entered, heaved a colossal brass flugelhorn to his lips, and produced a loud, off-key blast. The Viceroy appeared.

"Tarrababart, Functionary Supreme, Viceroy of Oval-Earth!" the Herald shouted. The retinue burst into a hymn of acclamation:

> Terrible and Dreadful is he
> Whose Whimsy is his Law.
> He veers like winds in autumn.
> His orders come and go.
> Stunning is the Rancor of his Breath.
> His rules bind all but him.

Tarrababart was a squat, runtish, wrinkled figure with bulging eyes and a bulbous, pockmarked nose. A deep crease ran through the center of his forehead, as if someone had once buried a hatchet in his skull just at that point. A fat, wormlike vein zigzagged over the crease. At the bottom of his face, a soft, shapeless chin was partially hidden by a dangling lower lip that tended to quiver uncontrollably.

Over his shoulders was draped a red, gold-threaded robe that resembled the canopy over the throne; he also wore a pair of puffy yellow pantaloons gathered up at his ankles. His shoes were long, thin, blue scabbards with tiny spikes protruding out of both the heels and toes, and his hat was a fluffy swag of green cloth. He carried a long, shapeless wooden scepter in his right hand. When he mounted the throne, he struck the scepter violently against the well-battered wall behind him. The Herald bellowed, "The Imperial Court is now in session."

The Imperial Quill-Drivers immediately began to write furiously on parchments spread before them on their desks, even though there was nothing to write about yet.

One of the Ejectors pointed his billy club at an unfortunate member of the crowd who was trapped up front when the court entrance began. The cordon was opened momentarily, and he was ushered forward to stand on a square mosaic floor panel called the "petitioner's box." He looked about nervously, knowing that his situation was hopeless. The Grand High Scrivener cried out in a high, wavering voice: "Present your petition."

"Your ... Your ... *Highness*," he said hesitantly, "I humbly—"

"SILENCE!" shouted the Viceroy. "Today I am to be referred to as 'Your *Magnificence*.' Eject him."

The Ejectors sprang forward, grasped the hapless petitioner, and dragged him to another mosaic panel on the floor, which sprang open, and the petitioner was tossed into the gaping hole. The panel slammed shut.

An Ejector grabbed a fisherman by his checkered sweater and pushed him forward. The Grand High Scrivener cried out again, "Present your petition."

"Your Magnificence," the fisherman stuttered frantically, "I *humbly* beg to represent the fishing village of Mommergent on the Midland Sea. Our fishing rights—"

"SILENCE! Humility will not do today. Only obsequiousness will do. One must '*obsequiously* beg.' Eject him."

The fisherman was ejected.

A mooseherd, a tall, middle-aged man dressed in a tunic of shiny white moose leather, was the next to be shown past the cordon. He had spent five days at court already and knew that his situation was hopeless as well, since he had again been trapped up front.

"Present your petition!" the Chief Scrivener proclaimed.

"Your Magnificence, I obsequiously beg once again—"

"SILENCE! No one is ever allowed to use the expression 'once again' in my presence. It implies that I have neglected my duty. Have I neglected my duty?"

"No! Your Magnificence," was the resounding chorus that arose from the entire court.

"Do I ever neglect my duty?"

"No! Your Magnificence," resonated again through the court.

"Am I a perfect model of a kindly, generous, ever-dutiful ruler?"

"Yes! Your Magnificence," they cried yet again.

"EJECT HIM!"

The moose herder vanished down through the hole beneath the sliding panel. A wood-gnome was shoved past the cordon.

"Present your petition," the Chief Scrivener shouted.

The wood-gnome, short and thin, with tufts of ragged hair sticking out at all angles from his head, held a parchment in his hand and trembled violently.

"Your Magnificence," he shrieked, "I am Cutty-Root of the hornbeam clan. I obsequiously beg to bring to your attention this matter of a murder.

My fellow clan member, Twigbottom, was the victim of a most deplorable murder—"

"Deplorable? DEPLORABLE?" howled the Viceroy. "What's so deplorable about a murder?" He broke out into coarse, hysterical laughter. The vein on his forehead bulged enormously. The Quill-Drivers began to laugh, followed by the clerks, and the crossbow bearers, and the guards, and the Ejectors. Finally, many in the crowd started to laugh. Laughter shook the entire building.

Guards dropped their halberds as they buckled over in laughter; the Ejectors guffawed as they hit the floor with their billy clubs; the Quill-Drivers hooted and pounded their desks; the Nib-Nibblers, Scroll-Rollers, Wax-Melders, Seal-Stampers, Parchment-Pleaters, Glad-Handers, and Claim-Adjusters cackled; the Malicious Doodlers, Blabbers, Pettifoggers, and Filibusterers rocked back and forth with uncontrolled merriment as they slapped one another on the backs. Only the Retroactive Rubricians maintained their composure, for part of their job was to laugh only at old and stale jokes, though it was difficult for them not to repress their smiles.

"SILENCE!" the Viceroy bellowed over the tide of laughter that flowed back and forth across the courtroom. There was immediate silence. "This 'deplorable' murder, as you so amusingly describe it, has already been investigated. Relevant dossiers and sealed writs have been forwarded to the Ministry of Insoluble Affairs. Under no circumstances will it be deemed proper to apprise the Viceroy of something already known to him. Eject the petitioner!"

Cutty-Root screamed, "How was I to know that you had been apprised about it already—" but he found himself swallowed up by the hole in the floor before he had a chance to continue his protest.

The next petitioner was brought through the cordon. It was a young woman dressed in a shabby orange gown and a blue cape. She looked frail and impoverished.

"Present your petition," the Grand High Scrivener cried out.

"Your Magnificence, I obsequiously beg you to redress an evil done to me. I am about to lose my small farm to a scheming neighbor. My husband is ill, my children are starving, my—"

"SILENCE! Petitioners must first state their name and village before declaring the details of their business. EJECT HER!"

"My name is Baractra. My village is—"

"EJECT HER!" the Viceroy screamed, "NOW!"

The two Ejectors were pulling at her arms when a deep, ear-rending "NO!" thundered through the courtroom. Hrudan stormed to the front of the crowd and shouted, "In all justice, you must hear her case!"

The court was mute with astonishment.

The squat figure of the Viceroy rose from the throne in disbelief. His dangling lower lip quivered uncontrollably; the vein on his forehead swelled up into a bright purple band. The mouths of Quill-Drivers dropped open. The halberds of the Imperial Guards shook and rattled.

The Ejectors were paralyzed. They let the woman loose, and she backed into the crowd. The Blabbers, Pettifoggers, Scandal-Mongers, and Filibusterers braced themselves for a signal from the Viceroy that would unleash an unruly din so loud that any further challenge to the court would be summarily drowned out.

Then the heads of all the people in the court arched suddenly upward. Through the broken window in the dome darted a hairy-winged fly, so huge that it looked like a gnarled version of a midsize bird. It whizzed grotesquely around the inside of the dome and with blinding speed dived down at the crowd. Hands and arms flailed at the enormous insect as it passed over the heads of the crowd. It dipped and butted in and out of archways and niches around the room.

The Quill-Drivers stopped their incessant writing and scrambled down from their desks as it flew by; guards began to swing at it with their halberds, hitting the walls and shattering the halberds or knocking one another down on the floor.

The hairy-winged fly arced and looped and plummeted directly into the face of the Viceroy, who tumbled off the dais and into the lower drapes of the canopy.

The Herald blasted his brass horn again and again in an effort to restore order, until the fly swept into the mouth of the horn for a second, squirted a jet of putrid fluid into it, and caused the Herald to cast away the horn and to bend over with spasmodic coughing and spitting.

The pandemonium in the crowd intensified.

The Viceroy managed by this time to pick himself up. He crouched beside the throne, holding on to the wooden frame. His face was contorted with anger. He screeched, "Can no one quash this insolent insect that dares disturb the tranquility and beneficent order of my court?"

Tundra-Bear stood forth from the crowd and said, "I can."

The Imperial Court was silent except for the hideous buzzing of the hairy-winged fly as it momentarily circled around in the upper part of the dome. Everyone stared at Tundra-Bear.

"I will need a crossbow."

The Sergeant-at-Arms glanced at the Viceroy. "Your Magnificence, I obsequiously remind you that nobody can hit a hairy-winged fly with anything, especially not with a crossbow!"

The fly dived down again.

Four crossbow men, provoked by Tundra-Bear's challenge and acting on their own initiative, discharged their weapons at it. Bolts struck the masonry walls and bounced off towards the crowd, which now clamored and stampeded back and forth in order to avoid the new threat of madly ricocheting projectiles. One stray bolt sliced a thin strip of scalp off one of the Ejectors. He screamed and held both hands on his bleeding head, while the other Ejector pointed at him with his billy club and laughed. Another bolt rebounded directly through the throne and vanished behind the canopy.

The Viceroy gaped at the hole left by the bolt. "Sergeant-at-Arms, give him your crossbow. Young man with the deep hood, if you can kill the fly, I shall grant any petition you might have."

The magnificent, ceremonial crossbow was delivered into Tundra-Bear's hand. Its perfection of design and excellence of craftsmanship immediately reminded him of Hrudan's Axe. It must have been made in some prior age. It rested lightly but powerfully in his arms.

With his hood still pulled well over his head, he advanced to the petitioner's box to get a central position, steadied his feet, and made sure the crossbow and bolt were properly adjusted. He raised the crossbow and prepared to fire. Carefully lining up his sights, he aimed at some invisible spot high in the dome of the courtroom.

Then he stood there completely motionless. Everyone watched him with rapt attention. They were mystified by his stillness. They expected that his crossbow would be flailing around wildly, trying to follow the erratic flight of the gigantic fly.

The hairy-winged fly still darted around the room at furious speed, changing its direction instantaneously, rising and dipping through the crowds and the guards, none of whom dared to move.

All the while, Tundra-Bear's eyes were following it as he maintained his aim at the invisible spot. At one point, through its hundreds of ups and downs and backs and forths, the fly headed directly towards the invisible spot.

Tundra-Bear had already discharged the bolt when the fly passed through his sights. There was an ugly splat as the hairy-winged fly exploded into a shower of wet, slimy fragments that filtered down over the crowd. The bolt, having passed through the fly, struck the dome and ricocheted downward, landing with its point buried deep in the top of the Grand High Scrivener's desk.

The crowd gasped in admiration, even as it bent and twisted in its efforts to avoid the loathsome fragments of the dead fly. The Viceroy sank down into his throne again in relief. Tundra-Bear returned the crossbow to the Sergeant-at-Arms. He congratulated the Sergeant-at-Arms for possessing such a fine crossbow. The Sergeant-at-Arms was speechless.

"Present your petition," said the Grand High Scrivener.

Hrudan spoke for Tundra-Bear. "We desire entrance into the Ministry of Historical Records."

"Your purpose?" the Viceroy asked, as he slouched, broken and exhausted, in his throne. He had forgotten about his protocol. In any event, Hrudan had decided to ignore it, and the Viceroy was too intimidated by Hrudan at the moment to make an issue of it.

"To examine some antique deeds from the period prior to the War of Desolation," He answered.

"Deliver the written petition into the hands of the Grand High Scrivener."

Hrudan complied.

"Grant a court permit for this entry," the Viceroy commanded. One of the Imperial Quill-Drivers, using a quill whose nib had been finely honed by the teeth of a Nib-Nibbler, scribbled the permit on a piece of parchment. The Grand High Scrivener signed it and handed it to a Parchment-Pleater, who folded it and handed it to a Wax-Melter, who poured hot wax on the seam of the fold and handed it to a Seal-Stamper, who stamped the hot wax with an official seal and handed it on to a Notary, who blew on the seal until it cooled and handed it on to a Glad-Hander, who handed it on to Hrudan.

Hrudan called over to Baractra and asked her to join them. Like so many of the others in the assembly, she had been terrified by Hrudan's defiance of the Viceroy, even though he was coming to her defense. Moreover, she had shrunk back into the crowd while the commotion about the hairy-winged fly was going on. Yet, if she found the powerfully built, black-bearded stranger frightening at first, she found him reassuring as well.

She decided to accept his invitation — it was, after all, the only way for her to exit the courtroom safely. Tundra-Bear, Baractra, and Hrudan turned to leave. The crowd made a passageway for their departure. They watched in admiration as the three marched calmly through the passageway and out of the courtroom.

As soon as they had left, the Viceroy turned to three of his guards. "I could swear that the young man who killed the hairy-winged fly has purple eyes. He is from the Hills. Maybe he has some connection with the Hill people seen at the wood-gnome meeting only a short time before their tents were set on fire. Besides, a man who has an aim like that is dangerous. He could have placed a bolt straight through the pupil of my eye, if he had wanted to."

The Viceroy rubbed the bulging vein on his forehead frantically. "As for the bearded man with the black cape," he blustered, "he is even more dangerous. He dared to defy me. Follow those two and the woman with them. I suspect a conspiracy here. And send squadrons to block the four gates at the terminals of the boulevards. They must not leave the Capital."

"Your Magnificence, I obsequiously remind you that the gates cannot be blocked because they have all fallen down," one of the three guards whimpered as obsequiously as he could.

"Block them anyway!" the Viceroy hollered.

The three guards slipped rapidly through the rear door of the courtroom. The Viceroy turned to the Claims-Adjusters and ordered them to draft documents rescinding the permit granted to Hrudan, and then he directed the Retroactive Rubricians to blot out the rubrics of such a permit from the court registry. He charged the scribes to strike all accounts of the hairy-wing-fly incident from the court records and to promulgate an interdict against any memory of what had happened.

To make sure that his orders were understood, he demanded of the court: "Do you remember what happened here today?"

"No," was the aggregate reply.

"Do you remember what it was you were not supposed to remember?" he added.

"No," the court spoke in unison, though he considered for a moment that perhaps the proper answer to that question should have been yes.

But he was satisfied, thinking it was better for the court not to remember what it was not supposed to remember than to remember what it was not supposed to remember, which would still be a way of remembering, though by not remembering what it was not supposed to remember, there was a danger that it would remember what it was not supposed to remember anyway.

Well, it was all too confusing. The Viceroy slid further down into his throne and covered his head with his arms. His head ached viciously, and his vein throbbed voluminously. He crouched there for the next ten minutes in a distraught silence that no one—not even the Filibusterers, whose mouths constantly moved, as if they were talking even when they were not talking—dared to interrupt.

Once on the Imperial Plaza outside the palace, Hrudan, Baractra, and Tundra-Bear braced themselves against the cold wind and walked quickly into the northeast quarter of the city to find the Ministry of Historical Records. The sky overhead was still overcast and threatening to rain. The square was not difficult to find, even through the ravaged streets, because Baractra was familiar with this quarter of the city. Eventually Knarry was seen at a distance standing by the cart. He waved, and Hrudan, Baractra, and Tundra-Bear found themselves, or thought they found themselves, reunited with the others.

A moment later, Fox-Foot and Bomsiell came running breathlessly out of a side alley. Fox-Foot tucked her quiver back into the baggage, flung her robe of disguise around herself again, and hopped onto the wagon.

"Where have you been?" Tundra-Bear asked her.

"Nowhere special," she replied with a smile. Bomsiell also leapt onto the wagon and crawled under some coverlets. Knarry was mystified.

Baractra was introduced to the travelers. She advised them about an escape route through a breach in the northeast wall of the city and about an abandoned farmstead they could use for the night, since the weather was inclement. Knarry was pleased to have this information. It was decided that Baractra would go ahead of the others and would meet them there later in the afternoon.

After she left, the travelers rehearsed their roles as they had devised them back at Branch-Knot's house and turned towards the Ministry of Historical Records. It was a forbidding place—a low, badly deteriorated old building with a large central door. A tower of irregular stonework rose high above the door; it seemed to be tilting slightly to one side. Knarry rapped loudly on the door.

Only after several more raps, and about a ten-minute wait, the door swung open, and a tall, lean old man blinked out somewhat vacantly at the group of travelers. He had a long, pointed nose with enormous spectacles mounted uneasily about halfway down on it. One small, reddened eye was higher than the other, so that the spectacles leaned sideways on his nose as if to match the slant of his eyes. From the point of his nose, a long, grizzled whisker stuck straight up into the air. Knarry thought he looked like a moss-mouse turned into a human being.

"What can we do for you?" he retched coarsely at them, his whisker bobbing back and forth as he spoke.

"We need to examine some historical documents," Tundra-Bear announced. He had carefully memorized a speech composed by Tristan-Phoros for this occasion.

"Whatever would you need to examine historical documents for?" the old man returned.

"Madam, here," Tundra-Bear said, "has come to investigate and review the titles of some her many properties spread throughout the principalities of Oval-Earth. I am her secretary. Some of these titles are very old and thus are not to be found in the Ministry of Deeds."

"How far back do you need to go?" the old man coughed, his red eyes squinting at them through the thick, glassy spheres of his spectacles.

"We need to go as far back as . . ." Tundra-Bear hesitated. Knarry nudged him with his elbow to proceed. "To the War of Desolation."

"What! The War of Desolation?" the old man croaked.

"Even more . . . we need to find out something about . . . the Kingdom of Darkness."

"Whatever for?"

"To understand if it . . ." Tundra-Bear faltered.

Tristan-Phoros whispered, "If it has any claim . . ."

"Yes, if it has any claim to . . . to . . ."

"The aforesaid properties," Tristan-Phoros whispered again.

"The aforesaid properties," Tundra-Bear concluded. He was clearly relieved that his prepared speech had come to an end. The old man was incredulous. He also could not figure out where the whispering was coming from.

Knarry quickly spoke up, "Whom do we have the honor of addressing?"

"My name is Klorp. I am the sole functionary of this ministry. Nobody comes here. We have no history to record. We have no history worthy of recording. We have no history worthy of remembrance. You must go away."

"Where do the annual reports of the Ministry of Historical Records come from?" demanded Hrudan.

"They are made up by the Scribes of the Viceroy. They write whatever they want to write. They make up any history they want to make up. They obliterate any history they want to obliterate. I never see the reports. I don't care what's in them. What does it matter? Anyway, you must go away. I have work to do. The ungrateful populace of Oval-Earth does not appreciate how difficult it is to work all day when you have absolutely nothing to do."

Hrudan produced the court permit from underneath his black cape and handed it to Klorp. "A court permit," he declared, "authorizing us to enter the Ministry."

Klorp held the parchment in his trembling hands. He broke the seal, unfolded the parchment, and examined the permit with scrupulous care through his tilted spectacles. "I have never seen one of these before. It must, therefore, be a forgery."

Tristan-Phoros was all too eager to challenge the illogic of that statement, but Knarry muzzled him in time with a grasp of his shaggy hands. Hrudan replied, "It is not a forgery. We have just come from the Imperial Court, where we obtained this permit."

"I have no proof of that, and I have seen no precedents with which to validate the authenticity of this document. But permit or no permit, I can't let you in. It's a long-standing order. I could honor this permit only if it were accompanied by an imperially witnessed and notarized affidavit that remanded the prior statute."

Klorp felt rather proud of himself for having delivered such an officious pronouncement. The tip of his nose twitched variously up and down and waggled defiantly the single whisker at its tip.

Knarry frowned and looked at Hrudan. Knarry plucked from his cloak the brilliant blue diamond gemstone that he had found in the ruins of Gnarl-Oak's earth-house. He held it up before Klorp's tilted spectacles. At first, Klorp did not understand. Then his little red eyes glistened as if with tears, and his sole whisker shook with excitement. "You mean—you mean you are going to provide me with a . . . a not-altogether-inopportune consideration?"

"Yes," said Knarry, "a consideration, inopportune or otherwise."

Hrudan looked away, as Knarry extended his arm to Klorp in a mock ceremonial gesture.

Fox-Foot murmured, "All that effort at the Imperial Court for nothing!"

Klorp tenderly received the gemstone and rolled it around in his ungainly hands. He tilted his head to the side and closed his eyes. He trembled with emotion. "All these years and nobody ever came here, so I could never receive a consideration. Now I have. I feel that this is a milestone in my career—indeed, its crowning achievement. A real consideration! How it infuses my old and withered heart with a sense of . . . yes, having become at last a recognized and distinguished member of the civil service! Please do come in."

Fox-Foot climbed down from the wagon, where she had been sitting and followed the others as they entered the building. Klorp was uneasy about allowing a dog to enter the Ministry, but Tristan-Phoros moved too quickly to be prevented. Bomsiell stayed behind, partially hidden in the wagon. She could protect it, if need be, from any local or official brigand provoked to tamper with its valuable cargo. Hrudan closed the door of the Ministry securely behind the group after they had passed through.

The interior of the building consisted of numerous long hallways, gloomy in the half-light and stacked along the sides with cabinets filled with parchments and scrolls. Klorp admonished his visitors not to touch anything because it was all organized according to precise rules.

But what they saw was a disorder as thorough as a disorder can get. Many of the cabinets were tipped over, and their contents were strewn across the floor. Nothing was labeled, and mounds of dusty and shredded documents looked as though they had been tossed about with a pitchfork. Klorp conducted the Madam and her retinue through the tangle of clogged hallways to the indexes. Here he left them to pursue their work.

As soon as Klorp had turned the corner and was out of sight, Tristan-Phoros jumped up on his back legs and began to rifle through the indexes. Knarry and Hrudan joined him. Fox-Foot and Tundra-Bear wandered off to reconnoiter the cavernous building.

An hour or two of studying the indexes revealed very little of use. The indexes made no sense at all — they were simply scraps of disorganized information. Moreover, they gave no clues about where, in the Ministry, any document could be found. Tristan-Phoros sat on his haunches and panted a bit from the effort of the search. He turned to Knarry and said, "We've got to get Klorp back in here. With him, I doubt that there is much we can do, but without him, we can do nothing."

Fox-Foot and Tundra-Bear were sent to find Klorp and summon him back to the index area. He walked in sideways like a long-legged crab, peering at the group with his wide, tilted spectacles and little red eyes. The tip of his long, thin nose moved up and down in quick little spasms, shaking the whisker.

Knarry addressed him. "Klorp, you must be proud to hold such weighty responsibilities in the safekeeping of Oval-Earth. We are all grateful to you." All the rest nodded in agreement, and blotches of pink blush spread out all over Klorp's pasty, wizened face.

Knarry continued. "Our mission in the service of our beloved Madam requires that we seek out any document that is stored in this magnificent edifice that will give us reliable and definitive access to the entitlements of the Kingdom of Darkness upon the lands and peoples of Oval-Earth. Only in this way can we settle the claims that certain evil speculators are making to wrest Madam's properties away from her. We do implore your aid."

Klorp wrapped his frizzled head in his long, spidery fingers and pronounced, "Well . . . yes, there is something that might help."

Tristan-Phoros tilted his head. The others listened intently. Klorp sneezed so loudly that dust was blown off some nearby scrolls. "It is called *The Chartulary . . .* yes, *The Chartulary of the Kingdom of Darkness.* It is located in the tower collection. But it is strictly forbidden. Nobody can read it—except for myself. And I have never read it."

Knarry clapped his knobby hands together and exclaimed, "Well, now that sounds like just the thing to solve Madam's troubles for her. Please be so good as to read it for us!"

"Yes," said Fox-Foot, assuming a high-pitched whine. "Do be so kind. At last, my woes are over. Isn't that so, my sweet little Poochy-Poo?" She leaned over and kissed Tristan-Phoros on his big, wet, black nose. He, in turn, forced himself to wag his tail in assent but harbored in his mind some way to get revenge on her for this gratuitous and unnecessary insult.

Klorp giggled as if someone were tickling him. He was delighted to be of such service. He even wondered if Knarry might not have another gemstone in his pocket. It was not so much the value of the gemstone that interested him; to be bribed twice in the same day would simply be too exquisite! Still, he did not have the courage to ask. Instead, he turned around; and in long, angular, sideways strides, he led the wealthy lady and her retinue up the curving staircase that led to the tower room.

The room was dark except for a few narrow slits of dim light that came from the overcast sky through the half dozen embrasures that ringed the tower at regular intervals. One large cabinet seemed to be in reasonably decent shape—the rest having fallen over or decayed into what looked like worm-eaten mounds of sawdust. The tips of old scrolls projected upward through the heaps.

Klorp approached the one remaining cabinet and fetched a set of brass keys out of his robe. He fumbled with the large, clanking keys for a while until he isolated one of them, fitted it slowly into a lock, and, turning what must have been a massive bolt, opened a large, uneven drawer. He groped around in the drawer until he finally lifted out a scroll, and, waving it about in the dusty air, declared it to be *The Chartulary of the Kingdom of Darkness*.

Knarry and Tundra-Bear both reached out to grasp it, but Klorp quickly drew it away. "No," he croaked. "Only I am allowed to read it."

"Please do," said Tundra-Bear, and he drew a writing tablet and a stylus out of his robe to pretend to take notes. Tristan-Phoros winked at him as if to say, "Don't worry, Tundra-Bear. I will commit to memory everything he says." But Tundra-Bear would have to go through the motions nevertheless.

Klorp engaged in an excessively long clearing of his throat. Then he unrolled the scroll, edged it around to catch some of the light entering the tower through the embrasures, adjusted his spectacles, and began to read.

"*The Chartulary of the Kingdom of Darkness*," he read and looked up, quite pleased with himself for having made it that far.

"Yes, we know that," said Knarry. "Please go on."

"No author. No date. No table of contents. No place of publication. No house or venue of publication. Do you wish me to continue?"

"Naturally."

"No prologue. No epigraphs. No preambles. No watermarks. No frontispiece. No scholia. No devices or emblem or subtitles or prolegomena or recommendations or summaries or notices or colophons or dedicatory epistles or—"

"Please get on with it."

"Some of the first lines are illegible—the ink has run. Maybe it got rained on. The roof of the tower has a tendency to leak. I, and many generations of my predecessors in this august post, I do believe, have submitted the appropriate complaints and requisitions to the Ministry of Public Buildings, all to no avail—as is obvious."

"Read whatever you can."

"Besides these beneficent powers, beknownst unto all and of which I hitherto have discoursed in documents and registries suitably proffered, yea, even those powers of earth and under-earth and Song ..." Klorp looked up from the manuscript. "Am I doing well? Can you follow it? Does this make sense?"

"Just keep at it," said Tristan-Phoros, forgetting that he was not supposed to speak.

"Who said that?" Klorp replied.

"Oh, just me," said Tundra-Bear. "Sometimes my voice gets a little hoarse."

"Horse? Horses no longer exist. Sounds more doggy to me."

"No, hoarse — rough; you know what I mean."

"You should have Madam's physician look after it."

"I will. I will. But read on."

Klorp resumed his reading: "There are yet other powers, yea even powers not of things, but of the darkness of spirit, of spirit no longer shaped to things, but unto itself, spirit giving birth to spirit, spirit unsung, unshaped, no ties, no boundedness . . ." Klorp glanced up again. "I see nothing here about titles to properties. I see nothing here about property at all. Shall I go on?"

"Without question," Knarry grumbled.

"For these are the Rulers of the Darkness of this world, the Kingdom of Lo-El, the Principality of Lo-El over Lo-Els, for there is only one Lo-El, and it is all Lo-Els and makes unto itself all Lo-Els, for which reason it is called the Prince of the Power of Darkness, because it rules in the darkness of this world, and in consequence hereunto, they who are under its dominion are called the Children of Darkness and their domain thereto the Kingdom of Darkness . . ."

Silence.

"Still nothing about titles to property, or leases, or rents, or whatever. And all this strange talk! It means nothing to me. Are you sure you shouldn't go back to the Ministry of Deeds?"

"Positive," Knarry said. "Proceed!"

"If you insist."

"I do."

"Be it understood that Lo-El is Prince of Phantasms, Inhabitants of his dominion of air and darkness, and these demons, phantasms, or Spirits of Illusion verily even Lo-Els each unto itself in the mirage and delusion of Lo-El, Prince of Lo-Els, do thereby and at all times constitute yea even a confederacy of deceivers, and their terrain thereto the vales of sleep and dream, and to dreams they are, and dreams will be, even the dreams that trouble grievously the night of the spirit, for the spirit of the troubled does make them, and the spirit of the darkened does engender them, and none other does engender them, no, not that which was made at the Beginning of time which was all good and all beneficent, for they, and hear me, O blessed ones, dwell not beyond, but within, and those lie who tell you otherwise than this; for such as tell the untrue mingle with untruth and with the way of illusion, and they are like unto the Lo-Els whom they worship with their ways of lies; and the day will come, the day of the summoning, that dreadful day, when out of the hidden places of the earth, and out of the darkness where they have dwelt since the ages when the darkness began and it grew, until that summoning, yea, even that dreadful summoning, that Great Upwelling, shall arise over the earth the Lo-Els in all their might and in all their works and pomps—"

"MEEEEOOOOAAAUUU!" The high-pitched screech of a forest cat ripped through muffled silence of the tower room. It was Bomsiell, from down below in the wagon.

Klorp's head shot backward, spinning his spectacles upward into the vaulted ceiling of the tower room. Fox-Foot sprang to one of the embrasures and looked down. A throng of armed hirelings led by the three palace guards was advancing from the direction of the Imperial Plaza and was just about to enter the square in front of the Ministry of Historical Records. "Quick!" Fox-Foot shouted. "We've left our wagon and weapons down below. We've got to get out of here."

Fox-Foot and Tundra-Bear were the first to bolt down the curving stairs in order to help Bomsiell protect the valuable gear left behind on the wagon. They were followed by Hrudan and Knarry. Only Tristan-Phoros remained behind in the tower room with his teeth sunk in one end of *The Chartulary* as Klorp struggled with the other end. Klorp, now partially blind without his spectacles, cavorted around in hysterical convulsions, trying to shake the fangs of Tristan-Phoros out of the scroll. Tristan-Phoros, for his part, snarled and growled in a most doglike manner, rigidly digging in his front legs and yanking his head back and forth to get possession of the scroll.

Klorp cried out at last, "Let go, you stupid dog!"

Tristan-Phoros yelped, "How dare you call me a—" and lost hold of the document. Klorp flew backward with the scroll and landed with a huge puff in a mound of fine worm-dust, which set him to sneezing in rapid, compulsive jerks of his head.

"A dog that talks!" he gasped.

Knarry shouted from below for Tristan-Phoros, who, at that moment seriously considering that he might really be a "stupid dog," ran for the staircase, scudded all the way down, and leapt through the door that Knarry held open for him.

The armed mob had just rounded the corner of the square in front of the Ministry when Tundra-Bear and Fox-Foot, their disguises shaken off, their longbows already strung and armed and their green hair streaming loosely around their shoulders, discharged two arrows that penetrated the peaks of the plumed helmets of the two guards at the front. The helmets, lifted by the arrows, flew off their heads and across the square, colliding with a sharp metallic clang against the wooden wall of a nearby livery stable.

Two more arrows instantaneously deprived the third guard of his helmet, one arrow knocking it into the air and the other spinning it around suspended above the crowd, until it swung off and punched into the soft belly of a wildly gesticulating functionary with high boots and a pair of pince-nez attached to his uniform.

As he yowled in pain, the crowd of hirelings, almost in a single movement, became panic-stricken and dove to the ground for protection. Here they sprawled and wrestled over one another in an effort to abandon the square. They shouted and cursed and tugged at one another's coats. They abandoned their weapons, such as they were, all over the square. Tundra-Bear and Fox-Foot sent one more pair of arrows over their heads to make their flight even more panic-stricken.

The three helmetless guards, meanwhile, had raced over the backs of the recumbent and squirming multitude, breaking ribs and squashing fingers with their boots as they stampeded their way across the howling fugitives; they were the first to flee out of the square.

Tundra-Bear and Fox-Foot turned to join their friends, who were well on their way out of the Capital by now, following Baractra's directions through the breach in the northeastern wall. With their fleet stride, Fox-Foot and Tundra-Bear caught up with them, and the members of the band, now quickly divesting themselves of what was left of their cumbersome disguises and of the draw-cart, disappeared into the farmlands east of the Capital.

A slow, steady rain had developed over Oval-Earth by the afternoon, when the travelers found their way to the abandoned farmstead Baractra had told them about. She waited for them in an empty hay-shed, the only building left on the old farmstead that had a reliable roof covering it. She waved them over to the shed.

Inside it was dry, quiet, and fragrant, and the hay was soft to lean back on. Bomsiell climbed up high in the rafters and peered out through the cracks in the wooden boarding to see if anyone was coming. The others simply relaxed. They knew that search parties, should there be any, would end up avoiding the rain by frittering away their time in the various local taverns and would draft some false report to submit upon returning to the Capital.

Meanwhile, Baractra had been busy. She had collected some millet from an old storage grange and cooked up a hot porridge over a fire of fallen timbers she recovered from the ruined cottage on the farmstead. When everyone had eaten and had become reasonably dry and warm, they gathered together to mull over the day's events.

Tristan-Phoros opened his satchel and filled his pipe with fresh bilberry weed. He sat there puffing for a while, his back leaning against one of the posts of the shed and his forelegs folded behind his head. He listened to the pleasant sound of the rain on the roof of the shed.

Knarry turned to him. "Well, what do you think we learned, my erudite friend and esteemed philosopher?"

"A great number of things," Tristan-Phoros replied. "Not as much as we would have liked to have learned, of course; but a great deal nevertheless."

"For example?"

"Well, we don't know who wrote that document. We don't know why the document was written. We don't know when the document was composed, but its archaic flavor would imply that it is fairly old. Can we trust its authenticity? Perhaps it is a fraud. These are serious matters."

Knarry nodded.

Tristan-Phoros went on. "I think it may be genuine by the very fact that it states something directly counter to what we take to be, and have good reasons to take to be, the prevailing mythology about the Kingdom of Darkness. I cannot imagine, if the author were in bad faith, that is, if he were in league with *them*, why he would have said things that the forces of darkness would most ardently not have wished to be said."

Knarry looked at Tristan-Phoros. "I hope you don't burn down this shed with your pipe, Tristan-Phoros, though I know it helps you to think, and your thinking is of great importance to us now. In the meantime, be more specific."

"To be sure," Tristan-Phoros murmured. "Shall I itemize what we have learned, or what I think we have learned if we can count on that document and if my inferences from it are correct?"

"That may be appropriate."

"*Item*: We know the names of the forces of darkness. They are called Lo-Els. They have a Prince. Their Prince is Lo-El."

"What do you make of that?" asked Fox-Foot.

"Only this: there are many of them, yet the many is a one. I know that sounds like a contradiction. It means that our adversary is not simply a collection of individuals, though it certainly is that. But it is also a oneness, a condition, a phenomenon of being—hmm, let's just say being adversarial, of being the adversary.

"In any case, it is good to know that there is an adversary, that the adversary has deliberately set itself up as an adversary, that the adversary has a name, and what the name of the adversary is.

"That is a great deal, and yet not very much. But it helps to define not what we are talking about but that we are talking about something that can be talked about. Shall I continue?"

"Of course," Tundra-Bear remarked, though he had little idea of what Tristan-Phoros was talking about.

"*Item*: The Kingdom of Darkness has something ... I guess we should say 'invisible' about it. It is hidden—well, hidden until it no longer wants to be hidden.

"*Item*: The Kingdom of Darkness is somehow bound up with the illusory. It is no less real, in its own way, for that. Illusions are as dangerous as real things. Indeed, they are more dangerous.

"*Item*: The Kingdom of Darkness did not exist at the origin of things. It arose later in time. It is not natural, but rises, indeed, against the natural order.

"*Item*: Its power grows. Its power emerges from the energy of things already created—yet not so much from the physical energy of things but from the psychic energy of things that can think; that is, from creatures … creatures like us.

"*Item*: Its peril has some relationship to sleep—to sleep and to dreams." Tristan-Phoros hesitated after making this observation. Something strange and inexplicable began to puzzle him, and he seemed to be saddened by it. After a few seconds, he recovered himself again.

"*Item*: One day its power will come to a head—the day of the summoning, or what *The Chartulary* called the 'Great Upwelling.'"

Hrudan interrupted, "But hasn't that happened already? Wasn't that the War of Desolation?"

"I don't understand about the War of Desolation, Hrudan," Tristan-Phoros retorted. "*The Chartulary* didn't mention that. I presume, therefore, that the document was composed before the time of the War. Perhaps you are correct; yet it has always been assumed in Oval-Earth that one day the Kingdom of Darkness would return to have another war—an even greater war. Perhaps this is what is meant by the 'Great Upwelling.' We don't know, but we must find out. I suspect it will be very soon."

"But why now?"

"Now? Because Garug-Caroch accidentally stumbled upon a few words of the Song. These 'Lo-Els,' whatever they are, must have realized that. In some fashion, they recognized that someone knew something he shouldn't: something that would be very bad for the Lo-Els if it were known—namely, the Song.

"For the first time in thousands of years, the words of the Song were uttered. In their invisible kingdom, they could feel its tremors. That is why they went after the Ancestral Tree. To speed things up, they needed power over the seasons.

"But of course, they have now had their setbacks. According to all you have told me, Knarry, one of them went after Garug-Caroch with the Purloined Staff. But it was too late. Garug-Caroch already knew two verses of the Song—enough to destroy one of these Lo-Els, even when armed with such a formidable weapon.

"In any case, the seasons have returned to normal, and the Lo-Els no longer have the Staff—we don't know who has the Staff now. Should I continue?"

"Please continue," said Knarry.

"*Item*: We come now to the most important revelation for our purposes at the present time."

"Yes?" said Knarry.

"The Kingdom of Darkness does not lie beyond the Golden Mountains."

"Then where is it?" Hrudan exclaimed.

Tristan-Phoros took another puff on his pipe and allowed the smoke to clear. He pronounced solemnly, "The Kingdom of Darkness is in Oval-Earth."

"But that's absurd," Knarry said.

"There is nothing absurd about it. *The Chartulary* was very explicit on this matter. Do you not recall? '*For they, and hear me O blessed ones, dwell not beyond, but within.*' And, furthermore, why did Kasyan's people leave Oval-Earth?"

"Because they struggled against these ... these Lo-Els ... the Princes of Darkness?"

"Which makes them ...?"

"The Princes of Light!"

"And where is the Kingdom of Light?"

"Beyond the Golden Mountains!"

"So you see!" Tristan-Phoros said as he expelled another puff of smoke. "We have learned a great deal. Our adversaries are here in Oval-Earth; they are part of Oval-Earth—as much a part of it as we are. And our adversaries are invisible and dangerous, though they can appear as phantoms or specters or whatever you want to call them, and they can ingest, as you saw on the Northern Taiga, the substance of earthly creatures to enflesh themselves as ravening monsters. They are generated somehow right here in Oval-Earth, and the loss of the Song of the Eternal Aeons has something to do with that. In the presence of the Song they cannot live."

While Tristan-Phoros spoke, the others had sat in a small circle around him and listened to him in silence. They were all mystified to some extent by what Tristan-Phoros had said, Baractra most of all, of course, for she knew little of their prior adventures. They heard the soft sound of the rain as it fell on the shed and dripped from the eaves.

"What now?" asked Hrudan.

"To the College of Wisdom," replied Tristan-Phoros. "We will find out even more there, I suppose. Or perhaps we shall find out nothing at all. But we are not too far away. Tomorrow, let us be off. This evening, let's have a nice long sleep on this soft hay. After a night in that calamitous inn, we deserve it."

"But on our way to the College of Wisdom," Hrudan proposed, "we have one short detour we ought to make and some business to do. We have taken Baractra into our care and must make sure that some of her problems are resolved for the meantime, until we can return later on."

The travelers agreed to this course of action and dispersed to various parts of the shed to find places to sleep. Tundra-Bear and Fox-Foot found a small alcove on the hayloft up above and wrapping a blanket around themselves, nestled down together in the hay.

Tundra-Bear whispered to Fox-Foot, "Listen, Fox-Foot, what were you and Bomsiell doing back there in the Capital running off by yourself?"

She laughed gently and whispered back. "Tundra-Bear, I thought you might have to do a favor for the Viceroy, especially if something happened where Hrudan could not restrain his anger. Knowing Hrudan, I figured that was pretty likely to happen.

"Then I figured: What could be worse for the Viceroy than to have something enter his court that he could not control in any way and that would ruin all his—what did Toten-Haas call it?—his protocol? And who but Bomsiell could ensnare a hairy-wing fly in her claws and help me encase it in my quiver until I needed it?

"I had noticed the day before the broken window in the dome and realized, the following day, what my opportunity might be. And you, my beloved Tundra-Bear, who but you could hit a hairy-winged fly with a crossbow? And what a crossbow that was! I could see it from the window above."

"And who but you," Tundra-Bear added, "could climb a dome like that and release the fly at just the right moment through the broken window?"

She laughed again. "It was fun." They entwined themselves together. They became like one person. And they fell asleep.

Chapter VIII

The College Revisited

The journey overland to the College was tedious and difficult. Hrudan decided that it would be best for his companions to avoid the Eastern Arm of the Radial High-Road; instead, they should follow the winding lanes that led from village to village through the countryside.

The familiar scene of desolation met the travelers at every turn of the road: ruined farmhouses, collapsed barns, clogged drainage ditches, abandoned harvesting equipment rusting at the edge of burned-out copses, and villages littered with manure and rubbish.

The travelers were often forced to ford rivers where bridges had been washed away and never replaced. They spent nights in damp woodsheds and insect-ridden hollows carved out in riverbanks. They had to be calm when affronted by surly gazes and arrogant remarks addressed to them by a lethargic populace.

Their only comfort in this situation was the knowledge that the Viceroy's hirelings would never have the gumption to pursue them on such an arduous path; and if, by chance, they should encounter one of their paltry platoons, it would pose little threat to their safety.

Indeed, their efforts at concealment were more for the safety of their opponents than for their own. They did not wish to hurt the people they were trying to preserve by unnecessary confrontations and potentially violent encounters.

The journey was complicated by Hrudan's insistence that a small detour be made in order to help Baractra in her plight. Her village of Clement-Fields was reached on the second day out from the Capital. Hrudan and Knarry propped up her dilapidated cottage by replacing several decayed roof beams and floor joists with lumber freshly hewed by Hrudan's powerful axe.

Knarry, meanwhile, attended to Baractra's ill husband and applied some of his medications. The husband awoke from his fever, surprised to see the burly wood-gnome hovering benignly over him. He was soon able to talk.

Tundra-Bear and Fox-Foot accompanied Baractra as she scoured the neighboring fields and wetlands for food: they collected berries and mushrooms, seed grains from tall swamp grasses, and rich, succulent tubers growing in the dense undergrowth of the roadside hedges. By the end of the afternoon, they had mustered a sizable store for the use of Baractra's family.

Fox-Foot prepared a nourishing, if—by lowlanders' standards—unusual, meal for the family. The children were famished and appreciative of whatever was put before them, though they quickly found Fox-Foot's ginger and elderberry tarts to be unusually tasty. By evening, Baractra's husband was sufficiently recovered to discuss with Hrudan and Knarry how to reconstruct his barn.

Baractra was now able to direct her attention back to the management of the farm in the provident and resourceful manner to which she was accustomed. Her children spent the evening playing tag with Bomsiell and riding a bit on the back of Tristan-Phoros, who, just for this occasion, submitted to such an exercise of canine playfulness. They were rather surprised and especially delighted when he accompanied them to their sleeping loft and amazed them by telling bedtime stories.

After the evening meal, Knarry and Hrudan sought out Baractra's troublesome neighbor. He reacted to these strangers initially with arrogance, subsequently with abject fear, and finally with a cautious reverence.

Hrudan succeeded in explaining to him the rights and limits of the contracts he had arranged with Baractra in the past, and the responsibilities these rights and limits entailed. The neighbor, in good faith, promised never again to challenge Baractra's ownership of the tiny farm; in exchange, he was granted fishing rights in the stream that ran through the small barley field adjacent to the farm. He was happy about this because that is all he had really wanted in the first place.

Hrudan and Knarry left his domicile with the assurance that the feud between the neighbors had been resolved. They rejoined their companions, who spent the night at Baractra's farm and set off the following morning. Baractra and her family were sad to see them go; the children made

Tristan-Phoros promise that he would come back again someday and tell them more bedtime stories.

In midafternoon of the fourth day from the Capital, the band came into view of the College of Wisdom. Knarry thought back to his visit the winter before last, when he had to push through mountainous snowdrifts to reach the portals of the College. The others simply stared, looking for the first time at the distant buildings — the old Gate-Tower and the stone Library rising high above the others. For Tristan-Phoros, the scene seemed new and yet familiar, as if he had been there before. Behind the College they could see the misty threshold of the Moor-Plains to the east.

Their plan was, first, to visit the Library. They circled around the College in a wide berth so that they could approach the Gate-Tower directly from the east and enter unseen the walled alley that led to the Library.

As they passed through the arches of the Gate-Tower, Knarry looked up and searched the facade for the stone carving that had once flickered and danced before Garug-Caroch's eyes. But he could not see it; it was hidden by a dense growth of ivy. Hrudan studied the Gate-Tower with great care and asked Knarry a multitude of questions about it, most of which Knarry could not answer.

Tundra-Bear and Fox-Foot were astonished to gaze upon such an ancient and rough-hewn edifice with its old battlements and jutting casements, every nook and cranny of which was studded with innumerable bird nests. It was like a narrow, teetering mountain made by human beings and yet was surrounded by an atmosphere of something that must have been, in its origins, deep and wise and serene.

The alley was as choked with briars and stubble as ever, but Knarry cleared a way for the others, though Bomsiell darted ahead of him through the underbrush with ease. Within moments, the band stood at the great faded wooden doors of the Library.

Though there was nothing about the facade of the Library that looked intimidating, they remembered the story of Twigbottom and Garug-Caroch and readied their weapons for action. Hrudan stepped out in front and drew the glistening Axe from its linen covering, Fox-Foot and Tundra-Bear strung their longbows, and Knarry grasped the Splinter in his hands.

They did not know what to expect inside.

Had the Library been used since Garug-Caroch's flight the previous autumn?

Was there a new custodian?

How did the hornbeam clan know of Twigbottom's death?

Was the Library still haunted by some monstrous presence, perhaps one of those Lo-Els spoken about in *The Chartulary*, ready to lunge at them when they came through the doors?

Hrudan gave orders to the others as he prepared the strategy for entrance. He would be the first to pass through the door. He brandished the mighty Axe and swept his black cape back around his shoulders as he stepped forth, took hold of the latch, and swung the door open.

Inside it was dark and silent. A startled moss-mouse stood up on its back legs directly in front of Hrudan and was dazzled momentarily by the unaccustomed light flooding through the open door. It chirped and scurried off into the shadows. The band followed Hrudan into the central rotunda. Tristan-Phoros began to sniff around but stopped when he realized what he was doing. The door swung shut.

The others stood in awe, looking into the deep, book-filled recesses that surrounded them and peering upward into the high vaults above with their many mezzanines and balconies. Thin beams of yellow light pierced through the narrow windows into the darkness. The Library was suffused with serenity, and goodness, and beneficence. Whatever evil had been there was gone—gone, Knarry surmised, through the dogged, if ill-tempered, heroism of Twigbottom, who had dispelled it at the cost of his own life.

The band dispersed. Each member wandered through the Library. Neither Fox-Foot nor Tundra-Bear could read. Still, Fox-Foot pulled a book from a shelf in one alcove and thumbed through the pages. It was titled *A Treatise on Garden Seeds and Their Uses.*

Tundra-Bear chanced upon a book on astronomy, while Hrudan glanced at the woodcuts in a compendious volume on the architectural monuments of Ospeth's Capital. "Look!" he cried out. "Here is a woodprint of the Ministry of Historical Records. But it looks much better here than it does now."

Hrudan seemed to take great pride in the magnificent buildings whose pictures filled the volume. Tristan-Phoros, meanwhile, was studying the diagram of the alcoves under the inscription and soon was off to the section on philosophy and mathematics.

Knarry, still a bit wary, lit a torch with the end of the Splinter and descended into the lower vaults accompanied only by Bomsiell, who managed to resist chasing after the moss-mice.

Knarry was not able to descend very far. Fallen stone and timbers had filled the lower vaults. "One day, we will clean this out," he thought to himself. What treasures of knowledge must lie hidden here. He ascended to the central rotunda again and, along with Bomsiell, rejoined his friends.

Tristan-Phoros summoned the band together and announced that it might be a good idea to visit the College proper. The Library was safe; they knew that now. But access to the Commentaries on the Song in the lowest vault, as Knarry had reported, was blocked by the collapse of the subterranean vaults, and the remainder of the Library was simply too abundant in lore to allow them, at least in a short time, to find out more detail about the few facts revealed to them by *The Chartulary*.

Moreover, the holdings of the Library were also too attractive to permit them to focus their minds for long on the project they were obliged to pursue. Knarry recalled the months that Garug-Caroch had worked in the Library with relatively few results.

Tristan-Phoros was convinced that a visit to the College precincts might give them more up-to-date information about how things stood in Oval-Earth. The band agreed, though reluctantly, to this advice. Knarry cautioned them: the atmosphere of the College was sinister and dangerous. He suggested that only he and Tristan-Phoros should actually penetrate the College domain. The others could remain in the Library until, or unless, they were needed.

Something of a spirited argument ensued, but the result was that Tundra-Bear, Fox-Foot, Hrudan, and Bomsiell would remain behind in the Library, while Tristan-Phoros accompanied Knarry into the College quadrangle. Tristan-Phoros renewed his pledge to comport himself at all times as a dog—a promise, as it turned out, he did not keep for long.

Tristan-Phoros and Knarry traversed the briar alley. They passed through the Gate-Tower, rounded the corner of the College cluster, and entered through the service portal. The kitchens and larder were empty of their usual culinary staff. The quadrangle was empty, too, except for a student in a brown robe asleep and propped against the refectory wall. Its shabby condition had not changed in the last year. The cloisters, which surrounded the quadrangle, were also empty. Tristan-Phoros and Knarry entered the cloisters and walked cautiously around the quadrangle. For a moment, they thought the College must be on vacation because there was so little sign of activity. Or perhaps it was College naptime! They were not sure. The entire cluster of buildings seemed to be enveloped in an oppressive atmosphere of a long, nightmarish siesta.

Moments later, they became aware of a soft, droning, monotonous voice emanating from an open door of the Lecture Hall. They crossed directly over the quadrangle to the door and looked in. A few old dusty windows dimly lit it from above. Small groups of students, all dressed alike in their moth-eaten brown robes, sprawled here and there throughout the room.

Many were asleep; others watched one another idly, or occasionally peered upward through the gloom at the lecturer, who, unaffected by their lack of attention, continued to drone on. He stood on a kind of platform, with a lectern and a low table in front of him. On the table was a wooden board of the Game of Spheres. Mounted on the wall behind him was a large diagram of the Game etched on a sheet of dark slate. He did not notice the entrance of two strangers at the back of the Hall.

Knarry sat on one of the Lecture Hall stools towards the back and gently elbowed a student who sat beside him. The student shuffled and snorted in his half-sleep, and, jerking upward out of his slouch, blinked with just a hint of surprise at the large wood-gnome sitting next to him. "What do you want?" he mumbled.

"What's it all about?" Knarry whispered.

The student looked harder at Knarry. "Don't be such a blockhead, wood-gnome. There is only one thing around here that everything is about! It's about the Game of Spheres. That is the Senior Master Laus-Urop giving his lecture on the second quartile of the seventh outward loop of the third circle. It's his specialty. He's given this same lecture over eight hundred times during his tenure at the College. In fact, that's the only lecture he gives." The student yawned so violently that Knarry thought he could see clear down to his stomach.

Knarry nodded sympathetically. He said, "But why did you come if you have heard it already?"

The student was slouching over again on his stool, his head swaying and his eyelids closing, but he did murmur, "What else is there to do? The ale-hour is still three hours away."

In the meantime, Tristan-Phoros was inching his way nearer and nearer to the podium, partially hidden by the sprawl of stools and students scattered through the Hall. Only the white tip of his golden tail, raised a bit over the debris, gave Knarry any indication of his movements. He was listening carefully to Laus-Urop. The lecture was as dispirited as it ever was, but occasionally the lecturer shuffled over to the slate diagram and traced with his finger the movement of the emerald gemstone through the third circle.

Raising his voice slightly, as if arriving at an original and especially brilliant point, he proclaimed, "So you see, a successful passage through the second quartile of the seventh outward loop requires no fewer than fourteen different quadratic calculations to be made in one-sixth of a second, especially if you intend to enter the ruby gemstone in the fourth circle any sooner than twenty-two seconds prior to the completion of all the loops of the third circle. Consequently—"

"I beg to differ!" arose from the Lecture Hall.

"Who said that!" rasped Laus-Urop, instantly aroused from his routine torpor. Masters at the College took quick offense at any challenge to their authority.

"A successful passage can be made with only three calculations."

"Three calculations! That's absurd! Who dares to question me on this!"

"I do!" shouted Tristan-Phoros who jumped up on one of the stools right in front of the lectern. The students began to squirm around sluggishly, like clusters of pale maggots under a rock when the rock is suddenly lifted and a bit of sunlight pours in.

"Who does?" returned Laus-Urop. His gaze darted around the Lecture Hall. He ignored the canine visage directly down in front of him.

"I do!"

His eyes widened with astonishment as he realized that the dog was addressing him. "Who let that dog in here?"

"Don't evade the question! Who is, and who is not, a dog may very well be arguable under the circumstances, but in any case, such an argument is not relevant here! *Ad canem* arguments are not permissible in academic discourse."

Knarry groaned. He wanted to sprint forward and haul Tristan-Phoros out of the Lecture Hall by his hind legs. But now he saw it was too late for that without creating pandemonium. The students were awakening, jumping from their stools, and crowding around the podium to see what was happening. For all their sloth, they dearly loved a good quarrel now and then and only wished they had some ale to drink while observing it.

So deep was their apathy that the appearance of a dog standing in front of them and arguing with the professor did not seem to cause either much alarm or curiosity. It could have been a moose, for all they cared, or an oversized moss-mouse. It was the looming fight that counted.

Tristan-Phoros leapt up on the platform. "Do you want to see me do it?" he asked.

"That won't prove a thing," Laus-Urop snapped back. "We can't see into your mind to know how many calculations you are making in the sixth of a second."

"Then you will do it!"

"Me? How?"

"The forty-two unknowns engendered by the second quartile of the seventh loop can be reduced to nine if the sum of their bi-tertial coordinates is divided by the square of the ninth variable of the third quartile of the sixth loop multiplied by six hundred thirty-eight to the fourteenth power. With nine unknowns, only three quadratic calculations must be made, giving the player much more time to set up the eighth loop and shortening the period before the ruby gemstone can enter the fourth circle. Try it!"

"I don't believe it will work. I have spent my life studying the third circle."

"Try it! We won't complicate it by having the first and second circles simultaneously in motion. Just roll the third circle."

"Could you repeat the process for me."

Tristan-Phoros repeated it.

Laus-Urop looked suspiciously at Tristan-Phoros. He took the emerald gemstone in his fingers, fidgeted with it for a few seconds, and finally twirled it into the third circle of the game board. The emerald spun through the complex system of grooves on the board as Laus-Urop concentrated on making the mathematical calculations necessary to keep it on course.

The emerald entered the sixth loop and the seventh and zipped from the first into the second quartile; in an unprecedented flash, it had entered the third quartile, and Tristan-Phoros shouted, "Enough! You did it!"

Laus-Urop dropped backward from the board, his head beaded with sweat. "It worked," he conceded. The students cheered. Tristan-Phoros wagged his tail for a second until he brought it to a rigid halt.

Suddenly a voice from the rear of the Hall bellowed at the crowd clustered around the podium. "What's going on here?" The students quickly fell back, their faces white with fear. It was Arfla; it was the Grand Master himself who filled up the entire entrance with his blue-robed corpulence.

His face was puffed out and flushed. Under his heavy robes, he shuffled forward anxiously, brushing past Knarry without even noticing him. The students parted, and Arfla came face-to-face with Tristan-Phoros. "A dog!" he howled sarcastically. "How did a dog get in here? Dogs aren't allowed in College buildings."

"I beg your pardon," answered Tristan-Phoros, "but, as I previously have had to admonish your esteemed colleague here, my being, or not being, a dog is not relevant to the issue at hand. *Ad canem* arguments are not per—"

"*Ad canem* arguments!" Arfla squawked. "No arguments of any sort are permitted here, *ad canem* or otherwise, whatever such an argument is anyway! I never heard of such an absurdity!"

"But I have just shown Laus-Urop how he can roll through the third circle with greater simplicity than he had been used to doing. I believe that the students—"

"Your contributions to the College of Wisdom are neither necessary nor desired. I must ask you to clear the premises."

Tristan-Phoros suddenly felt himself overcome by a strange eagerness to sink his teeth into Arfla's belly. But he repressed the desire as being unworthy of a logician and philosopher. "You are, I take it by your insignia, no matter how stained they may be by turnip ale, the Grand Master of this institution."

"Correct!" Arfla snapped back at him.

"If correct, you must be willing to answer all challenges to your preeminence. Am I correct in this as well?"

"Correct where humans are concerned! Not correct where dogs are concerned!"

"Correct where anyone — dog or human — who can play the Games of Spheres is concerned! Isn't that so?"

"Correct! Correct!" the students chanted. Arfla glowered at them, and they were still.

"Then I challenge you to a Game of Spheres!"

Arfla laughed nervously, his eyes jiggling as he did. "Play against a dog! Well, I never thought things would come to this. This should be easy." The students cheered. They picked up fallen stools and jockeyed among themselves for advantageous positions from which to view the contest.

Meanwhile, a student had run out into the quadrangle and was shouting, "A championship match!"

"Where?" came back numerous cries.

"In the Lecture Hall! Where else, you preposterous dummies?"

Students and Masters wiggled out of every nook and cranny of the College buildings like an explosive infestation of brown and gray worms, squirmed across the quadrangle from every direction, and squeezed into the Lecture Hall, where they crowded in as close as they could to the podium. Still, the Hall was jammed right back to the entrance portal. Knarry, for all his sturdy weight, found himself pressed against the rear wall. One rather more alert student uttered, "What! A Moor-Plains Retriever! Is this a joke?" The other students didn't seem to notice or to care.

"You go first," said Arfla. He sat down heavily on a stool next to the board, and his eyes rolled around as he leered at the students. He expected the students to support him against the newcomer. But the students were prepared only to support a winner, and secretly most of them hoped that the golden-furred dog would vanquish the disagreeable Grand Master.

Tristan-Phoros mounted a stool opposite Arfla, where he sat upright, balanced himself back on his haunches, his tail touching the floor behind him, and freeing up his front paws for the action of playing the game. Laus-Urop handed him a complete set of gemstones. Tristan-Phoros studied them for a few moments, picking up each one in his paw and testing its weight and roundness. "A satisfactory set — not the best, but it will do," he pronounced. "And since, in my present circumstances in life, I do not have the advantage of an opposable thumb at my disposal, putting the right spin on these things may prove to be difficult."

He picked up the agate gemstone in his paw, shook it a little, and then swung it into the wide-arching first circle. It flew around the outer rim of the board with dizzying speed. It was followed in rapid succession by the topaz, and as the audience gasped in wonder, the emerald passed through the third circle with a velocity they had never witnessed before.

Laus-Urop saw this and buried his head in his hands as if he had just come down with a ferocious headache. The ruby went in, as all the stones whizzed back and forth across the board, Tristan-Phoros intent on the tens of thousands of calculations necessary to keep them in perfect order. The sapphire went in, and soon the amethyst was whirling through the grooves of the sixth circle. All the gemstones had begun to glow with a fierce inner light.

Tristan-Phoros picked up the blue diamond.

"He's going to roll the *Darii!*" the crowd shouted.

Arfla was sweating profusely, and his body was starting to quiver in horror.

Several students dislodged themselves from the crowd in the Lecture Hall and ran back out into the quadrangle, proclaiming "A *Darii!* A *Darii!* We are going to have a new Grand Master, and he is going to be a dog!" A few stray students and Masters, too lethargic to come at first, ran across the quadrangle to witness the prodigy, though they could not force an entrance through the door.

Tristan-Phoros shook the blue diamond vigorously and prepared to spin it into the board. But he did not have the chance to make his throw. Arfla let out a hair-raising scream and sprang to his feet, knocking over his stool as he did so and, at the same time, bringing his fists up underneath the game board and flinging it high into the vault of the Lecture Hall. The gemstones flew in all directions. Students ducked as the heavy wooden board descended and shattered on the paving stones of the Hall.

A second later, Tristan-Phoros had buried his teeth in Arfla's paunch. The two rolled in one ball off the platform, as Arfla bellowed in pain, and Tristan-Phoros snarled and tore at his flesh. A few students close to the podium tried to pull him off but ended up wrestling and punching one another. Around them, the fight spread, as a riot broke out from one end of the Lecture Hall to the other. Student fought against student, and the professors launched into one another with fists flying and feet kicking from beneath their heavy robes.

One professor grabbed hold of two students by their hair and appeared to be braiding their heads around each other. Another professor climbed up to one of the wooden beams that spanned the Hall and dangled there upside down with his knees hooked over the beam like the bloated version of a swamp-sloth. There, in the upside-down way he usually saw everything, he gazed with mingled horror and delight at the tangled, whirling mass of bodies underneath him (or above him, according to his perspective), and occasionally intervened in the melee by reaching down and sticking a finger in the eye of any unfortunate who fortuitously came within his range.

In the midst of the brawl, Knarry strode as steadily as he could through the crowd. He made his way through a tangle of flailing arms and legs, thrusting aside entire bodies that collided with him from every direction and trying not to tread on the writhing human flesh underfoot. He even warded off a potential jab in the eye by whisking his arm so powerfully at the sloth-like professor on the beam that the professor flew off his perch and landed with a crash on the podium.

When Knarry arrived up front, he got hold of Tristan-Phoros's hind legs and tried to yank him off, if not out of, Arfla. After a third pull, he shook him free, Knarry practically dropping backward on a mound of squirming students and Tristan-Phoros retaining a sizable piece of the Grand Master's robe hanging from his teeth. Arfla struggled to get up; his bare, bloody stomach spilled from his remaining robe. His face was contorted in a fearful grimace. He bellowed, "Summon the College gendarmes!"

It should be mentioned at this point that the transformation of the College gendarmes from a protective to a punitive role was an innovation introduced by Arfla shortly after the departure of Garug-Caroch. When Arfla assumed his position as Grand Master, his first declaration was to have the Hall of Games sealed off from general use. Somewhat later, several students violated the ban on entering the Hall of Games; they entered, and their disappearance amid unearthly screams alerted everyone that the Hall was a dangerous place to go.

The reform of the College gendarmes was enacted by Arfla ostensibly to protect the students against whatever peril lurked inside the building, but his real reason was to have the appropriate personnel to push unruly, uncooperative, or otherwise tiresome members of the College into the Hall, intentionally, for punitive reasons. Erendroop, former Senior Master and Dean of the Hall of Games, had been one of the earliest victims.

No one committed to the Hall of Games ever had to be punished again; one simply never reemerged. Only Arfla had the inexplicable ability to enter the Hall and come out alive. Whatever it was that was so dangerous in the Hall had obviously achieved some "understanding" with the Grand Master and his vengeful ways.

The gendarmes bludgeoned their way through the crowd with billy clubs and encircled Tristan-Phoros and Knarry. The fighting ceased as suddenly as it had begun, and all attention was directed towards the front. The prospect of new victims for the Hall of Games was even more intriguing than a fight.

Sympathy in the crowd now immediately and capriciously shifted from the Moor-Plains Retriever to Arfla, who, as much as he was feared and hated, could be expected to provide some quite delectable entertainment for the next half hour or so. And entertainment was valued more than anything else. Arfla ordered Tristan-Phoros to be fettered and dragged to the Hall of Games. He also pointed at Knarry and Laus-Urop and ordered them to be hauled away as well. "The gnome is obviously a friend of that dog, and Laus-Urop is a disgrace to the College," Arfla declared loudly.

Laus-Urop began to plead with Arfla; he cast himself down on the floor and beat his head against the stone pavement of the Lecture Hall. "Please, Arfla, kill me … torture me … banish me … anything, but not the Hall of Games!" From the flaps in his robe, Arfla drew a razor-sharp dirk and prepared to deliver a coup de grâce to the back of Laus-Urop's neck. But no one wanted to see Laus-Urop be dispatched with such ease. Students and Masters alike chanted, "The Hall of Games! The Hall of Games!"

"The Hall of Games it is!" Arfla roared. The crowd cheered. He slid his dirk back into his flaps and beckoned the gendarmes to proceed.

Tristan-Phoros whispered to Knarry, "You know, it might not be such a bad idea to get us out of this little dilemma."

Knarry whispered back, "Of course! But let me remind you that you got us into this dilemma in the first place. Anyway, I want to see what everyone is so excited about inside the Hall of Games."

Tristan-Phoros was dubious. "Well, Knarry, I'm not so sure that I want to see whatever that is. I have a feeling that we are being dragged off to a diabolical circus and that we will be the main act."

"A circus, maybe," Knarry answered. "But more likely, we are going some-place where we will be presented as the main course. They, or it, or whatever we find there, shall not find us, however, altogether too easy to digest. Have no fear."

The shoving, stumbling mass of collegians moved out of the Lecture Hall and across the quadrangle to the Hall of Games. Arfla led the crowd and was followed closely by the gendarmes, pushing Laus-Urop, Knarry, and Tristan-Phoros in front of them. As the throng reached the steps leading to the entrance, it grew hushed and expectant.

"The tongs," Arfla commanded.

Three gendarmes responded by fetching several long, crisscrossed iron rods from a nearby cloister, now converted into a guardhouse. They fixed the ends of the tongs to the three victims and opened the portals to the Hall of Games. Arfla turned around and gazed maliciously on the crowd. Then he whirled about and, with arms raised high, entered through the portals. The three victims were shoved in behind him at the ends of the tongs. The tongs were released and withdrawn, and the portals were shut and bolted from the outside. The crowd listened in delighted anticipation for the piercing screams that would soon come from the Hall of Games.

Inside, the Hall of Games was dark, airless, and musty. Knarry noticed the old gaming tables and boards tipped and littered carelessly about the room. He saw the balcony where Garug-Caroch once had imagined himself viewing the games below. But Arfla was now, as then, the center of atten-tion. He wailed and raved and flung himself down on the floor. His mouth foamed, his hands shook, and he cried out, "Come, Master, come; come, I have brought you nourishment. I have delivered my enemies over to you."

Tristan-Phoros spoke in a low voice: "Knarry, it's one of them; it is a Lo-El!"

At the far end of the hall, an undulating column of decaying yellow light emerged out of the darkness. It grew and quivered horribly against the distant wall. Its amorphous head towered up to the balcony, and its eyes were narrow slits of fierce green light. Its surface, indented by irregular oozing cavities and swollen oily pores of various sizes, seemed to change at every moment — fluorescent tints shifting from sickly brown to muddy green and back to pale yellow again. Its shape was that of an enormous transparent leech bending and flowing in the currents of a poisonous swamp.

Bodies, sometimes whole and sometimes as disconnected pieces, sometimes moribund and sometimes jerking spasmodically, seemed to float slowly around inside it. A leg here or an arm there would flex and bend and wriggle aimlessly through whatever medium it was that held the apparition together.

Occasionally, a recognizable human face, entrapped and agonized, became the face of the monster for a few moments until it dissolved and was replaced by yet another contorted face. A foul odor hovered over the apparition, and beams of sickly light undulated softly out of it and spread in little wavelike motions through the entire room.

Arfla prostrated himself before it. "Take them, my Master, they are yours. I know your hunger is great — for your time, and the time of your cohorts, is drawing near. Feed upon them, O Master!"

Tristan-Phoros whispered to Knarry once again, "I think the time is drawing near for us to make our exit."

"A worthy thought!" Knarry replied. "Shall we try to save Laus-Urop?"

"Another worthy thought!" Tristan-Phoros said.

Knarry snapped his iron fetters as if they had been made of paper coils and flipped the Splinter of the Ancestral Tree out of his jerkin. "I don't think I can destroy this malignant mirage, but I can put a protective cover over us." He waved the Splinter in a circle around himself and Tristan-Phoros and Laus-Urop, who was already in a state of petrified shock.

"Why not use the parts of the Song you know?" Tristan-Phoros protested vehemently. "We'll blow that garish ghoul clear out of Oval-Earth!"

"I don't want them to know how much of the Song we have — and don't have. That's for whatever still awaits us. The Splinter will be enough for now."

The shimmering specter was now undulating slowly and sickeningly down the Hall of Games. A low, barely perceptible hum—as of a cloud of noxious flies—seemed to emanate from its interior. It permeated the entire room with a nauseating stench, and Tristan-Phoros had to make every effort to keep from getting sick. Laus-Urop was bent over, belching uncontrollably. Arfla continued to prostrate himself, his arms waving back and forth and his head bouncing up and down on the filthy ground.

A long, lurid extension flowed out of the specter in an attempt to enwrap itself around the three victims. When it encountered the protective cover, the spirit flashed with livid, pinkish anger and emitted a low, coarse growling sound. It glanced around for an alternate victim; its hunger, so intensely aroused, would not go unsatisfied.

Arfla glanced up to see what the matter was. In an instant, without warning, the arms of the specter elongated in the direction of Arfla, who screamed for mercy and struggled to get to his feet. The giant appendages of the specter seized him and wrapped around his mountainous body, as his high-pitched screeching dissolved into suffocated gurgles and his flesh disintegrated into the specter in thick, sticky gobbets.

Soon parts and pieces of Arfla, still alive and quaking, were visible as they floated about, suspended within the monster's frame. When the absorption was completed, the specter's face began to take on the appearance of Arfla's face, and that face in the specter was filled with unspeakable agony and horror. Arfla was still alive somehow in the voracious emptiness of the Lo-El.

The transformation continued until the entire specter looked like Arfla, and it took on an obscene appearance of something temporarily sated but ready to do anything to stimulate its appetite again. Its eyes were now large spinning circles, and its belly was swollen monstrously large and malodorous.

"Enough of this circus!" Tristan-Phoros pleaded.

"And enough of this clown!" Knarry announced. He slipped the Splinter back into his leather jerkin, and with one block-like foot, as sturdy as a battering ram, he kicked right through the bolted portals of the Hall of Games. They swung open on their creaking hinges and tossed the two pieces of the broken bolt clear across the quadrangle.

The crowd, having relished the cries of terror that had emerged from the Hall, were astonished to see Knarry pitching out Laus-Urop and Tristan-Phoros. They dropped back in fear as two gendarmes, thinking that Arfla must still be alive in the Hall, charged at Knarry with their pikes.

He, in turn, grabbed simultaneously the hafts of the pikes just beyond the sharpened blades, and swung both pikes and the gendarmes still clinging to them through the open portals of the Hall. He called after them, "Don't hang around in there too long! I've got a feeling that grisly gourmand wouldn't mind some dessert." The gendarmes lost no time in crawling back through the portals as rapidly as they could and joined the other gendarmes, all of whom abandoned their pikes and retreated to their guardhouse.

Meanwhile, Knarry picked up several of the pikes, kicked the portals of the Hall of Games shut again and dropped the pikes into the slot where the huge bolt had been. Then he gently tore the fetters from Laus-Urop and Tristan-Phoros, while the stunned and now diffident crowd surrounding the entrance of the Hall of Games kept pressing backward into the far corners of the quadrangle.

Knarry and Tristan-Phoros descended the stairs and walked through the crowd towards the arcade that bordered the quadrangle. Tristan-Phoros shouted back at Laus-Urop, who sat moaning on the steps to the Hall of Games and whose headache had become even worse, "Don't forget about the sum of the bi-tertial coordinates! That's the key part."

As they passed through the Gate-Tower and walked up the briar alley-way, Knarry mentioned that leaving the College might not be a bad idea, but there was no hurry. The Library was safe, and it would take a while for the Masters and students even to figure out what had happened. Without a Grand Master, the College would be in disorder for a few days. Under any circumstances, nobody from the College would remotely consider going into the Library for any reason at all.

Knarry and Tristan-Phoros entered the Library. It was a scene of eager activity. Books were stacked on the floor of the rotunda, many of them open. Fox-Foot had discovered a richly illustrated book about flowers of the Hill Country. "You know, they took them apart and figured out how they are made inside. Also, from what I can figure out, they realized there were families of them — flowers related to each other — just like relatives in different villages! What a wonderful discovery!" The book was upside down, and Knarry turned it around for her. "No wonder it looked a little strange to me sometimes," she said.

Tundra-Bear was equally devoted to a volume showing pictures of glaciers in the Golden Mountains. He kept putting his finger on the pictures of the glaciers to see if they felt cold.

In an alcove on the second mezzanine, Hrudan had found a series of books on what was called "statecraft." He called down to Knarry on the main floor, "These are books about how to run a good empire. They were written by advisers to the Emperors. They talk about law, and justice, and right."

Bomsiell ignored all of this, of course, and slept on top of Twigbottom's old desk, occasionally awakening to glance at a moss-mouse that scurried across the floor.

Fox-Foot shifted attention for a moment from her book to Knarry and Tristan-Phoros. "I don't suppose you two have been up to much of anything," she said.

"Not much," Tristan-Phoros sighed. "It's a dog's life."

Knarry nodded. "It may be a dog's life, Tristan-Phoros, but at least you never have to worry about being called a 'blockhead.'"

"You've got a point there. Let's have some refreshment appropriate for the occasion. I need it. It's not every day one narrowly escapes being the main entree of a midafternoon college snack."

Chapter IX

The Battle of the Moor-Plains

After a night encamped in the Library, Knarry awoke the other members of the band. They shook out their blankets and wrapped up their gear. They had a small breakfast of berries and nuts, after which they gathered on the steps of the Library in the early morning light to confer about what they should do next.

Knarry suggested that it was prudent to leave the College of Wisdom and continue their quest. Hrudan concurred. Among the volumes he had consulted the previous evening, he had noted that the Gethsarbim, the tiny people who inhabited the magical city in the depths of the Moor-Plains, once had an important role in the life of Oval-Earth. In that distant age, all who had practical problems of any kind sought out the wisdom of the Gethsarbim.

Hrudan also noted that the Gethsarbim had been ruled by an aristocratic house of Grand Dukes. Once a year, the Grand Duke, accompanied by his regal consort, the Grand Duchess, embarked on an enchanted sloop moored close by the City of the Gethsarbim and sailed down the River N'ea to the Midland Sea.

On the Midland Sea, they paid a ceremonial visit to the Eye of the Universe — now called, of course, the Isle of the Drowsers — and sailed onward to the Imperial Capital. It was, apparently, an annual event of great pomp and festival in the cycle of lavish rituals that had prevailed in Oval-Earth.

Needless to say, such a ceremony had ceased ages ago. But Hrudan insisted that remnants of the ducal lineage might still exist, and if they did, they might remember the Song of the Eternal Aeons. A foray into the depths of the Moor-Plains might be well worth the effort.

Knarry at first disagreed. "The Moor-Plains, Hrudan," he said, "are at best a treacherous, unending series of bogs perpetually bound in by mists and rain. Even the wood-gnomes have learned to avoid them. The original causeway that led through the dense swamps to the City of the Gethsarbim has long since decayed and disappeared.

"There is, of course, another way to enter. One could skirt the Moor-Plains to the west until one met the point where the River N'ea flows out of the fens; we could build a raft there and attempt to follow the river backward into the fens until we arrive at the city."

"Against the current?" Fox-Foot asked. "That might be difficult."

"They must have sailed against the current when they returned from the annual visitation to the Imperial Capital," Knarry said.

"That would have been no ordinary vessel they were using," Hrudan commented. "The old parchment referred to it as an 'enchanted sloop.' It was navigated by mysterious, bejeweled hands that manned the rigging and served the voyagers exquisite delicacies found nowhere else in Oval-Earth."

Knarry dropped the idea of a raft. He went on to question the usefulness of Hrudan's suggestion. He noted that the rare persons who penetrated the swamplands — mainly clam diggers, lobster trappers, and others in pursuit of the abundant water life of the Moor-Plains — returned with stories about the Gethsarbim that did not especially recommend them for any profitable consultation. They were a people gone mad and chattering like lunatics. Their proverbs had devolved into unintelligible and often malicious barbs directed aggressively at people who had not asked to hear them. But even if some of the Gethsarbim could be found who would be of help, how would the band penetrate the watery maze of the Moor-Plains themselves?

Tristan-Phoros interrupted the conversation with an embarrassed cough. "This is a somewhat touchy matter," he said, "especially for me and considering my ... well, what I like to refer to as my present circumstances. As you know, my memory acts in a very strange way. Strictly speaking, I have no direct recall of an existence prior to my present 'state,' if you want to call it that. Yet I can remember all kinds of things that I don't remember ever having learned. For example, yesterday ... the Game of Spheres. Frankly,

I don't remember ever having played the Game of Spheres, yet it came as naturally to me as if I had played it a thousand times."

"You have yet to tell us about your adventures yesterday, Tristan-Phoros," said Hrudan. "And we are aware of how your curious memory works, but what does this have to do with —"

"Everything," Tristan-Phoros cut him short. "Now, this is *rather* awkward for me to have to point out, but ... you may not have noticed ... well, I suppose you have already ... that my bodily shape is that of a ... well, it is called a Moor-Plains Retriever."

Everyone nodded gravely, not quite knowing how to respond respectfully to this all-too-obvious observation.

"And?" said Knarry.

"And it appears," Tristan-Phoros went on, "that I have memories connected with that part of me as well. I know the Moor-Plains. I have ... as it were ... 'hunted' there before."

"Can you lead us to the City of the Gethsarbim?" Hrudan inquired.

"I can certainly 'point' the way," Tristan-Phoros replied with a slightly repressed chuckle. "I may even be able to 'retrieve' something for you now and then."

"Will it be difficult?" Tundra-Bear asked.

"Not for me," answered Tristan-Phoros. "Something tells me that it is, in one sense, my natural element. Do you see these big, splayed feet ... er, paws ... just right, you know, for treading on soggy ground. But, yes, the travel will be difficult — and very wet. It is a beautiful place, nevertheless, once you get used to it. Its birds — especially its long-necked cranes and its dense flocks of brightly colored hummingbirds — are unlike anything you could see anywhere in Oval-Earth. It will take us two days, I surmise, to arrive at the City of the Gethsarbim.

"Halfway through the swamp is an open space where a circular bank of reeds surrounds a wide, shallow lake with a tiny island at the center. It is called the Rabatana Pan. It is well stocked with lobster, shrimp, crayfish, crabs, and multitudes of other delectable crustaceans and shellfish. If we arrive there by evening, we just might succeed in scooping out a delightful dinner for ourselves. Of course, making a campfire in the drenched vegetation of the swamps will be almost impossible, but, Knarry, I trust you will not be loath to employ your revered Splinter once again in our service, even if only to boil up for us a few mature, succulent lobsters."

Knarry demurred. "Well," he agreed, "just for this occasion. With the Splinter I am confident I can heat up anything you want."

Hrudan concluded the discussion: "Under the circumstances, I can see no reason why we should not try to reestablish contact with these ancient people of the Moor-Plains. It cannot help but be vital for the future of Oval-Earth."

"Let's go!" said Knarry.

The band collected its accoutrements, exited the Library through the carved oaken doors, and walked down the briar alleyway through the arches of the Gate-Tower. Tristan-Phoros asked the others to pause there for a moment while he attended to some rather hasty business in the College. Before Knarry could object, he vanished through the service portal and into the College refectory. Soon they could hear raised voices and pots and pans being hurled and broken.

A few minutes later, Tristan-Phoros galloped out of the service entrance with a delighted look on his face and with something large stuffed in his pipe satchel. "A brief but compulsory visit to the College refectory and its adjoining larders," he remarked, "and I have 'retrieved' a little something for you that you may welcome later on in our journey."

No one thought to question him further about the purpose of this "brief visit." The travelers crossed over the fields in front of the College, descended a steep, grassy embankment, and entered into the damp mists and water-logged morass of the Moor-Plains.

Knarry immediately sank up to his knees in mud. The others foundered and tripped as they tried to pull their legs out of the thick ooze. Only Tristan-Phoros and Bomsiell seemed secure from the miry trap of the marshy bottomland. But Tristan-Phoros quickly had matters under control; he taught the others how to make oblong, oval mats out of bamboo shoots, to bind them to their feet with hemp, and to use them so that they would not sink down into the decaying plant life that covered much of the surface of the swamp. After some practice, they were slowly making their way successfully through dense bamboo groves and thickets of swamp bracken and fennel.

The air was filled with the melodious sounds of innumerable songbirds. Exotic butterflies spangled with marvelous colors fluttered out of the mist, circled around them, and disappeared back into the mist. Occasionally the band would see clouds of hummingbirds swirling through the undergrowth; they were like swiftly moving aerial gardens of flowers in their lusters of vermilion and gold and shimmering lime-green and lavender.

Farther along, the travelers saw raspberry-colored dragonflies as large as human forearms whose gold webbed wings and large bluish eyes glimmered in the half-light; the dragonflies would hover in the foggy air or perch on vine-garlanded branches of willows that hung low over the swamp.

At times, the mist would grow thin so that the sun could be seen through it looking like a pale orange wafer slung low among the mangrove trees. It was an enchanted landscape, filled with the powerful fragrances of jungle orchids and lush tropical fruits that ripened and spilled over into the rich, black loam of the fen.

By evening, the travelers had advanced to within a league of the Rabatana Pan. But they were too tired to continue and found a rise where it would be possible to camp for the night. Fox-Foot and Tundra-Bear began at once to clear a campsite, while Hrudan and Knarry searched the locale for firewood—which, as Tristan-Phoros had predicted, was not easy to find under the circumstances, since deadwood tended to rot quickly in the Moor-Plains.

Tristan-Phoros disappeared into the swamp and reemerged a half hour later; he had with him a small filigree net that was crammed with spiny-fish and three-eyed swamp frogs. Not long afterwards, these were cooked up—Knarry just a bit reluctantly surrendering the Splinter for the purpose of igniting what little useful wood could be found—and served to the weary travelers who were still trying to wipe the mud off their gear. The repast was certainly not as sumptuous as Tristan-Phoros had promised, but the next day would bring them to the Rabatana Pan and to a potential crab and lobster feast.

Around the fire at night, Knarry and Tristan-Phoros informed the others about what had happened at the College on the previous day. Hrudan, Tundra-Bear, and Fox-Foot were astonished. Why hadn't Knarry and Tristan-Phoros called for help? The situation was under control, Knarry assured them. Too many people would have been more of a burden than a help. Why hadn't Knarry informed them of this the previous afternoon in the Library? Knarry assured them again; he told them that he knew the Library was safe and he didn't want to distract them from their researches.

The conversation turned to the Game of Spheres. Tundra-Bear and Fox-Foot remembered Garug-Caroch's game board. Hrudan knew nothing about it at all. Knarry could recall only bits and pieces of information he had heard about it over the years, though on occasion he had watched Garug-Caroch play the game, sometimes for hours on end. Wood-gnomes generally ignored the Game of Spheres. They were immune to whatever attraction it had for humans.

Finally, Tristan-Phoros began to describe the game. He spoke about the gemstones, the intricate carving on the board, the methods for spinning the stones through the grooves, and the mathematical calculations necessary to guide the stones.

"But what's the purpose of it?" Hrudan interposed.

"A good question!" Tristan-Phoros replied. "It really doesn't have a purpose. It's a display of skill. It shows how brilliant you are."

"Isn't that a tragic way to abuse the gift of intelligence?" Hrudan asked.

"Yes, you could look at it that way," Tristan-Phoros answered. He mused for a while as he took out his pipe and bilberry weed. He tried to light the pipe, but the bilberry weed had become too damp. He put it away again.

"Part of the problem is that we have lost the actual history of the Game. A myth has grown up around Rorpigan the Shrewd, who invented the Game. It is supposed that he constructed it out of the pure genius of his intellect. Now, I would not want to argue that he was not a genius—assuredly he was. But, like many a genius, he was not always willing to acknowledge whose fund of knowledge he had successfully pillaged in arriving at his own discoveries.

"You see, what Rorpigan the Shrewd did not bother to tell his disciples was that the movement of the gemstones over the board is not the result of imposing sheer mathematical intelligence on their various circuits through the grooves of the game board. It may seem like that, but it is not. What the mind does in its calculations is to release the energies latent in the mineralogical properties of the stones. The designs on the board are mathematically precise replications of complex lines and fields of magnetic forces in the cosmos, and the stones are calibrated to vibrate along these lines with intense power and to interact with one another through overlapping and constantly shifting fields.

"Rorpigan admitted to none of this. He designed the board by doing research in the Library using the work of generations of scholars and natural philosophers. What he did was to summarize in an elaborate etching on a piece of wood the discoveries made over centuries about earthly and celestial dynamics. It was a stupendous achievement! But having done that, he behaved as if no further reference to that previous work was necessary, and that there was no further work to be done. It was easy, beyond this point, to pretend that the board was a self-contained thing, an act and product of pure intelligence without relationship to the world or to the cosmos.

"On this basis, Rorpigan the Shrewd was able to erect a false claim—one that the Master Sages at that time bitterly resisted but that was gradually accepted and, since that time, has become the only claim left in the intellectual life of Oval-Earth."

Tristan-Phoros sat up. He took a deep breath and uttered, "The claim is this: that the mind *imposes* order on the board and, through it, on the entire cosmos. It is the mind that is the source of order in all things. That is another way of saying that the cosmos itself has no order, no design, no purpose, no fundamental goodness about it, no meaning at all except for whatever we wish to think is there.

"The days, the ages—whichever it was—that I spent in the Barrows were devoted to thinking about little else but this. And I tell you, one learns soon enough in the Barrows how horribly mistaken Rorpigan was and what a dreadful legacy he left to the College of Wisdom and, through the College, to all of Oval-Earth. He left a legacy of delusion—a delusion that closes down the life of the mind.

"The fact is the opposite way around: the mind *finds* order in the cosmos— an order so intricate and grand that even the very best mind can grasp only a small part of it in a lifetime. In the same way, the mind finds order in the board, but only because the board mirrors, in a limited way, the order of the cosmos, and can make use of it, again in a limited way, even if that way requires phenomenal mathematical dexterity.

"Take, for example, the gemstones. The kind and sequence of the gemstones are assumed to be purely conventional—a purely arbitrary tradition that it would be most unsportsmanlike to violate. To the contrary, no matter how prodigious a mathematical mind a person might have, no matter how many tens of thousands of simultaneous calculations he would be capable of, he could not roll a *Darii* with anything else but the blue diamond, or the first circle with anything else but an agate. It just wouldn't work.

"The success of the game depends on the ability of the mind to interact with the intrinsic qualities of the stones and their motion within certain preset patterns, as determined by even higher patterns identical with the movement of stars and planets through the universe.

"Of course, how does the power of the mind transfer to the motion of the stones? Rorpigan the Shrewd simply recognized that it did and made use of it. He never tried to plumb that mystery. Some scholars in the ancient times approached the threshold of this question; but they knew that the answer lay with those most mysterious of Oval-Earth creatures: the rock-gnomes."

Hrudan tossed a final piece of wood onto the low, smoldering campfire. Its dampness hissed in the hot coals. Around them, the fens seemed to slumber in the deepest silence. Fox-Foot turned to Tristan-Phoros and said, "But why has all of this affected the life of the College so much?"

"It has affected all of Oval-Earth," he replied. "But we don't know yet exactly how. As for the College, once the Game of Spheres was fully accepted, it transformed the wondering mind into a calculating mind steeped in the illusion that calculation was the product of the mind pure and simple.

"The world outside our human consciousness was no longer interesting or important. Hence, the Library was eventually sealed off by the retainer wall, and one of the two lecture halls was converted into the Hall of Games to take its place. The minds of the Masters and students alike, no matter how brilliant, became shriveled, stunted, dwarfed to the exercise of a single faculty.

"Moreover, they were turned in on themselves, into themselves, a deeper and deeper regress into the vast emptiness of a self that no longer exists in relationship to other things. It was as if the eyes of the mind had rolled backward in their sockets and could only look inward. And inside was only emptiness and shadow and sleep—yes, nothing but sleep. That is where the Game of Spheres finally takes you—into sleep … a deathlike sleep … a sleep from which one doesn't wake … a sleep of death."

"But why sleep, Tristan-Phoros?" Fox-Foot inquired.

"Because the mind, in denying what is most evident about reality—its order, its design, must end up denying the evidence of its own reality, of its own order and design. It must not only extinguish its awareness of everything other than itself but must also extinguish awareness itself. It must gradually, permanently induce itself to fall asleep."

"And why would anyone want that?" she pursued the question.

"It's the only way to get what is sought—perfect control, perfect domination, perfect empowerment. In the cessation of consciousness, there is nothing left to control, or dominate, or exercise power over. And over nothing, nothingness can prevail. Of course, it's all a delusion."

"What happens then?"

"The most brilliant practitioners of the Game of Spheres, with a few exceptions, such as Garug-Caroch, ended up at …" Tristan-Phoros faltered.

"Where?" asked Fox-Foot.

"The Isle of the Drowsers." At this, Tristan-Phoros bent around and looked vacantly into the dark shadows of the swamp. He said not another word that night.

Knarry murmured quietly, "And in that sleep of death what dreams may come!"

"Let's go to sleep," said Fox-Foot. Knarry stood at the fringe of the campsite, steeping himself in serene gnome-sleep. Hrudan lay down close by the campfire, while Fox-Foot and Tundra-Bear wrapped themselves in a blanket and in one another's arms and fell asleep. Bomsiell stretched out and yawned on a nearby log. Tristan-Phoros, in a doglike crouch, held his head erect, staring wakefully into the deep quiet of the swamp for the remainder of the night. In the distance, he could hear the occasional plop of a three-eyed frog into a puddle or the hum of a lantern-fly as it skimmed the surface of some far-off pool and shed its pale glimmer over the sodden foliage of the jungle.

The dawn broke gray and dim in a heavy fog that floated thickly through the vine-tangled branches and over the matted hillock where the travelers were encamped. Tristan-Phoros awoke the others. Their blankets were soaked with the heavy dew, and their skin and hair were as wet as if they had been swimming. Fox-Foot wrung out her waist-long hair while Hrudan distributed damp elderberry muffins and cold fish cakes. There was no thought of trying to make a breakfast fire.

They were all content to resume their journey as soon as possible and presently were sloshing through the swamp again on their bamboo pads, sometimes jumping from one cluster of fallen branches to another and often falling into the mud, sinking up to their knees, despite the pads, and extracting themselves again with much effort.

They relied fully on Tristan-Phoros's guidance, for they could see very little through the fog; frequently they had to call out to each other just to keep the band together. After two hours or so of difficult travel, Tristan-Phoros announced that they were approaching the Rabatana Pan. By this time, some of the fog was beginning to burn off, and pinkish shafts of sunlight penetrated through the mist.

Several minutes after Tristan-Phoros's announcement, the band found themselves surmounting a shallow embankment. From the top of the embankment, they could make out a large, calm lake that vanished from their sight in the wispy orange fog that shrouded it.

Tristan-Phoros said, "This is it. We will walk directly through it, for it never gets more than a few paces deep, and the bed underneath the water is firm. Bomsiell can ride on my back. We will rest at the small island in its center and then continue. Meanwhile, I will gather some victuals for lunch as we proceed."

The travelers removed the bamboo pads from their feet and were about to descend from the embankment into the shallow waters of the lake when Hrudan asked, "Tristan-Phoros, what is that over there?"

About three hundred paces from them, a large, humped-over creature, about the size of a large dog and covered by a scaly shell and with a dozen crooked legs, stood in the water and trained its beady eyes on them. Long, groping antennae swayed slowly over its narrow head.

The fog prevented them from getting a clear view of the creature. Tristan-Phoros assured the others that the Rabatana Pan was inhabited only by many small crustaceans and by the beautiful, long-necked cranes that fed on them.

"If that is so, then what in Oval-Earth is that thing?" demanded Hrudan.

Tristan-Phoros looked sharply through the fog. "I would say that that creature is a shrimp," he said.

"A shrimp!" Hrudan exclaimed. "That's the biggest shrimp I have ever seen!"

"There's no question it is a shrimp," Tristan-Phoros responded. "Maybe something about the fog, or the water, is magnifying it. But I don't understand. A shrimp should not be standing *out of* the water. Ordinarily they swim around in the water."

Suddenly the shrimp turned and scurried off into the fog. They could hear its loud splashing long after they could see it no more.

Hrudan faced the others. "That shrimp, or whatever it was, was acting as a scout. I think we are in for serious trouble."

Tundra-Bear had already strung his longbow and uncovered his quiver. He said, "If shrimp around here come that big, I wonder what their crabs and lobsters look like!"

Tristan-Phoros added, "If shrimp around here come that big, then we are dealing with something other than shrimp."

Fox-Foot strung her bow, and Hrudan uncovered the Battle-Axe. Knarry removed the Splinter from its casket and slid it into his leather jerkin in case he should have need of it. He took a crooked tree bough that lay nearby on the embankment to use as a club.

Hrudan assumed command. He removed his black cape and folded it up on the embankment. "Tristan-Phoros and Bomsiell," he ordered, "remain here on the embankment. I will move out in front. Knarry, you come in behind me about twenty paces. Tundra-Bear and Fox-Foot, each of you fan out on the sides."

Hrudan lowered himself into the lake and began moving through its cool, knee-high waters. Despite the water, the footing was smooth and stable. Tundra-Bear and Fox-Foot followed him in a widely spaced arc. Knarry followed behind. Around them, the orange mist began to lift slightly from the lake's surface.

After a hundred paces, the small formation stopped and listened. In the distance could be heard an ominous splashing sound that gradually increased into a steady wavelike roar. The water became turbulent and frothy.

As Hrudan gave out more detailed orders about the plan of defense and they all started to back up slightly towards the embankment to tighten their formation, they saw materialize out of the mist a sprawling host of shrimp, crayfish, lobsters, prawns, and crabs ranked in powerful phalanxes.

The foggy air was alive with thousands of bright antennae quivering with anger and hostility. Savage claws were reared high above the army and snapped powerfully at the sky. The enemy host was fully decked out in its glittering natural plates of armor — black and brown, gray and green, red and yellow. And a long, terrible, dismal uproar arose from its bristling ranks.

A squadron of shrimp burst from the crustacean battle line and swatted loudly over the surface of the lake towards the band. There were at least five hundred of them, each one as big as the shrimp scout they had all seen originally.

At once, Tundra-Bear and Fox-Foot discharged arrows, which hissed across the watery surface and pierced the thin armor of two shrimp; they somersaulted over one another and flailed their legs in their death agony. But Tundra-Bear and Fox-Foot knew that their supply of arrows would soon be exhausted if they continued to fire at so many opponents, so they prepared to use their bows as staffs. A moment later, the shrimp squadron plummeted right into the band itself.

Hrudan, positioned out front, swung his Axe back and forth with lightning speed, cutting a huge swath through the squadron. The Axe hummed and sang in the misty air while the joints and appendages of unwary shrimp flew in every direction, splashing down into the water dozens of paces away and floating on the surface in tumultuous array, the severed muscle tendons still contracting and writhing in the murky lake.

Knarry, joining Hrudan, batted the shrimp right and left with his tree bough, shattering their shells and pitching hunks of them over the embankment behind him.

Tundra-Bear and Fox-Foot worked their sturdy longbows like sharpened staves, catching shrimp after shrimp and flinging them, shattered and broken, to every side. One shrimp managed to scramble up on Tundra-Bear's back and held him fast around the neck with a dozen little legs as its pointy black eyes curled around in front and looked directly into his eyes.

But it was wrenched off a second later — the tip of Fox-Foot's bow through its soft belly. She tossed it off into the mist. The few shrimp that landed alive on the embankment quickly discovered how fast and dangerous a forest cat could be with her razor-sharp claws, and how expeditiously the fangs of a Moor-Plains Retriever, philosopher or not, could dispatch a hapless foe.

The skirmish did not last long. The remaining ranks of the shrimp foundered and panicked. Their bodies littered the embankment. As quickly as they had attacked, the remaining contingents attempted to regroup, trampled one another in their retreat, and managed to withdraw back to the battle line, leaving hundreds of their sheared comrades bobbing up and down on the turbulent waters of the lake.

Hrudan hastily reorganized the defense as best he could, though he realized that tactics would have to evolve according to the situations they faced. Tundra-Bear and Fox-Foot retrieved some arrows out of the corpses of the shrimp, for they realized that their resources were few and had to be conserved. They were also aware that the arrows probably could not penetrate the thick skeletal armor of the larger species. Knarry gathered for himself several more boughs from the nearby fenland to use as weapons in case some of them broke. Bomsiell and Tristan-Phoros tested the waters of the lake to see if they could participate more immediately in the action.

A flailing mob of crayfish now pushed methodically through the water, raising a great frothy wave before them and swaying their massive one-armed claws back and forth. Fox-Foot and Tundra-Bear shot off a few arrows but were appalled to see them bounce harmlessly off the crayfish's armor.

Hrudan ordered them to retire the longbows and to fetch boughs of trees and work as a team in using the boughs as levers to pitch the crayfish upside down. He determined to concentrate his own axe blows on the soft joint ligaments that supported the single great pincers of the crayfish.

The opposition closed with each other. Again, Hrudan slashed and swung the razor-sharp Axe as crayfish antennae hurtled wildly through the air, sometimes splashing down in the water hundreds of paces away or landing with a gruesome thud on the embankment. Knarry, with heavy blows, crushed one crayfish skull after another.

Tundra-Bear and Fox-Foot, operating as a pair with their boughs, could only disable the crayfish temporarily. Tundra-Bear would plunge his bough underneath a crayfish and lift it partially out of the water; Fox-Foot would then use her bough to flip it over on its back.

If Hrudan was not quick enough to sever the great claw at its base, the crayfish would struggle for a few seconds to right itself and then be back again, reaching out with its line of jagged teeth in an attempt to wrench off limbs and cut through joints. Tundra-Bear received two deep gashes in his thigh, and Fox-Foot, at one point, was grappled and pulled down below the shallow water, but Knarry saved her by bringing his club down on the skull of the crayfish with an enormous blow and throwing it to the side.

The band slowly retreated under the pressure of the assault. As the fight pressed backward against the embankment, Bomsiell and Tristan-Phoros joined in by jumping from the embankment and from crayfish to crayfish, avoiding their swinging claws, and tearing off their small black eyes, leaving them to thrash around blindly in the bloodstained water.

But Hrudan, wielding his Axe, lopped off so many limbs and wreaked such destruction among the crayfish ranks that the attack soon faltered, and the crayfish retreated. They scuttled noisily through the shallow water back to their own battle line.

Hrudan summoned the companions together on the embankment. They were exhausted. Tundra-Bear and Fox-Foot sat together on the embankment, as Fox-Foot tended to Tundra-Bear's wounds. Knarry leaned heavily on his tree bough and seemed short of breath. Hrudan still stood in the water, clutching his Axe. He was covered with dozens of small bleeding cuts. Bomsiell was ready to commence action again and nervously paced back and forth along the top of the embankment, but Tristan-Phoros lay on his side, his rib cage lifting and falling as he panted. They peered out over the misty lake that was awash with thousands of fragments of dismembered foes.

The fog had lost its orange tint and was lifting high enough to allow shafts of sunlight to filter in. Patches of blue sky opened up here and there. Far off they could see a long, serried phalanx of gigantic lobsters massing along the battle line for a direct frontal attack. The air shook with tens of thousands of antennae, and the huge claws jerked back and forth as their armored plates clattered in fevered anticipation of the engagement ahead. Hrudan gazed over the shimmering waters at this foreboding sight and bent his head. "We won't be able to take on that battle line when it comes. We should retreat beyond the embankment."

Tristan-Phoros rose up from his side. "If we do that, the enemy will cross over the embankment as well. Then we won't have a chance in the swamps. They will hunt us down and destroy us." He turned to Knarry. "We should use what we have of the Song. Those creatures are possessed by Lo-Els. They won't be able to stand up to the Song."

"That is why we shouldn't use it. We don't want them to know we have that kind of strength ... not yet anyway," Knarry responded. "Our gourmand friend in the Hall of Games at the College has alerted its fellow Lo-Els to us, and some of them decided to waylay us here in the swamps. They ingested the bodies of the water life in this lake to attack us physically. They clearly don't want us to get to the City of the Gethsarbim."

"What should we do?" asked Hrudan

Knarry looked doubtful. "There is the Splinter. The most I could do with the Splinter is to use its force to knock several of them over or to make a protective shield. I don't know the extent of its power yet."

Tristan-Phoros objected. "I think we can do better than that. I saw you ignite a torch in the Library with it. You know it can provide heat. The Splinter, I would guess, has powers we have not yet tried. After all, it comes from the Ancestral Tree. It has absorbed sunlight for aeons of time. Its capacity for generating thermal energy may be boundless. We could destroy the entire host of the crustaceans with it."

"How?"

"It is simple. There is only one way to do a good lobster — or a crayfish, or a shrimp, or a crab, for that matter."

"Yes?"

"Steam them! Use the Splinter. Dip it into the lake and call upon its ages and ages of stored sunlight. It will understand. It will deliver."

Knarry pulled the Splinter out of his leather jerkin, gazed upon it for a few seconds, leaned over, and dipped it into the lake. "I suppose you might call this 'heating the Pan,'" he said.

Hrudan, who was still standing in the water, sprang up onto the embankment. "That's working fast," he observed. Knarry climbed out of the lake water a moment later.

Over the broad expanse of the water, the great ranks of the lobsters had begun moving slowly down the lake. Their antennae whirred. Their commanders waved them on with sweeping motions of their gigantic claws.

Slowly, steadily, formidably, they approached. When they were not more than a hundred paces from the embankment and their black little eyes burned with the ecstasy of imminent battle, their forward motion abruptly stopped.

The lobster commanders began to lift their legs and bodies out of the water, arching their backs and buckling with surprise and pain. Lobsters in the front line started to pull back, squeezing into the line behind them. Antennae spun around rapidly in confusion. All at once, panic spread through the ranks, and the battle line dissolved almost instantaneously. Entire battalions turned and started to splash and push in the opposite direction.

It disintegrated into a thrashing rout as lobsters climbed up on one another's backs and clawed and fought among themselves. The crab ranks broke, followed by the crayfish and the shrimp and the prawns. The entire army fled backward from the steaming waters, away from the embankment and towards the island in the center of the Pan. Soon the steam of the Pan grew so intense that nothing could be observed any longer.

"Now let it cool a bit," said Tristan-Phoros, stroking fondly the bulging object in his satchel. Knarry used the Splinter to heal the deep gashes in Tundra-Bear's thighs. Then he applied a salve to Hrudan's many scratches and cuts.

The band rested on the embankment for a while until the steamy vapors lifted 5end floated away from the surface of the lake. The waters had cooled, and the sky overhead was momentarily clear. The blue sky was a pleasure to see. The sun shone brightly over the vast, now placid surface of the Rabatana Pan; tiny pieces of bright flesh floated everywhere.

The band, following Tristan-Phoros, waded out into the lake. Bomsiell declined the offer of a ride and splashed and swam through the shallow waters. As they approached the island at the center, they saw that it was piled high with steamed shrimp and lobster, crayfish and crabs — all transformed back to the normal size for those creatures.

"You see," said Tristan-Phoros, "as the possessing spirits departed the dying bodies of the innocent creatures they had ingested, the creatures once more assumed their natural size and disposition. And, right now, their disposition is to provide for us that long-awaited feast I promised you. Knarry, may I borrow the Splinter for just a moment?"

"For what reason, may I ask?" said Knarry.

"To melt some moose butter, of course," said Tristan-Phoros as he drew a wax-sealed jar from his satchel. "I figured that old Arfla, of beloved memory and late Grand Master of the College, just might have some delicacies hidden away for his private use in the College larder. Arfla could scarcely be expected to do without a supply of moose butter — his own supply, I should add, and not the rancid stuff served up to the students. Anyway, he won't be needing it now, and what is a good steamed lobster without butter?"

The band cleared a space on the island and sat down to a delicious feast. But they were not the only ones to have a feast. Overhead they noticed large flocks of waterfowl — fluffy-winged gannets and two-beaked ibises, purple-striped flamingoes and yellow swamp-pigeons — circling the Pan and descending to feed on the profuse, if sad, remnants of the great battle.

One flock of broad-winged birds circled high above the little island. Moments later, a dozen long-necked cranes landed on the surface of the Pan. They stood on tall legs in the water close by. They were fine, magnificently plumed creatures; they had azure bodies, crimson wings, and golden tufts rising from their heads.

The members of the band took pleasure in cracking open lobster claws and throwing large succulent pieces of flesh to the cranes, which gobbled them down with obvious delight. Tristan-Phoros made the point that no one need worry about the future of the cranes or of any of the other water life in the Pan.

"The Rabatana Pan," he said, "is the perfect habitat for breeding water life in ceaseless abundance. It will quickly be restocked by the crustaceans from the surrounding fens, all of whom shall again thrive. The cranes and other waterfowl will not lack proper sustenance. Besides, we will be leaving behind us enough leftovers to last them quite a while."

More birds arrived at the Pan: lyrebirds and red-breasted eiders, crabivorous plovers and terns and shrikes, Ospeth's ospreys and golden-manacled geese, mocha-mottled bowerbirds and snapper-pipers and orange-pursed wrens and a hundred others. They circled around the island in resplendent panoplies, filling the air with songs and dazzling color and joyous aerial dance. They swooped over the waters. They landed on the arms and heads of the travelers and chirped and flew off again into the brilliant sunlight.

Fox-Foot jumped up onto a little knoll at the center of the island; the birds swirled around her. "Hooray!" she cried. "Hooray for the birds and the sky and the sun and the trees and the stars! Hooray for the creatures of the waters that nurture us! Hooray for Oval-Earth and all the universe that surrounds us!"

The others could not help but share in her celebration. Only Tristan-Phoros sat at the edge of the island, focusing his attention steadily towards the east. A gentle, early-afternoon breeze had picked up, wafting away some of the mist that had still hovered over the eastern shore of the Rabatana Pan. Tristan-Phoros pointed his paw in that direction. "Look," he said to his companions.

They all looked and saw, arising far off out of the dense fronds, a small forest of thin, brightly colored minarets capped with little gemlike cupolas.

"That," Tristan-Phoros announced, "is the City of the Gethsarbim."

Chapter X

The Sayings of the Gethsarbim

By late afternoon, the companions had traversed the final leagues that separated the Rabatana Pan from the City of the Gethsarbim. Here and there, as they groped through the gathering mists of the evening, they stumbled upon the ruins of the ancient causeway that had once penetrated the depths of the vast fenland.

Sections of the old stonework lay tipped and sodden in murky pools and backwaters. The tall iron cressets that had once stood at regular intervals along the causeway and had guided visitors through the dense fog with their blazing flares were bent and rusted posts projecting forlornly out of the swamp grass. But the original foundations of the causeway, though covered in places by tangled undergrowth and shallow, brackish water, provided some stable footing for the travelers and made the journey a bit easier.

The foundations came to an end at the edge of a wide lagoon that surrounded the City of the Gethsarbim like a moat. Here, a slender bridge had once arched across the lagoon to the city gates. A pair of towers, inlaid with precious and fanciful mosaics, had supported the long, silken cords from which the bridge was suspended. Now, except for the tilted remains of the towers, stripped of their former adornments, and one silken cord that drooped down like a forsaken fishline from the farthest tower, the bridge was little more than a line of masonry projecting fragmented chunks out of the water at irregular intervals. The companions had to descend into the lagoon and wade through the sluggish moat to the city on the far side.

As much as the splendor of Ospeth's Capital had been celebrated throughout Oval-Earth in days of old, anyone who had ever visited the ancestral home of the Gethsarbim had to acknowledge that there was little that could compare with it. The Gethsarbim had lived in these swamps since time immemorial.

They were a diminutive, impish people whose ivory skin and scarlet hair set off amber eyes that glowed like little gold coins under their brows. Aeons of time had adjusted their eyes to see at great distances through the fog of their homeland, and the travails of life in the swamp had turned them into a hardy people, filled with practical wisdom and inexhaustible energy.

Their city had been considered a marvel of building skill. Its colorful houses arose from a web of tiny canals like dovecotes piled zigzag on top of each other; everywhere, balconies, esplanades, and buttressed gardens led to thin minarets that soared by the hundreds over the city with their brightly gem-studded cupolas. Little footbridges and viaducts had spanned from minaret to minaret like a skein of silken threads cast softly over the city. And everything—walls, towers, gates, balconies, and esplanades—had been adorned with a riot of colorful mosaics depicting, in brightly hued pieces of colored glass, the glorious flora and fauna of the great swamplands themselves.

It had been an enchanted place—a city of luxuriant flowers and glittering lanterns and singing fountains whose canals were plied by glossy gondolas with silver embossed oars rhythmically stroking its emerald-tinted waters.

Knarry was the first to haul himself out of the lagoon, dripping with water and bedraggled with swamp grass. He passed through the gates. The others followed behind. What met them was a damp, forlorn slum. The canals were clogged with rubbish. Many of the minarets had fallen over or leaned at angles or were broken off at the top or in the middle like snapped reeds, and most of the upper footbridges and viaducts had collapsed into the narrow streets, where they lay like ramshackle barricades.

One could still see on the houses their colorful porcelain sidings and carved balconies, but the porcelain had fallen off in many places, leaving great patches of crumbling brick exposed to the damp air. The streets and canals were lifeless, stagnant, and empty.

It began to rain. A heavy downpour drove the travelers into the sheltered alcove of a nearby building. As they stood in the darkness of the alcove, shivering with cold and shaking the rain from their garments, Fox-Foot became aware of a pair of twinkling golden eyes peeking at her from a door that was slightly ajar in a nearby dwelling. The tiny eyes, glistering in the sullen darkness, seemed to be fixed on her with a strange mixture of wonder and desperation. But when Fox-Foot turned to speak to the hidden figure, the door slammed shut.

Hrudan declared, "We must seek out the ducal palace. Otherwise, we have no purpose being here." The others agreed.

As soon as the downpour let up, they began to meander through the narrow, littered streets, now heavy with fog and impending night. Tundra-Bear and Fox-Foot took the lead in guiding the others through the dusky gloom. Tristan-Phoros admitted that he did not know his way around the city—that it had not been, as far as he could make out, his former terrain; only the hunting and fishing grounds of the Moor-Plains were familiar to him.

As the group passed through the streets, they could see an occasional candlewick dimly glittering in some isolated window, and they could sense here and there a pair of anxious golden eyes peeking down at them from behind a shuttered balcony high above. Otherwise, the city seemed to be deserted. Occasionally, to the rear of them, they could hear the scuffle of tiny feet—a single pair of them; and Fox-Foot would peer back into the shadows to try to see who was following them.

After a while of picking their way through the rubble of fallen bridges and vaulting over several clogged canals, they began to hear distant sounds of what appeared to be revelry—something like a combination of coarse shouting and a rough, clashing music floated through the dank air of the city.

They turned a corner and entered what looked like an open piazza. It was partially lit by an assortment of torches that sputtered uneasily in the dampness.

At the far end of the piazza was a large palace capped by a dozen towers of different sizes and shapes. The facade of the building was marked by a line of tall windows along the full length of the second story. They were covered with rusted latticework. An ornate porphyry balcony ran along the base of the windows. On the ground floor, an elaborately jewel-encrusted gate appeared to lead into an inner court. Several torches flared at the entrance. The tall windows above glimmered with a pale but uneven crimson light. A throbbing, disorderly racket emanated from the building and disappeared into the muffled desolateness of the city.

"I think we have found what we were looking for," said Hrudan dismally, after he examined the coat of arms over the bejeweled gate. "This must be the ducal palace. I think I recognize the coat of arms from the volume I consulted in the Library. But the coat of arms has been partially defaced, and the carousing we are hearing scarcely sounds ducal to me at all."

The group ventured through the gate and entered an inner court encircled by thickly smoldering torches. A set of obverse curving staircases on either side of the courtyard arched up in a horseshoe pattern to an inner balcony and to a large palatial door on the second floor; beyond the door was a spacious banquet hall lit with wide-armed bronze chandeliers filled with blazing candles.

Clusters of tiny Gethsarbim scurried back and forth along the inner balcony from a side entrance, carrying platters, bowls, and wine ewers in and out of the candlelit hall. The raucous din emerging from the great hall behind that door was more rambunctious than ever.

After they had absorbed this bewildering sight, the companions ascended the ducal staircase and entered the candlelit hall. The boisterous clamor suddenly stopped. Tundra-Bear and Fox-Foot stood in front. Knarry and Hrudan stood just behind them, and Tristan-Phoros and Bomsiell came around the sides. They stared at the spectacle before them.

Thousands of glinting golden eyes stared back at them in astonishment. The cavernous banquet hall was now recognizable as a throne room with a raised dais at the far end. Innumerable blazing candles from the chandeliers and the wall sconces were mirrored in the fiery red hair and brightly hasped robes of the Gethsarbim who sat at long, richly appointed tables.

A Gethsarbim gentleman, a majordomo, if his dissolute garb and sommelier's medallion could be trusted, bounded up in front of the strangers. He was a bulbous fellow with two skinny bowlegs giving him the appearance of a frog. He grabbed onto a badly frayed tapestry, pulled himself partially off the floor, and grimaced at them with his colossal teeth. "Poor folks' guests return home early!" he screeched.

He swung his ungainly body with its big potbelly protruding out of his shredded and spattered livery and landed on his back on the floor, where he rocked and spun around in hysterical laughter, kicking his spindly legs in the air.

A furious uproar broke out; the Gethsarbim screamed at the travelers and then at one another. A stumpy woman, as round as a ball, whose red hair was piled up into a pyramid on her almost indistinguishable head, pounced on the group and railed at them, "Guests, like old fish, soon go bad."

Thousands of Gethsarbim bounced and joggled on their seats, swilling their wine and banging their goblets and slapping their plates against the tables. The servants bearing food and drink once again scurried among the tables as the feasters tripped them, snatched food from the platters, and seized the ewers and splashed wine into their goblets, overfilling them while splattering the tables and themselves. They were howling nonsense at one another, baring teeth, and waving their arms and legs back and forth.

One pinheaded imp in a torn green garment jumped on a table and ran its full length, stepping on dishes and breaking them while kicking food into the laps of the ones who were seated and overturning wine; at another table, several feasters competed with one another by flooding a long stretch of the table with wine and then dashing along the top of the table, going into a skid, and seeing who could slide the longest distance on the slippery surface of the table.

The feasters responded by yammering in compulsive high-pitched laughter. Throughout the crowd, feasters surged and tore at each other, giggling, shrieking, and pitching food across the banquet hall.

The leggy majordomo somersaulted and cavorted into an upright position again. As if adhering unconsciously to some code of deportment germane to his office but whose purpose was now mostly forgotten, he leapt to a nearby table, where he seized several men and women by the hair and yanked them away from their places.

He cleared the table by turning it on its side, letting all the plates and glassware smash into pieces on the floor. Righting the table, he snapped his fingers, whereupon a score of servants flocked to him with fresh utensils and food. In an instant, the table was ready, and the travelers were beckoned to take their places at the feast, though it was difficult for them to sit at the short table since their knees were much too high.

Sizzling platters of hummingbirds, roasted and basted in their many-colored feathers, were thrust in front of them. Miniature goblets of cool, delectable wine were shoved into their hands. Baskets of tiny fruit pastries were dumped on the table and piled into their laps.

The majordomo continued to shout abusive proverbs at them, even as he was having them served. But they were glad to partake of the Gethsarbim's delicacies; this much of the Gethsarbim tradition had been preserved, and the new dinner guests, however distressed by the appalling noise and riotous behavior, were eager to taste their famous cuisine.

Someone in the ducal kitchens, Knarry observed, was doing something right. The servants who waited upon them, oddly, had a certain air of dignity about them, even a willingness—however secretive and repressed—to treat the guests with respect, though they were compelled by the majordomo's unrelenting harassment into the kind of frenzied service they were providing.

One of the servants, an elderly but pleasant-looking man, saw to the needs of Bomsiell and Tristan-Phoros. As Bomsiell began to lap some honeyed orchid dew from an old crystal bowl, a nearby feaster howled at her, "Who laps last, laps longer" and broke into a storm of shrill laughter.

After they had eaten, the newcomers tried to talk to the Gethsarbim who were sitting near them, but intelligible discourse seemed impossible. The Gethsarbim could not sit still for more than a moment and could not focus their attention in any direction for more than a few seconds at a time. The only things they spoke were garbled proverbs that made no sense.

One Gethsarbim woman raced past them and yelled in their ears, "A bitch in slime craves brine." Another shouted, "If you can't bite, don't show your teeth" and pulled his lips back with his fingers, showing a ghastly array of rotten teeth.

Hrudan motioned to the others over the persistent noise that they should leave; nothing good could come of this.

They were about to get up from the table, when the majordomo began to pound chaotically on a brass gong that hung by the doorway. In front of the room stood an elevated platform—once the dais for the throne. A flimsy stage of sorts had been erected near it, and now a troop of Gethsarbim mummers pranced into the room from a side door and, springing onto the stage, began performing acrobatic tricks of various kinds.

Now and then, as the mummers shouted some unintelligible joke, the audience would, in turn, be convulsed with riotous giggles. Members of the audience began to do imitations of the actors and to make jokes about them, so that attention was often diverted from the stage to an impromptu act exhibited somewhere else in the room.

The audience gradually became more and more insulting. When one acrobat overleapt the edge of the platform, the nearby feasters grabbed hold of him and began to toss him from table to table, much to the amusement of the entire crowd.

The entertainment took a more vicious course as servants were dragged up onto the stage; there they were pinched and kicked, and their hair was pulled. The audience was convulsed with laughter. "I cannot watch this anymore," Tundra-Bear proclaimed. "Let's leave this place."

At this moment, a filthy, scared-looking girl appeared at the main entrance. Her clothes were in rags and her skin was blackened by large sooty smudges. Her hair was a stringy tangle of dirty red braids. But her clear golden eyes sought out the eyes of Fox-Foot and gazed into them.

Fox-foot immediately thought she recognized the eyes of the bedraggled creature: it was the girl who had looked out at her in the dark alcove an hour earlier. She wondered: Had this child followed them all the way through the city?

When the majordomo noticed the urchin at the door, he sprang at her and tried to chase her out of the hall. He snatched at her hair, but she ducked underneath him and flew in the direction of the guests. There she flung herself into Fox-Foot's arms and stared defiantly back at the majordomo. Fox-Foot cuddled the wet, smudged child against herself. She was now certain that this was the person who had peered at her so forlornly through the open door when the band had just entered the city.

Attention in the hall suddenly turned from the entertainment to what was happening close to the front entrance. The Gethsarbim feasters climbed up on the tables to see better.

When they recognized the girl, their mood quickly changed. They became outraged and bitter, and they shouted threats and obscenities. Some began to throw dishes and food at her, but Fox-Foot protected her by batting away various projectiles, while Knarry and Hrudan stood up to quell the commotion.

Hrudan withdrew the Battle-Axe from its slipcover and raised it high above the assembly. At once, the Gethsarbim collectively let out the most woeful howl Hrudan had ever heard; they fell on the floor, holding their hands over their heads. Even the majordomo ceased his antics for a moment and threw himself down on the floor prostrate before the Axe.

Fox-Foot tried to talk to the girl, but she would not reply. She motioned to Fox-Foot that she wanted to go someplace. She pointed to the dais at the front of the hall. Fox-Foot held her hand and rose from her seat to accompany her, but the girl made her sit again. She whispered to Fox-Foot, "The right words in the right place are best."

Then, alone, she began the long walk to the front of the hall.

The Gethsarbim feasters were terrified of the newcomers, especially of the powerful figure who wielded the great Axe, so they would not touch the little girl as she walked down the aisle. But gradually, one by one, they started to rise and shout at her. The crowd did not want her to approach the dais and certainly would not have let her, if the powerful figure with the great Axe did not stand there as her surety.

One wizened old man hollered at her as she passed by him, "A bad penny never gets lost," while another, climbing over his shoulder and puffing his cheeks, screamed, "The worst wheel squeaks loudest." A woman stuck her head up from under a table and threatened, "A nail that sticks out soon gets flattened."

The tide of abuse mounted slowly and steadily until it became one great deafening roar. The Gethsarbim stood up again and screeched and stamped their feet; they bashed the tables with their chairs. They flung their heads backward and closed their eyes, waggling their tongues in their mouths as they howled. They flung dishes against the walls and smashed them. The hall thundered and shook with the outcry.

Meanwhile, the girl calmly walked between the waves of the crowd and mounted the dais. Knarry, vaguely aware of what was going to happen, reached into his haversack and pulled out a stylus and a piece of parchment.

He motioned to Hrudan. "I think we are going to get part of what we came here for."

Hrudan answered, "You are right, Knarry. I read about this in the volume about the Gethsarbim. Among them, the Song may be spoken only from the ducal dais, and only by someone very special. Her gumption shows that she is someone very special."

The outcry reached a new pitch of intensity and anger. The stamping became rhythmical and methodic, scorching to the ears in its incessant and oppressive clamor. Rhythms and counter-rhythms developed, producing a pounding, thumping cacophony almost beyond human endurance. Both Bomsiell and Tristan-Phoros held their paws over their ears, and Tundra-Bear thought that even the roar of the Rock-Falls was not as bad as this.

The girl turned on the dais and faced the crowd. Her eyes gleamed golden and shimmering bright across the room. She held herself straight and regally. As the din in front of her peaked in a chaotic blast of almost unbearable noise, she opened her mouth.

The very first syllable she spoke burst through the crest of the uproar as clear and as sharp as a ray of pure light puncturing the misty darkness of the fens. Immediate and dead silence followed, vibrating only with the melodious intonation of her voice:

> *For earth is the maiden,*
> *The daughter of light,*
>
> *Bride of the blazing*
> *Archways of heaven.*

The palace shook to its foundations. Tapestries dropped from the walls; decaying portions of the frames around the windows crumbled and slid to the floor in clouds of dust.

The Gethsarbim collapsed to the floor, where they held on to one another and whimpered and moaned and cried. Sweat poured out of their faces, and their little golden eyes were soaked in tears.

A small group of them clambered up to the dais and knelt down before the girl and bowed to the ground. They spread apart to make a passageway through them as the girl descended the dais and returned across the banquet hall to Fox-Foot.

Fox-Foot received her again into her arms and wiped away some of the soot from her face. She asked, "Who are you?"

The girl answered, "The Lords of the Land have left but a single seedling. Her name is Dolopeia."

Hrudan glanced at the others. "She knows some verses of the Song. That can only mean that she is a descendant of the Grand Dukes. The Gethsarbim know this—that is why they did not want her to ascend the dais, because she could recite the verses only from there. And she is a mere girl—and an orphan at that, we assume—but she must be the sole heir to the throne; she must be the Grand Duchess of the Gethsarbim herself."

The leggy majordomo threw himself at her feet. With a quavering voice, he said, "He who knows not he is a fool is the biggest fool of all."

Dolopeia extended a hand to him and answered, "He who knows he is a fool is not the biggest fool there is."

The majordomo withdrew. He started to pick up broken chairs and set tables upright again. The Gethsarbim imitated him. In shame and silence, they began to clean up the banquet hall. They removed their jewel-hasped cloaks. They swept the floor of its debris. They sat the servants down upon benches, graciously offered them food and drink, and laid the jewel-hasped cloaks around their shoulders. They whispered to one another in low voices as they worked and once more exchanged the ancient proverbs of the Gethsarbim, but now spoken sensibly again.

Several Gethsarbim ladies, some of those who had been servants, approached Dolopeia and invited her into an adjoining room. She went with them as the visitors waited for her and watched the remorseful cleansing of the banquet hall.

An hour later, Dolopeia reemerged. Her matted red hair was combed out into sparkling curls; a chaplet of golden filigree, as delicate as dragonfly wings, adorned her head; her face beamed with the fragrant oils of a bath; and she wore, gathered around her shoulders, a resplendent shawl woven with many-colored butterfly and hummingbird designs. The crowd gasped in wonder and fell to their knees.

Dolopeia beckoned to the guests and led them out of the great throne room and down the marble staircase into the inner court. There she exchanged words with the majordomo, who nodded submissively to all she said and returned back up the stairs to the hall. Many of the Gethsarbim were filing quietly out of the palace and returning to their homes along the darkened streets.

Dolopeia turned to Fox-Foot and said, "Plant the fields before you build the house. To travel with a purpose is to be wise." With that, she gathered some torches for Tundra-Bear and Hrudan to carry and led the band through a secret entrance and down a long passageway that tunneled under the palace. It was black and damp, and the walls were covered with layers of age-old moss. The passageway had not been used for centuries.

At the far end of the tunnel, they could see a faint pearl-like glow. Here they emerged in a little harbor surrounded on three sides by tall stone walls. On the fourth side was the lagoon. The lavender moons, shining softly down through the mist, illuminated a tiny silvery sloop tied at the dock with silken cords. Its sails were like embroidered tapestries and its gossamer-like rigging swayed gently in the breeze.

"Who sails the ship must first embark," Dolopeia said with a laugh, and she skipped across the diminutive gangplank that rang with a dozen silver bells. The others followed her. Only Tristan-Phoros hesitated, but Tundra-Bear urged him on. He trotted across the gangplank as the bells tinkled cheerfully.

The gangplank slipped away on its own power, the sails were raised, the finely filigreed cressets fore and aft were suddenly ablaze with golden light, and the sloop magically glided out of the hidden harbor and into the misty waters of the lagoon. Minutes later, the rudder shifted on its own, and the ship entered the lavender-hued headwaters of the River N'ea.

"So this is it," Hrudan murmured, "the magical vessel of the Grand Dukes. How well preserved it is, as if it were a thing that has a life of its own!" He settled himself into a corner of the poop deck. The others found places to settle down for the night.

Only Fox-Foot accompanied Dolopeia into a picturesque little cabin in the forecastle. Because of her height, she had to bend down to enter through the door. There she talked with Dolopeia for a long time, as the invisible hands lit miniature candelabra and served crystal bowls of fruit sherbet. Later she emerged from the cabin. The others sat up and waited to hear what she had to report.

"I am not sure I understand everything she said," Fox-Foot decreed, "but I do think I know a few things now."

"Tell us about it," said Knarry.

"As Hrudan guessed," Fox-Foot responded, "Dolopeia is the sole surviving descendant of the Ducal House of the Gethsarbim, and that makes her the Grand Duchess. Her parents died not long ago. Like so many generations of the Ducal House, they lived as outcasts in the city, despised by everyone and kept away from the palace, and from the royal dais.

"It was the custom of the Grand Dukes to recite once a year the Song of the Eternal Aeons from the dais; it was this practice that maintained the strength of the Gethsarbim.

"For generations, members of the ducal family have tried to regain the dais. But they could never succeed; they had to eke out impoverished lives in the worst back alleys of the city, hunted, persecuted, often at the brink of starvation. In time, most of the Song was lost, except for the two verses that Dolopeia sang before the Gethsarbim assembly. She knew that even two lines would restore the people to some degree of sanity."

"And what does she want to do now?" Hrudan asked.

"She wants what we want — the rest of the words."

"Does she know how long it is? I wonder how much there is to find?"

"She does know how long it is. It is twelve verses all together."

Knarry interrupted, "Then what we have heard from Kasyan is correct, and we now have half the Song — the two verses that Garug-Caroch sent with Bomsiell on the night of the great winter storm; the two we heard from Kasyan in the Barrows; and now the two that Dolopeia just recited at the banquet. But where should we go to find more verses?"

Fox-Foot replied, "We must trust Dolopeia's judgment. She left the majordomo with orders to restore the palace and the system of governance. Those servants you saw being so mistreated and later honored — they were descendants of the old chivalric orders of the Gethsarbim, families noted for their wisdom and generosity. The majordomo will see to it that the chivalric orders will again be reestablished to govern the City.

"Meanwhile, Dolopeia wishes to accompany us in our quest. I have told her what is happening in Oval-Earth and about what we have discovered already. She is not at all surprised. And she thinks the time is short."

"What does she advise us to do, Fox-Foot?" Knarry queried. "The Gethsarbim were always known for their practical insight."

"Dolopeia says there is only one thing for us to do," Fox-Foot answered. "We must visit the water caverns of the Hydro-Sylphs. Dolopeia says that the enchanted sloop will know how to get us there. Only several leagues from here, the headwaters of the River N'ea are joined by a tributary that flows out from the Golden Mountains. We must sail up that tributary and pass through a thin, lacy waterfall to enter the water caves. Dolopeia does not think that anyone has visited the Hydro-Sylphs in recent memory."

"The Hydro-Sylphs!" Hrudan exclaimed. "Illyria had heard of them. The folklore of the Downs has preserved a memory of that name. And we have seen them depicted in ancient carvings and murals. Who were they? What were they?"

"Dolopeia does not know much about them either. They were distant neighbors of the Gethsarbim, a princely people who inhabited watery realms and had the bodies of seals—a doglike mammal with flippers instead of forefeet and a tail like a fish's. Dolopeia described them as 'poetic' creatures who love to play on lyres and sing melodies preserved over millennia of time in their strange memories. If they still survive in the depths of their water caves, they might know the most ancient of songs itself, or at least part of it. It's worth a try."

Everyone agreed. Knarry turned to Tristan-Phoros. "You might feel at home there," he said with a chortle, "even though you have no flippers, and your tail is hardly like that of a fish."

"Not likely," Tristan-Phoros groaned.

The moonlight was gradually obscured by a bank of mist that moved heavily over the vessel. The cressets glowed brightly through the mist, however; and the little bells tinkled in the breeze. The companions found places to sleep on the tiny deck. Bomsiell climbed the mizzenmast and sought out a snug place to spend the night.

Far off in the misty darkness, they could hear the sound of a light, airy waterfall descending from the tall cliffs of the Golden Mountains. Later they felt a passage through a veil of light spray that hovered momentarily over the sloop. Afterwards, they were enveloped in a deep, silent blackness as the sloop glided into the innermost depths beneath the Golden Mountains.

Chapter XI

The Hydro-Sylphs

The companions awoke in the deep recesses of the water caverns. It was early morning. High above them arched a rough-hewn, golden, quartz-like sky, and the river they floated upon was as gold-tinted as the crystalline quartz above them. Beams of golden light, mingled with orange and purple and crimson rays, slanted downward through the crystal sky at many angles and skimmed playfully over the waves of the river and against the verdant banks on either side.

Tristan-Phoros was the first to rise. He stood up on his hind legs, resting his forelegs on the railing of the deck, and gazed upward at the crystal sky. At first, he was puzzled at what he saw. After a few moments' reflection, he announced to his sleepy companions, "It's a matter of simple deduction, my fellow mariners. We are beneath the Golden Mountains! We discover, much to our surprise, that they are translucent, and the sunlight is being refracted all the way down through their craggy precipices, coloring the river a deep golden hue and filling the air with beams of light."

The others arose to view the spectacle of light and water. Only Bomsiell remained high in the rigging of the mizzenmast, yawning and stretching her furry feline legs.

The caverns were suffused with serenity. The river brushed gently along its banks, where it was joined by dozens of little rivulets gurgling downward from the rocks above. Waterfalls abounded and laced the golden air with thin, airy scarves of water that reflected in the river below. Streams rippled out of narrow crevices, over which delicately tinted rainbows hovered like little gossamer bridges. In small coves and inlets along the river, sapphire-blue mists glided over the cool waters. Here and there, a lissome waterspout wound its way across the surface of the river like a fountain of spray and air dancing in the sparkling light.

The banks of the river displayed bright golden-green groves of fruit trees heavy with peaches and luscious water-plums, with pink-veined olopalins of sweetest pulp, and with dappled moon-drops and apricot-cherries glowing in the foliage. The fragrance of the fruit wafted on the soft breezes that flowed through the caverns.

As the enchanted sloop rounded a bend in the river, the companions noticed up ahead a series of lofty pavilions built along the banks of the river. High on the cliffs surrounding the pavilions were innumerable terraced ponds and streams. Along these streams were hundreds of loggias and promenades. Spans of finely chiseled crystal stone arced over the streams and the river in many places. Several floating islands bearing little gardens of speckled white flowers rocked gently in the waves of the river.

In a small inlet was a harbor — a series of silvery quays where a flotilla of lavishly canopied skiffs and schooners were moored. Luminous rings, reflected from the river and from the many little streams and cascades, formed brilliant bands of color that moved gracefully over this festival of watery splendor.

Not the slightest sense of decay or ruin impaired the beauty of this sight. Yet a doleful mood hung in the air, an irrepressible sadness, an inexplicable gloom, for the caverns resonated faintly with the sweetest and yet most mournful songs that any of the companions had ever heard.

As the sloop moved closer to the harbor, the companions saw, among the pavilions, arrays of lavishly carved and gilded tables overflowing with salvers of fruit and bearing high-necked crystal carafes glowing with a pale-blue wine. Next to these tables and poised close to the watery banks of the river were silk-covered divans surrounded on all sides by thick, finely woven carpets of intricate design.

On these divans reclined richly gowned creatures with long, lithe bodies of brown, furry skin and wide-finned tails and flippers. Large, dark eyes—browless but soulful—reposed in sleek, silky heads that tapered forward into petite black noses perched over exquisitely curried fronds of soft papillae. While some of these creatures lifted goblets of wine to their lips or partook of fruit piled high on the salvers, others regaled themselves with music on their lyres and with songs of the most woeful measures.

Hrudan was the first to speak. "So, these are the mythical Hydro-Sylphs," he said, "yet now no longer mythical for us, for we see them with our eyes and hear them with our ears."

The sloop passed under one of the crystal bridges, bending down its masts as it went under, and tipping the still sleepy Bomsiell out of her perch. She landed on the deck with a thump and looked around curiously at the others, who were, however, too rapt in the wonder of the scene to pay her much heed. Only Tristan-Phoros nodded at her, just a bit self-righteously, as if Bomsiell had deserved such a rude awakening for lounging too long in her privileged nest high in the rigging.

On the pavilions, the Hydro-Sylphs were so preoccupied with their sad songs that they did not even notice the unusual sight of a tiny ship sailing up the golden river right into their midst. But the sloop knew where to go; it veered to the left and docked itself directly in front of the grandest pavilion of them all. The gangplank rolled out and slid onto the wharf with only the slightest tinkling of its little bells.

One by one, the companions disembarked, Dolopeia skipping first across the gangplank, and the others following. They left on the deck of the sloop their various accoutrements—the haversacks and baskets and quivers and longbows and Hrudan's Axe—for they felt they would have little need of them in what was clearly a gracious and hospitable environment. Only Knarry carried his satchel containing his parchment and stylus and the jeweled casket containing the Splinter.

The companions stood in a group on the wharf, and when they had overcome their momentary diffidence about intruding uninvited on what appeared to be someone else's elegant reception, they approached an especially ornate esplanade suspended over the waters of the river. Here, a small cluster of Hydro-Sylphs reposed on beautifully embroidered divans close to the balcony's edge.

One of the Hydro-Sylphs wore a scarlet turban around his head, and his long brown body was sheathed in a green silken sarong, bound at the waist by a scarlet sash. He was the first to notice the strangers. With one bejeweled flipper, he laid down his lyre on the rich carpet at the side of the divan, and with the other, he sadly beckoned his unexpected visitors to approach. The other Hydro-Sylphs on the balcony observed his action and, in turn, laid down their lyres and watched in silence as the strangers approached.

"Welcome to the rueful realm of the Hydro-Sylphs," said the Hydro-Sylph with the scarlet turban. "I am the sovereign of this realm. My name is Prince Witzlau." A long tail with wide manicured fins projected from underneath his green sarong.

He gestured to a delicately attired Hydro-Sylph on a divan next to him with big brown eyes and long eyelashes. "This is my consort, Princess Tiphaine the incomparable, the jewel of my principality." She glanced mournfully at the strangers, lowered her lids, and, in homage to the guests, bowed her smooth, furry head with its long, exquisitely pointed nose. Golden and pearl earrings dangled from the edges of her shallow ears.

Prince Witzlau proceeded with his courtly speech: "Allow me to introduce you to the guests at my pavilion today. For here is the noble Fredegar, and there the aged Fichapel of Suevrum, a councilor whom I hold in highest esteem. To your left is Hannac, the Grand Drogo of Lianne'neas—I don't know what I would do without him; and to his right, his consort, Natu, a sublime fountain of beauty and wit.

"On the divan next to Natu reposes the doughty Coskaer of Eudo—a peerless warrior in battle, if ever we happened to have a chance to do battle—and Bac'haol, his squire, and the Lady Engonia of Anschetil. And did I miss Creac'h here, my sunlit clearing of laughter in a forest of sighs? For he is our jester and brings to our woe a ray of delight. But all are worthy gentlefolk you see arrayed before you, all sires and damsels of high degree."

With a melancholy wave of his bejeweled flipper, he indicated the tiers upon tiers of loggias that lined the terraced canals in every direction. Thousands of Hydro-Sylphs reclined on their divans and watched with interest the proceedings below them.

Knarry introduced himself and the band of travelers to the court. The green-haired Hill couple, miniscule Dolopeia, mighty Hrudan, the forest cat, and the Moor-Plains Retriever were all greeted with delight and curiosity. Knarry apologized for their intrusion at what was obviously a special occasion.

A murmur of polite and perhaps even embarrassed laughter rippled through the loggia. Creac'h responded, "No need for an apology. I speak for Prince Witzlau and all the court when I say that your presence is most esteemed and would be most esteemed even if this little salon of ours were a 'special occasion,' as you call it. But I hasten to inform you that this is the way we live all the time."

Prince Witzlau, meanwhile, was preoccupied with Tristan-Phoros. He found himself impelled to address him. "You, I assume, are what the denizens of Oval-Earth call, or used to call, a 'dog.' Am I mistaken?"

"There is some ambiguity about the appropriateness of that designation, Prince Witzlau," Tristan-Phoros replied as graciously as he could, not wishing to discuss the matter. He found the presence of these humanlike creatures in nonhuman form to be vaguely troubling.

"Ah, he speaks. For some reason, I suspected he could understand what I said and could reply. But I did not know that the dogs of Oval-Earth could speak. He is like us, then, is he not? But are we ambiguous?" Prince Witzlau glanced at the noble Coskaer of Eudo.

Coskaer answered, "Sire, whether or not we are ambiguous is itself an ambiguous question; but we do love ambiguity."

"We revel in ambiguity, Coskaer! It's so wonderfully lugubrious! Don't you agree?" Prince Witzlau directed himself back to Tristan-Phoros. "Are you lugubrious as well, my gallant and all-so-ambiguously doglike friend?"

"I am a philosopher and a logician," Tristan-Phoros retorted. "I am neither gallant, nor am I, as ambiguous as it may appear, a dog. Please do not ask me to explain this latter point. In any case, I don't have time to be lugubrious. I am too busy for that. I have too many things I am trying to figure out."

"And I am a poet and a musician. Consequently, I have all the time in the world to be lugubrious," Prince Witzlau crooned. He turned to address his court. "We are *all* lugubrious, are we not?"

"Hear, hear!" came from the surrounding pavilions.

"We are veritably a polity of poets, bards of the baleful, jongleurs of joylessness, chanters of chagrin, minstrels of melancholy," Prince Witzlau proclaimed with a series of deep sighs. "Without stint, we pour forth the anguish of our souls though the sorrowful sorties of fathomless and unfathomable time."

"Is that all you do?" Hrudan interrupted, somewhat curtly. The indolent luxuriousness of his hosts had set him on edge and made him unaccountably irritable.

Princess Tiphaine, taken aback by both Hrudan's question and his tone, pointed her exquisite little black nose in the air and said, "No, that's not all we do. We sail upon the river in our lovely craft and harvest the fruit that grows along the shore. We visit far-off pavilions along the river, for it is a very long river that circles under the mountains, and partake of the hospitality of our friends and neighboring potentates, such as Hannac here, the Grand Drogo of Lianne'neas, who has come from a great distance to join us today. Often we have visited him and his consort, Natu, in Lianne'neas—an enchanting spot, by the way, if you should ever care to visit it."

"You would be welcome," said the beautiful Natu, who was admiring Hrudan. She curled up the tip of her tail in a most coquettish fashion.

"Speaking of welcome," Prince Witzlau exclaimed, "look how we have slighted our guests! We have simply allowed them to stand there. Bring divans for them and goblets of water-plum wine and salvers of our finest fruits."

Satin-vested Hydro-Sylphs, both male and female, emerged from the inner rooms of the pavilions, and sliding gracefully on their long tails, brought in divans followed by salvers of fruit and tall, thin-necked carafes made of elaborately embossed silver coils entwined around crystal stems. They gave wide, shallow goblets fashioned out of fragrant sandalwood to the guests, who sat down on the divans and had their goblets filled with the bubbly water-plum wine.

Tristan-Phoros struck a particularly dramatic pose as he stretched back on his divan. He had begun to enjoy the company of these strange creatures, with whom he could not help but feel some affinity.

Tundra-Bear and Fox-Foot reclined on the same divan together and experienced the usual confusion and amusement when encountering soft cushions and silken cloth. They viewed the pale-blue bubbly wine in their goblets with some suspicion. They had never seen effervescent wine before and wondered how it would compare with the Hill wine they made in their mountain vineyards.

Creac'h, who sat opposite them, squirted an almost imperceptibly thin jet of wine from between his teeth at the Hill couple, who were surprised and laughed as they batted away the fragrant stream aimed so deftly and unexpectedly at them.

Knarry, Hrudan, and Dolopeia sat at the edges of their divans without reclining back on them. They were eager to get down to business. Bomsiell jumped up into the lap of Natu, who at first did not know what to do but, after a short hesitation, began instinctively to stroke Bomsiell with one of her long, elegantly polished flippers. She was surprised to find Bomsiell purring in response.

"Do you know many songs, Prince Witzlau?" Knarry asked.

"Yes," he sighed. "I know many songs. They are all so sweet and all so sad."

"Assuredly," Knarry said. "But do you know songs of the ancient times, songs of the ancestors?"

Prince Witzlau tilted his fine-turbaned head. "Songs of the ancient times? Songs of the ancestors?" he repeated. He had not given much thought to the ancient songs, not at least since his youth, and he was startled by such an abrupt question about them from a stranger, and a wood-gnome stranger at that. He pursed his lips. "Whose ancestors?" he asked pointedly. He raised, as far as he could, his flat, oval ears.

"All of our ancestors. The origins of Oval-Earth. Things that happened far in the past."

"I know you may find this strange, but I do know something about *your* ancestors, my most estimable Knarry. There is a song, I think. Ah, yes, there is a song—I may know some of the words of it, but my memory is dim. The jongleurs who live along the river where the Golden Mountains ring the Northern Taiga have preserved bits and pieces—just a verse here and there."

"But I am not interested so much in my ancestors, Prince Witzlau. The wood-gnomes have been around since primal times and have not changed much for all of that."

"There you are mistaken, my intrepid Knarry, for they have changed, and one of the ancient songs makes that reasonably clear. Indeed, your very statement jogged my memory of that song. It is called the 'Song of the Children of Elyr.'"

"But 'Elyr' is the ancient *gnomenie* word for 'woodland.'"

"Aha! I did not know that, but it makes perfect sense. For the wood-gnomes were the children of the woodland. They were the first inhabitants of Oval-Earth, back when the Golden Mountains arose like blossoms out of the crystalline womb of the earth. How spacious they were in those days, so far apart, so much wider—"

"Wider?" Tristan-Phoros snapped abruptly, sitting up in his divan. "Wider? How could they have been wider?"

Prince Witzlau peered at Tristan-Phoros in astonishment. "Do you mean you didn't know that the Golden Mountains contract and expand over the aeons of time? Oval-Earth in its history has been much wider than it is now, and even much narrower. We are in one of the narrower cycles at the present. Here beneath the mountains, we see everywhere the remnants and signs of its geological history and its various phases."

"But what power could be so great as to move the mountains?" Tristan-Phoros exclaimed.

"The same power that drives the great Rock-Falls of the western perimeter," Prince Witzlau answered. "It is the power of the rock-gnomes beneath the surface of the earth and their connection with the planetary forces that impel the universe and the World beyond the Worlds. But alas, we digress. We were speaking of the Children of Elyr."

"World beyond the Worlds!" Tristan-Phoros repeated. "Excuse my impertinence, but that sounds like something we should know about!"

Prince Witzlau ignored the comment. He reached for his lyre. It was a beautiful instrument made of inlaid woods, polished to the brightest hue; golden cording was wrapped meticulously around the columns that supported bronze crossbars of intricate design.

Words in an ancient alphabet were carved on its base. Hrudan could not help but think that it reminded him, in its distinguished craftsmanship, of the Battle-Axe. Tundra-Bear was reminded of the imperial crossbow he had fired in the Viceroy's court.

Prince Witzlau positioned the lyre on his lap, holding it in place with one flipper and gently stroking its quivering strings with the other. He began to sing in a gentle but flawless tenor voice; the melody was strange and ancient.

> *To the Children of Elyr in the primal dawn light*
> *When the forests abounded, from rim to far rim,*
>
> *Wuldor gave beneficent command:*
> *The Seed of the Tree, Life-giving Offshoot,*
>
> *Eternal progeny of the Children twice blessed*
> *Wood-sprite and woodland forever conjoined,*
>
> *Till . . .*

Prince Witzlau grew silent. "I think that is all I can remember, my most esteemed Knarry. In fact, I am surprised I remembered that much. The ancient songs are like that in my memory—bits and fragments evoked inexplicably sometimes by a word or phrase, and I don't remember how and when I learned them, if I ever did learn them at all. As for the song itself, I don't know what it means, but it seems to point to a time when your most remote ancestors, the Children of Elyr, I assume, had not yet fully evolved into wood-gnomes."

"It is as much a mystery to me as it is to you," Knarry observed. "But it has something to do with the Ancestral Tree being planted in Oval-Earth. I had always thought that wood-gnomes evolved from trees, but, if we are to believe the words of the song as far as we are able to understand these, it seems to have been a joining, perhaps very primitive at first, of a woodland sprite and forest sprigs engendered in the primal shadows of the Ancestral Tree. But who is this Wuldor mentioned in the song? I have never heard of Wuldor before."

"I don't know who Wuldor is, but I do know part of a song wherein Wuldor is mentioned. In fact, Wuldor is mentioned in a great many of the ancient songs." Again, Prince Witzlau swept the strings of his lyre with his flipper and began to sing:

> *Wuldor of Aeons Primeval I chant,*
> *Who held the Unfolding of Time in his hands,*
>
> *The World beyond the Worlds in primal delight,*
> *Who fashioned glorious Micelihiu, the Strong,*

> *To bind the Betrayer in Rifts of shame.*
> *For the Glory of the Works of the Light*
>
> *Was Pain to the Servants of the Fallen One;*
> *And he it was . . .*

"Oh, dear," said Prince Witzlau, "I think I have forgotten the rest." He laid down his lyre and glanced dolefully at the others. "We have forgotten so much. We live in bits and pieces of memory."

Knarry offered his consolation: "That's all right, Prince Witzlau, but when was the last time you recited it in its entirety?"

Prince Witzlau sighed. "I can't remember that either. Maybe I never recited it in its entirety."

"It is clear, in any case," Knarry said, "that the isolation of your people has preserved you from the ills that have beset the rest of Oval-Earth. You remember things that the rest of us don't, even if in fragments. For you, in these magical mountain caverns, nothing has changed."

"Nothing has changed?" Prince Witzlau cried out in a wavering voice.

"Oh, nothing has changed at all!" muttered Creac'h sarcastically. He bent his tail fins so far around that they touched the back of his head and looked like little wings coming out of his ears. The retinue laughed for a second, before swallowing up their laughter in a chorus of dejected wails.

"Everything has changed!" Prince Witzlau lamented. "Everything! Everything!"

"What has changed?" Knarry responded, stunned by the reaction to his comment. "Tell me about your ancestors. Tell me about your own history."

"Please, please, do not speak of our ancestors. We cannot bear to think about them," Prince Witzlau moaned while dramatically covering his eyes with one flipper and casting his head backward into the silken cushions of the divan.

"It's simply too humiliating," said Coskaer of Eudo.

"Simply too mortifying," said Fredegar.

"Simply too embarrassing," said Lady Engonia.

"A disgrace," said Bac'haol.

"A source of limitless shame," said Natu as she stroked Bomsiell with her radiant flipper.

"But I don't understand this," Knarry remonstrated. "Your ancestors were admired in Oval-Earth. Hrudan has found out that they used to travel down the River N'ea to the—"

The courtly retinue burst out in an anguished groan. They buried their heads in their flippers.

"To the Midland Sea," Knarry resumed, after a moment's hesitation, "where they accompanied the Duke and Duchess of the Gethsarbim in their enchanted sloop to the Eye of the Universe and from there to the Ospeth's great Capital to celebrate the annual festival. It must have been a wondrous event." Dolopeia assented vigorously. Her golden eyes twinkled.

"Too wondrous indeed," said Prince Witzlau. "You make our pain too acute by reminding us of what they could do and we can't."

"Why can't you?" Fox-Foot complained. She had sat patiently on her divan next to Tundra-Bear during these various exchanges but now seemed at the end of her patience. "What's wrong with all you … people, or whatever you are? Why are you so sad?"

Princess Tiphaine blinked at Fox-Foot with tearful eyes. "I know it must be hard for you to understand. But …" She hesitated and studied her own finely ribbed flippers.

"Tell me, Princess Tiphaine. I promise I will understand," Fox-Foot urged.

"Very well, I will tell you. The Hydro-Sylphs, you see, well … the Hydro-Sylphs are natural to these watery caverns with all their wonderful channels and streams and waterfalls. And once, as Knarry said, we used to travel down the River N'ea and into the Midland Sea to join the peoples of Oval-Earth in their celebrations. We no longer do any of that."

"But why not? You have all these boats tied up at the dock and sailing craft."

"We didn't use boats back then. We had no need of boats. When we accompanied the Gethsarbim to the Capital, we didn't use a boat. A boat is to us as a set of crutches is to a man with a broken leg."

"Then what is broken?"

"You may have noted us sitting all the while on these divans and carpets gazing longingly at the golden waters of the river."

"Yes."

"You may have also noted that we … well, we just look, that's all."

"Now that you call it to my attention, I do notice. Your physiques are all too clearly made for—"

"No, Fox-Foot, please don't say the word; we can't endure it!"

"I will say it!"

"Please don't!"

Fox-Foot jumped up from the divan, looked Princess Tiphaine directly in the eyes, and declared, "You are made for *swimming!*"

A loud tremulous cry echoed from one end of the water caves to the other. Princess Tiphaine sobbed, great wet tears rolling down her sleek furry face; Prince Witzlau covered his eyes with his flippers; Natu hugged Bomsiell in her remorse; Lady Engonia wept; Coskaer of Eudo sank his head down onto his chest; the surrounding pavilions wailed with woe and lamentation.

"I know what we are made for, Fox-Foot," Princess Tiphaine sputtered through her tears. "But the problem is—*we don't know how to do it anymore.* Ages and ages ago, something happened. We lost the ability. There is no explanation."

The courtly retinue moaned in agreement.

"But there is nothing to it. Just plop into the water and flap those flippers," Fox-Foot asserted firmly. She moved her arms rapidly in an undulating motion. Tundra-Bear had to restrain her from diving into the river to demonstrate.

"We are afraid to. It won't work," said Natu.

"One of these days, we may try it again," Prince Witzlau added morosely.

"One of these days is none of these days," Dolopeia spoke sharply.

Prince Witzlau arched his long shiny neck around and glanced sadly at the tiny Gethsarbim princess. "I suppose, my most delightful Duchess, you're right. But what are we to do? We are accustomed to call this most unfortunate loss of skill our 'bereftment.' It has made us so unhappy ever since." The sorrow of the moment was temporarily assuaged as carafes of water-plum wine were passed around and the sandalwood goblets filled to the brim.

Hrudan was impatient to get on with the purpose of their visit. He addressed Prince Witzlau in a voice stern with command: "Prince Witzlau, it is vital that you attempt to answer several questions we will pose to you. We are bound on an important errand, one that holds the entire safety of Oval-Earth in its pur-view. We depend on whatever you can bring out of your memory to help us."

"I will be glad to help. You are clearly a person of consequence, noble Hrudan. I knew that the moment you stepped off the ship. Please proceed," Prince Witzlau said.

"What do you know about the War of Desolation?"

"I have never heard of it."

"I guessed as much," Tristan-Phoros yapped.

"Quiet, Tristan-Phoros," Hrudan ordered. "I must conduct this inquiry without your interruption. We are not here to solve logical puzzles, as much fun as it is to do that. Prince Witzlau, have you ever heard of something called a Lo-El?"

"Never."

"What do you know about a supposed immigration of the People of the Wind over the Golden Mountains?"

"The Hydro-Sylph princes of ancient times were good friends of the People of the Wind. They were a noble race. Shortly before the unfortu-nate 'bereftment' of my own people made communication with the outside world too shameful to be pursued any longer, we heard that the People of the Wind were planning such a migration. I have no further knowledge of what may have happened."

"Why were they planning this migration?"

"I don't know that either."

"I do," said the aged Fichapel of Suevrum. "They said that something called the Kingdom of Darkness was taking control of Oval-Earth."

Hrudan turned to him. "Where did they say this Kingdom of Darkness was to be found?"

"In Oval-Earth itself," Fichapel replied.

"I guessed that too," Tristan-Phoros yapped again.

"Muzzle your mouth, you mangy mutt!" Hrudan declared, in an unusual display of irritation.

"What marvelous alliteration!" Prince Witzlau remarked, glancing at Hrudan with admiration. "What rhythm! Do you mind if I ask what meter you put that in?"

But Tristan-Phoros looked hurt.

"I'm sorry, Tristan-Phoros. I didn't mean that," Hrudan apologized.

"That's quite all right," Tristan-Phoros sighed. He adopted the melancholy pose of a Hydro-Sylph.

Fichapel of Suevrum went on: "The People of the Wind also wanted to leave because they had a special devotion to the Emperor and were ready to serve his purposes. But the line of Emperors disappeared—nobody knows why; and government was given over to a Viceroy. The People of the Wind thought that the system would soon decay into something unworthy of either human or creaturely dignity."

Prince Witzlau again interposed himself into the discussion: "The People of the Wind were valiant. Wherever they have gone, if they survived the passage over the Golden Mountains, they have created a civilization worthy of the greatest respect. They would always be ready to serve the imperial line, should it ever be rediscovered. They were astute trainers of birds; their dream was one day to domesticate the giant scarlet eagles that used to nest in the highest bastions of the Golden Mountains.

"Before the ancient horse became extinct, as its pasturelands in the Downs were diminished by the contraction of the Golden Mountains, the People of the Wind had trained them to be ridden, as later happened in Oval-Earth with the tall white moose, whose original range were the forests of the western foothills around the Claha-ain Plateau. But the horse was the most beautiful animal in Oval-Earth—no offense intended to dogs, my laudable Tristan-Phoros."

"No offense taken," he replied.

"Splendid creatures indeed," Prince Witzlau rhapsodized, "creatures with fine long manes and beautiful legs, magnificent as they galloped in mighty herds across the heathlands of the Downs. They are associated, too, with Wuldor, and the beginning of all things in the World beyond the Worlds."

Knarry perked up at this. He wanted to find out more about horses. "Prince Witzlau, does the mention of horses ever appear in any of the songs you know?"

"Not that I can think of."

Knarry looked at Hrudan for a cue. Hrudan assented with a nod of his head. It was time to press the cardinal question. He turned back to Prince Witzlau. "Do you know anything about what is called the Song of the Eternal Aeons?" he asked.

Prince Witzlau's scarlet turban slid off the back of his head in his astonishment. "Your request surprises me; I have never heard such a request before. I know the name. I know that it was the most important song in Oval-Earth, a song bequeathed to the Oval-Earth peoples by Wuldor, the same Lord of creation who bequeathed the Seedling of the Ancestral Tree to the Children of Elyr.

"The Song is even more ancient than the Ancestral Tree. But the words have been lost. How often I have thought that if we had not lost the words, our 'bereftment' would never have happened. As far as I can remember, the Song was safeguarded and sung every morning at the Eye of the Universe in the center of the Midland Sea. You should go there to find it."

"It's no longer the Eye of the Universe, as you call it, Prince Witzlau. It's called the Isle of the Drowsers—a very different kind of place from what it once was." Knarry said. "But your memory seems to treasure all kinds of things, even if in fragments. Couldn't part of the Song be in there, unbeknownst to you? Just a verse or two?"

"Many things are in my memory for which I can give no account of how they got there. Music preserves many things."

Knarry prodded him further. "A friend of mine, Garug-Caroch—the former Grand Master at the College of Wisdom—sent me, as perhaps one of the final acts of his life, two verses of the Song. When he did this, he included other scraps of parchment along with them. On one such scrap was prominently written the word 'horses.' I presume that the word was part of a line of the Song. That is why I asked you about horses. Can you remember anything with that word?"

"Horses?" Prince Witzlau repeated.

"Yes."

"Horses . . . horses . . . horses," he mumbled slowly. He thumped the side of his head with an elegantly bejeweled flipper.

"You've got it."

"I am afraid, my intrepid Knarry, that I haven't got anything at all! Horses … horses? Sorry, nothing in the old noggin about horses!"

"You're quite sure? This is important."

"Horses? Oh, *horses!*"

"Yes, *horses!*"

"You said 'horses'?"

"Indeed, I did!"

"Horses … horses … with manes?"

"Sounds good … horses have manes!"

"Manes … yes … black …"

"Black … horses? Black …?"

"Steeds?"

"Steeds? I don't know about steeds." Knarry was puzzled.

"Another word for 'horses,'" Hrudan interjected. "Illyria sometimes calls them steeds. I wish she were here. She knows all there is to know about the memories and legends of horses."

"Illyria? Who is Illyria? A queenly name that, like our little Dolopeia here," Prince Witzlau said.

"Stay with the horses, Prince Witzlau!" Knarry reprimanded.

"So … horses … steeds … black … cosmic …"

"Go on, go on, get them into combination! Can you get them into combination?"

"Cosmic … fiery … black … horses … steeds!"

"Into combination! Only the combination will work!" Knarry exclaimed.

Prince Witzlau shivered from his head to his tail in excitement. His eyes rolled in his head. He flapped his flippers and struggled upright in his divan. He reached for his lyre and deposited it in his lap. Slowly, as if in a trance, he began to pluck one harmonious chord after another. It was an ancient music, mysterious and serene.

The other Hydro-Sylphs rose high in their divans and listened with rapt attention.

Tristan-Phoros whispered to Knarry, "It's going to happen — get ready!" Knarry grabbed for his haversack and pulled out the stylus and parchment. He prepared to write.

Prince Witzlau began to sing in a pure and melodious voice, and the sound of his song resonated magically throughout the length and breadth of the golden vaults that towered high above him:

> *Out of the black-maned*
> *Horses of darkness,*
>
> *The fiery steeds*
> *Of the cosmic deep*

A pure and blessed stillness reigned throughout the water caverns. The golden river gurgled to its depths. Nobody dared to move. The entire nation of the Hydro-Sylphs seemed frozen in position on their loggias and divans.

Suddenly, Prince Witzlau slid up high on his powerful tail; he dropped his lyre to the side as he glided faultlessly out of his green gown and scarlet sash. His shimmering deep-brown body rose off the divan in a smooth vertical line, hovered for but a moment high above the esplanade, coiled and arched over, and descended through the glittering air, noiselessly slipping into the dazzling waters beneath the pavilion.

The onlookers could see him sluice faultlessly through the deep, clear currents below them. Just as suddenly he burst out of the river with a high, joyous splash, bolting so far out from the water that his tail barely touched it anymore, before bending over again in a perfect arch and plunging once more into the depths.

He was followed by Princess Tiphaine, whose lithe form rose out of her gown and curved backward high through the air and downward into the water. The two of them disappeared for a few moments and then reared upward through the surface of the water simultaneously, rising together in perfect form and coiling over once more into slender dives deep into the currents of the river.

Then Coskaer of Eudo, and Bac'haol, and the Grand Drogo of Lianne'neas plummeted flawlessly into the river. The sublime Natu, who gently shed Bomsiell from her lap and her embroidered gown at the same time, coiled upward and around, flipped her elegant tail high above her, and cut down through the waves without raising a drop of water in her descent.

The whole court, followed by hundreds and hundreds of Hydro-Sylphs, slid out of their gowns and off their divans and into the water. The Hydro-Sylph servants soon shed their satin vests and joined their fellow countrymen. They turned and twisted though the tremulous waves, riding up the waterfalls and spouts, hurling themselves into the air and twirling in graceful diving pirouettes into the golden river. The caverns resounded with the joy and rapture of their swimming.

"I think it is time for us to be leaving," said Fox-Foot somewhat regretfully as she looked out at the spectacle before her. She was eager to dive into the water herself and to swim and play with the Hydro-Sylphs.

The others agreed. There was much more to be learned from the Hydro-Sylphs; maybe their memories would now be restored to their fullness and their moods made infinitely less morose.

Dolopeia assured them that it would be a while before the Hydro-Sylphs, in their present state of joyful recovery, would be calm enough to be of much assistance. The companions arose from their own divans—the stay had been such a pleasure, and they certainly could watch for hours the wonderful sight that dazzled their eyes.

They made their way to the enchanted sloop and crossed the gangplank, which hurriedly withdrew itself back into the ship. Soon they were swept swiftly under the crystal bridge and away from the pavilions along the golden river. The Hydro-Sylphs sported around the hull of the sloop and slapped their tails playfully against the surface of the water.

As the sloop turned the bend of the river to head for the waterfall and the open reaches of the River N'ea, Prince Witzlau and Princess Tiphaine flashed out of the golden waters and leapt clear over the bow of the sloop, waving their flippers in farewell and inviting them to return as soon as possible. They plunged into the river again on the other side of the sloop and vanished out of sight.

Tristan-Phoros was sad, in a way, to leave these new and curiously bi-form friends. "Now my songs shall be sad," he muttered to Bomsiell, "and their song shall be, at last, happy again. But that is as it should be." Bomsiell blinked her eyes; she could not understand what he had said, yet she was sympathetic with the somber tone of his voice.

Hrudan knew that if Oval-Earth were ever to return to good order and sanity, the Hydro-Sylphs would have an important contribution to make. Despite his impatience, he would have liked to stay longer. But he wondered if he would ever return.

Hrudan again expressed his apologies to Tristan-Phoros, who wagged his tail and told Hrudan that all was well. He conceded, "I was talking out of turn, Hrudan, and I deserved your rebuke. And I do like to turn things into logical puzzles sometimes, ignoring the bigger and more pressing issues at hand."

"Whatever you may or may not have deserved," Hrudan answered, "I had no right to impugn your dignity. Let me assure you, Tristan-Phoros, that you are neither mangy nor a mutt. Nor was I right to allow the manner of the Hydro-Sylphs to set me on edge like that."

After a few moments' thought, Tristan-Phoros observed, "About my being mangy or being a mutt, my golden fur and pure-bred retriever blood may well belie that, but I do fear that such terms may also describe some aspect of my soul. I feel that there is much that I will have to answer for, in my own way, when all of this is over, if it ever gets over.

"As for the manner of the Hydro-Sylphs, I can understand, Hrudan, why a man of action like yourself would get impatient with their mode of life. But they have goodly spirits, and whether you like it or not, their life of glamorous leisure is the source of their creativity.

"Action is not the only thing in life. Oval-Earth will have much need of them, as well as all of those, even like myself, whose task it is to probe and celebrate what is eternal and true and beautiful. You must understand this well, Hrudan."

"I will try to understand this, Tristan-Phoros," Hrudan replied, "and I stand, moreover, justly rebuked by you. May I always remember what you have said."

"I think you shall, Hrudan. And anyway, Prince Witzlau was delighted to hear your alliteration. There once was an ancient people here in Oval-Earth who wrote all of their verse using such alliteration. No doubt, in Prince Witzlau's mind, some shred of that memory remains."

When the magic vessel emerged from under the thin veil of the falls that curtained the entrance to the water caverns, it was early evening in Oval-Earth. The sun was going down over the Golden Mountains at the far western horizon. The sloop glided smoothly through the manifold bends of the River N'ea. Around it, the Downs were beautiful as the golden gorse and purple heather that carpeted the windy moorlands glimmered in the evening light.

Occasionally the sloop passed by some riverine hamlet where boatmen tied up their skiffs for the night and watched with startled curiosity the magic vessel as it slipped quietly past. Gradually, on the sloop, the companions came together in the center of the deck.

Knarry spoke to them. "It is clear from what we have been told by Prince Witzlau that, in our search for the remainder of the Song, we must go to the most important place of all. We must sail to the Isle of the Drowsers."

Tristan-Phoros sat up and looked anxiously at the others. "I don't want to go there," he said.

"Why not?" Tundra-Bear responded.

"I don't know why. I just don't want to go there." He groaned in misery and lay down again. He rolled into a very doglike curl, his bushy tail wrapped up over his nose and fell into a twitching, uneasy sleep.

Night fell soon afterward. The companions were served a fine Geth-sarbim dinner by the same invisible hands that sailed the enchanted sloop and always seemed to know just what to do and where to go without being asked. Once again, the companions found places to be comfortable for the night. Dolopeia retired to the diminutive cabin, and Bomsiell perched high in the mizzenmast. The sloop glided farther onward down the river. Its silver bells tinkled in the breezes that wafted across the poop deck, and its fiery cressets fore and aft sparkled like little rubies in the glow of the lavender moonlight.

Only Hrudan and Knarry talked together deep into the night. Hrudan expressed his hopes and anxieties about the future for Illyria and Erudan, and about Oval-Earth in general. He dreamed about what Oval-Earth might once have been—a prosperous, beneficent place, rich in produce and goodly habits, citizens generous to each other and willing to share in their goodness, a place of wisdom and reverence and festivity, where all could come together in noble pageants to celebrate their fruitfulness.

He told Knarry that it was up to them — to Tundra-Bear and Fox-Foot, to Dolopeia and Tristan-Phoros and Bomsiell, to Knarry and himself — to try to make things good again. Finally, Hrudan grew silent as well, and Knarry slept on his mighty wedge-like feet. The twin moons waned low over the Golden Mountains.

The morning sun rose like an orange disk over the radiant white waters of the Midland Sea. The sloop had reached the estuary of the River N'ea. The travelers awoke and were greeted by Dolopeia, who danced excitedly around them and cheerfully dispensed her proverbial lore about early rising. Invisible hands began to produce fruit tarts and finely wrought cups brimming with moose-milk brew, piping hot and flavored with ground cinnobar-nuts.

The travelers shook off their sleep and welcomed this early morning repast. Even Bomsiell, who slept contentedly in her comfortable little roost among the silken sails, was brought a bowl of cool moose milk to lap up there in the silver rigging.

Knarry pointed at a blue spot on the horizon. "There it is!" he shouted. "The Isle of the Drowsers!"

At that moment, there was a heavy splash from the starboard side of the sloop. They all ran to see what had happened. In the water, they saw a furry golden head and a black nose — and a few feet away, a furry golden tail with a white tip. The pipe satchel was floating loosely around his shoulder. Tristan-Phoros looked back at them and shouted. "Don't worry about me. I will meet you at the felucca dock at the other end of the Sea! Good luck!"

Bomsiell let out a desolate yowl. Fox-Foot cried out, "Take care of yourself, Tristan-Phoros!"

He barked. He actually barked. Then he turned around and swam through the estuary waters to the shore. The enchanted sloop raised its own great spinnaker sail, which ballooned out gallantly to the winds. With a swoop, it rose up over the shining, mother-of-pearl waves and headed for the island in the middle of the Sea.

Chapter XII

The Brotherhood of the Drowsers

By midday, the enchanted sloop had rounded the eastern shore of the island and hove to in a small natural harbor — a sheltered cove that faced northward towards the Capital. In this inlet was the dock where the felucca, whose sole purpose was to transport new members for the Brotherhood across the milk-white waters of the sea, traditionally landed.

The felucca itself, however, was always moored in an obscure fishing village at the far shore of the mainland, for few members of the Brotherhood were known to return to their native lands. In recent ages, none had ever returned. Nevertheless, a signal flare stood at the far end of the dock, should the occasion arise when the felucca had to be summoned. Of course, it was never summoned.

An elderly fisherman had the task of piloting the felucca back and forth and of watching for the signal flare, should it ever beckon him. His position as ferryman was hereditary; it was passed on from generation to generation in his family; and his disposition — disagreeable, miserly, and exorbitant — seemed to be equally hereditary. But he executed his duties with care and vigilance and waited patiently for the signal that never came.

From the gunwales of the sloop the travelers had viewed the approach to the island with curiosity and fascination. They had not realized that the giant blue spruce trees, which covered the island with their dense groves, were so tall.

The serenity of the towering trees — their great boughs swaying in the sea wind and gathering into the depths of their great verdant arms the bright sunlight of Oval-Earth — reminded Knarry, and those who had ventured with him into the ancestral forest, of the Northern Taiga. He mentioned this resemblance to Fox-Foot and Tundra-Bear, who nodded their agreement.

Indeed, they thought the island was as beautiful as anything they had seen in Oval-Earth; no wonder the Brotherhood rarely returned to the mainland. Yet why, in the midst of all this marvel, would one be inclined to live out one's life buried in sleep?

The sloop pulled up at the dock in the middle of the sheltered inlet, and the invisible hands cast silken cords around the piers and tucked the silver-belled gangplank neatly into place. Dolopeia was, as usual, the first to cross it, followed by Bomsiell, who was glad to be back on *terra firma* and to be entering a forest once again. The others came in turn.

A narrow footpath led from the dock into the heart of the spruce forest. As they walked along the path, the tall, swaying trees arched far above them. Their trunks were massive and straight, and there was no undergrowth—only the solemn pillars of the spruce trees reaching high into the heavens. Beneath the trees, a brooding darkness was occasionally pierced by a wisp of sunlight that flashed momentarily through the shaggy boughs overhead.

Knarry meditated deeply on this forest—he had always known that the spruce-gnomes on the mainland of Oval-Earth were a clan apart, a reserved community who rarely came to the Claha-ain Plateau for the an-nual meetings. It was said that they were taciturn gnomes, often rapt in the contemplation of some mystery that seemed to surround them. It was also said that, in the lonely enclaves where they made their homes, they had some special concourse with the rock-gnomes who lived deep under the soil of Oval-Earth.

While on the Northern Taiga, Knarry had not noticed the presence of spruces, but then again, it was often rumored that at the time of their metamorphoses, spruce-gnomes went to the extreme northernmost fringe of the Taiga, where they made their solitary domicile.

Yet it was possible to wonder—as Knarry did—whether they came here at the time of their metamorphoses. The perpetual sough of the wind in the swaying branches overhead was like the sigh of a lover in the presence of his beloved.

After the companions had walked for an hour along the path through the forest, Tundra-Bear noticed a clearing ahead. Fox-Foot affirmed what he saw, though the clearing was still far away.

In another half hour, they stepped out onto a wide greensward covered with clover, at the center of which stood a broad, perfectly round Tower rising high above the vaulted rooftop of the forest and made entirely of a deep-black obsidian that glittered beautifully in the sun.

A narrow staircase wound up along its outermost wall to its summit. Knarry reflected on the pearl-white Midland Sea, and the blue of the spruce forest, and now the black Tower so brilliantly placed in the exact center of Oval-Earth. "We have arrived, I take it," he announced, "at the 'Pupil' of the 'Eye of the Universe'!"

Dolopeia darted out in front, scrambled across the greensward, and began to climb the steps of the Tower. She loved to be in front. They all followed her; they had grown to trust the courage and spunk of the tiny Gethsarbim duchess.

The Tower itself was about two hundred paces tall. The staircase was made of narrow white slabs of marble that projected directly out of the Tower wall. It curved up the side of the circular wall and had no railing or banister, though it was firm under the tread of unfamiliar feet.

The summit of the Tower was a wide, inky-black shallow basin several hundred paces wide. A red marble railing surrounded it. It was obviously an observation deck only, a place to look out from — and indeed, as one turned around, one could see the entire length and breadth of Oval-Earth, all curiously magnified.

On every side, the distant peaks of the Golden Mountains glittered from afar. To the south, the Hill Country rose into its many-colored uplands; to the north, beyond the spires and domes of the Capital, could be seen the Northern Taiga and its majestic forests; to the west, the sparkling glimmers of the Great Rock-Falls made a sharp contrast with the somber mists that, to the east, hung over the Moor-Plains. Overhead, it seemed that one could look infinitely deep into the universe beyond.

"What must it be like at night, when the stars are out?" gasped Fox-Foot.

Dolopeia replied, "When the eye is sound, the soul is sound as well."

"But it's *not* sound; no indeed, not sound at all!" said a strange voice.

"Who said that?" asked Hrudan.

They all glanced around, searching for the source of the unusual voice, curiously high-pitched, shy, just a bit quavering, but kindly.

"I did," said the voice. "Who else out here can *actually* talk! That is, until all of you showed up and began to engage in what, to my ears, sounds like—excuse the expression—*frightful* blab, even though you have said practically nothing at all. But I adore it, I assure you. Please blab on. It's just so quiet out here, and I am delighted to hear the sound of human voices once again and have the opportunity to use my own at last, after all these hundreds of years."

Everyone swiveled their attention around to the center of the observation deck, and there, standing up to his waist in a stairwell that led down into the interior of the Tower, was a somewhat rotund young man. He had a big smiling face, a shiny bald head, and ears that protruded rather far from the tipped-up edges of his enormous smile. He was garbed in a copious but ill-fitting black robe that reminded one of a Master's robe at the College of Wisdom, except that the hood was so long and thin that it hung down his back and well into the trapdoor where he stood.

"Welcome," he twittered with a slight bow and a gesture of swinging a great berobed arm around and tapping his forehead with his dainty white fist. "Welcome to the once-renowned 'Eye of the Universe,' as that rather excessively burly wood-gnome amongst you so appositely called it—except that you are about a millennium too late to observe it in the state of affairs that would have merited such a laudable designation.

"Now it is called among the populace of Oval-Earth, if I am not mistaken, the Isle of the Drowsers. *And how right they are!* You see, everyone sleeps here; they sleep *all* the time, except for a little *frightful* interlude each day when they—how should I say it?—actually *get up*. After all, everyone does need some rest from *whatever* one is doing, doesn't one?

"But they don't really get up. They constitute, in their *Blinking*, the most sorry surge of somnambulant sops the universe has ever known. Anyway, I must say I am charmed to meet you. You are the first people I have had a chance to talk to since I awakened—I mean really awakened."

The young man with the protruding ears glanced cheerfully at each member of the band. His smile widened even more, and he poked a stubby finger so deep into one of his jowls that it practically disappeared.

"But you are certainly the *weirdest* conglomeration of people I ever saw—if you are people! Now, I'd recognize a wood-gnome by those wedge-shaped feet and bark boots from a league away. But who are this man and woman with the long green hair and bronze-colored skin and great longbows strapped around their shoulders? Are those eyes, or are those rather oversized amethyst gemstones aglow in their heads? And a large, gray-striped cat with four ears! And a miniature maiden with scarlet hair and golden eyes—aha! a Gethsarbim, I would be willing to bet. I now recollect a description I heard so very long ago, though I've never seen a real one before. But what a most *darling* shawl you have, my dear, with all those lovely butterflies and hummingbirds embroidered on it!

"And then obviously a real human, with a beard as black as night and eyes like a hawk, who is carrying with him a *frightful* axe that looks as if it could split, with one blow, all of Oval-Earth in half! I hope you are not a woodsman bent upon leveling our gorgeous spruce forests.

"What a very *peculiar* lot! What on earth ever brought you here to our isolated, *frightful*, and moreover, desolated abode?"

Knarry began to stride over to the stairwell to get a closer look at this prodigious fellow who still stood up to his waist in the aperture, but the young man removed his finger from his jowl, leaving a little crater behind in it, and waggled it in the air as a gesture for him to stop.

"Uh-uh! Not so close, my all-too-inquisitive wood-gnome! I mean, not for my sake—but for your sake. You see, we eat only one thing here—garlic! I just thought it would be polite that I should admonish you. You just may not find my olfactory *penumbra*, if you would deign to call it that, all too pleasant. I'm sorry, but there is nothing I can do about it."

Knarry replied, "Well, whatever you say! But who are you? And what do you mean by saying that you awakened?"

"First, allow me to emerge from this ever-so-inconvenient and *frightful* stairwell. I was just underneath when I heard footsteps, as well as your talking, and came up to investigate. One hasn't heard footsteps up here for heaven knows how long! In point of fact, one has *never* heard footsteps up here before. Of course, until recently, I would not have heard footsteps even if there had been some, because I was fast asleep.

"Now, which way is the wind blowing? Ah, yes — could you all move over to that side of the Tower? That's good. A little further—yes, that's better. You wouldn't *want* to be downwind from me if you could possibly help it."

The young man emerged, or rather, he kept emerging, from the stairwell. He was of medium height but huge in girth and had broad shoulders that hung over his bodily frame like great, sloping cliffs in the high mountains. His heavy black robe was torn and threadbare. As he turned around to the travelers, bunched together at one end of the observation platform, his huge smile stretched out even further and made his ears twitch a bit.

"My name," he said, "is Weyland. I am a member of the Brotherhood of . . . well, frankly, I don't quite know what to call it. 'The Brotherhood of the Drowsers' will have to do, I'm afraid, except that I am no longer drowsy. In fact, having slept a great deal, as I calculate, centuries of sleep perhaps, I need very little sleep at all.

"I awoke last winter at the time of the solstice when the most *frightful* storm was just positively bellowing over Oval-Earth. Yes, I was jolted right out of my bed — right out of my bed, I tell you, and stood there amidst the dreadful snoring of my brethren, wondering what on earth was going on. I had been having a particularly bad dream — I don't remember what the dream was all about. But there I was — awake, and feeling *awfully* good to be awake, I must admit. I am the only person who is awake on this island — except now for all of you, of course!"

He laughed, and at that moment, a gust of wind spiraled around him and blew back in the direction of the others. The travelers fell backward, holding their noses and choking. Bomsiell coughed and spat, while her tail stiffened and the hair rose along her back.

"I told you so!" he said with another cheerful smile.

"Listen, Weyland," Knarry muttered as he recovered from the unseemly gust and pressed a lapel of his cloak around the bottom half of his face, "we are here on important business, and we need your help."

"I would be delighted to be of service."

"We are looking for the words of an ancient song. Perhaps you have heard of it; it was called the Song of the Eternal Aeons. We understand that, in times past, the Brotherhood had the custom —"

"I know! I know! The custom of chanting the Song at dawn from the summit of this noble Tower. There was once a parchment, too, upon which the words of the Song were written down. I know all about it, but ..."

"But?"

"I don't know the words of the Song, if that is what you are leading up to, as well I suspect it is. How remarkable that you should ask about them, however! I have been looking for them myself. Somehow, I think I have recently heard some of them. Somehow, I have the impression that my bad dream was dispelled by a few words of the Song. What a *frightfully* odd impression, don't you think?"

Weyland paused and pushed his finger back into his jowl in the identical spot (which had just recovered from the previous puncture) in order to express his obvious puzzlement. Another gust swirled around, and the visitors fell farther back from him.

"In any case," he said, "I have spent the last five months since my awakening searching our archives and trying to figure out what has happened here on the island over the past centuries. I have discovered a great deal of evidence referring to the parchment upon which the words of the Song were reputedly written, but I have not been able to find the parchment itself. It seems to have disappeared.

"An ancient tradition appears to have held that, generally in Oval-Earth, the Song could be transmitted from generation to generation only by memory. There was one exception to this rule: a parchment preserved with care — or once upon a time with care — on this island. I also understand that extensive commentaries were written on the Song, and these were preserved both here and in the Library at the College of Wisdom. But the commentaries assumed that readers already knew the words and simply alluded to them here and there. What a *frightful* misfortune for us that they made that assumption."

Once again, Weyland removed his finger from its temporary pocket inside his jowl. "I wonder," he added, "if perhaps a tour of our lovely, albeit presently malodorous, domicile would not be of *some* assistance to you! You arrive here, obviously, knowing a great deal that I do not know. Perhaps something you will observe will help make a connection for you. Meanwhile, I feel I have a lot to learn from you. Furthermore, I do rather look forward to being a tour guide; I have never been a tour guide before, yet I feel an inclination towards it, as if it were in my very blood and bones, even though I must marshal you through something that even the most tolerant of persons would have to concede is, at times, just *frightfully* gruesome.

"Before you descend, however, I strongly recommend that you all attach some kind of covering in front of your face—even that gamesome four-eared cat should do so. I don't think she is too fond of garlic."

The companions needed, at this point, little urging to prepare face covers. They searched through their packs, found suitable pieces of cloth, and tied them into place over their noses and mouths. Bomsiell, as could be expected, resisted this effort but finally cooperated.

"Has the Brotherhood always subsisted on garlic, Weyland?" Fox-Foot asked.

"*Heavens no!* Back when things were right—whenever that was—the Brotherhood lived on a most varied and nourishing diet. I have been able to learn from the archives that the greensward around the Tower was once a fruitful garden of delights. The ancient members, in fact, were particularly fond of a certain kind of crimson-fruited melon—very sweet and juicy and eaten very cold. This garlic thing happened only when they all began to sleep.

"You see, they get up once a day for about a half hour and walk about in a stupor, blinking their eyes and bumping into one another incessantly. I have grown accustomed to calling this brief period of time the Blinking.

"One can never quite predict when the Blinking is going to happen. It all starts with a deafening gong that makes one's ears ring and that reverberates throughout the manifold chambers of our establishment.

"I have never discovered who sounds that gong and why it goes off whenever it does. But it initiates the Blinking, and this, in turn, provides enough time for the brothers who tend the garlic to do their tending (it grows in subterranean beds by the light of a glowing quartz crystal), and for the garlic preparers to prepare the garlic, and the water-drawers to draw the putrid water that collects in a series of ghastly cisterns located disconcertingly not all that far from the fraternal cloaca.

"When that is done, we assemble in the refectory, and there we ingest the garlic and imbibe the putrid water. It's all *frightfully revolting*, if you get my meaning—and not just the cuisine. It's the bumping, too. Don't you just *hate* to get bumped?

"Then the Blinking is over. Of course, there is sometimes another five minutes or so for other niceties, some of which, I dare say, defy the most euphemistic description one could possibly devise for them.

"Occasionally, we must make up a bed for a new arrival—they keep dribbling in, you know, mainly from the College of Wisdom. One or two a decade, at most. It's the Game of Spheres that does it to them—it fries their poor brains to a cinder. They take the little felucca over the Midland Sea. It is ferried by a *frightful* fisherman—he charges the most *ridiculous* fees, though I suppose he doesn't get much business!

"'Dribble' is the best word to describe the arrival of novices. They are usually half asleep upon disembarking from the felucca. They stumble through the forest, bumping into trees as they go (good practice for later bumping into one another, I must say), and then lurch across the greensward, up the stairs, across the observation platform, and down the stairwell. It's a miracle they find their way.

"Then it is our job down below, in the midst of the Blinking, to drag this latest instance of a drooling, drooping, limp swag of a human being into the dormitory and dump him into some bunk recently vacated by a deceased member of the Order. Wash the bedclothes? Of course not! It wouldn't do any good anyway, given the quality of the water.

"By the way, I hope you didn't arrive here by way of the felucca. You would *never* have fit in that little shabby barque. Perhaps you noted on the greensward, as you passed, a small garden filled with the most luscious melons; yes, I have revived the art of growing them, to say nothing of the art of devouring them. I didn't get quite this *frightfully* fulsome, as I supposed you *may* have noticed, on garlic alone, I can assure you. As a matter of fact, you wouldn't happen to have a few little tidbits of something or other with you? I should *love* to eat something other than melons and garlic!"

Dolopeia stepped forward, pulling out some fruit tarts from underneath her shawl and, trying not to get too close, tossed them to Weyland.

"Why, thank you so very much, my dear," he said as he snatched them out of the air with his hand and flipped them into the air again and into his mouth. whereupon he gobbled them down. "What *sheer* pleasure! I assure you I shall celebrate in song and story the generosity of the Gethsarbim damsel to the end of my days. Now, follow me!"

The group approached the stairwell and descended a spiral staircase into the Tower. At the first landing along the spiral staircase, they entered into a large circular chamber lit by orange-red gemstones that were placed regularly along the wall. Long, narrow curving tables made of a black, polished marble surrounded the spiral staircase at the center. Carefully stacked documents, maps, and scrolls covered the tables. Little gemstone lanterns shed a cheerful light over the glossy black surfaces of the tables. It was obviously a reading and writing room.

"Welcome to the *quondam scriptorium* and *biblioteca*! What a *mess* it all was before my awakening!" exclaimed Weyland as he flailed his rather robust arms about. "And so much work to clean up! The room hadn't been used for centuries. And then, of course, I have been poring through these documents to see what I can learn. *So much* was assumed, you know, and without that, you can't easily make sense of it all."

"You are not the first to be making these observations," Knarry said, thinking of Garug-Caroch's travails in the Library.

Weyland sat, rather heavily, on one of the benches at a circular table and motioned the others to do likewise. Dolopeia sat next to Fox-Foot, and Hrudan and Tundra-Bear sat on either side. Bomsiell simply lay on the floor, pawing impatiently at her face covering. Knarry stood in the rear, firmly anchored on his knobby feet, and listened attentively.

Weyland took this opportunity to learn each of their names and to ask about the nature of their mission. Both Hrudan and Knarry alternated with one another in trying to give a coherent account of what they knew. Weyland's questions, posed at regular intervals during the discussion, attested to the quickness of his mind in understanding, sometimes even better than they did, what they had experienced.

At times, he reminded them of Tristan-Phoros in his lucidity and penetration of seemingly discordant facts. In turn, Weyland found their accounts of Tristan-Phoros rather especially interesting. It was soon apparent to the travelers that, behind the supercilious surface, Weyland possessed a serious and discriminating mind.

Knarry initiated a turn in the discussion. "Weyland," he asked, "can you tell us about the Brethren of the Wakeful—that is, before it all got turned into the Brotherhood of the Drowsers? Why did they come here? What was this all about in ages past?"

"There is a great deal here that I don't understand," Weyland began. "For example, how did this extraordinary Tower get built? What explains the strange power of vision afforded from its observation platform?

"I do know that the black obsidian of the Tower did not come from the mainland. It rose up from underneath, from the depths of the earth below, for it is a single gigantic block of obsidian that was somehow, in subsequent ages, partially hollowed out to make its interior chambers and passageways. To this day, I might mention, there is a tunnel that leads from the bottommost chamber of the Tower down into the impenetrable darkness below.

"And then all these glowing gemstones that give light to this chamber, and similar ones that give light to the chambers at the lower levels—I imagine that you have never seen a gemstone radiate light of its own, unless you have had the dubious privilege of witnessing the Game of Spheres, when the gemstones begin to glow as they spin through the circles. Down here, it is the normal thing for a gemstone to do.

"I suspect that what this all means is that there is some connection, however mysterious, between this great obsidian 'Pupil' of the Eye and the rock-gnomes who live beneath the earth and have some powerful link with cosmic forces. *They* built it for the Brethren of the Wakeful—of this I have little doubt. But I don't think anyone has ever seen a rock-gnome or even knows what one looks like.

"But what had been the purpose of all of this before the ages of sleep descended over the Eye of the Universe and the inhabitants of its wonderful 'Pupil'? They came from the College of Wisdom, where, like all the rest of the students, they had studied with zealousness the things that could be known and understood in Oval-Earth and in the universe observable from its confines. What happened to some students is that they realized there was something even more than that to be known—something multiform and gorgeous in its variety and beauty.

"They called it the World beyond the Worlds. And there was something even beyond that—not so much to be known, as to be watched—yes, simply watched and admired, as one watches and admires something or someone who is loved.

"For the Eye of the Universe is not just the Eye of the Knower; it is the Eye of the Lover. They came here to gaze with love up into the World beyond the Worlds."

Weyland's face grew sad for a moment. "Things *have frightfully* changed, haven't they!" he remarked. "Why did they change? Well, you all have heard, I am sure, the standard explanation. There was the Kingdom of Darkness, whose dreaded minions stormed across the Golden Mountains and waged the War of Desolation against the populace of Oval-Earth! After that, nothing was the same.

"And as Oval-Earth awaits the renewal of the onslaught, it languishes in its defenselessness, its impotence, a victim of its own fearful anticipations. And everything, in due course, fails and collapses."

Knarry interrupted, "But, Weyland, we have found out that the Kingdom of Darkness is not beyond the Golden Mountains—it is within Oval-Earth itself. An ancient document at the Ministry of Historical Records told us this. And this information was, in turn, confirmed by Prince Witzlau of the Hydro-Sylphs."

Weyland waved his hand in front of his face and proclaimed, "I *know* that already, Knarry. When I began my researches in these archives soon after my awakening, it was one of the first things I discovered. But one day, you shall have to tell me more about the document you consulted and also about the Hydro-Sylphs. I have read about them in our archives too. But I can tell you something else equally important."

"What is it, Weyland?" Hrudan pleaded.

"What is it?" Weyland repeated. "It is this: the War of Desolation never happened. The War of Desolation as an event in the past is a *frightful* illusion. It is an illusion fostered by the Kingdom of Darkness itself to steep the peoples of Oval-Earth in illusion heaped upon illusion. That is why we have no history."

"Those who do not write their own history will have someone else write it for them," Dolopeia pronounced.

"Exactly—for the Kingdom of Darkness has written what little history we have left in order to obscure the one element of truth it does actually, though indirectly, reveal—the War of Desolation is *in the future!*"

"But we have heard a hint of this. What will it be called when it comes?" Hrudan cried.

"It will be called the 'Great Upwelling.'"

"Just as *The Chartulary* told us!" Tundra-Bear remarked. They all wished that Tristan-Phorus were with them. He would understand better than any of them what Weyland was disclosing and would know the right questions to pose to solicit even better information.

Weyland paused; he folded his arms and looked resolutely at the floor. After a moment of brooding silence, he turned to the others and said, "I would, if I could, partake in your quest for the words of the song. But I must remain here, for I am, whether I want it or not, whether I like it or not, the sole active inhabitant and therefore, in some sense, the sole warden of this *frightfully* derelict institution.

"Knarry, I should very much appreciate it if you would inscribe a copy for me of the eight verses you told me you now have of the Song. According to your account, we are still missing four verses, and we don't know what order those eight verses should be recited in, so I am not sure what help I, and you, can finally expect from what we have. But I may find some further clues among these ancient scrolls and documents, and having what you have of the text would be helpful for me."

Knarry saw the wisdom of this suggestion and immediately proceeded to remove stylus and parchment from his haversack and write down on a separate strip of parchment the eight verses in the order in which he had received and heard them—first from Garug-Caroch, then from Kasyan, and Dolopeia, and Prince Witzlau. He handed this to Weyland, who tucked it into his robe.

Weyland had further advice to give. "As I consider the information I have at this point, it occurs to me that there are two courses of action that I could recommend for you to do if you are to complete the task that I understand you have set out for yourselves—and both courses of action will be dangerous. In fact, to preserve your energy and resources, I would most heartily advise that you split up into two groups.

"I suggest that one group descend into the depths of the earth to visit those creatures whom no one has ever seen before — the rock-gnomes. We know they are beneficent creatures; but they may be difficult to find and to identify and even more difficult to speak with. The journey may be dangerous, for the route is unknown and the perils unfamiliar."

"I wish to visit the rock-gnomes," Fox-Foot blurted out. "I wish to go on this journey."

Weyland cautioned her, "It will be a subtle and mysterious adventure, requiring ingenuity, speed, and sympathetic sensibilities. I do not know why I mention speed, but I think that at least one member of the group who descends among the rock-gnomes should be the swiftest among you."

"The swiftest among us is Fox-Foot," Tundra-Bear acknowledged, "but I hardly could desire that she go off on such an unknown quest without me."

"I am not as swift as you are, Tundra-Bear," she objected.

"Indeed, you are as swift as I am, and much swifter even, and you know that well," he rejoined. "At our summer meets in the Hills, Fox-Foot, there is no one as swift as you are. Only Bomsiell here, and she is a forest cat, could outpace you. If you are to go, Bomsiell must accompany you."

"But go I shall, despite your fears for me, Tundra-Bear, for I have often wished to see the rock-gnomes, and often I have said so. Bomsiell shall be at my side, as she was in the Capital. She is a trustworthy companion. And I would like Dolopeia to come with me too, for her wisdom and her eyesight in those lower regions will be important."

Dolopeia agreed. Weyland was pleased as well. "It is good to take the Gethsarbim damsel with you, for she is wise beyond all of us and will see things the rest of us could not. And it is good to take the four-eared cat, for I sense that, in the realm of the rock-gnomes, strange things may happen and sheer animal intelligence, about which we know so little, may be of great value to you." Bomsiell appeared to understand and wiggled her four ears.

Weyland continued, "We know practically nothing about the 'Habitat' of the rock-gnomes, for so it is called. We do know that a passage from our Tower leads downward into it.

"I also know, from studying some of the ancient charts I discovered in this chamber, that another passage leads out of it and returns to the surface of Oval-Earth close to the Great Rock-Falls. I suggest that your company of voyagers meet up again at that destination."

Weyland turned to the others, "For Hrudan and Tundra-Bear, I recommend an adventure that will demand unflagging physical strength and endurance, for the two of you must journey across the Golden Mountains to visit the Kingdom that lies beyond.

"According to one of the ancient scrolls I have uncovered, the only pass over the mountains is known as the 'Needle,' for it is a narrow defile that cuts through the mountains just a day's journey north from the Great Rock-Falls.

"I have every reason to believe that, on the other side of the mountains, beneficence shall also be found, but not until after violence beyond anything known in Oval-Earth has been confronted and surpassed, for this group must thread another 'Eye' — what is known as the 'Eye of the Needle.'

"This is not the eye of the living looking outward but the eye of the dead looking inward. It is not the serene and clear eye of love; it is the rancorous and beclouded and glaring eye of hate.

"I urge you to consider this. Remember, there is not much time. If there is to be a War of Desolation in the future, the things you have told me about the weather, and about Garug-Caroch, and about the wood-gnomes show that the time is close and the matter is pressing."

Tundra-Bear remarked, "That is the pass and that is the Eye that Kasyan was trying to tell us about when we were in the Barrows. But what is this Eye? How do we contend with an Eye?"

Weyland replied, "I think you will figure that out only when you get there, Tundra-Bear. But between you and Hrudan, with his imperious Axe, I think a way will be found."

"I do not look forward to this task, but I will do it," Hrudan affirmed.

"And my job, Weyland? What do you assign to me?" Knarry inserted.

"Your job is to stay rooted in Oval-Earth, Knarry, for that is the source of your resilience and strength. Perhaps when you rejoin your dog friend on the mainland, you could convince him to be the third member of the group that traverses the mountain. But I think you should stay with Fox-Foot and

Dolopeia and Bomsiell after their return from the Habitat. You should go somewhere that is safe and wait there until you see what happens after the journey beyond the Golden Mountains is completed."

Weyland's mood abruptly changed; his cheerful smile returned, and his ears twitched merrily once again. "Now it is time for our little tour. But I warn you, it will not be terribly pleasant. The Brotherhood, of course, is asleep. Tighten up your nose guards for the air gets *frightfully* nauseating beyond this point."

Weyland led the companions back to the spiral staircase, and they descended deeper into the Tower. At the foot of the stairs, they found themselves in a narrow chamber surrounded by many doors. "Follow me carefully," Weyland warned them, "and don't get too far behind, or else you'll get lost."

They entered one of the doors and began a long, circuitous journey through endless rooms, all lit by magically glowing gemstones of different sizes and colors and arranged with one another in intricate mazes. Knarry immediately recognized the resemblance of the Tower's arrangements to a wood-gnome's earth-house, except that it was far more complicated. Weyland explained the former function of each room in the complex and active life once lived there. The rooms were now idle and useless and often littered with refuse.

Eventually, the group was ushered into a large chamber aglow with eerie green emeralds and lined on all sides by dining benches and tables. "The refectory," Weyland announced. At each end of the refectory was a long cavern-like structure. In one such structure, a blazing quartz stone hung over thin beds of garlic plants. The garlic sprouts looked pale and unhealthy in the quartz light. The other structure was some kind of meeting or assembly room. It was large enough to seat several hundred members of the Brotherhood. "Our Chapter Room," Weyland commented. "I doubt it has been used in the last thousand years. It was once the scene of many a lively discussion and debate."

Finally, they passed through an archway and down a wide staircase to another large chamber—the subterranean dormitory of the Drowsers. A dozen rows of hundreds of beds each ran the full length of the dormitory. In each bed, a berobed and hooded Drowser lay, smothered in a deep but uneasy sleep. Their bodies twitched; their faces were sometimes buried in their hoods, sometimes peering upward out of the folds of their heavy robes with pained and terror-stricken grimaces or with slavering lips or with eyes quivering behind darkly sealed lids.

Sometimes their eyes were open, even in sleep, but were blankly white with pupils somehow rolled so far back in their sockets that they could not be seen. Many of the Drowsers mumbled or talked or even, now and then, shouted incoherently in their sleep. They snored loudly and heavily, ground their teeth, and trembled as if with fever. It was not a scene of peace, but of tormented slumber weighing heavily like a disease upon tortured victims.

"And to think that only the most brilliant and creative minds in Oval-Earth have come here through the centuries!" Knarry said.

"Why, thank you *so very* much for such a flattering comment!" Weyland answered.

"Don't mention it."

After crossing the dormitory, the group descended a short flight of stairs into another dormitory. It was small and clean. Here the air was pure, as if some cool draft from the inner earth rose to freshen it. A few beds were located at intervals inside secluded niches that were carved into the obsidian walls. Small diamond gemstones flickered in the darkness above the alcoves.

"Some of these members of the Brotherhood have been here for the longest time of all. All this sleeping extends one's life span for a very long time. In any event, these fellows are special, for reasons I don't quite understand. They never get up at all, even for The Blinking," Weyland explained.

Fox-Foot approached the farthest alcove in the chamber and gazed down at the sleeping figure on the bed. By the faint glimmer of the diamond gemstones, she could barely make out a man with a short, stubby beard and coiled up in heavy bedclothes. She was curious about him, for reasons she could not explain. The alcove emanated a tone of serenity and even familiarity. "Who is this, Weyland? Do you know?"

The others approached and likewise gazed down at him. Dolopeia stared at him with her brightly shining golden eyes. Bomsiell stood up on her hind legs and probed his heavy robe gently with her claws. She was purring softly. Weyland replied, "He has been here so long that his name was forgotten centuries ago. But it is rumored that he was the greatest player of the Game of Spheres in the history of the College of Wisdom. That he could role a *Darii* whenever he played was simply taken for granted; the question was: How fast could he do it? He knew all kinds of remarkable shortcuts. They say he was a masterful logician and philosopher."

Knarry leaned closely over the sleeping figure with the practiced gaze of a physician. He noticed a small object protruding from a pocket in the robe. He reached down and drew it partially out of the pocket. It was a blackbriar pipe. He slid it back into the pocket before the others noticed.

Weyland added, "Unlike the other members of the Brotherhood, he sleeps peacefully. Sometimes a smile lightens up his face; sometimes a scowl, as if he were working out some philosophical problem or another. Then he smiles, as if to say, 'Aha! I've got it!' I have a sense that he is always thinking and finding a happiness in his thinking."

Suddenly, a gloomy, deafening "bong" resonated throughout the dormitory. "Oh, *goodness,* it is The Blinking! Come with me!" shouted Weyland. He hurried his guests out of the small dormitory into a yet farther chamber that was empty except for an elaborately engraved portal that led down into the lower earth. Near the portal were suspended several ruby gemstone lanterns. Weyland pointed to the portal and said, "That's the way into the lower earth. I remind you that there is another passage in and out of the lower earth. It emerges from underneath the earth at the cavern that runs under the Great Rock-Falls. Those of you who will embark on the mission to the lower earth should exit from there."

Hrudan remarked, "Yes, that is the cavern I showed you, when we made our way beneath the Falls."

Knarry and the others looked anxiously at each other. Fox-Foot laughed. "Dolopeia, let's take some of these lanterns. I am eager to meet the rock-gnomes. And you come along, Bomsiell. We'll meet the rest of you at the Great Rock-Falls. Don't begin the journey over the Golden Mountains until we have met up with you again."

"We must come with you," Tundra-Bear protested.

"No, you must save your energy for what is ahead. Don't worry; we can do it!"

Dolopeia swung one of the lanterns off the wall. "Without danger, danger itself cannot be vanquished," she proclaimed in her musical voice.

Knarry fetched the jeweled casket out of his haversack and gave it to Fox-Foot. "Take the Splinter with you. You might need it; you have seen some of its powers," he said. "Just ask it to do what you want. It will understand. Even if you don't know what you want it to do, it will act appropriately."

Fox-Foot packed the casket into her haversack. She lifted another lantern from the wall, turned, removed the veil from her face, and putting her arms around Tundra-Bear and pushing aside his face veil, nuzzled him in the Hill Country version of a kiss. "I'll be safe," she said.

She and Dolopeia said goodbye to the others and to Weyland, thanking him for the tour and for his sage counsel.

Dolopeia removed the face veils from herself and Bomsiell and, together with Fox-Foot, entered the dark portals of the inner world, their lanterns like two little specks of light in the boundless cavern below that gradually grew dimmer until they disappeared altogether. The others watched them as they departed.

"Now, as for the *rest* of you," Weyland said, "I shall escort you to the little harbor whence you came — if we can make it through the Blinking, which is in process just above. Prepare to get *bumped*. I simply can't *abide* getting bumped. But they can't see where they are going very well, not with all that infernal *blinking*! They are not really awake, you know; just in an advanced state of somnambulation. And firm up those face masks if you have any hope of surviving the imminent olfactory ordeal."

Knarry, Tundra-Bear, and Hrudan followed Weyland back through the dormitories and up into the refectory. Many of the preliminary activities of the Blinking had been completed, so most of the Brotherhood were already at table gulping down their garlic cloves and water. A few of the water-drawers were still active, walking into one another and spilling vats of muddy water all over themselves and all over the floor.

The visitors treaded carefully between the crowded, jostling tables of blinking diners and had just reached the door of the refectory when a sudden muffled outcry began to swell up among the Brotherhood. Some of the Brotherhood stood at the tables and gesticulated hysterically towards them.

The others began wailing and moaning and dashing their heads against the tables. Within seconds, they became transformed into a mute, swirling mob.

Weyland was astonished. "I have never seen anything like this!" he cried. "I think they are possessed. Perhaps we had better make haste to get out of here as quickly as possible!"

The mob, like the frothy water spilled by the water-drawers, surged backward into the great dormitory and, a moment later, spilled forward again into the refectory. They were all armed—with pillows!

They twirled their soiled and sodden pillows above their heads and thumped and pounded one another with them as they raged through the refectory in pursuit of the visitors, tumbling over tables and benches and one another, sometimes piling up in large heaps, and then frantically disentangling themselves. All the while, they clamored in dismal, unintelligible voices.

Weyland led the visitors deftly through the maze of antechambers, but not without having to change directions several times when a riotous charge of the Brotherhood was encountered in some passageway or rushing chaotically across some room. Often different groups of the Brotherhood collided together, and all fell down, or else batted at one another with their pillows, then gathered themselves together and rushed off, only to collide with yet another group.

Weyland was getting a bit out of breath as he led the visitors back up the spiral staircase and into the scriptorium and biblioteca. "I warned you about the bumping," he said, "but this *frightful* colliding and thrashing about is quite without precedent."

"What do they want to do with those pillows?" Tundra-Bear shouted at him over the din that was rising from the chambers below.

"I don't know!" Weyland heaved back, "but I *rather* suspect they have something like *suffocation* in mind. How appropriate for a Drowser! And those pillows are so filthy. You would think that they would *at least* find some clean pillows for their nasty business! Who would want to be suffocated by a filthy pillow? Of course, where would they find clean pillows?"

At that moment, a thin, flimsy Drowser sprang from a nearby door and seized Weyland with one hand while attempting to stuff his pillow into Weyland's face with the other hand. Weyland easily rolled the Drowser over his shoulders and flung him off into an adjoining chamber. "Get your sluggish slammers off me, you somnolent shmuck!" he called after him. He turned to the others with a big smile. "They may look threatening," he said, "but a diet of garlic and a lifetime of sleep makes them as dangerous as a splash of brackish water. You have noted, I assume, how utterly emaciated they all are. It's just so *frightfully* inconvenient to have to contend with them in this way."

"Then why are we running away from them?" Hrudan demanded. "We can easily hold them off."

"I know we can, most noble and magisterial Hrudan," Weyland shouted back, "but we don't want to hurt them, if possible. We are trying to protect them as much as we are trying to protect ourselves."

The companions wasted no time ascending the spiral staircase that led to the platform at the summit of the Tower and rapidly descending the outside stairs to the greensward. Weyland trundled quickly along behind them, though all this unaccustomed exercise was getting the better of him. The Drowsers were not far behind. They spewed out of the stairwell at the top of the Tower like a foul discharge of sludge erupting from a sewer, spread out over the observation platform, and funneling together again, cascaded down the outside staircase, tripping and falling, all in a wild, babbling pursuit.

Weyland shrieked, "I will divert them. You go to the harbor. I will run off to the opposite end of the island."

Hrudan shook his head. "No, Weyland, they are going to kill you. You said yourself that they are out to smother someone. I will be able to hold back the entire group by threatening them with my Axe."

Tundra-Bear added, as he drew forth his longbow, "I can help too. I can use my longbow as a stave to swat them away."

"No, no!" cried Weyland. "There must be no violence. These *are* my Brotherhood, after all. Anyway, remember that they are not really awake, and they cannot be active much longer in this somnambulant state. They are already out of breath. Many have not been in the sunlight since they arrived here on the island. The heat of the sun and the intensity of the light will drive them back in before too long. And anyway, you must be on your way. Trust me, I shall be *frightfully* safe. I can take on the whole lot, if need be, single-handedly." Weyland lifted his arms and flexed his muscles. "Me strong;

they weak," he declared with a gruff laugh. He was not too convincing about that; his arms were huge but flabby, and his hands, small and fragile. Still, he was up against an army of enfeebled wraiths who couldn't do much harm.

The Drowsers bunched up on the greensward like a cluster of gnats buzzing around one another, thumping into one another's pillows, blinking impulsively in the unaccustomed sunlight, and wondering what to do next. Weyland ran around to one side of them and shouted, "*Toodle-doo*, here I am! Come and get me! If you want to smother me, well, that's fine, but *do* be quick about it. I haven't got all day!" He shot a big ear-twitching smile at Hrudan, Tundra-Bear, and Knarry and whisked off through the spruce forest with the Drowsers trundling pell-mell behind him.

"I hope he will be all right," said Knarry.

"Something tells me he will get through this without any problem at all," replied Hrudan.

The three followed the path back through the forest to the enchanted sloop in the harbor. The sloop seemed glad to see them. It tinkled its little bells and flashed its little lanterns, and its invisible hands were quickly at work raising the sails and preparing for the voyage. A few minutes later, they were well out into the milky waters of the Midland Sea.

Tundra-Bear sat on the forecastle thinking only of Fox-Foot. Hrudan was thinking of Illyria and Erudan. Knarry was looking towards the north, where the sloop was headed, in the direction of the felucca dock on the mainland. He was thinking of everyone. As evening fell over Oval-Earth, the felucca dock hove into sight. There they saw a quite self-satisfied Moor-Plains Retriever sitting up against a pier, smoking a pipe, his forepaws behind his head.

"Hello there!" Tristan-Phoros called to them. "Did you have a good voyage?"

"We'll tell you about it at dinner," Knarry shouted back.

Tristan-Phoros leapt to his feet and dropped his pipe on the dock. "Where are the others?" he cried out in alarm. "Where are Fox-Foot and Dolopeia and Bomsiell?"

"We'll tell you about that at dinner too."

The sloop landed as perfectly as ever at the dock and tied itself up. The little felucca rocked in the waves on the other side of the dock. Knarry,

Tundra-Bear, and Hrudan disembarked from the sloop and went over to examine it. It was small, leaky, and badly in need of paint. A lateen sail, tattered and with clumsy makeshift patches, hung idly from its mast.

"So that's the famous felucca," Knarry said.

"It certainly is," Tristan-Phoros answered as he recovered his pipe. "As I was waiting here, the fellow who ferries it to the Isle of the Drowsers stumbled out of that dilapidated old shack over there and asked me if I wanted to ride to the other side. A disagreeable old fellow he was and is. He didn't even bother to look at me very carefully. If he had, he would have recognized the absurdity of addressing that kind of a request to a … a … well, forget it. You know what I mean."

Tristan-Phoros joined the others and examined the felucca sadly for several moments. "Why, I wonder," he asked, "do I have the sense that I have seen this contemptible little vessel before, perhaps even have ridden in it?" Knarry stood next to him; he didn't say a word. He was able, just barely, to resist patting Tristan-Phoros sympathetically on his head. Tristan-Phoros, on his part, was unable to resist sniffing a bit at his colleagues. "Where have you been?" he protested. "You all smell like the most abominable garlic broth ever brewed by the maladroit maestros of the College kitchens."

Tundra-Bear ignored his observation. "Anyway," he said, "we have heard that the ferryman is the most *frightful* fisherman."

"Who charges the most *frightful* fees!" Hrudan couldn't refrain from adding.

"Talking about fishermen," Knarry declared, "in a fishing village like this there *must* be a good place to eat. I am *frightfully* hungry. I suggest we seek that out, *right* away."

Chapter XIII

The Habitat

The cavern passageway underneath the Tower led downward into the dark recesses of the earth, from which a cool, aromatic breeze wafted softly around the three voyagers. As they walked, their tiny gemstone lanterns jostled and flickered in the hollow darkness like two tiny fireflies alone at night in a boundless wood.

Fox-Foot resolved that, in the present circumstances, she should take up the foremost position. Her waist-length hair hung loosely around her light-green linen tunic. At her back hung her longbow and quiver; by her side, slung with a leather strap from one shoulder, was her satchel containing the tiny, jeweled casket. The dim glow from her lantern was sufficient to allow her eyes to penetrate deeply into the darkness beyond.

Dolopeia followed close behind; her small, coin-like golden eyes often reflected the glimmer of her lantern. Though gifted with the ability for sight over long distances and through mist, she could not see well into the obscurity of the cavern.

Bomsiell, as was her custom, darted about on either side, sometimes advancing beyond the others, sometimes dropping back behind. She could see well into the darkness. Her four ears rippled gently on her head as she loped forward, curious yet not especially cautious, for already she sensed, as did the others, that they were descending into a habitat perhaps strange, though peaceful and generous.

Gradually, the tunnel began to undergo perplexing and beautiful altera-tions. It became wider; the stony walls glowed with a bewitching luminosity. Luminous veils of reds, golds, and greens floated through the air like slender iridescent clouds. Here and there along the length of the tunnel, the passage entered spacious grottoes that overarched lucent pools of crystal-clear water. Little incandescent fish, like sinuous threads of rainbows, darted about in the pools and gazed with bulbous sapphire eyes in wonder at the travelers as they passed by.

The pools were often connected from grotto to grotto by gurgling waterfalls that sometimes softly glided in pure sheets of water like flawless glass over the lip of one rock basin into another; at other times, the streams tumbled though tumultuous rocky channels that combined and separated and combined again, while the water frothed and danced and sang its own sweet melody in its winding course.

The tunnel itself became a series of ever larger and larger stately rock-hewn chambers, each one surpassing the other in their grandness of design; they were studded with myriads of glowing gemstones in intricate patterns that seemed to move and reshape themselves before the amazed eyes of the spectators, assuming living, vibrant patterns like some kind of kaleidoscope in perpetual motion. Some chambers were veined with thin-webbed rivulets of molten, fiery silver and gold, flowing across the marbled surface of the walls. Farther chambers were vibrant gardens of lapis lazuli and jasper and emerald flowers; garnet berries peered through shiny leaves of agate and aquamarine. It was a paradise of color and light, as the two gemstone lanterns that Fox-Foot and Dolopeia carried now dangled uselessly at their sides.

Dolopeia stooped at one point to admire an agate flower. She observed, "The beauty of a blossom will fade, but beauty itself will never pass away. Yet I think the beauty of this blossom could endure for many ages."

After a period of time almost impossible to calculate, the sequence of chambers finally terminated at a great, dazzling oval-shaped arch of ruby-bright crystals. Dolopeia was convinced that they had descended very deeply into the center of the earth. After a brief hesitation, the three voyagers moved forward and entered an enormous underworld cavern that stretched even beyond Dolopeia's capacity for sight. Around it flowed a river of molten gold so bright that the entire cavern shimmered in the waves of light that undulated peacefully over all of its surfaces.

The roof of the cavern spanned so high above them that it was like the sky over Oval-Earth itself. It was fashioned of a deep, flawless translucent jade studded with multitudes of fiery blue diamonds arranged in intricate patterns and constellations that moved and varied across the vast expanse and sparkled brightly in all that golden radiance.

From a great distance, Dolopeia could see an opening in the center of the diamond-studded sky through which a great shaft of light seemed to enter into the underground cavern.

Fox-Foot, followed by Dolopeia and Bomsiell, crossed an emerald bridge that spanned the river of gold. At the far end of the bridge, they simply stood and gazed at the spectacle in awed silence.

Then Fox-Foot and Dolopeia heard music, faintly at first but ever and ever more clearly as their ears seemed to open to receive it. And it *was* music, though they had never heard music like this before.

Fox-Foot was familiar with the reedy dance music of the village festivals high in the Hill Country, and Dolopeia knew of the stamping, thumping riots that had come to be accepted as music among the Gethsarbim after its ancient tradition was forgotten.

Music like this—solemn, delicate, intricate, and beautiful as the bejeweled paradise that surrounded them—was something utterly unknown to them, yet their ears immediately could rest and take joy in its enchanting loveliness. It seemed to invite a person inward into it to explore its boundless and interactive depths and layers of sound.

As Fox-Foot and Dolopeia listened to the music in rapture, they noticed that Bomsiell was behaving very strangely. Her ears were quivering, and she was deeply attentive to what she was hearing. She was enrapt with the music too. But something else was happening: the music seemed to be speaking to her. Bomsiell, in an uncharacteristic gesture, rose up on her hind legs and bent all four ears forward to attend to what she was hearing.

But what was the source of the music?

Fox-Foot ventured from the bridge and began to walk over the porphyry-red surface of a great plain that stretched beneath the vault of the cavern. She could see nothing on this plain except for tall, conical, brightly hued stalagmites that dotted the plain and looked as if they had been there from time immemorial.

Each one had a distinctive shape and size and color and curved upward like a flame or a tongue of stone—a fluid, wavelike motion sculpted into a perfect marmoreal utterance that gave the impression of being both a spontaneous eruption out of the plain below and, at the same time, the product of endless ages that would endure forever. Some of these conical stone formations were tall and others short; some radiated with an inner green light, and others gleamed with delicately enameled yellows and reds and organdies and damson purples.

Dolopeia and Bomsiell followed after Fox-Foot. As she advanced farther out into the plain, she noticed that the music changed—it was the same music, but subtle alterations in tone and pitch occurred as she walked. Her ears seemed alive and sharp as they had never been before. Sometimes she heard entirely new melodies.

Then she noticed Bomsiell sitting at the base of one of the stalagmites; the cat's eyes were wide open as she stared up at the tip of the many-hued cone of rock. She was listening to the music. Fox-Foot realized that the music changed as one passed by each stalagmite. Then it occurred to her: the stalagmites, the conical rock formations, were the source of the music!

Dolopeia had made the same discovery simultaneously, for she exclaimed, "The words of the mouth are the windows of the soul!"

Fox-Foot grew dizzy when she realized what they had discovered. The music was speech. The stalagmites were talking to them in music.

Beyond this, she came to the most astonishing realization of all: what she had taken to be simply cones of many-colored rock were the rock-gnomes themselves!

They were living creatures in some sense, glowing with shifting light and resonating, like the strings of a lyre, with the most beautiful music she had ever heard. And that music was their speech, their song, their joyful acclamation in their paradise at the center of Oval-Earth.

Dolopeia and Fox-Foot hurried to join Bomsiell at the foot of the mysterious conical shape that towered over her. Bomsiell sat back on her haunches and looked anxiously into their eyes as if she wanted to tell them something.

A glorious music flooded around them. They could not understand it; but Bomsiell could, and she was trying to tell them what it meant. Yet she, too, could not speak in the way that humans would understand, and so, in the midst of what they might be hearing as the most perfect discourse of which the universe was capable, both Dolopeia and Fox-Foot were as deaf as if they had no ears at all.

"What are we going to do, Dolopeia?" Fox-Foot said. "We cannot understand anything."

"A locked door requires a key," Dolopeia replied.

"And where will we find a key? And is there a key?"

The towering rock-gnome pulsated with rays of light as if it had heard these questions and answered in several melodious musical phrases. Both Fox-Foot and Dolopeia shrugged their shoulders and looked at each other in dismay. Bomsiell rolled over on her back and put her paws over her head. If a cat could understand, how could a human not understand!

Dolopeia pointed to the distant opening in the dome of the heaven-like vault of the cavern and made it clear that perhaps they could discover something at the base of the porphyry plain beneath that opening where the blazing pillar of light seemed to intersect with the plain.

Yet how far away could that be?

It could take minutes, hours, days to get there. Fox-Foot made a gesture to Dolopeia to remain where she was while Fox-Foot explored deeper into the vast plain that stretched beyond them. She thought for a moment of taking Bomsiell with her but then decided it would be best to leave her with Dolopeia. She also removed her satchel and gave it to Dolopeia, as well as her longbow and quiver. She was confident she would not need any of these, and they would impede her journey.

After taking a careful look at starry formations on the vaulted roof of the cavern so that she could find her way back, she began a soft, loping run across the plain and through the hundreds of solemn, cone-shaped figures towards the center of the cavern. The distance was much greater than she had realized at first, and the plain seemed to enlarge towards the center, to become more spacious and boundless and varied in its hues and shapes.

As she ran, she noted that the conical figures grew larger and more impressively shaped—possibly, she thought, because they were older. The music that they made became ever more subtle and magnificent in its iridescent harmonies. Her soft, loping run gradually turned into a fast steady pace, then almost a sprint, as she raced across the surface of the plain with the speed of a mountain wind.

She realized she was covering vast distances, and yet the distances were growing even vaster as she went. Furthermore, the whole plain seemed to be moving, to be whirring about in ever faster and faster circles as she penetrated more deeply towards the center.

Suddenly, without warning, after a span of time that she could not even begin to figure out, she found herself caught up short at the brim of a wide, glimmering whorl of light that revolved around a central axis at a speed that was, at one and the same time, breathtakingly fast, yet as gentle and slow as a softly churning pool of crystal waters.

She hesitated for a moment at this brimming disk of light, and impelled by the strangest of impulses, she stepped onto the broad, shimmering disk itself.

Instantly she knew where she was. She was directly underneath the obsidian tower on the spruce-forested island. The shining disk looked up through this "Pupil" of the "Eye of the Universe" into spheres beyond spheres, and into universes beyond universes, up to the World beyond the Worlds itself, all moving to the measure of ineffable harmony and grace. Fox-Foot felt herself being transported upward into realms of dazzling splendor and beauty.

Yet oddly, a thousand homely thoughts crowded in on her, thoughts of every detail of her life; she thought of Tundra-Bear and of her children and of Oval-Earth and all she had known and loved in her life, and it all seemed to be there, transmuted into an eternity of light and mystery.

She could sense an overwhelming cosmic force embracing her, infusing her, connecting her to everything in the created universe. She could hear no words, no language, no speech, but she felt she was hearing the Song of the Eternal Aeons itself as it existed in its most primordial form—a form before utterance itself was formed, a form out of which utterance itself could arise, perhaps in multitudinous and radiant expressions throughout the many worlds.

She now felt that she understood who the rock-gnomes were, and how they were connected with this World beyond the Worlds, and how their time and their space and their language were not the same as humans could know, at least not for now, though all of creation shared in it, and was part of it, and could, in a way appropriate to each thing, understand it.

A moment later, or an eternity later—she did not know which—she found herself out at the rim of the disk once again, charged with an energy she had never known before.

She raced back across the great porphyry plain and through its undulating waves of golden light with the speed of a meteor on a starry night, traversing its intricate time-space fields, its churning galaxies of light and song as if darting through the multifarious worlds themselves, greeting the rock-gnomes who glowed with light as she passed and who greeted her in turn with a music of incomparable grandeur and joy.

When she arrived back, Bomsiell and Dolopeia thought she had been gone only for several seconds and looked at her curiously. She did not try to tell what she had experienced at the center of the great cavern; she knew she would never be able to tell anyone about that experience.

But what she did know now beyond any doubt and what she could tell about and use was that they could entrust themselves fully to the rock-gnomes and whatever they had to say. She turned to the rock-gnome who was in front of them and simply asked, "Is there anything you can tell us that will help us in our quest?"

The rock-gnome burned with a heavenly light and emitted a short, beautiful melody.

"Is that all?" she asked.

It repeated the melody.

Fox-Foot, in turn, hummed the melody. The rock-gnome glowed in response.

Fox-Foot turned to Bomsiell and hummed the melody. Bomsiell indicated that she understood. Fox-Foot realized that what had been communicated was simple but important.

"We thank you!" she sang out to the rock-gnome, who again glowed in response and emitted another melody, which Fox-Foot assumed meant "You're welcome!"

"Let's go!" she said. She collected her bow and quiver and strapped the satchel around her shoulder. The three travelers somewhat reluctantly crossed back over the emerald bridge. In the distance, at about a quarter of the way around the cavern, Dolopeia discerned another opening in the cavern walls—it was, she assumed, the underground passage that led to the Rock-Falls in the west.

They hiked for a long time along the outer bank of the molten river of gold until they came to the entrance of the passage, and with a last look at the palatial cavern of the rock-gnomes, they entered the passage and began the long trek underground to the Rock-Falls.

The sharp little beams of the gemstone lanterns became necessary again as the passageway grew darker and narrower. The fiery ribbed walls and the clouds of shimmering light gradually gave way to wet, jagged rock faces, slimy with mildew.

The air grew heavy, and as the passage narrowed even further, the journey became unbearably tiresome. Fox-Foot found herself often stopping to rest and panting for air—an experience certainly unfamiliar to her. Dolopeia was just barely able to drag herself along, and even Bomsiell's usual vivacity was transformed into a lethargic crawl. The passageway was scarcely straight: it wound up and down and back and forth and was joined by dozens of other passages that entered into it at different angles. The three companions tried hard to keep to the central passage, for they figured that many of these side passages could lead into mazes out of which they could never find their way.

Fox-Foot figured that by now it must be nighttime in Oval-Earth. She wondered what Tundra-Bear and the others were doing and whether they would find themselves spending another evening lodged in some dismal inn near the Capital. They had a long journey ahead of them in order to reach the Rock-Falls. Her own journey underground with Dolopeia and Bomsiell would also be long, though she knew that time and space at these depths in the earth had a different meaning than they did up above.

After what seemed like hours of difficult groping through the dark passageway, she suggested to Bomsiell and Dolopeia that they rest for a while. Bedding down on the cold rock floor of the passageway was not at all attractive, but Fox-Foot slipped the jeweled casket from her satchel, withdrew the Splinter, and did as Knarry had instructed her to do. A warm, though invisible, protective cover arched over them.

Dolopeia removed her shawl and spread it on the ground beneath them. They pressed closely together as they sat down on the shawl and gathered the gemstone lanterns close to their feet. They shared a few provisions from Fox-Foot's satchel and the remaining fruit tarts that Dolopeia still carried with her. After these meager rations, all three snuggled together for comfort and warmth and fell asleep.

Moments or hours later, they awoke to the same dripping blackness in which they had fallen asleep. They had not the slightest idea of how long they had slept, nor what time of day or night it might be in Oval-Earth. They picked up the lanterns and the shawl. Fox-Foot erased the protective shield with the Splinter, and they forged ahead into the interminable darkness of the tunnel. The air was still stifling, and breathing was difficult.

After pressing forward for what seemed to be endless leagues through the narrow passage, Fox-Foot noticed an anxious twinge on Bomsiell's face. Her whiskers began to twitch, and her ears began flicking back and forth. Then she stopped and glared into the inky obscurity in front of them. Fox-Foot lifted the gemstone lantern and also peered into the darkness. They began to smell rancid and terrible odors.

The passage was blocked!

Before them, stuffed into the narrow tunnel, was a bloated ptoloch. Its swollen, eyeless body, with a thousand sucking mouths and tens of thousands of little squirming tentacles, slid slowly in their direction, belching and puffing. Putrid brown bubbles frothed at each of its gruesome apertures. Its coarse, slippery skin rubbed horribly against the jagged rocks that squeezed tightly against it on every side.

Fox-Foot tried to remember what she could about ptolochs even as she drew an arrow from her quiver. She knew already that an arrow could have little effect on a beast of this kind, but she discharged it directly into its soft, wobbly flesh. The arrow simply disappeared into it, as if it had been fired into a quagmire. The ptoloch flinched but immediately recovered. The arrow had left a little puncture, which squirted out some putrid liquid, after which the puncture immediately sealed itself up.

Fox-Foot was bewildered. Weyland had led her and her companions to believe that formidable dangers could be expected in the underworld journey. Perhaps he had been thinking of an encounter like this: face-to-non-face with a loathsome ptoloch. But she also recalled the few things that Knarry had said about ptolochs—that Twigbottom apparently had been gruesomely ingested by one—yet what little was known about them in gnome lore, according to Knarry, suggested that they were harmless creatures, even if repulsive.

Of course, it could be true that the ptoloch that had engaged Twigbottom in the depths of the Library had been possessed. The actual threat to Twigbottom came not from the beast itself. All of these things ran through Fox-Foot's mind as she and the others backed up away from the approaching beast.

After a moment's reflection, she drew the jeweled casket from her satchel and once again used the Splinter to draw a protective cover. When the ptoloch slithered heavily into the protective cover with a gruesome thump, it simply remained where it was, its diminutive tentacles squirming more frantically than usual. Fox-Foot glanced at Dolopeia and Bomsiell. They knew they were safe; they also knew they were stuck.

Fox-Foot felt that they had no other choice than to return to the Habitat of the rock-gnomes and ascend to Oval-Earth again through the Isle of the Drowsers. Dolopeia disagreed, and taking the Splinter from Fox-Foot's hands, she pointed it at the ptoloch. It had no effect. But as she nudged the Splinter forward towards the protective cover, the cover itself began to move and to push back against the ptoloch. The ptoloch edged backward. Dolopeia continued to move forward, as the ptoloch moved backward in the tunnel. She looked at Fox-Foot and smiled. Fox-Foot smiled, too, but shook her head sadly. Dolopeia nodded; she understood that, at this speed, it would take an endless amount of time to get out of the tunnel.

Of course, they knew some verses of the Song. Maybe that would make a difference. But Fox-Foot hesitated to use them. The ptoloch was obviously not possessed and, therefore, in a sense, was harmless. It was only doing its natural thing—sliding through an underground channel and living off the mould and slime that it gathered with its thousands of mouths. It was not even aware of the three travelers there, except that some utterly unknown thing had pricked it a moment ago and that some unknown force was now blocking *its* way.

It occurred to Dolopeia that they could back up into a side passage and let it pass by; but she soon revised her own thinking when she considered that the ptoloch would most likely not remain in the central passage all the way to the realm of the rock-gnomes, and, if it detoured into the same side passage that they chose, then even a return to the cavern of the rock-gnomes would be debarred.

Fox-Foot thought again of the rock-gnomes. She remembered standing on the glowing disk at the center of the Habitat and looking right up into the World beyond the Worlds itself. She remembered the glorious music and the sense of well-being and beauty that flowed from it. She felt that, indeed, the rock-gnomes were with her at this very moment as her mind entered into their mind and their knowledge. She felt as if she could commune with them, just by thinking of them.

The tunnel suddenly grew larger and larger and larger, and she cried out, "Let's run for it!" The ptoloch was now stranded in the middle of the tunnel, and lacking the pressure of tunnel walls necessary for its movement, it rocked back and forth, quivering and desperate, all its tentacles and mouths seeking out contact with something.

Skirting the left flank of the slimy ptoloch and trying not to touch it or even get too near to it, Fox-Foot, Dolopeia, and Bomsiell ran along the edge of the tunnel for a hundred paces or more until they had passed the huge creature. The tunnel immediately began to shrink back to its normal size, and it pressed in around the ptoloch once again. But before it closed all the way, Fox-Foot cried out, "Thank you, rock-gnomes!" She thought she heard the melody for "You're welcome" in the far distance coming up the tunnel from deep below. Dolopeia replaced the Splinter in the jeweled casket, and Fox-Foot tucked it away in the satchel. They continued their journey.

The air was now fresher in the channel; the ptoloch had been blocking the air current from a great distance. The three travelers felt much more enlivened. Also, a curious current of energy seemed to propel them along. They bounded quickly through the darkness, their gemstone lanterns dangling cheerfully at their sides. The passageway tilted upward at a slight angle. They were climbing back towards the surface of the earth.

After many more hours of clambering upward, they heard a distant roaring sound. "The Rock-Falls!" Fox-Foot said. Dolopeia offered her shawl to Fox-Foot, who tore the beautiful fabric, somewhat regretfully, into three pieces and made ear coverings for their heads. Soon they were very close to the Falls, as the whole tunnel trembled with its force overhead. They were glad when they saw sunlight.

They dashed out of the tunnel's mouth into the bright evening, which now spanned over the Golden Mountains and left the Rock-Falls in the deepest shadows. Already the sparkling beauty of the nighttime cascade of rocks was beginning to show. It had been a long trip, but the wonder of the Falls reminded the travelers of the great cavern whence they had come. They could feel a powerful force arising out of that cavern and generating the massive revolution of the boulders as they plummeted into the abyss and rose again through the mountains to be spewed outward into the brilliant skies.

When Fox-Foot, Dolopeia, and Bomsiell turned to the east, they saw three figures waving at them from a distant cliff. They were Tundra-Bear, Knarry, and Hrudan. Their heads were wrapped in coverings against the thunderous clamor of the Falls. Tristan-Phoros was there, too, his head wrapped in cloth and a pipe dangling casually from his mouth. He permitted his tail to wag—well, just a little.

Later that night, out of earshot of the Falls and gathered around a campfire, the companions settled down and prepared to exchange stories. Fox-Foot returned the jeweled casket to Knarry, who replaced it in his haversack. Hrudan, Tundra-Bear, Tristan-Phoros, and Knarry did not have much to tell; they had avoided the Capital altogether by re-embarking on the enchanted sloop that took them to a small port south of the Capital, after which it returned, on its own, to the felucca dock. On the roads westward, there had been one or two unpleasant incidents with the Viceroy's officers, but otherwise not much had happened. Hrudan had an altercation with an Imperial emissary who was collecting illegal tolls along the Western Arm of the Radial High-Road System. The altercation had ended with Hrudan tossing the emissary into a nearby frog pond.

Tristan-Phoros was pleased to offer, like one of the more cantankerous Gethsarbim on the night of the banquet, "It's a frog-eat-frog world." Dolopeia's eyes sparkled with delight at the story. Knarry had a bag of fresh provisions—biscuits and smoked fish from the Midland Sea, of which Fox-Foot, Dolopeia, and Bomsiell were glad to partake.

The latter told their stories—of their descent through magical caverns into the underworld, of the porphyry plain, of the rock-gnomes and of their strange speaking in music, and of the gruesome, but innocent, ptoloch they had encountered in the passageway and how the power of the rock-gnomes had widened the passageway for their escape.

Knarry pressed Fox-Foot for information about the rock-gnomes, but there was little she could say, and Knarry was left more puzzled than ever. "I never thought," he said, "that they would be so stationary, so attached to the ground, so immobile, yet it makes sense, in a way."

Fox-Foot, after some consideration, asserted, "Yes, they seem embedded, enrooted in that great plain, and yet, as I ran across the plain to the center, it seemed, not as if I was moving, but that they were moving around me at faster and yet faster speeds.

"They live their lives, lives that have no time, in song that never ends; yet they also seem possessed of great energy and speed, like the stars that seem so fixed, yet fly through endless spaces with a glory and a liberty we cannot imagine.

"And as the red plain swirled about me, I saw their shapes change, and their curving marble forms flickered and flowed like fountains of sheer light. I think, Knarry, that the ceaseless, self-renewing torrent of the Great Rock-Falls shows just a small part of their power. And what is more—each had its own song, yet all the songs throughout their shimmering habitat were harmonious together."

Tundra-Bear wanted to hear more about the whorl of light at the center of the cavern. "Tell us more about that, Fox-Foot. What did you hear? What did you see there?"

"I think I heard the primal Song there, the Song of the Eternal Aeons, Tundra-Bear, but without words, beyond words. And what I saw I cannot describe," she replied.

"But there must be something you could say!" he pleaded.

"I saw light there."

"Just a light?"

"No, I saw life there, life inside that light—the life that is the life of all the worlds."

"And what did it look like?"

"It looked like many things. It looked like circles within circles within circles, all of different colors and all layered on top of one another, yet all could be seen at the same time. It looked like a human face. It looked like the petals of a mountain laurel. It looked like a hawk high against the brassy face of the sun. It looked like you, Tundra-Bear. It looked like love when love is at its fullest, yet who, Tundra-Bear, who, in all the world, can say what love looks like?"

The companions were silent for many minutes after Fox-Foot had spoken these words. Tristan-Phoros broke the silence. "Did you bring back any message from the rock-gnomes, Fox-Foot?"

She admitted that she had, but that she was not sure it would do them much good.

"What is it?" Knarry asked.

She answered by humming a tune.

"That's a very nice melody, Fox-Foot, but what about the message?"

"That is the message," she said.

"I think you are right. That won't do us much good," Knarry demurred, "as beautiful as it may be."

"Oh yes, it will!" said Tristan-Phoros. "Someone around here understands it. Look at Bomsiell — she knows what it is! I would understand it, too, if — pardon me for mentioning it — my dog part were less, how should we say, 'compromised.' Some things are understood only in a deeply visceral way, the way animals hear them. We must coax Bomsiell to tell us about it."

Bomsiell needed little coaxing. She pranced into the middle of the camp-site and began to cavort and meow to fix their attention. When everyone was attentive, she moved off into the forest and galloped at full speed back into the campsite and, with a leap, landed in Knarry's lap. She being a rather large forest cat, Knarry was practically knocked over by this action, as powerful and steady as he usually was.

"She has run to you, Knarry!" said Tristan-Phoros. "What does that mean?"

"Nothing, at the moment," Knarry muttered, as he recovered from the unexpected assault. "The last time she ran to me like that was ... well, through the storm at the winter solstice."

"From Garug-Caroch — is that correct?"

"Correct."

"Then I believe this message has something to do with Garug-Caroch."

Bomsiell meowed and went to the side of the camp, where there were two flowers. One flower was alive, and the other was drooping over on its stem. It was dead. She batted the live flower with her paw.

"Something is alive!" said Fox-Foot.

"Precisely!" Tristan-Phoros affirmed.

Bomsiell now bolted across the clearing in the direction of Knarry, who prepared himself for another leap into his lap. But Bomsiell slid to a halt at the haversack that contained the Splinter from the Purloined Staff. She scratched at it.

"Something about the Splinter, I would say," said Tundra-Bear.

"Or maybe something about the Staff from which the Splinter came," Hrudan added.

Bomsiell came back to the fire and lay down on her side, looking very contented. Her task was finished.

Tristan-Phoros lit up his pipe, took several meditative draws, and concluded, "There you have it. The message is complete."

"Yes?" said Hrudan, incredulously.

"Yes?" said Knarry, even more incredulously.

"Garug-Caroch is alive and has the Staff!"

There was a long silence.

"We thank you, Bomsiell, for interpreting the message for us," said Tristan-Phoros.

She meowed.

"And we thank you," Hrudan said to Fox-Foot, "for delivering the message in the first place."

Fox-Foot hummed another little tune. It was the rock-gnome melody for "You're welcome."

Chapter XIV

The Eye of the Needle

The following morning, the companions trekked northward from the Great Rock-Falls towards the territory of the Barrows. By late evening, after a long, arduous journey through the now familiar but difficult terrain, they arrived at the plain of desert mounds; yet they were cautious not to venture across its border. Even though the method for escaping the bizarre space-time matrix of the Barrows was now understood, they wanted no further complications at a time when their task seemed to demand their undivided attention.

As Fox-Foot gazed at the Barrows, she recognized a peculiar similarity it shared with the porphyry-red plain of the rock-gnomes beneath the earth. The mounds were curiously barren and blunted replicas of the glorious stalagmites below, but without their beauty or their luminosity, their song or their vibrant inner life.

Another evening was spent around a campfire, making plans and posing alternatives, point by point and angle by angle. Everyone had a contribution to make: the deft reasoning of Tristan-Phoros, the practical adages of Dolopeia, the prudent governance of Hrudan, and the sage gnome-wisdom of Knarry. Even Fox-Foot had her say, and Tundra-Bear's occasional nod or murmur of assent assured the companions that the innocent clarity of mind of the Hill people was being confirmed in every major decision. All agreed that Weyland's advice should be followed.

Knarry would remain in Oval-Earth with Fox-Foot, Bomsiell, and Dolopeia. He would retain the Splinter for their protection. The four of them would travel towards the escarpment of the Northern Taiga and then follow along its base until they reached Branch-Knot's earth-house near the foot of Kyn Ardagh.

Knarry remembered the cavern hollowed out in the escarpment nearby. They could live at the earth-house — no one in Oval-Earth could be relied on more fully than Branch-Knot; if an emergency arose, they could retreat to the safety of the cavern. With the escarpment to their back, and a protective shield formed by the Splinter to their front, they would have not only a small, fortified redoubt of their own but also a good lookout point over much of Oval-Earth. From there, they could also watch, especially with the assistance of Dolopeia's long-sighted eyes, for the return of the others from across the Golden Mountains.

Hrudan and Tundra-Bear, as had already been planned, would venture across the mountains. Tristan-Phoros was of two minds about his participation in this venture. On the one hand, he was eager to go, if for no other reason than that he was curious about what lay beyond the mountains. On the other hand, he saw his participation as a liability, for he might be able to contribute little and might even be a burden for the others.

His ability to negotiate mountain heights was limited and even impaired by his flat, almost webbed paws, and he could not contribute much to the defense of the others if danger should arise, as most certainly it would. Nonetheless, in the end, Hrudan and Tundra-Bear wanted him to come, for they would appreciate his sharp intelligence. In the end, he consented to go.

The companions also tried to face the possibility that, for Hrudan, Tristan-Phoros, and Tundra-Bear, there might not be a return. To be sure, the ancient race of Kasyan, the People of the Wind, had ventured high into the mountains and had disappeared there.

Had it traversed the mountains successfully, or had it perished in misery among those icy pinnacles? No one had ever returned to inform the peoples of Oval-Earth.

Kasyan's witness to this episode had scarcely been reliable. And what unspeakable terror, mentioned by Weyland, blocked the passage that had made Kasyan himself turn back, only to be entrapped for ages of time in the nubby wastelands of the Barrows?

Finally, what did lie on the other side of the mountains?

Had the ancient and noble People of the Wind flourished there, or had they deteriorated like those of Oval-Earth, perhaps even more so? All of these questions could not be answered. The companions were acting on guesses; but guesses were all they could hazard in this situation.

The early morning brought a sorrowful parting. Tundra-Bear and Fox-Foot spoke silently with one another for a while before turning back to the others. They talked at length about their children and about the uncertainties of the future. For the first time in their lives, a parting was truly painful for them. It was like one person coming apart into two; they knew that the chances of their never seeing one another again were very real.

Hrudan drew Knarry aside to give him a special charge to look after Illyria and Erudan in case he should not return. He lay out a series of instructions for Knarry, including some messages to be relayed to them. If Hrudan never returned, Illyria would know what to do, for she had shared in everything that Hrudan did. But Hrudan pressed Knarry to remain at her side, even as he would want him to be at his side, for he thought that the wood-gnome's mature and sagacious intellect could be part of one's strength and one's counsel.

Tristan-Phoros sat with Bomsiell for a while. He found it curious that he had a desire to speak to her, as if, after all, they did share some bond together. But he said nothing, though he knew, in a way, that that was exactly the right way to speak; he did stroke her once on the head with his paw, and she purred quietly. As all of this was going on, Dolopeia packed a large supply of provender into the various haversacks and satchels for the journey.

Afterwards, the companions hiked together along the edge of the mountain massif until they reached a narrow footpath that led up into the heights. It was not the same as other paths that led up into the mountains and served hunters' and trappers' needs. It was strangely marked by natural boundaries: by rocks and bushes and pebbles that followed a fault line deeply cut into the mountainside.

The band concluded that it was the path that both Kasyan and Weyland had referred to as "the Needle."

Hrudan, Tundra-Bear, and Tristan-Phoros spoke their last farewells to the others and began the ascent. Within minutes, they were lost in the early mists that curled softly over the ledges above. The others watched them as long as they could. Then Knarry, followed by Fox-Foot, Dolopeia, and Bomsiell, led the way in the opposite direction to the Northern Taiga.

The mountain path was steep and slippery. Indeed, it was difficult to imagine that an entire populace with its women and children, its aged and infirm, and whatever possessions it had managed to bring with it, could have clambered up and through the confines of such a cramped and jagged way.

At times, the path narrowed into a shelf of ledge so thin that there was scarcely room for a sturdy foothold between the rock face on one side and the precipitous drop on the other. Tundra-Bear, who was accustomed to mountain travel, moved out in front with his supple stride. Hrudan had much more difficulty. His large frame and powerful limbs allowed him less room in a tight situation, and his balance was scarcely equal to that of Tundra-Bear. The great Battle-Axe swung uneasily from his shoulder.

Tristan-Phoros had the most difficulty of all. His balance was excellent, but his wide, flat feet—appropriate for travel on Moor-Plain swamps—were difficult to manage on the slender, rocky path. Moreover, for all his dexterity in handling a pipe, he did not have the benefit of fingers to grasp the rock face for added support.

At a resting place, Tundra-Bear prepared a safety rope for Tristan-Phoros by stripping and winding several mountain vines together. It was now possible to pull Tristan-Phoros, when necessary, over obstacles or lend him support through especially difficult stretches. But Tristan-Phoros began to feel bad about gradually becoming, as he had foreseen, a burden for the other two.

By midday, the three climbers had surmounted the initial stage of the craggy massif. Before them lay a wide region of upland pastures. These were covered by dark-green foliage and a dazzling spectrum of brightly colored wildflowers. Many brooks flowed through these pastures. Herds of mountain goats grazed in the distance. It was a peaceful place—lonely but beautiful, and the climbers enjoyed this part of the ascent.

At the edge of the upland pastures lay the glaciers whose melting ice fed the many brooks that flowed across them and whose translucent walls stretched high above the grassy meadows. The climbers rested here for a while and shared their noon repast. They gazed with wonder over what they could now see of Oval-Earth.

Tundra-Bear drew some small hornbeam hobs from his haversack and attached them to his sandals and to Hrudan's boots. They would provide traction on the ice fields that they were soon to traverse. Tristan-Phoros would have no difficulty here, for his wide paws would be secure on the ice, and his small, canine claws would finally be of some use to him in stabilizing his paws on the well-packed snow. Tundra-Bear also prepared his bow and quiver for rapid response and advised Hrudan to uncover the Axe. Since the glaciers were winterbeest territory, they would have to be on the alert.

At this moment, they regretted that Bomsiell was not with them, for a forest cat always knew when a winterbeest was near. Tundra-Bear reminded the others of how dangerous a winterbeest could be; but winterbeests were solitary creatures and traveled alone. A winterbeest would be no match for two people armed with a longbow and an Axe of such extraordinary power. Tundra-Bear reminded Tristan-Phoros simply to get out of the way of any action that should occur and not to assault the winterbeest at all. Such an assault would be fatal. Once again, Tristan-Phoros felt bad about his incapacity to be part of their defense.

They continued to follow the trace of "the Needle" as it wound up into the forbidding terrain of the glaciers. They passed through huge glistening-white canyons, where lofty shafts of ice leaned perilously over them. Often, they had to bend down as they walked through tunnels and caverns formed by mountain winds in the icy blocks. It was cold. Tundra-Bear wished he had his winterbeest robe to gather around his thin linen tunic, but he unwrapped his blanket and wound it around his shoulders.

Tristan-Phoros, for once, was glad he had fur to protect him. The travelers were fortunate that the winds were mild that day and that the early summer sun softened the chill atmosphere of the glaciers. In any case, they moved swiftly, so that they would be beyond the glaciers by nightfall.

Later, the path led out of the glacial ravines and on to the ice fields that glowed with light so strong that the climbers had to shade their eyes, even as they watched their footing over the slippery surface. The sun sank rapidly in the west, and the ice fields turned a fiery orange and red, as the mountains above cast long shadows over them. While the shadows deepened, the climbers made their way from the ice fields to an area of gravel and mountain scree that stretched up to the darkened outcrops of the mountains themselves. When they reached a small niche carved out in the slope by spring rains, they decided to set up camp and bed down for the night.

Tundra-Bear gathered some twigs from the patches of gnarled and stunted krummholz that dotted the surrounding area. He made a fire, and Hrudan prepared to warm some fish cakes and muffins. Tristan-Phoros sniffed around the locale a bit, to see what he could learn. He returned not long afterwards. He conceded that there was little he could tell from doing that sort of thing—he just didn't have much experience with it. Still, he had detected some odd and especially rancid scents.

Tundra-Bear was a bit bewildered by that information; they had now progressed too high to be still in winterbeest range, but an occasional beast might sometimes stray up this far. Its scent would remain behind it for days. Tristan-Phoros relaxed and lit a pipe. After they shared their meager dinner together, Tundra-Bear and Hrudan talked into the night — not about the situation in Oval-Earth, but about their families and villages and their memories of the past. Tristan-Phoros listened in silence. He wished he could remember his own past.

The fire died down. The night was long and cold. A clammy, acrid wind blew steadily from the high mountain peaks.

As dawn glimmered faintly over the eastern mountains, Tristan-Phoros suddenly raised his head. A foul smell floated vaguely through the mountain air. It was followed by the rapid successive crunches of a gigantic bulk thrashing down across the pebbly scree. Tristan-Phoros barked! Tundra-Bear bolted so fast from his reclining position under his blanket that Tristan-Phoros could scarcely follow him with his eyes.

In what seemed like only a second or two, an enormous, white-furred winterbeest crashed belly-down into the center of the campsite directly onto the smoldering twig-fire. A cloud of hot ashes puffed out in every direction from underneath the beast, and the bitter smell of burning fur filled the air.

The winterbeest quivered for a moment and lay still. A bloody arrowhead protruded out of the back of its shaggy white pelt, and its hot, slavering snout was buried deep in the pebbles of the scree. Hrudan, who was still asleep when all this happened, jumped up from underneath his cape and seized his Axe. Tundra-Bear remarked, his voice trembling just a bit with surprise, "It's all over now, Hrudan. The beast is dead. I wonder why it came up from the glaciers like that. It's not usual for a—"

Tundra-Bear did not have a chance to finish his comment. Tristan-Phoros gave out another frantic yelp. A second winterbeest was barreling across the scree in their direction and was almost upon them. Tundra-Bear turned to discharge another arrow, but he could not take a direct shot. Tristan-Phoros was between him and the hurtling white mass of fury.

"No!" he cried out, but Tristan-Phoros had already lunged at the heavy beast with his teeth bared. The winterbeest batted him out of the way with a single great swat of its long claw. Tundra-Bear's arrow, deflected by Tristan-Phoros's lunge, missed the winterbeest's heart and passed through its upper shoulder. It howled in pain but drove on and swung its other huge claw at Tundra-Bear, who ducked down as the swing passed over him. But he knew that a second swing would follow instantaneously, and he braced himself for the deadly swipe.

The swipe never came.

The carcass of the winterbeest, spurting a fountain of blood, collapsed on top of Tundra-Bear. Hrudan had buried the blade of the Axe deep in its skull and split its head in two. Its eyes popped out and bounced like puffballs over the scree and down the slope, and soft, steaming brain tissue spilled out like an acid over Tundra-Bear, blinding his eyes temporarily and singeing the linen tunic covering his chest.

With Hrudan's help, Tundra-Bear extricated himself as fast as possible from underneath the dead winterbeest. The upper half of his tunic was soaked with blood. He wiped his eyes clean and immediately looked for Tristan-Phoros.

As soon as he saw him, he and Hrudan ran to the injured dog, who lay on the scree about fifty paces away. He had been thrown an enormous distance by the winterbeest. His left side had been torn open by its razor-sharp claws. He panted softly, as his blood ebbed slowly out of the wound.

Tundra-Bear gently lifted his head to make his breathing easier as Hrudan probed the wound. Hrudan shook his head; the wound was very deep and had penetrated into the inner organs. The force of the blow had broken many of Tristan-Phoros's ribs.

Tundra-Bear murmured to Hrudan, "I have never heard of winterbeests coming in pairs. I was unprepared for that. But I should have paid more attention. I should have —"

"It's not your fault, Tundra-Bear," Tristan-Phoros managed to mumble, almost incoherently, with a wry smile. "I shouldn't have done what I did, should I have?"

"There's not much point in talking about that now, Tristan-Phoros, for the damage has been done," Tundra-Bear answered. "Yet you did no less than a loyal friend would do. You were trying to protect me."

Tristan-Phoros glanced up at Tundra-Bear. "Tundra-Bear," he said, "I think I am going to die."

Hrudan looked up from the wound and over at Tundra-Bear. Tundra-Bear said, "Listen, Tristan-Phoros, it is very bad. But we will help you. Do not worry."

Tristan-Phoros laughed painfully. "I'm not worried. I am dying. I know that. There's no help you can give me, Tundra-Bear, even though I know how much you would try if you could."

"We will return to Oval-Earth," said Hrudan. "We will carry you there, and Knarry will heal you with the Splinter."

"No! Not in the name of all that is good in Oval-Earth and in the universe! You must complete your journey. You must leave me here to die. I am a philosopher. It was said by a great philosopher in the past that the art of arts is the art of dying. I know that art and have meditated it with scrupulous care. I know how to die. Anyway, I would never survive being carried back to Oval-Earth. You must believe me about this! You must listen to me! I know what I am talking about!"

"But Tristan-Phoros, we can't leave you like this," Tundra-Bear said.

"Yes, you can. I want to be alone. There are some things I still need to think about, and I don't have much time left," Tristan-Phoros replied. "Bring me up to that ledge over there and lay me down. I don't want to be so close to the winterbeests. And bring me my pipe. I need my pipe."

They did as he said. They lifted him carefully and brought him to a small ledge that looked out over Oval-Earth. They wrapped him in Hrudan's cape.

They brought his pipe and lit it for him and placed it in his mouth. He puffed several times on it, and his eyes lit up.

"Thank you," he said. "You had better be going. What you have to face above is worse than anything we have yet seen. Greater sacrifices than this may have to be made. My life has been a paltry thing—a thing I have not understood. Something in it went wrong somewhere a long, long time ago, but I don't know what that was. In any event, my life will not be missed. You had better be on your way. The time is short."

Tundra-Bear and Hrudan returned to the campsite and pushed the bodies of the winterbeests over a precipice into an ice ravine at the edge of the glacier. They gathered their equipment and came back to say goodbye to Tristan-Phoros. They stayed with him for a while, sitting in silence and gazing out over Oval-Earth.

Tristan-Phoros remarked, "It is to you, Tundra-Bear and Hrudan, and to the those we have left below, that I owe what has been best in my life. For once, whatever gift of mind I was privileged to possess was put to a noble purpose. Your quest became my quest. What more can I say than that? Say farewell for me to all our friends—to Knarry and Dolopeia and Fox-Foot and Bomsiell. I insist that you be on your way."

Tundra-Bear extended his hand to Tristan-Phoros's head and held it there for a moment. Then he stood up and walked away, his arms folded and his head bowed. Hrudan also stood up.

He looked at Tristan-Phoros and spoke, "You have participated in shaping the destinies of Oval-Earth, Tristan-Phoros. You shall not be forgotten. You shall never be forgotten."

With the great Battle-Axe, Hrudan drew a line in the scree around Tristan-Phoros. He uncoiled a small piece of the brass cording that surrounded the haft of the Axe, twisted it into a small round medallion, and secured the medallion to the cape that covered Tristan-Phoros's shoulder. "With this medallion, I honor you, Tristan-Phoros, in the name of all the peoples of Oval-Earth."

Moments later, Hrudan and Tundra-Bear were slowly making their way up the remaining skirt of scree that led to the mountain outcrop. Their hearts were heavy with grief. Far below them they could see the figure of

Tristan-Phoros. He was looking out over Oval-Earth and still smoking his pipe. Later, they could no longer see him, but they could see the thin wisp of smoke from his pipe. Soon they could no longer see that, for the wisp of smoke had ceased, and nothing but a cold wind blew over the mountain ledge where they had left him.

The Golden Mountains rose steeply out of the loose scree that lay at their base. They were composed of yellow limestone and crystal that glowed from within with a kind of mellow iridescence. Both Hrudan and Tundra-Bear remembered how diaphanous they had been when seen from within the realm of the Hydro-Sylphs.

Under any normal circumstances, the Golden Mountains were impassable, for their cliffs rose up as sheer as glass. But the narrow pathway of "the Needle" cut its steep, jagged way into the precipice. Once again, Tundra-Bear and Hrudan had to edge along a thin break in the rock face.

Tundra-Bear had never before been up this high, since the Hill people always regarded the mountain outcrop as a barrier beyond which they could not advance. Furthermore, the cliff wall gave few or no handholds for balance, and the path was often slippery.

As the altitude increased, the wind began to blow furiously and erratically. Hrudan and Tundra-Bear found themselves hugging the cliff as gusts whirled around them. But they moved slowly and silently, their thoughts often turning to the memories of their lost friend below.

After several hours of climbing, they noticed that the pathway cut sharply inward to the cliff. Here they entered a narrow defile whose walls rose up straight and pure on either side for thousands of feet. As they advanced up along it through the mountain outcrop, they realized why it was called "the Needle"; it was so narrow that Hrudan sometimes had to draw in his breath to pass through certain sections. The defile also acted as a wind tunnel, for a powerful wind roared through it, making the ascent even more difficult.

Gradually, the defile widened until it was about twenty paces across, and Tundra-Bear could get a better sense of where it was going. It continued to rise above them for several thousand more paces, where it seemed to peak at the edge of a high ridge. At this point, a natural rock bridge spanned over the defile, making a jagged, oval-shaped aperture through which they would have to proceed.

"That, I suppose," said Tundra-Bear, "is the 'Eye' of the 'Needle.' It looks like the small opening at the end of the thin bone I use when stitching together my quiver or sandals with leather thongs."

"Perhaps," Hrudan replied, "but I suspect there is something more to it than that. I suspect that there is a great deal more to it than that."

At that moment, something appeared to be stirring in the aperture beneath the rock bridge.

"What is it?" said Tundra-Bear. "I cannot see it clearly."

"That may be," Hrudan added, "but whatever is the case, I have the feeling that it can see *us* very clearly."

They climbed another thousand paces or so, watching the bloated monstrosity that now squirmed feverishly and grotesquely in the aperture.

When they were close enough for Tundra-Bear to see it clearly, he shouted, "It is an eye! *It is an Eye!*"

Hrudan peered at it but still could not make it out. "What do you mean, it is an eye?"

"Just an Eye!

"A colossal Eye without a body!

"An Eye filling up that entire space … an Eye as large as fifteen winter-beests stacked on top of each other. And not a friendly eye … an evil Eye, a diseased Eye!"

It was a distended and swollen Eye whose engorged pupil was so large that the inner part of the Eye could be seen through it. The inner part was a writhing mass of decayed sight organs tumbling and swirling over one another. Its iris was a livid pinkish-red surrounded by a white that was webbed with thickly pulsating blood veins.

Around the gigantic Eye was a steaming, bloody border, as if the Eye had just been ripped from the body of some unearthly and titanic figure. In the rocky aperture formed by the pathway and the natural bridge, it quivered like diseased jelly and oozed a black, malodorous bile that discolored the rocks on either side. And, though it was an eye without lids, without anything but its own throbbing mass, it was an eye that was sluggish and dimmed, that suggested unbearable weariness, that had rolled around in itself and upon itself in a remorseless and deathlike sleep.

Hrudan and Tundra-Bear were nauseated. Their limbs trembled, and their hearts pounded. Hrudan expected to vomit as he leaned his arm and head against the wall of the defile. Tundra-Bear seriously thought of turning back. His resolve wavered as he stood gazing at the distant Eye. But he composed himself by methodically arming for the fight. He strung his bow slowly, testing its resilience and strength. He drew forth his sharpest arrows. Hrudan was put somewhat at ease by these preparations.

He understood how one could divert the attention of the mind until the conflict actually began. He uncovered the Axe, polished the blade with the linen slipcover, and swung it around his head several times in order to limber up his muscles. The inner power of the Axe tingled in anticipation.

Tundra-Bear looked at Hrudan for some indication of how to advance. At this moment, Hrudan could not think of a strategy for encountering the monstrosity that faced them. He had no idea how the Eye would engage in battle. They would simply have to come in closer and see what would happen. But whatever happened, Hrudan knew that Tundra-Bear waited upon his commands.

They began to move steadily up the defile. Several hundred paces from the Eye, Tundra-Bear fitted an arrow to his longbow. Stretching the bow as far as he could without breaking it, he discharged the arrow with enormous force directly into the center of the Eye. The arrow was swallowed up in the sordid blackness of the pupil. The thick-webbed blood veins flashed for a second. The Eye seemed unharmed. Again and again, as they moved closer to the Eye, Tundra-Bear fired his arrows, but all to no effect. The arrows simply vanished into the livid pulp of the Eye, without impact or injury.

Tundra-Bear and Hrudan stopped about a hundred paces from the Eye. It continued to glare intensely at them. Tundra-Bear stepped forward another four or five paces in order to discharge one more arrow when, suddenly, one of the blood veins in the Eye flashed out from it as a bright-red tentacle that whipped through the air and coiled itself around Tundra-Bear's right leg, knocking him down and dragging him rapidly forward. Hrudan leapt after the tentacle and lopped it off with the Axe.

Tundra-Bear sprang to his feet and stumbled backward to safety while the severed end of the tentacle sprayed steaming red fluid and writhed about independently on the ground. The remainder of the tentacle retracted back to the white of the Eye. A long, thin strip of Tundra-Bear's leg was severely burned where the tentacle had coiled itself.

"At least we know its range," Tundra-Bear said, trying to ignore the inflamed and searing flesh of his leg.

"And its method!" Hrudan added. "It wants to pull us into the pupil with those tentacles. And that red fluid is poison, Tundra-Bear! Be careful of it!" Tundra-Bear used his blanket to wipe the remaining drops from his leg; the drops burned holes in the tough fabric.

Once again, the two men advanced several paces. Just as suddenly, three tentacles shot out though the air. This time, Hrudan was ready for them, and with three whizzing flashes of the Axe, sliced off all three tentacles. They slapped against the walls of the defile, splattering hot red acid and sticking for a moment against the walls before sliding hideously to the ground, as they writhed in agony.

The Eye shrank and the veins around it swelled as it belched a jet of thick, black bile out of its pupil and into the space in front of it. It rolled upward and twisted in the rocky aperture, then wrenched itself around again and shot out five more red-hot tentacles.

Hrudan jumped back out of their reach as Tundra-Bear scrambled backward and aimed his bow again, sending an arrow straight into one of the largest veins that circled over the top of the pupil. It burst, squirting hot poison down over the iris. The Eye buckled and squirmed, but its tentacles still flailed about in the defile, looking for their prey.

Hrudan sprang forward again and cut them down on every side, though not without being stung by one before he hacked it off. The defile steamed with poisonous fumes from the severed tentacles that lay either convulsing or motionless along the ground like half-dead or dead snakes simmering in pools of frothy venom.

The men pulled back to catch their breath, to wipe off their weapons, and to try to determine what they should do next. They were choking from the poisonous fumes. Hrudan said that they would be able to do nothing as long as the Eye was wedged into the aperture. It must either be drawn out somehow or else forced out. Tundra-Bear agreed, adding that the arrows would be more effective if they could be shot from close range directly into the main arteries that fed the system of veins.

"The rock bridge!" Hrudan exclaimed. "We must use the rock bridge. Can you get up there, Tundra-Bear?" Hrudan remembered the enigmatic words of Kasyan about drawing out the Eye, as others circled behind it.

Tundra-Bear examined the sheer walls of the defile. He was a skillful climber, but these walls were unusual in their lack of hand- and footholds. Then he noticed a curious line of iron rungs pounded into the surface of the wall. They were badly rusted and blended with the yellow color of the limestone. "Someone else has faced this difficulty before and has tried to solve it in the same way. It must have taken unimaginable courage to do that work," he said. The rungs led upward to the rock bridge.

Hrudan noted an unusual pile of limestone boulders scattered around the front of the aperture. "They must have hacked those boulders out of mountain outcrop and dropped them down on the Eye, once they managed to dislodge it from the cover of the bridge. It was driven away. What cost of life to get so close to that monstrosity!

"And if Kasyan was ordered to draw it out so that they could hit it with the rocks, what a risk he took! To this day, he probably does not credit himself with such bravery. Yet the very act itself probably cost him his sanity."

Tundra-Bear strapped his bow to his back and pulled himself upward to the first rung. Bracing his feet against the rock face, he managed to work his way around so that finally he was able to pull himself up and stand on the rung. Now he could lean on the rock face and step from rung to rung in the direction of the rock bridge. The line of rungs rose steeply so that it would be out of the range of the tentacles. "We'll see if this works," he called down to Hrudan, as he swiftly moved along the rungs.

"And I will try to draw it out a bit from the aperture, if I can!" Hrudan shouted back.

Hrudan moved forward again, and again the tentacles shot out, writhing and snapping in the narrow defile. He severed several more as they attempted to coil around his arms and legs. Hrudan continued to move closer. More and more tentacles were scattered through the air by the swishing strokes of the Axe. They littered the base of the defile and stuck to its walls, sliding down slowly and leaving a sticky substance behind them or sometimes dropping abruptly to the ground with a sharp hiss.

Ten minutes later, Hrudan noticed a figure moving across the stone bridge. It was Tundra-Bear. He unstrapped the bow, and, once more stretching the bow almost to the breaking point, released an arrow into the top of the Eye. Bile, blood, and steam sprayed upward, causing Tundra-Bear to recoil. The Eye squeezed and trembled in the aperture and tried to look upward. Tundra-Bear darted forward again with another arrow and shot downward into an artery that throbbed like a swollen river on the upper side of the Eye. Another jet of hot poison erupted over the Eye, which wrenched itself violently backward and forward.

The Eye suddenly dropped forward out of the aperture, and propelled by some invisible coils beneath it, it plummeted downward towards Hrudan.

Tundra-Bear cried out, "Watch out, Hrudan! Here it comes!"

Hrudan was ready for this. He grasped the handle of the Axe with both hands and prepared for the onslaught of the Eye. He sprang forward to meet it.

The Battle-Axe began to glow with an inner fire—almost, as it were, speaking to Hrudan, imparting to him an inner strength and confidence he had never known before and revealing to him, even in this brief moment of deadly crisis, the unfathomable secret of its own identity, and of Hrudan's identity in possessing it.

He positioned the Axe behind his back, braced his legs between two boulders, whirled the radiant blade over his head, and thrust it down through the Eye as it fell upon him.

From the rock bridge, Tundra-Bear could see only the tangle of gnarled, blackened arteries on the back of the Eye as it appeared to collapse downward on Hrudan, and Hrudan disappeared behind it.

A second later, it was cleaved in two; and like the halves of a vilely rotten soft-boiled egg, it fell apart, spilling out into a flood of poisonous bile and blood. A thick, broiling tarn of writhing innards spread out over the floor of the defile; it reeked and smoked.

In the midst of this seething poison, Hrudan suddenly reared up, his body dripping with the searing acids of the monster. He staggered forward, holding the Axe in his right hand. His face was scorched; his skin hung like shreds around his body; muscle tissue was exposed, where jagged fragments of white bone projected out of his mangled limbs. His entire left arm was missing. He was spouting blood from his severed joint.

"Tundra-Bear," Hrudan cried, "I know what the Battle-Axe is. Defend Oval-Earth with it. Pass it on to my heirs—to Illyria and Erudan! Tell Illyria that my last thought was of her."

With one final effort, as he heaved the Axe high into the air, where it spun around, arching toward the rock bridge, he collapsed forward into the poisonous mire, and his body was swallowed up and dissolved in it. Without a gasp, without a sigh, without the faintest murmur of protest or disappointment, Hrudan, the mighty smith, had perished.

The Axe handle slapped squarely into Tundra-Bear's grasp, as if it had propelled itself that great distance and guided its own trajectory to come to rest in its perfectly appointed destination.

Tundra-Bear knew that Hrudan was dead.

He let the Axe fall from his hands and sank to the ground, pressing his head against the stony surface of the rock bridge. He was not familiar with grief. Only rare tragedies ever troubled the life of the Hill people, and these were viewed as natural to what they did and how they lived. But the death of his two companions—of Tristan-Phoros and Hrudan—was not natural to anything that he could recognize.

Tundra-Bear did not know what to make of it, and he had never really mourned before. It seemed right to get close to the earth and press himself against it. He pushed his head against the rock. He pulled and tugged on his long green hair and rubbed dirt over it and over his face and shoulders. And strange salty water sprang from his eyes, water he had never known before, water like a mountain creek, and it ran in funnels down his face.

Minutes later, he picked himself up, turned around, and sat on the rock bridge, holding the Axe in his lap. He thought for a long time. The idea came to him that people and even animals were like the wood-gnomes somehow, and that they did not actually go away but changed their form and lived somewhere else and were waiting for their old friends to join them.

In the depths of his heart, he knew that there was more to life than could be explained by life itself. Was this the World beyond the Worlds that Prince Witzlau and Weyland had spoken of and that Fox-Foot had actually seen in the ancient habitat of the rock-gnomes?

He knew that nothing truly fine, nothing worthy of love, could ever be lost for long. But the Hill people knew that already; they had always known that in a special, gentle, natural way. Now Tundra-Bear knew it in a new way—a way of grief, a way of almost inconsolable suffering.

He also thought of Hrudan's last command. In that last great cry from the midst of the cloven Eye, Hrudan's voice had borne with it an authority and a power that Tundra-Bear could only recognize as having nothing else but concern for the well-being of others. Tundra-Bear shook himself and stood up again. He wiped his face and head. He strapped his longbow to his back and picked up the Axe in his hands.

He descended from the rock bridge and stood in the aperture where the Eye had once taken up its defense. It was stained and slippery with the remains of the Eye. Tundra-Bear looked down the defile to the fuming and still bubbling morass of blood and poison where Hrudan had made his valiant stand. He turned sorrowfully away and climbed the last few paces to the end of the defile.

There, in astonishment and awe, he gazed out from the mountain heights onto a land far below him and reaching to the horizon. It was a land of unspeakable beauty.

Fine, thin-towered, proud-bannered cities rose out of fruitful plains. As far as he could see were orchards and grain fields and rivers where little ships sailed calmly over clear, brilliant waters. Well-tended villages with gardens dotted the landscape. Roads wound through the countryside and over forested hills and down into little valleys checkered with vineyards and granges and pastures where sheep grazed peacefully on the abundant grasses.

Tundra-Bear saw below something rising slowly through the air towards him; at first, it looked like a red dot in the distance, then like a wisp of ruddy cloud, then like a crimson sparrow-hawk soaring on tiny wings.

As it approached, it got bigger and bigger, and he soon recognized it as a giant scarlet eagle. It was the kind of eagle that Prince Witzlau had described as once, in ancient times, nesting high in the Golden Mountains. Its magnificent wings had a span of least fourteen paces; its powerful head and golden beak were like the prow of a stalwart ship. Its fierce eyes glimmered like rubies as big as apples.

And it was not alone. Mounted upon the magnificent eagle was a tall warrior in bright silver armor decorated with a myriad of brightly colored feathers. The figure raised a blue and white speckled banner high above himself in salute. It was a border guard. The eagle ascended solemnly on its scarlet wings to the pinnacle of the mountain massif where Tundra-Bear stood.

The face of the guard, surrounded by a flaming red beard, looked stern and imperious, but, as the eagle came close to Tundra-Bear and hovered stationary in the air while balancing itself adroitly on some powerful updraft of mountain wind, the guard spoke in accents beneficent and mild.

"Welcome," he said to Tundra-Bear. "I am Cherogimogyan, Sentinel of the Mountains and Sub-Commander of the Legions of the Wind. Whom do I have the honor of addressing?"

"I am Tundra-Bear" was the answer, followed by an embarrassed silence. His tunic was torn and splattered with blood, his blanket cape had huge holes burned in it, his quiver was empty of arrows, his bow was twisted, his green hair was streaked with mud, and his arms and legs were striped with the bleeding welts left behind by contact with the poisonous tentacles of the Eye.

Cherogimogyan stared at Tundra-Bear for a moment. He had never seen a person like this before, or in this condition, or at these heights in the mountains. But he ignored all this and fixed his attention, with no little surprise, on the Battle-Axe that Tundra-Bear held in his hands.

"And why, Tundra-Bear, as you call yourself, do you bear that great Battle-Axe?" Cherogimogyan inquired.

"It is not my Axe," Tundra-Bear replied. "It is an Axe that belongs to my friend Hrudan, who has just lost his life in defeating with it the Eye of the Needle."

Cherogimogyan stood high in his stirrups from the saddle upon the back of the eagle. The scarlet feathers on his silver helmet fluttered in the mountain winds. "The Eye is dead?" he said in amazement.

"Hrudan destroyed it. He destroyed it with this Axe," Tundra-Bear responded.

"It was prophesied from of old that one day the Eye should be destroyed, and that it would be, and could only be, destroyed by that Battle-Axe and the one who rightfully possessed it. We have images and carvings of that Axe throughout our realm, and we honor it to this day."

"But what is this Battle-Axe?"

"You do not know this, Tundra-Bear?"

"No, I do not know this."

"Then I shall tell you. It is the Imperial Axe and Royal Scepter of the House of Ospeth."

"And who is its rightful possessor?"

"Its rightful possessor is from the lineage of Ospeth and is the heir to the Imperial Throne of Oval-Earth. This Hrudan, of whom you speak, was, in the possession of this Axe, the rightful Emperor of Oval-Earth, and even in our domain beyond the mountains, we would honor him as our proper lord and sovereign."

"And what people are you descended from?"

"My ancestors, the People of the Wind, once served the ancient emperors of that House, before the evil times fell upon Oval-Earth. As the ages darkened, the lineage disappeared, and my ancestors migrated over the mountains."

"And where am I now, and what is this land?" Tundra-Bear asked.

"Welcome, Tundra-Bear," Cherogimogyan responded. "Welcome to the Kingdom of Light."

The Third Codex

The Great Upwelling

Chapter I

The Summons

A gray, dim morning broke over Oval-Earth. Ashen clouds hung low against the mountains, and a drizzly rain fell sporadically over the Midland Sea, over the Hill Country, and over the Claha-ain Plateau to the west. But strange things were happening — strange and demonic things.

At the College of Wisdom, the roof of the Hall of Games burst asunder, and the specter of the Hall, still fashioned in the monstrous shape of an agonized Arfla, reared up out of the shattered timbers, roof tiles cascading from its shoulders and ratcheting down what was left of the roof from where they dropped into the quadrangle below.

The brass gong over the facade of the Hall of Games, rung by dark and invisible hands, tolled dismally in the damp air. The specter raised its arms. It bellowed in a voice perceptible only to the demonic presences for whom it was intended but loud enough to reverberate for them over the length and breadth of Oval-Earth. "The Eye is dead. We can no longer wait. We summon ourselves to the Day of our Expectation, the Great Upwelling."

The ages of concealment were over. The Lo-Els rose out of their abiding places to the summons of the demonic conclave. The Great Upwelling was at hand.

Oval-Earth erupted.

Out of the craggy wilderness, out of the dark defiles, out of the abandoned mineshafts and eroded fields and broken villages, out of the defoliated orchards and from under ruined bridges and the torn-up pavement of old highways, they came. They were a bristling multitude, an appalling host puffed up with the things they ingested, despoiling and devouring the land as they converged on their great conclave. Their banners were black, and their eyes were yellow glints of vacuous horror in the midst of their tumultuous voids.

Sky and earth shook with the uproar; darkness fell over the landscape; storms spread out over the hills and mountains; lightning flashed in the unnatural night. Meteors streamed blood-red through the sky. It seemed as if the very earth itself was being torn to pieces, as woodlands cracked and fields burned and the Midland Sea rose up and lashed its banks with gargantuan waves while villages all over the desolate plains of Oval-Earth were flattened and crushed.

At the College of Wisdom, the Lo-El with the ravenous visage of Arfla leaned across the quadrangle and peeled back the roof of the Ale Hall. With a single great inhalation, it sucked into its hungry maw more than a hundred students, most of whom still clutched their ale mugs tightly in their hands. With this added enfleshment, the Lo-El's power became so great that it wrenched its way through the southern wall of the College, scattering broken masonry over the quadrangle inside and the fields outside, and began its cumbrous journey to the Capital.

In the western part of the country, the moribund patrons of the Red Ruby Café were sitting, as usual, around their flagons of rancid turnip beer when the door flew open and a long, thin, wavering appendage inserted itself. They were too drunk to move until too late, when the appendage coiled itself lazily around and through all of them. A minute later, after the cries and screams of horror had subsided, a bleary-eyed Lo-El stumbled laboriously up the hillside towards Hrudan's lodge.

Absorbing twelve drunk miners and the cantankerous innkeeper had placed too great a demand on its capacity, for it was reeling back and forth, and it retched out one of the miners, who fell heavily to the ground and tried to run away, only to be scooped up and consumed once again.

When the Lo-El came to the lodge, it pounded and thumped against the door and tried to smash it in. But Knarry's seal worked well; the door held. The Lo-El turned and continued its drunken walk towards the Western Arm of the Radial High-Road.

Over all of Oval-Earth, the black-bannered host of gluttonous phantoms planted their unchallenged power. Only for the time being was the

Hill Country left alone. As yet, the Hill people did not know the desperate state of affairs in the rest of Oval-Earth, though they were surprised by the violent storms that had suddenly broken out from the overcast skies. As they watched the blood-red meteors and felt the tremors in the earth, they knew that their homeland would soon be seriously imperiled.

In Tundra-Bear's village, the beacon lights in the watchtower were kindled. Immediately, all over the Hills, the beacons blazed from one village to another. Erudan, son of Hrudan, and Illyria quickly found themselves rapidly drawn into the action. Their brief sojourn in the Hills had prepared them for working effectively with the Hill people. Erudan helped Badger-Claw and Red-Wolf coordinate the efforts of the signal men on the towers. Their purpose was to gather a militia of bowmen to close off the Regional Road leading up into the Hills.

Illyria began to organize the surrounding villages into defensive units. She took charge of evacuating some neighboring villages so that strength could be concentrated in a few. The Hill women brought their children to the fortified villages, oiled their bows with winterbeest tallow to make them limber and strong, and sharpened their arrows.

The Moor-Plains were also ignored by the Lo-Els for the time being. Ever since Dolopeia had sung two verses of the Song, the Gethsarbim populace had begun slowly to put back together their ancient way of life. The Lo-Els that had resided in the swamps had not forgotten their humiliating defeat in the Rabatana Pan only a week earlier, when Tristan-Phoros had come up with the idea of heating the waters with the Splinter, but they discovered they could not ingest the Gethsarbim, since two verses of the Song were fresh in the heads of the diminutive folk.

Instead, the Lo-Els evacuated the Moor-Plains, laying plans for a revengeful return, after which, they reckoned, not a single Gethsarbim would survive their assault. They also made plans for penetrating the water caves of the Hydro-Sylphs, who as yet were unaware of what was happening in Oval-Earth, though unfamiliar tremors shook their luxuriant esplanades and sent high-crested undulations coursing along the surfaces of their golden canals and rivers.

The Lo-Els' struggles with the wood-gnomes in all sections of Oval-Earth were the most tragic and severe. Some wood-gnomes, attacked unexpectedly or weak from advanced age, succumbed quickly to the raging power of the Lo-Els.

As a wood-gnome was ripped out of its earth-house by a Lo-El, its earth roots would grip and its psyche would tighten into the power of the soil and the elements. Many wood-gnomes survived like this, only to crawl wounded and shattered back into the ruins of their earth-houses. Others were shredded into the vastness of a Lo-El, and their earth-power became transferred to it.

The Lo-Els reveled in their triumphs and staggered over the land in quest of fresh provender. They grew as they filled their bottomless appetite, and their forms shuffled monstrously over the countryside, grunting and belching as they went. The Lo-Els that had vanquished wood-gnomes became the most vehement and destructive of all.

Meanwhile, on the Isle of the Drowsers, the sleeping Brotherhood pitched and tossed on their beds in feverish frenzy. The entire dormitory shook with their twitching, though the members remained fixed in a heavy, oppressive slumber.

Weyland ran through the dormitory, trying to still them, but he could not. He soon realized that the Tower of the "Pupil" itself seemed to be under assault and powerful forces were trying to tear it open. Weyland scrambled, as fast as he could, up the flights of stairs to the scriptorium in order to seal, from within, the entrance to the observation deck above.

A large square block of obsidian mounted on hinges was designed to slip easily into place for this purpose. But, as he attempted to slide the block into place, he could feel pressure from the outside resisting his movement. He pushed again and again without success, straining his massive rounded but flabby shoulders and arms against the smooth surface of the block.

Suddenly the burden became inexplicably lighter, and he could sense that someone was beside him and pushing along with him. It was a member of the Brotherhood. In his surprise, Weyland almost forgot about the slab of obsidian. Under the dense mass of the block, he managed to wedge himself around, to face the stranger, and to ask, "And just who would you happen to be?"

"Under what might validly be defined as 'pressing circumstances,' that matter can wait," the other answered as he persisted in shoving upward against the block. "Our logical priority is to seal this entrance."

The slab slid into place and was affixed with giant iron bars. The Tower would now be safe—for the meantime. Weyland faced the stranger once again. He was a short, scruffy-looking fellow with a tangled beard and bright little eyes that glittered even in the gemstone-lit obscurity of the scriptorium.

"I recognize you," Weyland remarked. "You had been asleep for centuries before I came here—a *frightfully* long time. As a matter of fact, only a short while ago, a curious band of visitors passing through here happened to notice you asleep in the lower dormitory and asked about you. May I be so bold as to inquire what your name is?"

"You may indeed be so bold," said the other. "My name is Phoros, philosopher and logician, at your service. I awoke yesterday in the early morning. I don't know why. Since then, I have been reacquainting myself with this noble edifice, though what I find is not so noble. However, it looks as though this scriptorium is in good order. I suppose that it would not be unreasonable to conjecture that this is the result of your efforts."

"It took some work to achieve that, Phoros, but I do thank you for noticing it." Weyland was pleased by the compliment and was eager to return it. "I understand that it has been said that you were the greatest player of the Game of Spheres that Oval-Earth has ever known."

"Before I address that information, may I ask what your name is?"

"Weyland. I should have introduced myself."

"No matter. I should have introduced myself earlier to you as well, for I noted you before I came to your aid a moment ago. Still, I was trying to understand a few things before I presented myself to you. Now, Weyland, I assume that by 'greatest player' you mean someone who has exercised the highest level of mastery of the Game since the time of its invention until now."

"This is indeed true, Phoros."

"Hence, for me to know who the greatest player of the Game might be, I would have to be aware of all players who have played until now."

"Assuredly."

"But I have been asleep—well, as close as I can figure it—about four hundred years. Is it possible for me to be aware of all the players who have played until now?"

"Certainly not."

"*Ergo*, I am unable to affirm or deny the proposition that I was the greatest player of the Games of Spheres that Oval-Earth has ever known. Sleep is not a state ideally suited to acquiring the knowledge necessary to affirm the truth of that, or of any other, proposition. I do have an odd sense that I have played the Game rather recently, though my effort to roll the *Darii* was impolitely interrupted by some impudent fellow in a blue robe, into whom I consequently sunk my ... Oh dear, what could I be thinking? A dream, no doubt. But I do know I shall not play the game again, if I can help it."

Phoros drew a pipe from his pocket and lit up. "And somehow your name, now that you inform me of it, is already familiar to me, Weyland. Somehow I have the impression that I have heard people talking about you—even mimicking you."

"Mimicking *me*? *How* absurd! What's there to mimic? I am sure that to most persons of sound mind, I am a *frightful* bore."

"A boar? Do you mean a pig?"

"No, a b-o-r-e. Do I exhibit a set of tusks? Frankly, I wish I did. Then I could bore, or gore, whomever I wanted to gore."

"That well may be true, but, Weyland, you really do ... well ... rather ... if you will excuse the expression ... reek."

"Reek!"

"Yes, reek. In fact, this whole place could hardly be recommended for its olfactory savor. What have people been eating down here? But my pipe shall, no doubt, fumigate that which needs to be fumigated, at least in our immediate vicinity. Anyway, let's get back down to the dormitory. I want to observe what's going on there. Something very strange is happening! So much commotion from sleeping persons!"

At the far end of the Midland Sea, the Capital was the worst scene of devastation in all of Oval-Earth. The minions of the Lo-Els rose out of the shabby city like angry weeds blossoming in the perverse light of some blackened sun.

The functionaries and hirelings and imperial scriveners of the Viceroy were gobbled up by the scores. Entire departments of the government vanished in minutes, and the throngs of thugs used by the Viceroy to terrorize the local population were swept up and devoured. The tax-collectors were regarded as a particular delicacy.

Sometimes two Lo-Els would share one whom they found hiding in a cellar or under a rock. They would pluck out the hapless tax collector from his hiding place, then scrupulously slice him in half, making sure that the division was precisely equal. Each one would chomp its treasured morsel with a look of exquisite satisfaction in its bleary eyes.

As they ate, they became bigger and bigger. One Lo-El perched itself on top of the Ministry of Historical Records. It had just raked its sole occupant out of the dusty, scroll-littered corridors and had finished him off. The Lo-El now looked just like Klorp, with the uneven reddish eyes, the tilted spectacles, the pointed quivering nose with the long whisker, and the thin, spidery limbs. The Lo-El, however, was momentarily discomfited; it choked and spat out a blue diamond, which landed with a little splash far off in the Midland Sea.

Another Lo-El had absorbed huge numbers of hairy-winged flies. Now in the form of a hairy-winged fly as bulky as a government building, it buzzed slowly and horribly around the city and occasionally alighted on a tower, where it teetered back and forth, preening its wings and rubbing its enormous hairy legs.

One especially large Lo-El filled up practically the entire Imperial Plaza. It had lifted off the dome of the Imperial Court like a lid from a pot and had the good fortune to have dined on the Viceroy himself and on his closest cronies — including the Ejectors, Herald, Grand High Scrivener, Quill-Drivers, Nib-Nibblers, Scroll-Rollers, Wax-Welders, Seal-Stampers, Parchment-Pleaters, Tale-Bearers, Glad-Handers, Claim-Adjusters, Malicious Doodlers, Retroactive Rubricians, Blabbers, Pettifoggers, Conflict-Mongers, and Filibusterers.

The hapless Sergeant-at-Arms attempted to prevent his own ingestion by firing a bolt from his ancient, finely crafted crossbow into the head of the monstrosity. The Lo-El batted the bolt away with a delighted gurgle and swept up the Sergeant-at-Arms without further ado, as the crossbow fell and skidded across the courtroom floor.

Then the Lo-El, satisfied for the moment, sat stuffed in among the buildings of the Imperial Plaza like a deformed and malignant tuber and laughed in its vainglory. Sarcastically, in loud but burred accents, it cried out, "Behold, I am Tarrababart, Functionary Supreme, Viceroy of Oval-Earth."

Its creased forehead throbbed with a gigantic bulging vein. It formed the center of the ghastly convergence that flowed in sluggish streams from every direction into the Capital.

The great conclave began. Titanic in size, bloated and engorged, the Lo-Els swaggered and sprawled over the tops of buildings and among the rubble. Their swollen bodies teetered and lurched back and forth like drunken men in a brawl.

In slurred human speech, they quarreled among one another, though they knew they were all the same as one another, and the cacophony of their whining and grating voices was but the internal chaos of a single voice, self-contradictory, vacant of sense, spinning in its own vacuous circles and colliding and rebounding in meaningless and ephemeral combinations.

Over the rubble they had created, they beheld one another in terror and disgust, knowing that each was a mirror of the other, ready to drag anyone and anything into the depthless anguish of its own inner self, including one another, including their very accomplices and associates.

For the only consolation of their condition was to impart their nothingness to all there was, even to themselves, nothingness swallowed up into an endless vortex of nothingness, nothingness lusting for nothingness, with no other purpose but that Oval-Earth should cease to exist, yes, even — though they did not know it yet — that the universe should cease to exist and that the World beyond the Worlds should cease to exist, *for that was the only rejoinder, the only answer, the only rebuke to the great primal offense, that anything should have ever been created at all.*

The demonic conclave came to few decisions. Only the Lo-El with the visage of Arfla managed to attain some ascendancy over the multitude. Standing on top of one of the buildings, it berated its accomplices and delivered a long, obscene harangue whose purpose was to compel what little order was possible in the effort to subdue the remaining realms of Oval-Earth. A Tribunal of Public Despondency was established in the Capital until such time as the work of the Kingdom of Darkness should attain its completion, after which no tribunal of any sort would be necessary. Indeed, nothing would be necessary anymore.

It was acknowledged that Oval-Earth would offer some stiff pockets of resistance. The Arfla Lo-El saw to it that special expeditionary forces were organized. A squadron of Lo-Els would ascend the glaciers to find winterbeests and to enflesh themselves on the bodies of those elusive but savage beasts.

This army of winterbeests, swollen to four or five times their normal size, would muster at the foot of the Regional Road and tramp up into the Hills to take on whatever defenses the skillful archers of the Hills would attempt to mount, for the Lo-Els knew that the innocence of the Hill people would make them immune from their spiritual power. Only physical destruction by their traditional enemies would be effective in the effort to conquer them.

Another expedition would gather at the frontiers of the Moor-Plains; their task would be to break down the resistance of the Gethsarbim, though none of the Lo-Els could fathom yet how this would be accomplished. This same expedition was also commissioned to search for and destroy the watery domains of the Hydro-Sylphs.

Yet another detachment would approach the Great Rock-Falls in the hope of finding the hidden pathway to the Habitat and of penetrating to the greatest source of power in Oval-Earth: the rock-gnomes.

A fourth group would turn northward to affront the Northern Taiga itself—its purpose being none other than to uproot and destroy the ensouled forest and absorb its beneficent powers into its own malignant force. This group was to be led by the Lo-El that had, only weeks earlier, fled the Taiga after having felt the blows of Hrudan's Axe.

The Lo-Els, of course, rejected any notion that their respective missions might be difficult. Arrogance and presumption were the roots and firm support of their incapacity to understand anything they did.

Finally, it was resolved that, while a large contingent would stay to consolidate power in the Capital, the remaining Lo-Els, hundreds of them, would simply fan out over Oval-Earth to break down the power of those wood-gnomes who had managed to hold out against their initial assault. The humans would be easy to handle after that was over.

The conclave adjourned. The Arfla Lo-El, well-satisfied with its outcome, roared in laughter. The triumphant host screeched, railed, bawled, bleated, howled, yelled, piped, whistled, screamed, and rasped its bloated tongues in response, before it dispersed to finish its business in Oval-Earth.

Near the base of Kyn Ardagh, Knarry, Fox-Foot, Dolopeia, Bomsiell and Branch-Knot abandoned Branch-Knot's earth-house for the natural shelter recessed in the great escarpment behind it. They carried with them provisions necessary for what might be a long siege.

From there, they watched with alarm the storms that passed over Oval-Earth and knew that the War of Desolation was well in progress. They could hear the cries and shouts that passed over the land and could see the distant fires, the funnels of dust and smoke that rose up in dark, convulsive shafts, and the shattered fragments of buildings and towns that exploded into the skies.

They were afraid — afraid for those whom they had left at home and for those who had crossed the mountains. They felt the agony of helplessness of those who see untold destruction passing over a land and who can envisage the suffering it was causing, without, at the same time, sensing either the power or the ability to know how to stem the flood of anguish that was occurring. They also knew that their presence would soon be detected and that finally the enemy would come and encamp in their midst.

The darkness over the land was abetted by nightfall. Heavy, sullen clouds gathered over the mountains. The twin lavender moons struggled to emit their light through the overcast skies. Occasional patches of sky opened here and there, and the stars glimmered brightly for a moment and then were lost behind the turbulent cloud cover.

At the same time, the slobbering, teetering forms of the Lo-Els, each with its own lurid internal glow and yellow eyes, thrashed their way up the Northern Arm of the Radial High-Road — an insatiable host holding aloft their fluttering black banners. When they gathered close to the base of Kyn Ardagh, one of the pack peered through the darkness and noticed the enclave carved out in the rock face and the small group that held out there. In a jumbled series of snorts and belches, he pointed out the shelter. The expeditionary battalion stopped and redirected its force.

Inside the shelter, Fox-Foot prepared her arrows, though she knew that they could have little effect. Bomsiell stood erect on a rock nearby, not knowing what to do but ready to run a message, if necessary.

Dolopeia, who could now add six extra verses of the Song to the two she already knew, was prepared to chant them when necessary, though the order of the verses was still unclear. Knarry advised her to wait until they had more definitive information about what was happening in Oval-Earth. Correct timing of any initiative was critical, and what might be their most powerful weapon should be held in reserve until it was known both how and when to use it.

Branch-Knot sharpened stakes for the entrance to the shelter, in case the power of the Splinter should fail. Meanwhile, Knarry extended over them a protective shield with the Splinter.

The affront began with little success. The defenders of the alcove in the escarpment felt dwarfed by the immense figures clumsily tripping their way over the nearby woodland and hovering above them. The darkness of the night made them difficult to see at times, and often only their yellow slits of eyes were visible through the hazy gloom. Fox-Foot could see clearly in the dark and noticed that one of the adversaries looked like Klorp, whom she remembered from the Ministry of Historical Records. She saw that his thin nose, now a dozen paces long, pointed its trembling and menacing whisker directly at her.

But when the Lo-Els hit the protective shield, they recoiled in astonishment and their lurid forms flashed angry transparent colors. Fox-Foot let fly several of her arrows, but they passed directly through the Lo-Els and out the other side without harm. Knarry stood in front, waving the Splinter and making certain the shield stayed in place.

The Lo-Els pressed in again.

The size of the protected area seemed to shrink, even though the Lo-Els were once again rebuffed. They retreated in confusion, striking out at one another. One flushed and angered Lo-El leapt upon another in frustration and tore it into great gobs, which it fed upon in gruesome ecstasy. Three Lo-Els clambered up onto an overhead ridge, from which they prepared to roll massive boulders down into the opening of the shelter. Knarry knew that the shield might not be able protect them against this type of purely natural force.

Branch-Knot tried to think of some way of escape. His earth-house had a secret passage that led out into a distant canyon. But it was too late—the band had already been cut off from the earth-house. A Lo-El had occupied it and was destroying it piece by piece, shattering its vials of ointments and slurping down any medication that promised to augment its drunken frenzy.

The Lo-Els began their third assault. Swaying and throbbing, they oozed like mist through the dusky woodlands and over the crags from every side. The Lo-Els in the darkness above rolled great boulders to the brink of the ledge. The defenders shrank deeper into the shelter, while Knarry again called out to the Splinter for its protection and Dolopeia prepared, under any circumstances, to sing at least two verses of the Song.

Suddenly, Dolopeia's little mirrorlike eyes lit up with a brilliant purple-orange light. She darted out of the shelter and through the protective shield. Ignoring the advancing Lo-Els and the gasps of her friends, she pointed to the mountains in the west and cried out: "When the dawn appears, there comes the sun!"

Everyone looked to the western mountains — the Lo-Els on the plain and on the cliff abruptly ceased their activity and turned around and stared. Fox-Foot and Knarry and Branch-Knot ran from the shelter and stared. Bomsiell on her rock rose upright on her back legs. Her eyes, like those of all the others, were fixed on the mountains.

Over the mountains, in the dark-gray mantle of the sky, there spread an aureole of purple hue that burgeoned in a semicircle upward from the highest peaks. The purple became reddish-pink and then reddish-orange as it grew larger and larger. Bright yellow rays shot from its center and spangled the nocturnal skies with rainbows of colors. In the midst of the semicircle of dazzling light was a tiny dot.

The dot became a figure, and the figure was a man mounted on a scarlet eagle whose wings hovered like fiery clouds streaked with the dawn. The man on its back stood in his stirrups and brandished an Axe over his head. His long green hair flowed down over his shoulders, and the Axe in his hand exploded with flashes of lightning.

"Tundra-Bear!" Fox-Foot gasped.

As he rose higher in the sky, he was followed by wave upon wave of silver armored knights mounted on scarlet-plumed eagles. The banners they bore were blue and gold, the points of their spears were sparkling blue diamonds, their swords were like shafts of the sun. Out of the great darkness of the west an unspeakable splendor burst with the beauty of a golden galaxy over the lands of Oval-Earth.

It was the Legion of the Wind.

Chapter II

The Legion of the Wind

The clash of arms rang over Oval-Earth. The hosts of the Lo-Els, marshaled in squadrons under their sinewy black standards, met in the charge of mortal contention the Legion of the Wind, those eagle-mounted knights whose silver armor glittered like starlight and whose swords slashed and spears thrust in the perilous affray. Cherogimogyan and Childerician they were, Sub-Commanders of the silver-helmed regiments; and with them, Hildebrian and Marderosian and the Lord High Commander himself, Gutornitolyan.

The eagle-mounts darted and swooped and plummeted again, wheeling in circles at vertiginous speed as blue-diamond tipped spears sparkled in the dense night of battle; and swords, whose blades were forged in the furnace of fiery sunbeams, clove the darkness like shafts of flame.

At the head of the Legion, Tundra-Bear rose high in the stirrups of his eagle-steed and brandished among the ranks of the foe the Imperial Axe, that weapon that alone, among all the weapons of Oval-Earth, had slain, and could have slain, the Eye of the Needle. Its engrafted blade, its inner energy propelled by the urgency of battle, flared like a stupendous torch over the dusky enclaves of the land.

For only it and the enchanted weapons of the Legion could vanquish the spirits of the Void; the Lo-Els were sundered and broken as they burst into sordid fumes, their limbs flying and their torsos split, spraying their gruesome entrails into the air and over the plains and woodlands. All across Oval-Earth, monumental and torturous spouts of fire rose high across the land as the enemy imploded in one thunderous flash after another.

After the first clang of battle, after the Lo-El expeditionary force to the Great Rock-Falls was decimated, Tundra-Bear's eagle veered to the right and soared through the beclouded skies towards the Northern Taiga, followed by a combat contingent of eighty knights bristling with their powerful weapons.

In less than a minute, the speed of the giant eagle brought him to the shadowy ridge where the cumbrous Lo-Els, in their pale luminosity, were barely visible. They had piled their boulders and were about to drop them on the shelter at the base of the cliff.

Tundra-Bear, irradiating the entire cliffside with his flaming Battle Axe, thrust it into the Lo-Els with a series of rapid blows that catapulted them sheer over the edge of the ridge. They plummeted in streaks of pallid light into the ravines below, where they exploded into lurid splatters of sparks and flames.

The Lo-Els that had besieged the shelter at the bottom of the escarpment saw, in its lustrous formation, the approaching attack and scrambled in panic over the rocky terrain towards the Northern Arm of the Radial High-Road.

They had scarcely reached the Road when they collided with the glittering contingent of eighty knights on their eagles who sliced into their core like a scythe of fire cutting through a patch of dank, loathsome weeds. After passing through the ranks of the enemy, the contingent separated into two luminous flight formations and looped around rapidly though the darkness into position for a double-pronged attack on the Lo-Els' flanks. The Lo-Els foundered and thrashed about in a helpless rout; their flanks contracted together and then, unaccountably, burst apart and scattered in every direction, only to be shredded to pieces by the attack from the air.

A single mighty Lo-El stood at the center of the Radial High-Road and held its ground; it was a massive buzzing, glowing nebula of violently ingested wood-gnomes of the oak clan. It burgeoned with the earth-power of the oak gnomes and was fearless in its resistance. It had taken on the appearance of a gigantic oak tree flailing its powerful branches and was knobby with colossal boles that projected out of its thick-groined bark.

It withstood the assault by batting down the first six of the scarlet knights and their eagle mounts with a single blow. They fell to the earth in a sprawling heap, as the following knights swerved to the sides around the Lo-El and regrouped behind it. The stricken knights tried to pick themselves up and remount while the Lo-El stooped forward quickly to slurp them up into its gaping, yellow-eyed mass.

One wounded eagle, its scarlet feathers flying in every direction from the fluttering of its broken wings, had already been ingested when Tundra-Bear appeared directly on front of the Lo-El's blank yellow eyes; he reared up in his saddle on the great scarlet bird, swung the Axe in a wide circle over his head and brought it down on the Lo-El, sinking it deep between those lurid eyes.

An explosive shaft of grimy ash sprayed upward from the severed trunk. Within moments, the nebula had burst into a million squirming shards of wood while the corpses of a half dozen oak-gnomes and a badly mangled scarlet eagle were left strewn upon the ground.

The other knights who had been batted down were discomfited but not seriously harmed, though one knight had to search through the gloom for his lost weapons and missing helmet. The knight whose eagle mount had been killed climbed up on the back of another eagle behind its rider.

As soon as they had regrouped themselves as a unit and with their spears blinking fiercely in the dun coverlet of the night, their mounts rose with a flap of their wings against the earth, and they rejoined the battle contingent. The entire contingent circled in a twinkling corona of diamond tips around and over the Northern Taiga to check for intruders and to wait for Tundra-Bear to resume his command.

Meanwhile, Tundra-Bear's mount lowered itself slowly to the shelter in the cliff. Here, the eagle hovered only a few paces above the ground for a few moments and then settled into a landing as Tundra-Bear greeted all of the companions.

He dismounted.

He knew he had to return quickly to the battle, but he also knew that he had to impart the dread news about Hrudan and Tristan-Phoros. The companions had already divined as much, seeing Tundra-Bear in possession of the Axe and not seeing Tristan-Phoros with him. Further, they saw an expression on Tundra-Bear's face they had never seen before—a visage of solemnity and mourning that rarely occurred among the Hill people. He gathered them together and told them briefly what had happened. Lit up by the rays of the Axe like a lantern in the darkness, they assembled and listened to what Tundra-Bear had to say.

They stood for a while in silence together. Even Bomsiell, who seemed to understand, lay on the ground, covered her head with her paws, and purred softly. Knarry murmured, "There will be time for grief, for very much grief and possibly even greater grief than this, no matter how things turn out. But now we must act and save our grieving for later. What should we do, Tundra-Bear?"

"Stay here, Knarry, with the others until we can return to you," Tundra-Bear replied. "Your healing powers and those of the Orugug gnomes will be much in demand; and you, Fox-Foot, would you consent to join me?" Fox-Foot consented with a silent nod of her head; he clasped her hand and led her to the scarlet eagle. Here he mounted and swung her up behind him on the saddle. She bore with her the longbow and her quiver of bright, sharpened arrows, though she knew they would be of little use, at least for now.

"Farewell," he shouted, and with a single slap of the wings against the ground and a broad puff of dust and leaves, the eagle lifted straight upward, hovered for a moment a few paces above the ground, and then shot forward into the deep nocturnal sky again as it arched its wings out high against the upper rim of the escarpment and headed southward to the Hill Country. The sparkling flight formations of knights that had accompanied Tundra-Bear had just completed their circle over the Northern Taiga and fell in right behind him. The Northern Taiga was safe for now, and the knights had even noted below them in shadowy clearings dozens of tiny saplings sprouting throughout the woodland.

Knarry removed the protective covering over the recess in the escarpment with the Splinter and accompanied Branch-Knot, Dolopeia, and Bomsiell as they groped their way back though the darkness to Branch-Knot's earth-house. Branch-Knot lit up a torch and set to work putting things back into order, but there was much to do. The Lo-El, who had destroyed his house, had also broken most of his precious crystal vials and consumed his potent tinctures and ointments.

As ever, though, the eye in his chin twinkled as he worked. He could hear from adjoining glens and clearings the sounds of other Orugug gnomes stirring in the night and rebuilding their houses by the light of their lanterns; fortunately, as he learned later, none of them had been victims of the Lo-Els.

Dolopeia was Branch-Knot's industrious assistant, singing her proverbs and giving advice for anything about which advice could be given, though Branch-Knot, of an ancient and more earthly race, largely ignored it. He was too preoccupied with what he had to do. But soon she would be doing what she could do best: helping the stricken human beings muster their resources and energies for recovery. Bomsiell accompanied Branch-Knot and later Dolopeia on their rounds but was able to do little more than watch intently what they were doing.

Knarry went out to the foot of Kyn Ardagh to attend to a more tragic work. Where a Lo-El force had once been, there now lay, heaped up in contorted shapes in the darkness, mounds of wood-gnomes, humans, and animals, including the one giant eagle. He moved about in the dank mist and practiced what healing powers he could with the Splinter but was successful in reviving only an occasional human or animal. He managed to bring around a groggy moose, which stood up, shrugged its head, looked at him warily, and trotted off into the night-enshrouded woods, stumbling occasionally and bumping into some trees before it was able to orient itself again to its normal activities.

The wood-gnomes could not be helped, for they had already begun their transformations. Deceased before their allotted time, their bodies could not make the journey to Kyn Ardagh but would, instead, compost into the rich loam of the lowland while their ensouled sprouts would soon appear on the Taiga itself.

Knarry was glad that the Lo-El force had been turned back before reaching the eternal woodland, for the power it may have gathered there would have made it invincible.

The human cost was another matter, and its harvest was bitter. Knarry gathered the many dead and bore them to a field, where he laid them down in rows for eventual identification and burial. He could identify only one of them: it was Klorp, the solitary habitue of the Ministry of Historical Records. Knarry could not help but feel sorry for him, for death itself had endowed his appearance, ironically, with a dignity he had not possessed in life.

As for the lifeless eagle, even with his massive strength, Knarry could not budge him, though he knew that the silver knights would return in time to tend to their own losses.

Far away in the cavernous subterranean dormitory underneath the Isle of the Drowsers, other transformations were happening. One member of the Brotherhood after another was jumping from his bed—awake! Others rolled out of their beds and hit the floor. They shook the sleep out of their heads and rubbed their eyes, looking up at one another in astonishment. Hundreds of them were arising—confused, sometimes startled, perplexed at their being so suddenly wide awake.

Weyland and Phoros trundled back and forth down the length of the dormitory as the members arose, dazzled, confused, ungainly, tripping over one another. They helped to steady them and lead them into the refectory so that they could sit down and take stock of what had happened.

The members of the Brotherhood hardly recognized one another. They laughed with joy, but they did not know why; they exulted, but they did not know the reasons for their exultation. An old and terrible sleep with its frenzied dreams had lost its hold on them; some dread enchantment was coming to an end. They pointed at one another in gleeful shouts.

"There's Ranan-Throp," one cried out. "He used to know all about the geology of the Downs!" Ranan-Throp shook his head in his hands as if he had come down with a searing headache. "Maybe so," he cried back, "but it seems as if some purple-eyed bloke with green hair and riding on a big red bird just busted me between the eyes with an axe, and it hurts!"

In the Southern Hill Country, the army of possessed winterbeests, swollen to four or five times their usual size, strutted hideously up the Regional Road into the Hills. In the meantime, the twin lavender moons had succeeded in breaking through the clouds and cast a morbid purple gloss over the vales and plains of Oval-Earth.

The white-furred army of winterbeests, now hued by a ruddy-bluish cowl of moonlight, growled and rasped as it went, waving its long claws back and forth and twisting its paunchy, rodent-like snouts in the brackish air. It lusted for blood; it craved blood; its huge, engorged bodies plodded and shambled along in the darkness hungry for blood. As the front battle line of the monstrous army turned a long bend in the road, it was met by a storm of arrows and bolts.

For a moment, the Lo-Els were shocked by the attack; they had forgotten from the experience of the Rabatana Pan that, when they went into the body of a creature rather than absorbing that creature into themselves, they were subject to the injury that normal human weapons could do to the creature, even though their own spirits could not be destroyed in that way.

When the arrows and bolts tore into the white furry flesh of the possessed winterbeests and splattered them with their own blood, they howled and yammered with pain while the front battle line fell backward on the troops coming up from the rear.

There was confusion until the pressure from the rear simply pushed the front line forward again. Though they could feel severe physical pain, their massive composite bodies, made of many winterbeests absorbed into one, could not be killed by the missiles that the Hill people fired at such long range.

As the winterbeests regrouped and prepared for attack, Erudan posted his militia in the darkened coverts and hollows of the Hills so that they could not be seen easily, especially at night. The winterbeests thrashed about on the hillside, mottled with moonlight and shade, looking for the opposing forces in vain, being stung again and again by the relentless hail of projectiles from the militia.

The delay was only temporary, however. As Erudan saw that the winterbeests were not being killed by their assaults, he was forced to command a withdrawal of his forces to a position higher in the Hills so that they could plan a more effective strategy to fight the hostile force. The withdrawal was swift and effective; the winterbeests never laid eyes on the retreating militia.

Throughout the Hill Country, the beacons flashed from the watchtowers and alerted the fortified villages that the defenses of the Regional Road had been temporarily withdrawn. At this news, thousands of Hill maidens took their stations at the village stockades, strung their bows, and wrapped their arrowheads with fiber wadding, which they dipped into winterbeest tallow to make fire-arrows.

On the Regional Road, the men erected a second line of defense across the road, this time using the high ground on one side of the road in the hope of driving the winterbeest army off into the gorges that ran along the other side of the road. Their attack would be lateral, rather than frontal.

The winterbeest army pushed heavily forward in the moon-blotted night towards the site of the ambush and again was repulsed momentarily as wave upon wave of glittering arrows and bolts jabbed and pierced at it, driving a dozen winterbeests off the road and into the deep gorges below. There was also shoving and pounding in the darkness as the army recoiled upon itself in anger and squeezed many of its own members off the side of the treacherous embankments to their deaths in the gorges. But once more it blindly regrouped and propelled itself violently ahead through the ambush. The possessing spirits of the dead winterbeests fled back down into the lowlands.

The Regional Road was now open. The first village accessible from the Road was that of Tundra-Bear and Fox-Foot. Erudan pulled his men back again and mustered them in the small valley that led to the village.

In the village itself, emergency procedures were enacted. The village gates facing the Regional Road were sealed, while, at the rear of the village, evacuation channels were opened toward the forested hillsides. Children were already being moved through the channels by teams of older inhabitants. Meanwhile, buckets of fire were passed from hand to hand along the stockade parapets so that the Hill maidens could ignite the fire-arrows when the command was given.

Illyria directed operations from the watchtower; beacon fires were blazed to warn the other villages that an attack was imminent. Illyria also flashed signals to Erudan's militia to coordinate their movements and to secure their positions. Illyria's assessment of the situation, however, was grim. Erudan's militia was in a dangerously exposed position. Further, if the defense of the village did not work, the defenders would have little opportunity to withdraw. The winterbeest army would still have a long way to go before taking the entire Hill Country with its dozens of fortified villages, but the first village would be destroyed and, with it, hundreds of the lives of its defenders. And she knew that both she and Erudan would be lost as well. But she was fully prepared for this possibility.

Just when the winterbeest host reeled into view along the black crest of the valley, another sight appeared in the sky from the northwest. Swerving down from the jagged peaks of the Golden Mountains, like a swift thunderhead in the humid nights of the summer heat, a battle contingent of eighty silver knights, with Tundra-Bear and Fox-Foot at their head, swooped down on their wide-spanned eagles from the mountain heights above.

One of the Hill maidens in the watchtower saw from a distance the powerful battle contingent spangling the starlit night with its weapons. With her sharp, even if astonished, eyes, she recognized her fellow villagers leading the attack from the air. She ran to inform Illyria, who, in turn, alerted the defenders of the stockade and ordered them to prepare to discharge their first volley when she lowered her torch.

With perfect timing, as the battle contingent swept overhead, she lowered the torch and thousands of maidens discharged the flaming arrowheads, launching a fiery barrage of arrows into the darkened sky just ahead of the wing-borne assault.

The curtain of fire-arrows rose, arched over like a long coiling surf of flame, and plunged down into the ranks of the winterbeests. They fell backward, stumbling and crawling over one another. Erudan's militia sprang to the attack. The air filled with the acrid smoke of burning fur and flesh as the fire-arrows seared into the shaggy moon-livid hides of the winterbeests, only to be followed by the ponderous crash of diamond-pointed spears and the golden-shafted blades of the swords.

Tundra-Bear thrust and slashed with the Imperial Axe, while Fox-Foot drew arrow after arrow, discharging them at close range right into the hearts of the winterbeests. The eagle dipped and looped around them from every angle.

By the hundreds, the winterbeests tumbled, bellowing, into the gorges, for now not only were the bodies of the possessed beasts feeling pain and being destroyed, but the Lo-Els that possessed them were being destroyed as well. Some fled back down the Regional Road, only to be harried and dispatched by the pursuing knights.

Tundra-Bear and Fox-Foot brought the eagle down and alighted outside their village. As they dismounted, the village gates were opened, and a throng of Hill people bearing torches through the night raced out to greet them. Cheers and embraces surrounded them on every side. Their children, who had been evacuated to the hillside behind the village, ran around the outer perimeter of the stockade and threw their arms around their parents.

Only minutes later, Erudan and Illyria made their way through the crowd and stood silently facing them. They were happy with the victory, but some strange impulse told them that all was not well. They saw that Tundra-Bear was carrying Hrudan's Axe. Tundra-Bear, turning aside from the jubilation, asked Erudan and Illyria to come into his house in the village. Fox-Foot accompanied them. The others remained behind to celebrate the victory and to watch with unbounded curiosity as the battle contingent landed their eagles in the nearby field and rested. As they dismounted, their brilliant silver armor gleamed in the torchlight.

After reaching the house, Tundra-Bear lit several tallow candles and asked Erudan, Illyria, and Fox-Foot to sit down around the large wooden table where the family took its meals. Then he, with much difficulty and hesitation, told them about what had befallen in the mountains, about the valiant philosophical dog named Tristan-Phoros, and finally—though the implication had been there from the start, about the heroic death of Hrudan.

Initially Erudan and Illyria accepted the news with a kind of impassive steadiness and resolve. It didn't seem to surprise them. Somehow it seemed as if they knew this could happen and had already reconciled themselves to its eventuality. They had many questions to ask: about the mission into the mountains, about the Eye of the Needle whose destruction had claimed Hrudan's life, about the meaning and substance of his words and actions.

But soon enough, this courageously sustained impassiveness broke down. Erudan tried to comfort his mother as she wept in their presence. But, in her strength of character and bravery of spirit, she never uttered a word of complaint, or recrimination, or even regret. Hrudan's noble sacrifice would be her noble sacrifice too, and she would accept it with the same resolution as he had and with the same devotion to him that he had expressed about her in his final words.

There was great sorrow in that house that day. Fox-Foot embraced Illyria and sat with her for a while. Tundra-Bear walked outside with Erudan; he tried to console the son about the death of his father, but he didn't quite know how to do so. Consolation was rarely necessary in the life of the Hill people because they saw all farewells as temporary. He told Erudan about who his father was and about the imperial lineage and the Axe and what it meant.

Tundra-Bear concluded by saying that he would obey Hrudan's command to use the Axe until the great battle with the Lo-Els was over. Thereafter, the Axe would return to the House of Ospeth for all ages to come.

A while later, after making arrangements for two of the silver knights to bring Illyria and Erudan on the backs of their eagles to the outskirts of the Capital when the war had subsided, Tundra-Bear and Fox-Foot assured their children and countrymen that they would soon return and departed through the village gates to remount their eagle. They were accompanied by villagers bearing torches to the field where the battalion was resting.

The combat battalion remounted at the same time, and at a single command, the eagles slapped the ground with their wings and bolted into the nighttime skies again, hovered for just a moment, and with a startling burst of speed, took off towards the center of Oval-Earth.

Here battles raged hotly in many quarters. The assaults on the Gethsarbim and other outlying regions of Oval-Earth had already been repulsed, and many of the Lo-Els had entrenched themselves in the Capital, expecting to hold out there. The Gethsarbim had not needed the aid of the Legion of the Wind for their defense, for their own good sense, restored to them by Dolopeia, had been enough to vanquish any Lo-El whose impudent irrationality had made it so presumptuous as to approach one of them. One apposite proverb was enough to render the malicious vacuity in question more or less as permanently extinct as it ever was.

To the west of the Capital, the Lord High Commander of the Legion of the Wind, Gutornitolyan, was marshalling his corps for a massed offensive against the final stronghold of the Lo-Els. His plan was that they would come in at the Capital from all directions in four great prongs but at different altitudes so that the entrenched forces would be cut off from each other in all directions and on all levels. The training and flight precision of the eagles was so perfect that the Legions would not have to worry about midair collisions as the four flight formations passed through each other at breakneck speed.

Tundra-Bear and Fox-Foot would lead the southern assault team, which would come in at the highest elevation. Within moments, the attack was organized and underway. The Legion circled the Capital in a huge show of force, glittering and spangling in the moonlit skies, and then split off into the four prongs of the offensive. The four battle groups flew outward from the Capital, swerved around in a complex maneuver, and sheered back inward with the speed of arrows. The Lo-Els groaned in horror as they saw what was happening. They did not know what direction to turn to face the assault. Confusion reigned as many rioted through the city. Some tried to bury themselves in the dusky rubble; others ran for the murky outskirts, only to be cut off by the first glistering wave of knights that dove in towards them. At the center of the city, the corps met and sluiced past each other, carving hundreds of Lo-Els into pieces that collapsed into vile vaporous steam and powdery ashes over the rubble.

A few Lo-Els put up a stiffer resistance. The gargantuan Lo-El that had fed off the Viceroy and his cronies wedged itself deep down into the Imperial Plaza as the Legions whizzed over it. It rose rapidly out of the rubble brandishing a steeple from a nearby government ministry as a club, which it swung in the direction of Cherogimogyan. His eagle could feel the blow coming from behind and dipped suddenly underneath it, swerving upward at a steep angle and veering off to the rear. It rounded with enormous speed over the head of the Lo-El, and Cherogimogyan stood up in his stirrups.

With both hands braced against his spear's haft, he thrust the diamond-pointed tip directly down through the blotchy top of the Lo-El's skull, aiming directly at the immense gnarled vein that bulged inside the crevice of the forehead.

The Lo-El exploded, spewing the hideously mangled corpses of dead hirelings and functionaries all over the Imperial Plaza. The Viceroy was one of them; he splattered up against the palace facade and stuck there like a swatted fly. The Ejectors fell from the sky and were pinned on ceremonial pikes that extended from one of the upper bastions of a nearby ministry.

Scriveners and Quill-Drivers and Malicious Doodlers and Retroactive Rubricians floated in a river of inky bile. A stifling odor like a rotting balloon-fish permeated the air. Cherogimogyan did not linger to watch all of this; he spurred his mount and rejoined his assault team.

Hildebrian and Marderosian led their battalions into the most terrifying spectacle of all, for as they circled through the musty air of the low-lying swamps just east of the Capital, they were confronted by the sudden emergence of a colossal hairy-winged fly from the shadows that buzzed out at them like a flying mountain of monstrosities, containing within itself the voracious ugliness of all the hairy-winged flies in Oval-Earth.

The fly collided with an entire battle contingent of eighty knights, knocking them by the dozens off their mounts, strewing knights and eagles around in the swamps below. The six legs of the fly whirred and quivered as it descended towards the swamps and plunged immense suckers into the bodies of the downed knights, squeezing them up through its hairy apertures.

Marderosian had clung to the sides of the fly after the collision and was tangled up in the borders of the orange stripes along the fly's bluish body; his eagle had already been consumed and an antenna of the fly was groping backward and seeking him out. When it reached him, Marderosian used his single free arm to hack the tip of the antenna off with his sword.

Thousands of enormous dead flies sprayed out of the severed antenna and all over Marderosian, who attempted to deflect them as best he could with his sword. Then he disentangled himself from the damp hair of the huge fly and ran up its back, hoping to thrust his spear into the soft ridge of the fly's neck, but the fly rose up rapidly from the swamp, twisted, and turned upside down in its heavy flight and Marderosian was thrown off its back. The mud of the swamp cushioned his fall, but sharp pains in his legs told him immediately that they were broken.

Hildebrian's corps, however, was poised at the ready and pounced on the belly of the upside-down fly. Forty eagles plunged downward and affixed their talons in the fly, and simultaneously, forty diamond-headed spears impaled its belly.

The fly wrenched itself away from the talons and the spears of the attacking contingent, twisted upright with several spears still dangling from its belly, and flew upward, darting around in wild figures against the sky until it blew up into a dense cloud of millions of hairy-legged flies that fell like a heavy hail of fist-sized corpses over all the adjacent swamplands. Several dozen knights and eagles, having been ingested by the fly Lo-El, also toppled downward into the reeking mud. Hildebrian's contingent landed immediately to help the wounded and collect the dead.

Meanwhile, the Legion of the Wind wheeled around for another attack, their diamond-pointed spears gleaming like stars in the expanse of the night over Oval-Earth. When Tundra-Bear and Fox-Foot's corps soared though the Capital once again, a rotund and bloated Lo-El dressed like a Grand Master of the College of Wisdom reared up out of the ruins of the city.

It was the Arfla Lo-El.

Tundra-Bear directed his eagle mount around and upside down in a curving dive towards the Lo-El. Remembering the incident recounted for him about the Hall of Games, Tundra-Bear shouted, "Take this for Knarry and Tristan-Phoros!"

He hooked the Lo-El directly in the chest with the Axe and split it down the center. The chest cavity ruptured, leaving a gaping black hole out of which flowed a bitter, smoking bile filled with students in their robes still holding on to their ale mugs.

Tundra-Bear and Fox-Foot thought they saw a corpse floating in the erupted stream of bile—a corpse that was identical in appearance to what the entire Lo-El had looked like a moment earlier. The expression on the face of the corpse was curiously at peace, as if it were glad now to be released from its all-too-imperious master.

Finally, as the massed corps of the Legions swerved around again and sped in towards the center of the city for a third assault, instead of passing through one another, in one astonishing movement they all funneled upward like a great fountain of silver splayed high in the star-studded night.

At the very top of the funnel were Tundra-Bear and Fox-Foot. Next to them was the Lord High Commander. As Gutornitolyan pointed at them with his dazzling sun-sword, he gave them this charge: "Go upward! Keep going upward!"

Neither Tundra-Bear nor Fox-Foot understood what he was asking of them, but their scarlet eagle did, and in the next moment, the eagle was spiraling directly upward into the sky, spinning faster and faster until its wings flattened backward and its beak extended outward, so that its whole body was like some fiery arrow moving with immeasurable velocity into the great dark of the firmament over Oval-Earth. Tundra-Bear and Fox-Foot held on with all their strength as they flattened themselves against the feathers of the eagle.

They rose higher and higher, so that Oval-Earth became more and more diminished in size. They could see that what they called Oval-Earth was only a small part of a much larger planet, and then even that planet grew smaller and smaller until it was little more than a small ball suspended in space.

Around them was the vast luminous night of the universe, which sparkled in a resplendent panoply of stars and planets speeding past them. Wider and deeper the firmament grew around them; the more infinite the space, the faster the movement of the eagle through the vastness that surrounded them.

Suddenly, the eagle slowed down and resumed its usual posture with its wings spread out; everything around them grew light and airy; they seemed to drift gently through golden clouds where many-hued shafts of light danced to a music of an exquisite enchantment. Fox-Foot whispered to Tundra-Bear, "It is just like the music of the rock gnomes, but it is even more wonderful. I recognize it, Tundra-Bear!"

The eagle glided peacefully through the resplendent rays of light that played around them.

Tundra-Bear and Fox-Foot looked up and saw a distant but strange figure standing on a brilliant crimson starbeam. As they came closer, they saw it was two figures, one astride the other. One was a tall, majestic, long-legged creature of flaming red hide with mane and tail and eyes of glowing black. It reared up on its hind legs and pawed the bright-hued spaces with its great hoofed forelegs. It was the most beautiful animal that Tundra-Bear and Fox-Foot had ever seen. "A horse!" Fox-Foot whispered in amazement.

Astride its back was an elderly, bearded figure dressed in a long collegiate robe. He bore a Staff in his hands. The Staff was alive; it danced and sparked as it was held aloft over him and over his cosmic mount. The magisterial apparition's voice carried through the interstices of the many-colored space with the clearness of a musical instrument played with an absolute purity of tone.

"Listen," he said. "What has happened in Oval-Earth is only a part of what is happening throughout the World beyond the Worlds. Take the Staff and return it to the Ancestral Tree. Sing the Song, and the Staff will be rejoined, and Oval-Earth will be sound once more. My task is in the World beyond the Worlds, for the great struggle has just barely begun. Farewell."

With that, the bearded figure raised the Staff high above his head, and twirling it around and around, loosed it whirling into the lofty spaces that surrounded him. It spun slowly again and again through the intricate shafts of light and music, as if moving to the rhythm of a song.

Fox-Foot, holding firmly to Tundra-Bear's shoulder with her left hand, stood up in the saddle, extended her long, slender arm, and plucked the precious object out of the space above her with her right hand. Waving it in triumph, she cried out, "Thank-you, Garug-Caroch, and may you fare well in the World beyond the Worlds!"

The crimson cosmic horse with the glossy black mane and tail and eyes and the Grand Master who rode upon it disappeared with a colossal bound into the infinite reaches of space; the eagle, without as much as a single command, suddenly flipped upside down, narrowed itself again into an arrow-like shape and plummeted straight downward through the firmament towards Oval-Earth.

Tundra-Bear and Fox-Foot hugged themselves close to the eagle and to each other, holding tight to the Axe and the Staff, their green hair streaming about them. Below they could see Oval-Earth as a tiny point of light in the distance. It became larger and larger until they could see the oval band of the Golden Mountains and the Midland Sea with its blue island and the black obsidian Pupil looking up into the universe as though directly at them.

Before they knew it, the eagle spread out its wings, shaking out its scarlet feathers, and glided down over Oval-Earth.

Holding the Axe and the Staff aloft, Tundra-Bear and Fox-Foot soared through the now serene skies of Oval-Earth in the early dawn to show the peoples that the War of Desolation was over, that peace had returned, that justice was restored in the breadth and the length of the land, and that all things could be renewed and brought to fruition once more.

They flew over the Moor-Plains, and across the Downs and the Southern Hills and past the mighty Rock-Falls in the West. Tilting its magnificent wings, the scarlet-plumed eagle sped over the Northern Taiga and veered off towards the Capital. The peoples of Oval-Earth gazed in wonder at the green-haired man and woman who flew over them, wielding the instruments of glorious power that had brought them forth, and would still bring them forth, out of the ages of their captivity.

The battle was over. The Legion of the Wind landed on a wide, fallow cornfield just west of the Capital. The knights dismounted from their eagles and were wiping off their silver armor and cleaning from their weapons the rancid dust and bile of the Lo-Els that coated them. Other knights were bringing in the bodies of the dead and wounded and laying them out at one edge of the cornfield. The sun was just rising over the eastern mountains.

The scarlet eagles stood on their great curled talons with their tails resting on the field. They blazed in the thin rays of sunlight and threw long shadows across the ground. The Sub-Commanders, Cherogimogyan and Childerician, walked back and forth in their clinking silver armor, their fine-plumed helmets held under their arms as they inspected their ranks.

Casualties had been few among most of the battalions; only Marderosian's battalion had been seriously decimated, losing more than half its men and eagles, with many wounded in addition. The dead knights were laid out ceremoniously at the edge of the field to await transport back over the mountains for obsequies and burial. The bodies of the scarlet eagles, including the eagle that was lost close to Branch-Knot's house, were collected, and all were stacked tenderly together, where a massive funeral pyre would later return their eagle spirits to their homes in the wind.

Tundra-Bear and Fox-Foot brought their eagle down into the cornfield and rejoined the Legion. They dismounted and brought the Staff and the Axe to the Lord High Commander. Erudan and Illyria were already there. Cherogimogyan raised a banner, and the knights formed in a perfect circle around Gutornitolyan.

The Lord High Commander received the Imperial Axe of the House of Ospeth from Tundra-Bear's hands and turned towards Illyria. He placed it into Illyria's hands.

Gutornitolyan pronounced in solemn words, "Illyria, it is now your responsibility to rule here in Oval-Earth. The House of Ospeth ever acted with perfect justice. We all know that we can entrust to your wise judgment and prudence a governance of Oval-Earth that will restore justice to its populace and beneficence to its times and seasons. And I charge you, Illyria, to ensure that your son's nurture is such as to provide for you a wise and humble successor for the citizens of Oval-Earth."

Illyria stepped forth. "How are we to thank you, Gutornitolyan, and all your men, for what you have done?"

"It is we who must thank you, Illyria, and the noble companions who have brought Oval-Earth out of the grasp of the Kingdom of Darkness," Gutornitolyan answered. "And to your princely husband all ages hereafter must profess their gratitude. It was he who fulfilled the ancient prophecies vouchsafed to my people. Without that fulfillment, we could do nothing.

"As long as Oval-Earth dwelt in darkness and was dominated by the Eye that looked inward and that would not look out into the universe, we could only marshal our strength and make ourselves ready through the long aeons for the day of the onslaught.

"Oval-Earth was also our home, and the completion of the work of the Kingdom of Light could only attend upon the redemption of the ancestral heartland — the heartland given to us and to all the rest of our fellow peoples by the powers that rule beyond the stars. It is the noble band of companions who has saved Oval-Earth. Your husband, Hrudan, slew the Evil Eye.

"I request that this field be made a monument for future generations, for here the House of Ospeth has been restored. May this field be called evermore the Field of Hrudan. My knights this very day will begin to seek out the remains of your husband in the Golden Mountains and bring them here for burial. We shall return within several weeks."

"It will be done as you bid," said Illyria, her eyes welling up with tears.

Gutornitolyan took the hands of Illyria and Erudan and held them up high in the air. "Behold, the restoration of the House of Ospeth! May it ever seek the counsel and the good of its peoples and foster their energies, their talents, and their hopes!" he exclaimed.

The heads of a thousand knights bent in reverence. The formation dissolved and the knights returned to the task of preparing the dead for transferal and caring for the wounded. A column of brilliant crimson smoke soon wound up into the skies from the pyre of the eagles. All the birds of Oval-Earth, the cranes and owls and plovers and sparrows and countless others, arose from the woodlands and Moor-Plains and downs and gathered in immense flocks as they circled in solemn flight around the pyre in commemoration of the slain eagles.

Meanwhile, the Staff of the Ancestral Tree wiggled and squirmed in Fox-Foot's hand. She quickly understood. She followed the knights and approached the wounded men and eagles with the Staff.

Many of them were instantly healed by the merest touch of the Staff. Others were relieved of their pain but would need a period of convalescence before they would be well again. Marderosian's broken legs were rejoined, but he was still too weak to walk. Later, Fox-Foot went back to where Gutornitolyan was standing with Tundra-Bear and the others.

Gutornitolyan looked at Tundra-Bear and Fox-Foot. "What will the two of you do now, after accomplishing some of the most courageous and harrowing tasks Oval-Earth has ever known?"

Fox-Foot sighed. "We have work to finish. We must take this Staff back to the Northern Taiga, where it came from. After that, we want to go back to the Hills and live our lives the way we used to. Isn't that so, Tundra-Bear?"

"It is so," he replied.

"Then we shall depart," said Gutornitolyan. "We shall return soon with Hrudan for burial. And not long from now, as soon as we can organize it, we will begin to fashion a great highway over the mountains. Our peoples will come back together again."

Gutornitolyan motioned for the Legion of the Wind to mount. Fox-Foot suddenly cried out, "But the words of the Song!"

Tundra-Bear answered, "We had them all the time, even as Kasyan told us—they are inscribed on the head of the Imperial Axe."

"But we can't read them! No one was able to read them—not even Tristan-Phoros. And the two of us, Tundra-Bear, we can't read anything at all!"

"Not so, Fox-Foot. I can read them now. Cherogimogyan taught me how. And I will teach you."

Cherogimogyan beamed an enormous smile and nodded his bushy red beard. Then he turned to Gutornitolyan. "We must not forget to pick up Kasyan from the region of the Barrows and take him over the mountains. If he had not made that headlong flight out of the ravine, aeons ago, the Eye of the Needle would never have been distracted long enough for our ancestors to find a way around him."

Gutornitolyan agreed. "We won't forget him."

The corps of the Legion laced on their helmets and mounted their eagles. Many of the wounded knights had to be lifted onto their mounts or to ride behind another knight. The dead and the more seriously wounded were bundled into litters that were suspended underneath the eagles. Tundra-Bear and Fox-Foot's eagle was mounted by a knight whose eagle had been lost; it positioned itself among the other eagles and readied itself for flight. Gutornitolyan swung himself up over the back of his eagle and raised his blue and gold banner in salute to the Imperial family. The Sub-Commanders did likewise.

Then Gutornitolyan gave a signal to the Legion. The signal was repeated by the Sub-Commanders. The eagles slapped their wings against the ground, and in one great surge of wings and air, the entire corps arose simultaneously straight upward, hovered for a moment high above the field, and circled slowly around it. At another command, they wheeled around in one great movement and sped off, like a flash of light, through the air and soon vanished over the glistening peaks of the mountains.

Only one eagle lingered behind and dipped down in the far west over the Barrows. Moments later, it soared up high into the western sky and likewise disappeared over the mountains. It bore its silver-armored knight, and, seated behind him, the frail figure of a burnt-out man dressed in tattered feathers. He held in his hand a Hill Country arrow and waved it over his head in triumphant farewell.

Chapter III

The Incantation

Oval-Earth was devastated. Villages had been flattened in the storm of battle; fields were burned and farmsteads ravaged. What had been left of the Radial High-Road System was now little more than long lines of twisted rubble traversing plains and wooded hills. Large, gaping holes dotted the landscape; they still seethed with puddles of bubbling bile, while noxious vapors floated from their surfaces, wilting plants and poisoning animals for leagues around them. Local rivers and streams were jammed with the flotsam of torn vegetation, and both human and animal carcasses bunched up into steaming heaps at bends in the watercourses, creating momentary dams that backed up the flow of water into jagged pools mottled with debris.

Here and there, the burnt timbers of a storage grange, a barn, or a woodshed rose up like narrow blackened spires from the smoking ashes that surrounded them. Surviving livestock drifted aimlessly from field to field looking for whatever sparse green fodder still poked through oily mud or along old fences whose posts occasionally stood out lonely and barren against the far horizon. Odd pieces of household ware—a rocking chair, a brazier, a lampshade punched with holes, a cradle—littered the banks of streams or were caught among the branches of a tree and dangled uneasily in the breeze. Along with them might be found an assortment of objects: a child's doll, a carpenter's awl, or a farmer's threshing hook.

The earth-houses of the wood-gnomes were pits filled with broken vials and scattered medicaments; their curious asymmetrical chambers and tunnels were ripped open like warped honeycombs pulled violently out of a beehive.

In the Capital, most of the governmental ministries had been crushed. The Imperial Plaza was a cloaca of simmering liquid refuse in which little could be distinguished but clogs of torn uniforms and broken stone and masses of paper slips and parchments. The Imperial Court, with its once majestic dome, was in ruins.

Already hordes of insects buzzed low over the decaying city, while predatory rodents swarmed out of the sewers, only to sicken and die in the morass of putrid remains. The blue-coated, orange-striped hairy-winged fly, however, did not show up to feast on what should have been its most desirable nutriments; in fact, the hairy-winged fly was never seen again.

Gradually, cautiously, the populace of Oval-Earth began to emerge out of its hiding places — from out of deep root cellars, from under broken buildings and coverts and out of isolated hay sheds and hidden groves in the woods. They had been frightened as they had never been frightened before; but now, as if fright itself had been its own antidote, they shed their fright.

They gathered their dead from the fields, the clogged streams, the broken houses, and the rutted streets and byways. They mourned their dead with ceremonies as simple as they were brief, and they buried them in places where the memory of them could be sustained and honored for future generations. They attended to the wounded, bringing them to the few shelters they could still find intact, wrapping them in coverlets and brewing thin steaming potages of roots and seeds that would help their flesh to heal and to restore their spirits.

Local wood-gnomes were quick to organize special emergency hospices for the sick and the injured; others set up commissaries in the open air and, having lost most of their ointments and other healing agents, set up makeshift pharmaceutical distilleries. They were surprised by the willingness of men, women, and children to collect herbs for them and the firewood necessary to heat the brass pots where the medications would be prepared.

The human inhabitants, no longer willing to be passive, uncooperative spectators, helped the gnomes build large lean-tos for dressing stations. They built litters for the wounded and helped move them to safety.

The wood-gnomes, aware that plague might develop in the unsanitary conditions now prevalent in most of Oval-Earth, worked hard to restrain its outbreak. They directed efforts to clear the watercourses and streams and to quarantine areas that might be unusually contaminated.

Residents of the Capital had no other choice but to abandon the city; as they evacuated, they avoided the steaming puddles of harmful effluvia that collected in potholes on the streets. The stench was so excruciating that they wrapped their heads in cloth and made their way as quickly as possible to the outskirts of the city for relief. Reclaiming the city would require efforts of large-scale organization and relief, and, in those first hours and days after the conclusion of the hostilities, it was difficult for the citizenry to discern where that relief would come from. Yet, unbeknownst to them, such relief was being organized and soon would be underway.

In the foggy wetlands of the Moor-Plains, even before the conflict, the Gethsarbim had already begun the reconstruction of their enchanted city. The streets were cleared of the old debris, and the delicate little bridges spanning the canals were slowly being erected once more.

The chivalric orders helped to organize the effort and laid plans for rebuilding the ancient causeway through the fens. They knew that the peoples of Oval-Earth would soon seek them out, though they also knew it would take years before their wonderful old city would be ready to receive its visitors in the style and comfort it could once offer them. The thin-spun bridge from the causeway over the lagoon would have to be slung again from its towering piers. The myriad little hostels for the guests would have to be outfitted with their exotic dining alcoves and delicious Gethsarbim delicacies and wines, and the torches that once led the travelers through the mists of the swamps would have to be rekindled.

But the Gethsarbim went to work with enthusiasm and joy, and throughout the Moor-Plains, they plied their tiny craft in search of materials with which to build.

Beneath the Isle at the center of the Midland Sea, the feared Brotherhood of the Drowsers, now at last restored to the original name of the Brethren of the Wakeful, gathered in the great Chapter Room to decide their future. Gemstone lanterns were cleansed of oily deposits and shed their light again through the ancient meeting hall. Its carved oak benches were dusted off and polished.

The mood of the Brethren was sober and humble. They didn't know yet a great deal of what had happened in Oval-Earth or what had occurred just within the last day to alter that state of affairs, but they knew that, in some special fashion, they had been responsible for what had occurred in Oval-Earth, though they were still unable to explain these events to themselves.

They elected Weyland as their superior. The original name of the "Brethren of the Wakeful" was officially restored and promulgated.

After a long session of gentle but firm debate and remonstrance with one another, they exited the great Chapter Room and ascended through the various stairwells to the observation platform of the Pupil. Here, as a group, they gazed upward and tried to recollect the meaning of the Brethren, its purpose from time immemorial, and why the Isle had once been called "the Eye of the Universe."

But something vital was missing, and they all knew that. Whatever it was they were supposed to see from the observation platform, they were unable to see it, as if some form of blindness still held them in its grip. Only Weyland, in his months of research among the archives, knew what this was.

After helping to reorganize life in the Pupil, Weyland asked Phoros to accompany him across the Midland Sea to seek out the band of strangers who had visited only weeks earlier. He hoped to find out whether the words of the Song had been recovered from across the Golden Mountains.

Phoros readily accepted the invitation; traveling came naturally to him, he observed, though he didn't know why. He took his pipe and his leather pouch and accompanied Weyland to the harbor. There they lit the signal lamp that summoned the felucca from the fishing village on the opposite shore. An hour later, the felucca arrived.

Weyland was pleased to see that the disagreeable fisherman who used to ply the delicate craft through the milky waters of the Sea had been replaced by a rather cheerful young fellow with a curious twitch in one cheek. The new ferryman, with a quite unconcerned chuckle, allowed that the former ferryman had been a victim of "un o' dem ghastly ghouls."

Weyland was content not to dispute the tone with which this sorry fate was announced, and Phoros, for once, felt no impulse to debate with the young ferryman about what, precisely, he meant by "ghouls."

When, after a laborious transit over the milky waters (Weyland did rather weigh down one side of the skiff), the felucca hove to the mainland dock, Weyland noticed Dolopeia's enchanted sloop, which was still bound by golden bands to the other side of the dock. The sloop dipped its sails in courteous salute and jingled its tiny bells. It obviously was waiting for the return of its diminutive Duchess. Phoros scrutinized the extraordinary craft rather carefully, cocking his head first in one direction, then in another, not unlike … well, no need to mention it!

In the Hill Country, the villagers organized bands to repair the damages to the Regional Road and to salvage what was useful from the thousands of winterbeest carcasses that littered the landscape and clogged the highland gorges. They skinned pelts, smoked and dried whatever meat had not spoiled, and rendered the thick but precious tallow.

What they could not preserve they picked up and destroyed as rapidly as possible, so that the streams would flow with clean waters and the forests would be free of blights and contamination.

Though the winterbeests were their traditional and dreaded foe, they could not help but feel some compassion for the hapless beasts, to say nothing of hoping that enough survived so that an important source of sustenance for them and their way of life had been preserved.

Fox-Foot and Tundra-Bear's children eagerly anticipated their parents' return; Swallow-Flight organized provisions for a welcome-home festivity. Badger-Claw was glad to help out.

Throughout Oval-Earth, amid all the horror of the aftermath, there was a new morale abroad in the land among the people. There was, and would be, much sorrow at what they saw, sorrow such as they never thought could be so deep; but the sorrow itself was salutary.

They were no longer inclined to shrug their shoulders at misfortune, to accept it apathetically and unresponsively, to reside in a perpetual numbness of intellect and in the atrophied emotional life that such numbness both fed and fed upon; rather, they recognized, in all its fullness, the depth of loss they had experienced and resolved to transform their grief, as grief itself was ever meant to be transformed, into energetic activity. Only in that way could the memory of the dead be justly hallowed and preserved.

Farmers who normally watched their crops decay in the fields shook the lethargy out of their sinews and started to prop up their barns and mend broken fences and gates. Carpenters sharpened their worn-out tools and set to work. Men and women began to go to the fields to replant the crops and salvage what was left of the old. Villagers gathered for meetings. They appointed groups to clean up the village squares and replace the fountains, many of which had not worked for centuries. Small, temporary bridges were erected over rivers and streams so that limited commerce could begin again.

Most of all, the old apathy seemed to have been driven out, and an energy renewed, a zest for being alive and making things good again. There was much to be done, for not only would the destruction of the war have to be repaired, but the dereliction of centuries would have to be reversed. It would take generations to complete the work.

On the cornfield outside the Capital, Illyria and Erudan took tentative steps to form a temporary administration. At first, this effort consisted of little more than setting aside one corner of the field and marking it off with a boundary of reeds.

While Fox-Foot worked with the ill and the wounded, Tundra-Bear, with Erudan as his apprentice, was deft at constructing a fence of woven rushes along the reed boundary to surround the area as well as to define some passageways through it. The purpose of making the enclosure was no more than to make a space that could be clearly identified as a base camp.

The space was marked by internal divisions that would, according to Illyria's directions, correspond to the various tasks that would have to be performed there, and the passageways would provide direct and orderly access to these. What exactly these tasks would be she didn't know yet, but she knew that, before long, diverse functions would have to find their headquarters in a place where they could be directed from a central location and be coordinated with one another. Here, at the base camp, materials and information could be gathered and then redistributed as effectively and efficiently as possible.

From among the stream of refugees flowing out of the Capital, Illyria and Erudan were able to extract a small number of people who were willing and possibly able to provide at least a modicum of coordination in settling the huge outflow of population into organized groups.

Within hours, a rudimentary center was established within the rush-fence enclosure for collecting and distributing medical supplies, for rejoining families that had become separated, for food and sanitation, for resettling groups farther out in the countryside in order to avoid crowding and bottlenecks, and for the identification and burial of the dead.

Illyria's task was considerably facilitated when a delegation of wood-gnomes—a dozen or so of the taut, wiry, sharp-eyed members of the hickory clan—appeared at the perimeter of the base camp and offered their services. They were renowned throughout Oval-Earth for their ability to organize activities of all kinds; this group must have felt instinctively a need for their talents in the outskirts of the Capital and were quick to respond.

They soon had matters under control—or at least under as much control as was possible under the circumstances. The human volunteers appreciated their help, for they were overwhelmed by the extent of the problems, as well as by the unfamiliar functions and responsibilities they were attempting to assume.

Meanwhile, Fox-Foot, throughout all of this, was active using the Staff for medical treatment; she was joined by one of the hickory gnomes, who helped her with the sick and the wounded. Eventually, a contingent of other wood-gnomes, from the juniper and elderberry clans, arrived and worked with them in setting up an open-air hospital replete with straw beds and long, neat rows of roomy lean-to shelters.

On the following day, Illyria and Erudan felt somewhat awkward yet confident about leaving this tumultuous scene for a while, especially now that the hickory-gnomes were in charge. But they had another task to fulfill. They joined Tundra-Bear and Fox-Foot and sought out the Northern Arm of the Radial High-Road. Fox-Foot bore the Staff, and Erudan carried the Imperial Axe of Ospeth over his shoulders. Together they began the journey northward. The last momentous act of the companions still remained to be performed.

The High-Road was barely passable. Huge blocks of dislocated stone jutted up out of the roadbed like miniature mountain ridges. Trees on all sides had been torn down and lay across the roads at intervals. It was a different scene from the time when, only weeks earlier, the band had traveled southward in disguise with Hrudan pulling the draw-cart and Tristan-Phoros trotting behind everyone else, trying with all his power to pretend he was a dog, while being, in effect, a dog anyway.

On the journey, Tundra-Bear and Fox-Foot told Illyria and Erudan about their many extraordinary adventures. Especially painful was Tundra-Bear's account again of the ascent over the Golden Mountains. Sometimes Illyria would falter in her grief and would have to turn away from the others for a few moments. There were moments also when Fox-Foot regretted the times she had patted Tristan-Phoros on his head, even though she had been well-intentioned when she did it.

They spent the first night on the road in the ruins of an abandoned inn. Tundra-Bear made a fire, and they foraged in the neighborhood for a few things to eat. The inhabitants were well-disposed to them, even though they did not know who the strangers were, except for some who thought they recognized the green-haired man and woman who had flown overhead in the dawn several days earlier on the back of a scarlet eagle. In any event, the local people had little food, but what little they had they shared. Later on, some of them began to bring their sick and wounded to the abandoned inn. Fox-Foot applied the Staff to a wound or to a diseased organ and immediately healed it.

The following day, in the late evening, the travelers approached the foot of Kyn Ardagh and turned off the road. Here they discovered Branch-Knot's earth-house, half demolished by the ravaging Lo-El, but already being reconstructed by Knarry and Branch-Knot as Dolopeia darted about, still giving her advice.

A large hospice had been set up nearby where Knarry and Branch-Knot and the whole clan of the Orugug wood-gnomes had been attending to the ill.

The work had ceased for the day and a table with candles was set out in front of the earth-house with several vials of gnome-spirits and a simple pudding boiled up from the local roots and berries. Bomsiell, her four ears twitching, noted the travelers coming from afar and bounced out to meet them as soon as they left the road.

The reunion was an occasion for many tears, for Tundra-Bear told the story of what happened in the mountains once again. They all mourned for

Hrudan and for Tristan-Phoros. Even Bomsiell seemed to understand and climbed high in a tree to wail beneath the waxing lavender moons. Later, the group sat down to its skimpy but nourishing meal of brambleberry and root pudding, and Fox-Foot told Knarry about the meeting with Garug-Caroch up in the sphere of music high over the World beyond the Worlds. She also told him about the magnificent cosmic horse that Garug-Caroch was riding. Then she presented him with the Staff.

Knarry tenderly took hold of the Staff in his shaggy hands. If wood-gnomes could weep, he would have shed as many tears as a tree sheds raindrops in a summer shower. He shook his massive head and looked at the others.

Tomorrow they would ascend Kyn Ardagh and restore the Staff to the Ancestral Tree. In the meantime, Knarry pulled the jeweled casket out of his pouch and removed the Splinter. It fit perfectly into a thin gash in the side of the Staff. But it would not stay there. Perhaps it needed the Song to rejoin it effectively. He felt the heft of the Staff in his hands and the enormous power that lay in its fiber.

He could feel the wood tingle and quiver as he held it. It was vibrantly alive. How fortunate that Garug-Caroch had wrested it from the hands of the Lo-El in the winter storm! If the Lo-El army had had this weapon, the Legion of the Wind might have been turned back, if not by the Staff itself, then by the adverse weather that the Staff could have summoned.

The hour was late, and the travelers retired to small rooms deep in the lower parts of the earth-house that had survived. They would need rest for the following day. Before retiring for the night, Tundra-Bear assisted Knarry in writing down the words of the Song on a large sheet of parchment that they found in the partially ruined study of Branch-Knot's earth-house.

They placed several candles on the worktable. Knarry looked for a quill with which to etch the words on the aged vellum, but the quill in his haversack was missing. Having nothing to write with, he hit upon the idea of using the Splinter from the jeweled casket. It was shaped like a stylus and would do. He withdrew it from the casket and dipped it into an old pewter inkhorn.

The Splinter seemed to love what it was doing. It flexed in Knarry's hand and, on a few occasions, began to take dictation directly from Tundra-Bear and to hop into the inkhorn of its own volition to supply itself with fresh ink. Knarry was surprised. Looking at Tundra-Bear with a twinkle in his deep amber eyes, he said, "I think the Splinter may have a destiny of its own that we are not aware of yet."

Tundra-Bear did not pay attention to these words. In stumbling fashion, he translated the inscription that was carved along the blade of the Axe. They compared and corrected this translation with the verses of the Song that Knarry had already written down on separate pieces of vellum, though some of this correction was unnecessary, for, as Tundra-Bear stammered the words and made errors, the Splinter made the correction for him.

Soon, all was written down. They rolled up the parchment and tied it with a ribbon. They blew out the candles and joined the others in sleep. The Splinter jumped into the jeweled casket and curled the velvet cloth around itself as Knarry tenderly lowered the lid.

In the morning, everyone arose, and, after bathing in the icy-cold stream that tumbled near the earth-house and breakfasting on the remains of the former evening's pudding—now just a bit dry and cold—they began the procession to the escarpment and up Kyn Ardagh.

Branch-Knot accompanied them only as far as the base of Kyn Ardagh and returned to his home in order to rejoin his fellow clansmen in their medical work. For the others, it was a long and arduous climb. Boulders blocked the path and frequently had to be climbed up on one side and descended on the other.

The members of the band helped each other as they clambered over one obstacle after another, and as before, they relied on the climbing skills of Tundra-Bear and Fox-Foot. Dolopeia had the least difficulty and led the way as she skipped from rock to rock and hopped gaily over the small ravines and fissures that crossed the path. Bomsiell followed closely after her.

Somewhat behind the group, Knarry carried the Staff, and the jeweled casket and the parchment were packed securely in his haversack; as he climbed, he meditated on the need for repairing Kyn Ardagh and thought over how he would bring that subject up at the meeting of the wood-gnome clans on the Claha-ain Plateau next spring. He knew that the charges brought against him at the last calamitous gathering would soon be cleared.

They reached the high ridge of the escarpment about noontime. The Northern Taiga spread out ahead of them. It was a fine, beautiful day. The sun shone brightly over Oval-Earth, and a gentle wind out of the west rustled in the high forest canopy. The Northern Taiga had not been disturbed by the great battle just concluded, for the Lo-Els had been turned back at the base of the escarpment.

But the foreground of the forest was scattered with a large number of tiny saplings, and Knarry knew that these were the souls of wood-gnomes lost in the conflict. He noted too, and yet again, the little hornbeam that stooped rather precariously over the side of the cliff. Twigbottom would be remembered and would be honored for his sacrifice.

The hike through the magical woodland was easy and quiet. The silence and peace of the forest imbued each of the companions with a profound serenity; despite all the horrors that had beset Oval-Earth, the repose of the hushed and gently murmuring groves gave the impression of something stronger, something more enduring than the struggles they had experienced.

Within several hours, they came into view of the Ancestral Tree. It still reared its massive leafy branches into the sky above, even though the clearing that surrounded it was littered with dead and fallen leaves, and the gash in its side still trickled a bright sap that curled and sank into the ground. Many of its branches drooped and sighed in the gentle western breeze. At its base, the clearing was sprinkled with small saplings of some of the wood-gnomes who had perished in the Lo-El's encounter with Hrudan.

The companions gathered around the tree and gazed at it in wonder. Erudan and Bomsiell stood back and watched as the others approached closer to it. Erudan unsheathed the Imperial Axe and held it up as a kind of witness to the event. Knarry prepared to place the Staff into the gash on the Ancestral Tree as Fox-Foot unraveled the parchment and held it up in front of Dolopeia. Illyria received the jeweled casket from Knarry and opened it as Tundra-Bear removed the ink-stained Splinter from the casket and fitted it into the notch on the Staff. They moved forward. Knarry pressed the Staff into the side of the Tree.

Dolopeia began to sing. As in the great storm of the winter past, the words were right and true:

> *Out of the radiant garland*
> *Of stars,*
>
> *Out of the primordial*
> *Beauty of old,*
>
> *Out of the black-maned*
> *Horses of darkness,*
>
> *The fiery steeds*
> *Of the cosmic deep,*
>
> *Shone forth the aurora,*
> *The thunderous dawn,*
>
> *Shafts aflame*
> *In the brilliant-hued night—*
>
> *Arose then the sun-disk,*
> *Scarlet-plumed spawner*
>
> *Of orbits and worlds,*
> *For earth is the maiden,*
>
> *The daughter of light,*
> *Bride of the blazing*
> *Archways of heaven.*
>
> *She intones the glowing*
> *Song of the ages.*
>
> *The sacred aeons*
> *Dance in eternal delight.*

The ground underneath them seemed to shift; the whole forest burst with light, color, and music. The bark of the Ancestral Tree opened up and drew the Staff into itself, folding the bark gently around its edges until it was absorbed fully into the mighty trunk without seam or scar to show that it had been rent or torn.

All at once, the drooping branches of the giant tree lifted themselves high up again, and the leaves surged with vibrancy and color as they regained all their former vigor. The wound had been healed. The Ancestral Tree was itself again. The forest and the skies above rejoiced in its recovery.

But the Splinter refused to rejoin. After several seconds of reunion with the Ancestral Tree, it sprang out, leapt directly into the jeweled casket, still held open in Illyria's hands, and curling its ink-stained tip, pulled the lid closed.

"Oh no, you don't," Knarry chortled.

He opened the casket again. The Splinter lay there in its purple velvet bed among the folds of linen. But it was no longer a Splinter. It was a Stylus.

Illyria closed the lid.

"There is some reason for this," she said. "We had better leave it where it is. I think it has something to tell us."

Knarry agreed. "It has a special mission still ahead of it."

"Perhaps it has the job of telling a story," Tundra-Bear inserted.

"Perhaps. But we must go now," Knarry replied.

The jeweled casket was closed and replaced in Knarry's haversack. The companions turned and made their way through the now refreshed and invigorated forest. The descent of Kyn Ardagh was comparatively easy, for going down over all the obstacles was light and playful work.

Evening found them all gathered in Branch-Knot's earth-house. They stayed up late into the evening and talked about the Song. What did it all mean? Tundra-Bear concluded the evening by saying, "I don't know what it means. But I think it is good to try to figure it out." The others concurred and went to bed. Bomsiell curled up on a rafter near the hearth.

The following morning, the group said goodbye to Branch-Knot and resumed their travels. The journey back to the Capital along the Northern Arm of the Radial High-Road was, once more, laborious and time-consuming. Knarry found himself healing many injured people who were brought to the side of the road for his services.

Illyria and Erudan fanned out a great deal from the road. They wanted to find out as much as they could about what was happening and what needed to be done. Dolopeia was not lacking for the appropriate advice; and many villagers came to consult with her. Tundra-Bear and Fox-Foot mainly talked about getting back home to the Hills. Bomsiell trotted along behind them.

Within several days after arriving back at the cornfield just west of the Capital, Illyria set up a provisional seat of government. The makeshift base-camp of rush fences had served its purpose well, but in the meantime, a few enterprising city folks had remembered that some old warehouses outside the city gates contained a variety of tapestried pavilions once used for open-air ceremonial festivals and fairs of various kinds. These were raised up on the cornfield as living quarters and offices for the provisional government.

The largest tent was outfitted in the back with a raised dais to serve as a temporary throne room. On one side of the dais, the Imperial Axe was mounted. Illyria sat on a chair in the center of the dais, while Erudan stood at her right shoulder. Knarry sat on a rough block of wood to her left.

Small, ragged delegations were already arriving from all over Oval-Earth, looking for help and counsel. Knarry was indispensable to Illyria and Erudan and fell naturally into the role of prime minister and chief councillor, since his knowledge was necessary in helping to work out the hundreds of decisions that had to be made.

He also remembered the charge that Hrudan had given him before the ascent of the mountains. Illyria and Erudan were his special responsibility now. To help them in their work, he enlisted some more wood-gnomes, whom he added to the original band of hickory gnomes and whom he trusted to be his assistants in running errands and delivering messages.

Erudan made initial efforts to reestablish the Imperial Courier service by having some farmers bring his father's moose herd from the grazing fields near their lodge by the Great Rock-Falls and training both moose and riders to carry important dispatches to every corner of Oval-Earth.

Dolopeia was active, too, even though she knew that she must soon depart for the City of the Gethsarbim. She, Fox-Foot, and Tundra-Bear designed and produced simple white linen garments with a small insignia of the Imperial Axe affixed to the shoulder with red thread. These garments would help others to recognize the humans and gnomes authorized to work and speak for the provisional government.

One of the first delegations to enter Illyria's tent was from the Isle in the Midland Sea. Weyland and Phoros approached the Imperial dais. Weyland recognized Knarry and the others and pronounced his salutations. When he saw them back away slightly, he reassured him that his diet had changed. Then he stood aside for his companion.

The short, bearded man in a black academic robe stepped up and bowed before Illyria and said, "I am Phoros, philosopher and logician, at your service, Madam." He took a blackbriar pipe out of his pouch, filled it with dried bilberry weed, and lit up.

Tundra-Bear and Fox-Foot looked at one another with startled expressions. Bomsiell's ears shot up. The voice, to say nothing of the manner, was familiar to her. Knarry leaned over and whispered something in Illyria's ear. They turned their attention again to the front of the dais.

"We are here," Weyland spoke, "because there is something that we *frightfully* need."

"And what is that?" Illyria asked.

"We need the words to the Song of the Eternal Aeons. Do you have them?"

"We have them." Illyria nodded to a tall, spindly wood-gnome of the tamarack clan who shuffled across the tent and handed Weyland a parchment rolled up with a ribbon around it. "We have expected you. Make this document your most prized possession," Illyria added.

"Prized possession?" Phoros suddenly interjected. Illyria turned to face him. He continued, "With all due respect for the authority of your position, Madam, I must disagree with your contention that the document must be our most prized possession."

Tundra-Bear and Fox-Foot looked at Phoros in astonishment. Bomsiell opened her eyes as wide as the coin-like eyes of Dolopeia. Knarry chortled slightly and covered his face with one of his shaggy hands.

"Would you care to give the grounds for your disagreement with my statement?" Illyria replied.

"What does it mean to 'prize' something?"

"To give it value, to regard it as having worth."

"Correct. Now, if that is true, then it would follow that the 'most prized' possession is a possession on which the greatest worth or value is conferred."

"That is true."

"But can it be possible that a 'document' could be that upon which we confer highest worth or value?"

"I don't see what you mean, Phoros."

"A document is a parchment upon which something is written or inscribed, is it not?"

"To be sure, it is."

"Is the parchment valuable because of what is inscribed upon it, or is what is inscribed upon it valuable because it is on the parchment?"

"Assuredly the former."

"You are a wise woman, Illyria. For if the former were not true, then anything inscribed on the parchment would be as good as anything else inscribed on the parchment, and we would not want to concede that, would we?"

"Heavens no, Phoros."

"And we did not come here to *fetch* … ahem … to obtain a parchment but rather to acquire the words of the Song, which incidentally, happen to be inscribed upon the parchment in question. *Ergo*, our most prized possession is not the parchment, from which we can easily enough transfer the words to another parchment, but it is our knowledge of the words of the Song."

"I grant you that," Illyria said. She looked over at Knarry and back to Phoros. She did wonder why such an effort had been made to establish such an obvious point, but, then again, she could hardly claim to know what it was that made philosophers and logicians tick. On the other hand, the thought occurred to her that it is frequently the obvious that people do not see.

"Phoros," she continued.

"Yes, Madam!" He blew a thick cloud of smoke from his pipe.

"Phoros, I am going to ask you to leave the Brethren of the Wakeful—as I have been notified you people now call yourselves. I am asking you to leave permanently. I desire that you return to the College of Wisdom. And I charge you to restore it to its original calling as it was established in the ages of its foundation. As Empress of Oval-Earth, I hereby bestow upon you the position of Grand Master of the College with all its incumbent responsibilities and privileges. Make it once again the source of wisdom for all the peoples of Oval-Earth."

Phoros bowed gently before her. "I shall do all in my power to perform what you have asked. But, if what I have heard is true, I will need stone-masons. The wall around the Library must be taken down, and its doors opened once again. I understand that the Hall of Games has been destroyed. Let it remain that way for now, until we can rebuild it as a hall for learning and debate. The Game of Spheres shall become only what it always should have been—an entertainment for late on a winter night."

Phoros bowed again. He looked at Knarry and over to Tundra-Bear and Fox-Foot and Dolopeia. Finally, he looked at Bomsiell. He took another puff on his pipe, tilted his head slightly back and forth, and wrinkled his brow. Who were these odd characters? Why did he think he had run into them before?

Illyria turned to Weyland. "Weyland, return to the Isle with the Song. May the Brethren ever be wakeful, and as the peoples of Oval-Earth sleep from their labors, may the Brethren gaze, for the rest of us, from the Pupil of the Eye into the mind and heart of the universe. And may you all be pupils for evermore, never ceasing to learn from the font of eternal wisdom."

"It shall be done," said Weyland. He and Phoros turned to leave.

"The company one shares is half the fun of traveling," cried Dolopeia.

She ran from Illyria to Erudan to Knarry and kissed them and leapt down from the dais and ran over to Tundra-Bear and Fox-Foot. She jumped into their arms and kissed them, too, giving Fox-Foot a special hug. Then she kissed Bomsiell on the top of her head in the middle of her four ears. A second later, she was scampering alongside Weyland and Phoros. She waved goodbye again and disappeared from the tent.

Later that day, she sailed with Weyland on the enchanted sloop to the island, the "Eye of the Universe." There she left him off in the inlet. The sloop rounded the island again, and Dolopeia was on her way back over the Midland Sea to the River N'ea to rejoin her people in the Moor-Plains. As she entered the estuary of the river, she saw something splashing and disporting in the waters around her.

Suddenly two Hydro-Sylphs leapt into the air by the bow of the sloop. It was Prince Witzlau and Princess Tiphaine.

"We are on our way to the Capital to pay our respects to the Imperial House of Ospeth," cried out Prince Witzlau.

"We have some new poems, too," Princess Tiphaine added. "They are cheerful poems," she laughed.

They plummeted down into the water, only to rise again to the surface and stand full length on the water by treading with their wide-finned tails.

"Coskaer of Eudo is with us, and Natu, and the Grand Drogo of Lianne'neas, and Bac'haol," they shouted. "We will come to see you soon at the City of the Gethsarbim." They sank again into the estuary and, accompanied by the others, darted joyfully through the waves and into the mother-of-pearl waters of the Midland Sea.

Far away, on the Eastern Arm of the Radial High-Road, Phoros was walking in the direction of the College of Wisdom and making his way over the dislodged boulders, fallen trees, and open ditches. He was smoking his pipe. He was doing a lot of serious thinking.

In the Imperial tent, Illyria was approached by many more groups and individuals. One of them was a broad, heavy man with a wiry, disheveled beard. He wore what might best be described as the frayed remnants of an old uniform. It was maroon, and it still had one bronze button and a patch of gold braid loosely dangling from it.

Illyria remarked, "You must be from one of the ministries of the Capital."

"I am, Madam," he answered. "I am the former chief of the late Ministry of Insoluble Affairs, now of infelicitous memory and advantageously defunct. My name is Toten-Haas. I wish to be of service."

"How can you serve me, Toten-Haas?" Illyria inquired.

"My guess, Madam, having witnessed what went on in the Capital during the great strife, and knowing what things were like before all this happened, is that I may be your only link with the ministerial services as they existed in the past. The Ministry of Insoluble Affairs became a repository for all that the latter age of Oval-Earth could not fathom. In it, I learned a great deal about the past and about the original purposes of the ministries set up by the ancient emperors. Furthermore, I may be the sole survivor of the ministerial service.

"For some reason, those monstrous ghouls could not, and would not, tamper with the Ministry of Insoluble Affairs. I don't blame them. Even a ghoul would have enough sense not to want to become an insoluble affair, though, as far as I can gather, they were not much more than that, showing just how destructive an insoluble affair can be.

"But the building itself was destroyed in the final conflict, not by the demons, but by some of those silver-armored paladins on the scarlet eagles, if I am not mistaken. I was not sorry to see it go. Neither were they, if I can presume to form such a judgment from the obvious glee with which they demolished it."

Knarry took Illyria aside and mentioned to her that he recognized the man and that Hrudan had found him to be the only civil servant he had met who still possessed a sense of integrity.

Illyria turned to Toten-Haas. "I charge you to organize and clean out the Ministry of Historical Records. We must rediscover our history. Without that, we cannot reorganize the government. That will be your task, Toten-Haas. It is a serious obligation."

"I accept it with the greatest honor," he replied.

"As for the Ministry of Insoluble Affairs ..." she began.

"We will no longer have need of it," Toten-Haas interposed. "We will not file away our problems and leave them unsolved."

"But what if there are problems we cannot solve, Toten-Haas? I suspect there may be many."

"Then we will continue to try to solve them. We will not pretend they do not exist."

Illyria smiled, and Toten-Haas departed. At the edge of the tent, a hickory wood-gnome motioned him over into a small dressing room, divested him of his shabby uniform, and clothed him in a simple linen robe with the imperial insignia woven into its right shoulder. Toten-Haas was happy to the point of tears. He rubbed his hands vigorously together, clapped the hickory gnome rather soundly on the back and practically knocked him down, and set off with long strides towards the Capital. The Ministry of Historical Records, located by the edge of the western walls, was still standing, though its crooked tower had been swept aside early in the attack upon the Capital.

More and more individuals and delegations came. Illyria wanted desperately to help them all, yet her resources were so few and her knowledge as yet so limited that she knew there was little help she could give except for bolstering morale and holding out promises for better times. Also, she sometimes faltered inwardly when she thought of Hrudan and her heart filled with sadness. But the same thought gave her strength as well, and often she felt that Hrudan was standing by her side and helping her.

An elderly man approached the dais in the tent. He wore an old black robe with red borders and walked wearily, supporting himself with a crooked staff. His eyes were deeply sunken, and his beard reached to his waist. He bowed solemnly to Illyria. Illyria asked him what he wanted.

He spoke slowly, "My name is Port-Callant."

"Yes," she said.

"I am a lawyer."

"A lawyer?"

"Indeed, Madam."

Illyria was puzzled. "Port-Callant, I am honored to make your acquaintance, but I do not know what a lawyer is, though I have heard of such persons before, and I thought they had disappeared a long time ago. If I may be so impertinent, could you tell me what a lawyer is?"

The old man replied, "A lawyer is someone who tries to ensure that persons are treated justly in their relations with other persons, that they make agreements and assume obligations and honor these, and that something called the law is a just and equitable system of respect for all persons who come under its governance."

"That sounds like something that is right and good. And how do you happen to be this thing called a lawyer, when so clearly we have lived for centuries where no such law seems to have prevailed?"

Port-Callant replied, "That is a difficult matter to describe, Madam, for I am one of the few survivors of an ancient profession; it is a miracle any of us survived at all. And if the stories that have come down through the centuries are correct, we lawyers were by no means innocent of the troubles that came to beset the populace of Oval-Earth. We made the law serve our purposes, rather than those of the ones we claimed to serve. The Imperial Scriveners and their offspring were the result of our failure.

"But a small remnant of us gathered in the isolated woodlands of Mor-bihan a long time ago and did what we could to preserve and pass on the authentic tradition of legal inquiry and interpretation. Oval-Earth must, once more, come under a rule of law that is more than the tyrannical and temporary fancy of an individual or of a group. I am here to give what little help I can."

Illyria said, "Welcome, Port-Callant; a little help, under these circumstances, is much help. Your services will be invaluable to us and to the peoples of Oval-Earth." She directed the hickory gnomes to prepare a dwelling tent for Port-Callant and to tend to his needs.

Port-Callant was followed by a dashing, if excessively bedraggled, young fellow with a plumed yellow hat and a green velvet cape. Both his cape and his hat were torn and stained, though no less lavish and flamboyant for all of that. He introduced himself to Illyria with a sweeping bow.

"My name is Gommaspiel-Toron, Madam," he declaimed with a flourish of his hat. "My profession is to be Master of whatever Ceremony there is to be Master of. I specialize in pageants, revelries, mummeries, fairs, grotesqueries, fireworks, masked balls, village dances, beer-hall antics, bar-room ballistics, mischievous merrymakings, weddings, courtly intrigues, and all manner of splendiferous frippery.

"I can cavort and carouse, gibe and gambol, jest and gesticulate and lampoon at your pleasure. I must say that I, and my entire guild of fellow flaneurs, have been out of work for ages. What was there to celebrate? I am here to be at your service. I imagine that a great celebration is in order."

"Gommaspiel-Toron, the day will come when we will have need for your, no doubt, indispensable talents," Illyria responded. "But, alas, now we have little to celebrate. For all victories are defeats as well, and we must mourn, not only for our losses but even for the vanquished adversaries themselves, even those who appeared to be, willfully or otherwise, in collusion with the dark powers that acted through them, though about that we will never fully know.

"Save your celebrations for what we manage to restore in time, if we have the strength and the wisdom to restore it. And we hope to celebrate above all how and if we fulfill our resolution that victory will not make fools of us, as victory so often does to the victors."

Gommaspiel-Toron saluted Illyria with another flourish. "I already have good cause to celebrate your wisdom, Illyria, and shall await your pleasure on these matters. My panache is ever at your disposal." He skipped off in as gamesome a mood as ever.

When Knarry observed these interchanges, he wondered if Illyria really did need him. But he decided to take a respite and walked with Tundra-Bear and Fox-Foot outside the tent to a little grove of trees at the side of the field. They sat down on some fallen logs in the shadowy grove and were silent for a while.

Knarry spoke. "I know what the questions are that are in your mind. You are wondering what has actually happened here in Oval-Earth."

Tundra-Bear and Fox-Foot nodded.

"I don't think I can explain much of it, for there are things beyond Oval-Earth that are involved, and we don't understand what they are. Garug-Caroch made that clear to you when you saw him in the World beyond the Worlds. But I think I have figured out this much—and indeed, I knew this by the time we had finished our visit to the island, especially when Weyland said that he awoke on the winter solstice in the middle of the storm. You remember that *The Chartulary* spoke of Lo-El as a one and as a many. Whatever Lo-El is, it gathers to itself other things, both spiritually and physically. We don't know how Lo-El operates in the World beyond the Worlds, though the Eye of the Needle was not a thing of Oval-Earth. It came from beyond and was an important source of Lo-El's power in Oval-Earth.

"In Oval-Earth itself, the Game of Spheres seduced the best and brightest into believing that the mind and all it thought was self-created and had no relationship to anything beyond itself. This is what Lo-El wants everyone to believe, for then Lo-El can use them. That conviction induced the sleep of the intellect and a loss of all interest in things that exist around it and independently of it. It turned the eye of the mind inward upon itself and diseased it.

"Everything that happened after this happened as a consequence—the loss of reality, the spread of a world of illusions, the distortion of history, the incapacity for action. The best and the brightest drifted off to the Isle, there to become the Drowsers, rather than the most awake of all, which is what they were meant to be. And it was the immense psychic energy of the Drowsers, now under the dominion of Lo-El, the spirit of negation and emptiness, that created the demonic spirits that attempted to take over Oval-Earth. The Lo-Els were the enfleshed dreams of the Drowsers.

"As a Lo-El was destroyed, a Drowser woke up, because the power of the real reentered that person and the power of illusion was vanquished. You remember how Weyland woke up in the winter storm after Garug-Caroch destroyed the power of evil that was using his psychic energy. He must have been a great demon in his own way, wielding that Staff; for Weyland, as I realized about him when we first met him on the Isle, is a genius of the first order, even despite his somewhat silly demeanor. When we arrived on the Isle, it took astonishing intelligence for him to tell us the things he did, given the fragmentary evidence that was available to him.

"All of this has been going on in Oval-Earth for a very long time. Ospeth knew of its possibility and built the College of Wisdom to prevent its occurrence. The People of the Wind crossed over the Golden Mountains because they saw, but could not staunch, its growing dominion. The greatest triumph of Lo-El was to make people forget the Song, for as long as the Song was sung, the power of the real could be manifested among them.

"But Garug-Caroch rediscovered a phrase of the Song and said it out loud. The shock of the real was enough to set him on a whole new course of life—to find the entire Song. But the Lo-El in the College knew what had happened. The crisis of history was now forced. The War of Desolation, which had never happened, but whose illusory memory paralyzed the people, had to take place.

"The Lo-Els went after the Ancestral Tree and tore the Staff from its side. With that Staff they hoped to soften up Oval-Earth for the kill, as well as to destroy Garug-Caroch and hold off any other opposition to their power. But the Song prevailed; in fact, just those two verses, the written form of which Bomsiell delivered to me in the storm, were enough to prevail. We have much to be thankful for."

Tundra-Bear assented. "I am not sure I understand all of this, but I am glad that you have come to know these things, Knarry."

"But what about Tristan-Phoros?" Fox-Foot asked.

"Ah, Tristan-Phoros!" Knarry sighed. "That all became clear to me when I observed Phoros in the subterranean dormitory of the Drowsers. I knew that the spirit of Phoros was in the Moor-Plains Retriever, particularly when Weyland said that Phoros had been the greatest player of the Game of Spheres in collegiate history and when I saw the pipe in his pocket. You should have seen Tristan-Phoros that day in the Hall of Games with Laus-Urop and later Arfla. It was—well, one of the most remarkable things I have ever seen."

"But why the connection with a Moor-Plains Retriever?"

"His psychic energy could not be drawn into a Lo-El. It was diverted on its own internal bent and entered a dog. Because of this unusual concurrence of dog and philosopher, there was only one place for him to be in Oval-Earth—in the time-space matrix of the Barrows. And that's where we found him. Without him, our task could not have been accomplished."

Tundra-Bear looked puzzled. "But Knarry, why could his spirit not enter a Lo-El?"

Knarry smiled. "I know this is hard to understand. We wood-gnomes understand it sometimes. I'm sure the rock-gnomes understand it best of all. But the principle is this: *nothing truly reasonable can ever be evil.*"

"He was very reasonable," Tundra-Bear agreed.

"To be reasonable is to look at things the way they are, or at least to try to figure out how they are," Knarry went on. "A Lo-El is a spirit of delusion. It is the imagination when it no longer has any relation to the reality of the world. It wants things to be remade according to its own will; it is not interested in how things are. That explains its emptiness and its insatiable appetite, for, as hard as it tries, it can never make things be the way it wants them to be. Therefore, it wants them to be not at all. The Gethsarbim used to have an ancient saying: 'The sleep of reason gives birth to many monsters.' We now know how true that saying is."

Another long silence followed. Fox-Foot inquired, "But if Phoros is now alive as who he originally was, if the soul of Phoros returned to his body, what happened to the dog part, to … to … I guess his name would be Tristan? The death of Tristan-Phoros seems to have been as much a 'coming apart' as anything else."

Knarry replied, "I suppose we will never know the answer to that, Fox-Foot. But it is difficult not to think that the dog part of Phoros's soul was merely a body for him, and that the body died up in the mountains."

Fox-Foot pondered this answer for a few moments, after which she asked, "But what is a soul, Knarry? Isn't there a something that makes us a one thing, that makes us a whole thing, that makes us a different thing, so that what we feel, and how we are aware, and how we act all have a oneness, and not just any oneness but a oneness that isn't the same as any other oneness?"

"I would think so," Knarry answered, puzzled by this curious change of subject.

"And isn't that what we mean by a soul?"

"That much is certain."

"And doesn't a particular dog have a oneness like that, so that one dog is not many dogs, or that one dog is not any dog, but is this dog and not that dog?"

"My observation of dogs would confirm that."

"So, a dog is not just a body, but it, too, has a soul — perhaps not a soul like ours, but a soul."

"I think you are right."

"Then, if Phoros's soul was returned to his body, a body that it never really left, Tristan's body must have been returned to his soul, which also, in some way, it never left."

"That is a reasonable assumption."

"*Ergo* . . ." Fox-Foot proclaimed triumphantly.

"*Ergo?*" Tundra-Bear echoed in bewilderment, gaping at Fox-Foot with astonished eyes.

"*Ergo,*" she repeated, "Tristan may be alive somewhere in Oval-Earth, though I doubt we could ever find him."

Knarry paused and observed, "I think now, Fox-Foot, that perhaps Illyria should have sent you to the College of Wisdom, for your wisdom surpasses mine and you share the spirit of Phoros. In fact, you can think just like him."

Fox-Foot blushed. "You are very kind, Knarry, for saying that, but my wisdom is little. I should someday like to return to the College of Wisdom, for I would like to learn more about the families of flowers and plants, and of all living things, and how they, or rather we, all come from the same ancestral seeds, for that is a beautiful thing and makes us all one family together. I like to think that a rose is my cousin and a squirrel is my aunt.

"But I long for my children and my townsfolk, and for the mountain winds and streams, and it is there where I must go with Tundra-Bear.

"For, though in truth I have little wisdom, Knarry, I do have a love song in my heart, and now that I have heard the musical voices of the rock-gnomes and the music of the World beyond the Worlds and have heard the Song of the Eternal Aeons, that love song is even greater in my heart. And Tundra-Bear knows of what I speak, for he heard the same music too."

Tundra-Bear agreed. He turned to address Knarry: "We had a lot of luck, don't you think, Knarry? I mean, Garug-Caroch just happening to find those words, and we just happening to find Hrudan, and Tristan-Phoros, and everything else."

"I suppose so," Knarry answered. "But Garug-Caroch didn't really find those words by accident. According to his own account, he saw the starlike figures on Ospeth's Tower dance and glimmer before his eyes. His attention was *drawn* to them.

"And why was he walking in the field that day? Because he was restless, because he had some sense that things were wrong, because something was telling him that. And Hrudan knew at a certain point that there were things he had to do, and so he did them. Something has been telling us things, something has been guiding our steps and binding us together in a way that we needed to be bound together. Something else is out there in the World beyond the Worlds besides Lo-El, something that helped us at every step."

"I think I know what you are talking about, Knarry," said Fox-Foot. "There was a voice down in the Habitat of the rock-gnomes that seemed to speak to me in a way that I never understood before."

"Maybe it was the voice of Wuldor," Tundra-Bear reminded them. "Do you remember the mysterious songs of Prince Witzlau and how Wuldor was before the beginning of time?"

Knarry stood up from his log and folded his shaggy arms. "We don't know much about these things in Oval-Earth. In the days when there was still wisdom among our people, they tried to figure them out. That is why the Song was, and is, so important. It directs our attention to something out of time, beyond time, before time ever was. But, ultimately, despite all the commentary the ancient sages wrote about the Song, it seems they were never able to move beyond its mystery to its source."

"And nobody ever came to tell us," Fox-Foot avowed.

Knarry made no answer. He turned and gazed out of the grove at the distant tent. "I guess I should return to the tent," he said. "This is not going to be easy for Illyria and Erudan. They will need all the help that they can get, though their strength is much greater than they realize. Also, I need to convoke the Elders of the wood-gnomes. I think there will be no problem in clearing myself of the charges placed against me at the Gathering of the Clans. The wood-gnomes have come to their senses too."

"And we shall go back to the Hills; I have a wedding to arrange," said Fox-Foot.

"Please take Bomsiell with you. She will be happy to return to the woods and the hills. And stay at my earth-house on the way—if it is still there. It will be a good resting place before the journey into the Hills."

"Thank you, Knarry," said Tundra-Bear. "We will see you again when you come to the Hills."

Fox-Foot and Tundra-Bear accompanied Knarry back to the entrance of the tent and said farewell to him there. Fox-Foot and Tundra-Bear peeked into the tent and saw that Illyria and Erudan were hard at work, but they waved at them from a distance. Illyria and Erudan waved back.

After gathering their longbows and quivers and calling Bomsiell to their side, Fox-Foot and Tundra-Bear skirted the Capital to the west and started the journey along what was left of the Southern Arm of the Radial High-Road. Bomsiell followed along; she was sad to be leaving Knarry after spending such a long time with him.

The countryside was lonely and crushed. But here and there, they saw fields being plowed, orchards being pruned, and vines being strung along fences. Dusty villages were being swept out, the barns mended, the moose combed out and fed, the inns rebuilt. Most of all, the populace greeted one another and worked in unison. They were friendly to the unusual travelers and did not stare at them simply because of their bright-green hair and purple eyes. Children were laughing and playing in the village squares and often ran alongside the travelers. They patted Bomsiell on the head and listened to her purr.

After three days of difficult travel over devastated terrain, Tundra-Bear, Fox-Foot, and Bomsiell approached the village of Cantanteroff.

Remarkably, the village had been spared the more destructive effects of the War, even though it was close to the staging ground for the possessed winterbeests' assault on the Hills. As they approached Knarry's earth-house, they saw in a nearby field an old white moose grazing in the brush; they recognized it as Collielava. They were glad to see him still was hale and well.

Knarry's earth-house was in good shape, despite a few holes in the roof, punctured by a demonized and oversized winterbeest as it walked across the dome. The night spent there was pleasant enough. It was, after all, Bomsiell's old home. She pranced around the different rooms and jumped up on the dispensary table, knocking a few pharmaceutical vials to the floor. Tundra-Bear and Fox-Foot enjoyed a long bath in the wooden tub fed by the natural hot springs that Knarry had rigged up for his guests many years before.

In the morning, they prepared for the final leg of the journey homeward. It was a clear, breezy day, and they felt refreshed after the night of rest. They left Knarry's earth-house and had just come to the foot of the Regional Road when they happened to look up the path that led to the gazebo where, in the previous autumn, Knarry and Garug-Caroch had discussed the fate of Oval-Earth. The sun had risen in the east and shone directly through the pavilion at them, so it was difficult to look at.

But something was standing inside it, standing inside, as it were, the rays of the sun itself and looking down at them. It stood on four legs and was madly waggling a big, bushy tail. A moment later, it had burst out of the rays of the sun and was galloping down the path in their direction.

"It's a dog—a Moor-Plains Retriever!" Tundra-Bear cried.

"It's Tristan-Phoros! But without his pipe pouch!" Fox-Foot cried even louder.

Bomsiell meowed, scurried behind Fox-Foot's legs, and peered out curiously as this canine prodigy came bouncing wildly down the hill.

The dog came to a halt about fifty paces from them and sat back on his haunches. He was panting, and his tail was thumping the ground behind him. He was waiting for something.

"Not Tristan-Phoros," Tundra-Bear said. "This is only a dog. See how he is acting. He is enjoying being a dog! Fox-Foot, I thought you said we could never find him, never find … yes, Tristan — in case he survived somehow!"

"You are right, Tundra-Bear. I said that. And I still believe that. But I never doubted for a moment that he could find us," Fox-Foot replied. "And anyway, I am not sure it's really us that he was hoping to find."

Tristan bolted from his sitting position and ran over to them, jumping about, licking their faces and barking and rolling over and acting generally just the way a dog usually acts. Finally, and ceremoniously, he approached Bomsiell, tenderly touching noses with her, and she rubbed the length of her body along his leg. The two of them romped together back and forth across the road, chasing one another, batting and pouncing and barking and yowling and running off again.

Tundra-Bear and Fox-Foot laughed at them. Bomsiell and Tristan returned and joined them. Tristan barked, and Bomsiell meowed. The sun rose up over the pavilion and filled the little valley with bright sunshine. They turned to the Regional Road and headed together up into the Hills.

Valediction

My story is over. My charge has been fulfilled. I lay to rest the wondrous spirits of those, now gone, who trod upon this earth and enacted these wondrous deeds. May their memory never fail, their light never darken, their kindness be ever recompensed, their generosity be ever met with gratitude. In the World beyond the Worlds, their footsteps shall echo unto the end of all the aeons.

My pen, my quill, my beloved stylus, you move about, vital and warm, in my fingers that, heavy with age, stiffen with bark and fiber. I know that you wish to go, to spring free from my hands and through the open window of my chamber. I shall let you go unloosed to the elements, there to do your imperishable work.

One task behind you, another surely awaits you — one even greater than this — a greater sorrow than the sorrowing of these events, and a greater fear than the fearsomeness of those times that came upon the land, and a greater telling than these greatest of all tellings that we have yet known and that you made possible to me, because you were there when it happened.

That story, that story of the World beyond the Worlds, when it comes, shall be beyond me, beyond all we have seen or known as yet.

Go to it, my beloved stylus! I loosen my grasp.

You hesitate?

Ah, you look back only once!

Now you are gone!

The window, the fields and forests, the mountains and the skies, the universe are yours!

Farewell!

These final words I shall write with the woody twigs that have now become my fingers. I shall not write long, for all has been accomplished.

I fold the final leaf of my vellum and prepare a silken cord with which to bind it. In the last moments of my lamp's faltering flame, I shall melt a small vial of sealing wax to press the seam of this venerable parchment together. Then I shall affix the ancient seal with the signet ring of my clan. Nothing shall be left unfinished that could be finished, or undone that could be done.

My lamp shall be snuffed out.

The heaviness within me broadens my hands and feet. So dense, so cumbrous my being, I can barely tread upon my stony floor.

I need earth.

I need the pliant earth beneath my feet where I can rest, where I can set down roots, my toes curling gently down into the dark, rich loam, churning through its cool and fertile depths, drawing from it its moisture, its sap, its marvelous essences.

I shall betake myself to the Northern Taiga, there to take my place among my fellows; and I shall feel new blood run in my veins, earth-blood, nourishing, eternal, my fingers coiling upward, my arms lifted, sprouting branches and leaves, upward, ever upward, unfolding into the bounteous skies, into the bounteous sun.

Remember the words, my beneficent lector! Remember the words until the end of time! Remember the words of the Song!

About the Author

Johann M. Moser was born in Cambridge, Massachusetts, in 1940. He grew up in New York City and later in New Jersey. At Dartmouth College he majored in philosophy and studied with the poet Richard Eberhart. In 1970, he received a Ph.D. in comparative literature from the Catholic University of America in Washington, D.C., where he specialized in poetics and medieval literature. From 1970 until his retirement in 2000, he taught literature and philosophy at St. Anselm College in Manchester, New Hampshire.

Although familiar with many areas of the United States and having lived several years abroad, Moser spent his early summers in the Lakes Region of central New Hampshire, where he has now resided for over half a century. In these decades, he has formed an intimate bond with northern New England, whose mountains and lakes and lively populace have been a source of inspiration for him, even as he has devoted himself to a sustained pursuit and emulation of world literature in all its dense historicity and its universal aesthetic achievements.